To Sisterhood!

Gail R. Shapiro

BookLocker
Trenton, Georgia

Copyright © 2024 Gail R. Shapiro

Print ISBN: 978-1-958892-67-1
Ebook ISBN: 979-8-88531-728-3

All rights reserved. No part of this publication may be reproduced, stored in a retrieval system, or transmitted in any form or by any means, electronic, mechanical, recording or otherwise, without the prior written permission of the author.

Published by BookLocker.com, Inc., Trenton, Georgia.

This is a work of fiction. All incidents and characters, with the exception of some well-known historical figures and events, are products of the author's imagination. Where real-life historical figures appear, the situations, incidents, and dialogues concerning those persons are not intended to depict actual events or to change the fictional nature of the work. Otherwise, any resemblance to actual persons, living or dead, events, or locales is entirely coincidental.

BookLocker.com, Inc.
2024

First Edition

Cover photograph courtesy of The Second Wave records, M019, Northeastern University Archives and Special Collections, Boston, Massachusetts, Box 1, Folder 3.

Credit: Katharine Butler Hathaway, excerpts from *The Little Locksmith: A Memoir*. Copyright 1942, 1943 by Coward-McCann, Inc., renewed © 1974 by Warren H. Butler. Reprinted with the permission of The Permissions Company, LLC on behalf of The Feminist Press at the City University of New York, feministpress.org.

Dedication

For my daughters, nieces, and granddaughters – and yours.

Prologue

May 4th, 1969, Boston, Massachusetts

The Sunday classifieds in *The Boston Globe* read: "Help Wanted – Male," and "Help Wanted – Female." Fewer than 30% of married women with children work outside the home, and women earn 45% less than men for the same jobs. If a woman gets fired for refusing her boss's sexual advances, well, tough luck. There are no laws against sexual harassment in the workplace, or anywhere else. With rare exceptions, abortion is illegal in the United States. Birth control – unless one is married and has a doctor's prescription – is illegal in Massachusetts. "Domestic violence" does not yet exist as a term or a concept; wife beating is a private problem, not a public health issue. A responding police officer is likely to tell the batterer to "go take a walk and cool off." Married women cannot obtain credit in their own name. Most leaders of the anti-Vietnam War Movement are men. Men can refuse to serve; women can "say yes to boys who say no."

The second wave of the women's movement has just begun. A conference at Emmanuel College in Boston, sponsored by Bread and Roses and other female liberation activists, will change the way a group of four young women see themselves, live their lives, view society and their place in it, and develop friendships. They will hear about sexism and the oppression experienced by women – and what women can do about it. They will learn about self-defense, community organizing, class divisions, the influence of the media, and taking back control of their bodies from a male-dominated medical establishment.

One afternoon. The power of ideas.

✵ **One** ✵

Ellen stood in the dorm hallway, wondering if she should knock on Laurie's door or just walk right back in. Juggling her square beige Samsonite overnight bag, nightgown, and towel in one hand, she squeezed the water from her dripping long blonde hair into the towel with the other. She tapped the door gently with her foot.

From down at the end of the corridor, she heard Judy Collins singing, *Someday Soon*. Judy was on the cover of this week's *Life* magazine. Ellen had a copy tucked in her bag, saving it to read on the bus back home tomorrow afternoon. A few people had even told her that she looked like Judy, but Ellen, though secretly pleased, didn't think so. Ellen's neck was long and slender, her face thinner, though her eyes were just as blue.

"It's open!" Laurie called, and Ellen walked in to find Laurie sitting cross-legged on the lower bunk in striped, pink pajamas, chewing thoughtfully on a pencil, the Sunday crossword puzzle on her lap.

Laurie looked up, smiling at her guest. "Was there enough hot water?"

When Ellen said yes, Laurie said, "I'm almost through here. I need a quick shower, then I'll take you over to breakfast. I'm stuck. What's a five-letter word for 'miscreant'? The last two letters are o-n."

Ellen wrapped the towel around her head, turban-style. She pushed her glasses up and peered down at the puzzle. After only a second's pause, she offered, "Nixon?"

Laurie laughed and put down the puzzle. "I like you, Ellen. I do hope you get to transfer in."

"Me too." Ellen's calm answer belied how badly she wanted this. To be able to transfer to Radcliffe for junior year, to be part of this august institution, studying with the best professors, among the brightest women in the country, to graduate with a joint degree from Harvard…

Since the day of her Great Aunt Martha's funeral almost a decade ago, when a bevy of Martha's Radcliffe '23 classmates swooped into the church, looking like a flock of exotic birds, with their bright colored filmy dresses, curled hair, and high heeled shoes that absolutely scandalized the somberly-dressed, sensibly-coifed ladies of the parish, eight-year-old Ellen realized that getting into Radcliffe College – wherever that might be – was the ticket out of the life that was already planned for her in King's Lake. She still remembered pieces of those women's conversations, as she drifted among them, trying to hear without being noticed.

"…that new comedian Lenny Bruce, what a scandal, oh my, Martha absolutely loved him…" "Allen Ginsberg, yes that's with Grove Press, can you believe he finally had the nerve to publish it?" "…do you think your daughter is on the pill yet? Yes, they say it's finally going to be approved in a few months. Too bad it's too late for us…" And "Fidel is so sexy, don't you think?" "Ah, yes, but Miles Davis is God…"

At the time, Ellen had no idea what or who they were talking about, but clearly, it was a lot more interesting than crop prices, the rainy late-summer weather, and who in the county won first prize for best cheddar at the state fair.

To Sisterhood!

It had been her dream, way before she started this year at Ethan Allen State, the only place her parents would let her go. *Why do you want to bother with college? Why spend all that time and money, when you're going to work here at the store until you get married?* Ellen had worked hard all through school – earning the top grades in her high school class – because she knew Radcliffe took only the best students. But her parents wouldn't budge.

Ellen had tried again and again to explain her love of learning, her desire to be someone, to do something important with her life. They didn't understand. Letting Ellen attend junior college was a compromise, plus she had to live at home.

Ellen's plan was to apply for transfer admission and a scholarship. And if she got in – *when* she got in, please, please! – she'd enroll and then tell her parents. She could get a job to cover her living expenses if they refused to help her. She wanted this more than anything.

As Laurie left to shower, Ellen looked longingly at the room again, so different from her own room at home. On the wall over the desk was a red poster of a bearded man wearing a beret with a star in the center. The adjacent wall had a big red fist poster from last month's Harvard student strike, urging the students to participate for a host of reasons listed. Ellen especially liked, "Strike because there's no poetry in your lectures," and "Strike to make yourself free."

In place of curtains were navy metal Venetian blinds, open to let in the early morning spring sunshine. They matched the blue-and-white striped spreads on the twin beds. There was a colorful cotton rag rug on the floor, and a large spider plant sprouting a lot of babies hung in the window, but other than the two posters and the books spilling off the desk and covering every horizontal surface, the room was bare of decoration. No flowery prints, no chintz, no pastels, nothing girly Ellen loved it.

She dearly wanted to jump up and shout, "I'm here! I'm finally here!" but that definitely would not be cool. She sat still, and imagined that it was September, 1970 – 16 months from now – when she'd already been accepted, and really belonged here, instead of simply doing a weekend pre-admission visit. Ellen closed her eyes again, and tried to envision how she would decorate her own dorm room, here in Comstock Hall or wherever she'd be assigned.

She brushed her damp hair. It was thin and straight and never took long to dry. Then she pulled on a pleated khaki skirt and a short-sleeved white Villager blouse, an outfit which seemed smart when she packed it, but which she now feared would make her look overdressed, or at least a bit stuffy on this freewheeling campus. Then she tried to figure out what to tell her parents about the "field trip" she was supposed to be on this weekend in Boston with her art history class. Easy. She'd spend the afternoon at a Harvard art museum, pick up a couple of prints, and that should do it. They'd believe her. Their Ellen never lied.

Laurie returned in twenty minutes, looking anxious. "Do you have anything special you wanted to see today?" She wore a tee shirt and a short denim skirt with brown leather sandals. *I'm definitely wearing the wrong thing*, Ellen thought.

"Well, we've toured the campus. I sat in on a couple of classes on Friday. I was planning to go over to the Fogg Museum, I guess. I appreciate your hospitality, Laurie, but you don't have to hang around with me all day if you have other things to do. I have a friend from home I can call – that guy I'm going to stay with tonight."

"Boyfriend?" Laurie asked.

"No," Ellen said. "We dated in high school, but it's been over for some time. We're still good friends though. He goes to Boston College, lives someplace off Commonwealth Avenue."

Laurie was quiet for a minute. "Look," she said, "why don't you come with me? I ran into a girl from my history class. She said there's a women's conference today at Emmanuel College, across the river in Boston, being organized by women from a collective around here. I don't know if you're political or anything, but I guess a bunch of people from our class are going to go and you're welcome to join us."

"Oh, yes!" Ellen tried not to show how exciting that sounded. "I'd like that. I'll get ready. Is what I'm wearing all right or should I change?"

Laurie laughed. "You look fine," she said. "I'd rather wear jeans but 'Radcliffe students do not wear shorts or slacks to classes, or on the public streets,' or so it says in our handbook. Of course," she continued, "no one pays attention to that rule, especially since the strike, but I'm not going to push it right now. My parents are already freaked out enough that exams were cancelled, and one of my classes even stopped meeting. I just have to turn in a paper to get a grade…"

"Wow," Ellen said. "No exams? Lucky you!"

Ellen would fit in here, Laurie thought, as she fashioned her own long dark hair into one messy braid down her back. Ellen was kind of serious, but so were a lot of the other girls.

Laurie thought back to last September, when she first arrived at Radcliffe. There was much to learn – not only in her classes – even though growing up in nearby Newton, she'd been hanging out in Harvard Square since junior high. Some of the professors wanted to keep things formal, while others invited students for coffee. Lots of her classmates were highly competitive, and she was still figuring out who she could trust.

Laurie looked out the window onto Walker Street. It was a perfect spring day, welcome after those two record-breaking blizzards in February. And today should be fun. All she knew about the conference was that a Boston collective was bringing together a group to talk about women's common issues and to discuss how women could organize within and outside of the Movement.

Ellen walked over to stand next to Laurie. She, too, looked out the window, at the girls walking alone and in pairs. *Will I get to be one of them for real?* Only one more night before she had to head back north. In Vermont, it was still mud season. In King's Lake, she would be pulling out her Sunday dress, trying to get her hair to curl, and heading to church with her family. In King's Lake, Ellen would know every single person she ran into all day, and everything about them and their families. A women's conference? Absolutely yes!

※ ※ ※ ※

Nina hurried off the train and ran up the stairs out of Back Bay Station. She still had more than an hour before the conference started, but since it was her first time in Boston, she wasn't exactly sure how to get to Emmanuel College. She didn't want to be late. Doing a great job covering this story was important. It could be the one that launched her from lowly intern to low-paid freelancer, and on her way to a coveted staff position. *That* ought to shut up Muriel, who was always saying that Nina was an underachiever, whatever that meant. What Nina thought it meant was that Muriel and Herb were pissed off because they paid a lot for her to go all the way through The Dalton School, and now she was "throwing her life away," renting a pad in the East Village after dropping out of Sarah Lawrence, and working for free. That Nina was working at her dream job – well, at least at the entry-level to her dream job – at an important Movement organization was totally lost on her used-to-be-cool father and her Chanel-wearing, Establishment stepmother. Plus, all that tuition money was from Nina's mother's estate, so Muriel should lay off already.

Nina's mother had supported her dream. She'd had the idea to become a journalist almost as far back as she could remember, since long before her mother died.

Rod, Nina's supervisor, had written down directions from the station. "Turn left, walk two blocks to the Copley stop, take the inbound train to Park Street, then take the outbound car on Huntington."

But it was a truly gorgeous day – when she'd left New York early this morning it was still cool and overcast – so Nina decided to walk instead. It was only a couple of miles. Maybe she'd find a coffee shop on the way.

As she headed up Stuart Street and then down Huntington Avenue, Nina braced herself when she saw the construction site ahead. Head held high, back straight, wavy copper hair flashing in the sunlight, she walked past the site, ready to ignore the catcalls and whistles. She could handle a few piggy old guys, who were bound to notice and comment on her figure. She'd been good at handling guys all her life.

So she was surprised to hear nothing. Not even a "Hey, babe!" or a "Lookin' good!" But as she crossed to the next block, she realized she didn't even hear an electric saw or the crackling of welders or a jackhammer. *Good going there, Nina,* she chided herself, *it's Sunday, you silly girl.*

Laughing, she stopped at the next corner to grab a coffee, and frowned when she sipped the too-sweet, too-light brew. Apparently, "regular" did not mean "black" in Boston. She considered going back and getting another cup, until she checked the time. She had to be there early, to talk to some of the women before the conference started.

She sped up her pace, and fifteen minutes later, the plain red brick buildings of Emmanuel College were in view. Nina was delighted to see that the lawn in between the buildings was full of women, some sitting on blankets eating sandwiches with their radios on, and others playing Frisbee® with a couple of good-looking dogs. *So Movement women in Boston* do *have fun,* she thought. This was going to be cool. She rolled up her sleeves, gave her best jeans a tug, hoisted up her knapsack, and strode confidently toward her future.

※ ※ ※ ※

Diane sighed and cleared the mess in the kitchen from their late breakfast. Her mother had gone back to bed and her father'd disappeared right after he'd finished eating. At least he'd said thank you, with a wave of his hand, to indicate the pancakes and bacon, the

To Sisterhood!

coffee, and the "Happy 18th Birthday Theresa" banner decorated with red and blue balloons. Diane had stayed up late painting that banner, so she could see her sister's delighted smile this morning.

Diane yawned as she headed upstairs. She finished wrapping the new bathing suit. If it were up to their mother, Theresa still would be dressed in pink polka dots with bows. At the party tonight, she was going to give Theresa the new suit and the big stuffed Dalmatian Theresa had oohed and aahed over when she saw it in the window of the Coop last week.

Diane heard her sister getting out of the shower, and quickly hid the gifts under her bed. A few minutes later, Theresa bounced in.

"Wow, Dee, can you believe I'm eighteen years old today!" Theresa was wearing her new red sleeveless jumper over a crisp white blouse with a Peter Pan collar, and matching PRO-Keds®, white with a red stripe. Last week, Father had given Diane a check and asked her to buy Theresa a gift from him and Mother. He was surprised when Diane told him Theresa wanted fancy basketball shoes, but told her to go ahead and get whatever she wanted.

"I know, honey, almost as old as me. I got you presents." Diane had been working extra shifts at the candy factory, so she could get Theresa a few more things, and to pay for the big surprise.

"Can I have them now? Are you going to take me to Rome, Italy to see the Pope?"

Diane was touched by her sister's eagerness. "Well, not this birthday, honey, but I'm saving my money to take you there someday. I've got some other things for you, though, but you'll have to wait until the party tonight."

"Okay, I can wait." Theresa clutched her new red shoulder bag with both hands and looked out the window for the school van.

As Diane freshened her lipstick, Theresa came over to stand close to her. They could be twins. Black curly hair, teased and pulled into a bouffant style with side-swept bangs, round faces, and short curvy bodies. Theresa was proud that she could do her own hair, and Diane's too, and today she sported a red bow above the bangs.

Diane looked at her sister in the mirror. She was thrilled with all that Theresa had accomplished this year, and who knew? Her talent for doing hair might give her the opportunity to get a job in a salon, at least if Diane could find her a good training program. Theresa was also wonderful with small children. Perhaps she could work as a mother's helper, or in a nursery program, as long as there was supervision.

Diane couldn't wait to get Theresa out of this house. She'd been planning and saving for an apartment for the two of them for the past two years. But today was the big day. Theresa was finally eighteen. Diane planned to talk to her about moving tonight, right after the party.

"Have a great time today at Paragon Park!" Diane hugged her sister. "I know you'll have so much fun with your friends."

"I don't want to go on the Giant Coaster, Dee." She looked worried.

"You don't have to go on any ride you don't want to. Nobody will make fun of you, the teachers won't let them, you know that."

"But I like the horsies so much," she said.

"Yes, we had a good time on the Carousel when we went the last time, didn't we, honey?"

Theresa smiled, nodding yes.

"Now, Theresa," Diane said, "you remember that I'm going to a meeting in Boston today, right? But I'll be back in time for your party tonight. Isn't it great that the school trip turned out to be right on your birthday!" She slipped two dollars into her sister's pocket.

"Thank you, Dee," said Theresa.

"Now, don't stuff yourself full of cotton candy and hot dogs. Save some room for your birthday cake tonight!"

"I will." Theresa tried to look serious but her dark eyes were laughing.

"Love you, kiddo…"

"I love you too, Dee," Theresa said, and leaned over to give her sister a great big hug.

⁂ **Two** ⁂

Nina checked her watch. 11:30 am. The first-ever Boston Female Liberation conference was due to start at noon. She needed some background first, and got out her notebook. She approached two women about her age, possibly a couple of years younger, who were sitting on a blanket eating blueberry muffins.

"Hello," she said, smiling.

They smiled back at her, and one gestured for her to sit. Nina sat down, crossed-legged on the blanket. She held up her notebook.

"Nina Rosen. Revolution News Bureau. I'm here from New York to cover the conference. Do you mind if I ask you a few questions?"

"Ah, the Movement Press," said the brunette. The blonde looked puzzled, and offered Nina the box of Pewter Pot muffins.

"Forgive me," said the blonde, "but I don't know what that is. And hi, Nina, I'm Ellen MacDougall. This is Laurie."

"Revolution News Bureau," Nina told Ellen. "RNB. We write and gather stories about politics, culture, and other happenings, and distribute them to the underground press and college newspapers all over the country. We're up near Columbia, but this is the first time I've been sent out of the city on assignment. Actually, it's my first time in Boston."

"Cool," Laurie chuckled. "At least we'll get some reasonable press coverage. See those women over there? They're from the *Globe* and the *Herald*. Can you believe those rags sent guys first? Of course they were turned away. I don't know where they scrounged up these women, but they don't seem to know anything at all about what we're doing here today. Look at what they're wearing!"

Nina saw two women, from supposedly rival papers, huddled together and dressed almost identically in navy pant suits, heels, and pearls.

Just then, a short pretty woman with curly dark hair walked up. "Hi," she said. "I'm Diane. Diane Romano. I was supposed to meet a friend, but I don't see her, and I don't know a soul."

"Hi, Diane, welcome. Have a muffin." Laurie waved to the empty spot on the blanket.

"I'm Laurie Goodman. And this is Ellen. She came down on Friday from Vermont. Though not for the conference. She got lucky. We were with a group from my history class, but they met some friends from another school. They're all over there someplace." She gestured across the green. "This is Nina. She's a reporter."

"Hi, all." Diane made herself comfortable on the large blanket and helped herself to a muffin. "Thanks, yum!" she said, taking a big bite.

Ellen tucked her long legs under her before she spoke.

"Hello, Diane." She stretched out her hand. "I'm Ellen MacDougall, from up near Barre, Vermont. I'm here this weekend to visit Radcliffe before I apply as a transfer student. And look at what I ran into!" She gestured at the crowd, which was increasing both in size and volume. "Isn't it exciting?"

Diane nodded pleasantly.

"Wow," said Nina, amazed at the first real Vermont accent she'd ever heard, so different from her own fast, clipped New York speech. "You didn't come down here for the conference? You just happened to find out about it? Still, my first question was going to be, 'what brings you here?' You could be hanging out in Harvard Square. Why did you come across the river today?"

Ellen took a bite of her muffin and chewed slowly before answering. "I wouldn't call myself a radical or anything like that. Hardly. I'm not against men. I guess I'm *for* equal opportunities for women. I grew up in a small town. My father runs the general store. It was my grandfather's store before that. My mother's folks still farm, that's the house where I grew up. The plan for me was to graduate from high school, then go help out my parents in the store until I get married. But it's my younger brother – he's only eight – who will inherit the store, and probably the farm, too, someday."

Nina wrote down as much as she could.

"Look," said Ellen. "You can write about this if you want, but please don't use my name. I can't imagine that my parents would know anyone who would read your story, but they would clobber me if they found out. They don't even know I'm here this weekend. They think I came to Boston on a class field trip." She stretched once, then shifted to look at Diane, who was grinning. "Oh, listen to me babble on…"

"Why Radcliffe?" Nina asked.

"Well, I think I'd have the best chance to get an excellent education. And I'm excited about studying only with women."

"Not to mention all those cute Harvard guys," Diane added.

Laurie laughed.

Ellen blushed. "Actually, I have a beau at home."

"Is it serious?" asked Diane.

"Sort of," Ellen said. "Though he doesn't know yet of my plan to come to school here. We're sort of engaged to be engaged. I guess we'd be pinned but he's not in a fraternity. He goes to military school."

"The enemy!" said Laurie. "What are you doing with a military type?"

"He's a good guy," Ellen replied calmly. "We've been doing some anti-war activities together in Montpelier. I'm not sure yet what I want to do, but it *is* going to make a difference in the world, and it *isn't* going to be working in the general store in King's Lake."

How easy it is to talk to these women, Ellen thought. *They're strangers, but I can tell them things I can't tell Nick or my parents. And they seem to – well, they don't think I'm crazy or rebellious.*

"What about you, Diane? What brings you here today?" While Nina chewed her pencil, Diane told her about the community organizing work she'd been learning about, and the people working to keep Harvard from buying more property in her neighborhood.

Nina wrote faster as Diane added, "It sure looks like you're gonna get an earful today. My friend knows some of the organizers."

Laurie added, "They've got an impressive lineup of workshops. Look at this!" She offered a mimeographed program to Nina while she read her copy aloud.

"Control of Our Bodies."

"Self Defense: Protect Yourself on the Streets."

"Sexuality."

"Women in the Left."

"Community Organizing."

"That's the one I'm going to," said Diane. "My friend Patty and I heard about it from someone on her block. I don't know too much about this, and I haven't been active in anything like this before. But I want to work with women who are doing good things and helping themselves too." Diane was not ready to share her story with a total stranger. Especially not with a reporter. So she stayed friendly and upbeat.

"Do you know Cambridge?" Diane asked.

"No, not at all." Nina said.

"Cambridgeport is the neighborhood between Mass. Ave. and the river, from River Street, over toward Harvard Square, to MIT on the east," Diane explained. "That's where I grew up, and my family still lives there. Mostly working people: Italian, Irish, some Black, mostly families, some students. Now the area is starting to attract a few communes and collectives. The rents are still cheaper than the housing that's closer to Harvard or MIT. One and two-family houses mostly, some folks have put in apartments. There're a few apartment buildings like the one on River Street near Memorial Drive, but not many."

Diane shook her head. "Harvard is making plans to take over more and more of Cambridgeport. I came today to see what I can learn."

Laurie said, "That's great, Diane! I'd be interested in that too. I grew up in Newton, and hung out in Harvard Square most weekends, and I've been watching what Harvard's been doing to the community. Plus, since I'm at school there now, I guess I feel some responsibility."

Diane shrugged and said, "I guess we need all the help we can get. I still don't see my friend, maybe she's inside already. Let's go find out what this is all about."

※ ※ ※ ※

They went into Emmanuel's main auditorium together. Like Radcliffe, Emmanuel was an all-female school, and today the room was packed with women of all ages. A tall, solid-looking woman on the stage called for quiet. The room hushed as they all gave her their attention.

"Sisters," she began. "Welcome to the first Female Liberation Conference here in Boston. I'd like to thank the kind folks at Emmanuel College for allowing us to use their space today, and want to introduce our first speaker, who'll tell you why we are here..."

Cheers and clapping drowned out the rest of her words.

Nina whispered to Ellen, "Did you get her name?"

"Sorry, no."

Nina frowned.

The speaker climbed up to the podium. She was petite, with short dark hair. She wore dark jeans and a plain white T-shirt with a women's symbol in purple.

"Welcome, sisters!" A few people called back greetings.

"Most of us here are involved in the Movement in some way. Some are working to end the illegal war in Vietnam…" She was interrupted by both boos and some cheers. "Some are fighting to end the oppression of our Black sisters and brothers. Some are fighting for decent working conditions and living wages. Some are here because we want to determine for ourselves what happens in our communities. And no matter which struggle we are involved in, all of us have experienced another form of oppression – oppression as women."

Ellen sat forward on the edge of her chair, and Laurie excitedly grabbed her hand.

The speaker went on. "We want to learn to take control of our bodies, not have male doctors and the government make decisions for us. We want the right to walk down the street any time of the day or night without being hassled. We want to be able to work at jobs we love, and not have to worry about who will look after our children. Look around you, sisters. There are more than 500 of us here today! And this is only the beginning of the Movement for Women's Rights."

"Woo hoo!" someone shouted from the back of the room, as many others clapped and stomped their feet.

"Wow!" Laurie whispered to Diane, sitting on the other side of her. "This is so exciting!" Diane, listening intently, did not reply.

"For background of why we're all here today, I'm pleased to introduce Molly, one of the sisters who organized this meeting." Molly, a large white woman of about thirty or so, who was wearing overalls and a bright purple shirt, took the podium to enthusiastic applause.

"Beginning a couple of years ago," she said, peering out into the audience over her wire-rimmed glasses, "groups of women began gathering here in Boston for informal discussions about women's issues. When we began to talk honestly and openly about our own experiences, we began to realize that our *personal* problems weren't just personal. That is, in talking about our own lives in small groups of women we could trust, we began to identify the *social* nature of our oppression. We talked about things like the oppressive structure of the nuclear family – where the father goes out to work and kids go to school to learn to be good soldiers, and mother stays home and cleans up everyone else's shit."

Many of the older women nodded.

Molly continued, looking directly into the crowd. "In one of the sessions today, we'll be talking about the history of the nuclear family, in which the man gets to rule over everyone, like since the beginning of recorded time. It's not all that different today. It's even true in most communes, the alternative families we've tried to create ourselves. Who gets to talk at house meetings? Who does the cooking?"

A few women laughed nervously.

"For those of you sisters who have children, who makes the lunches for the kids every day? Who takes the kids to the doctor? Who changes the diapers?"

"Right on!" someone yelled.

"And you younger sisters, now in high school or college, think about this: Who talks the most in the classroom? Who gets called on? Who's encouraged to study math and science and who's told by her guidance counselor, 'Oh, you're not doing so hot in algebra? Don't worry. Take typing instead. After all, you don't need a college education, you are just going to get married and your husband will take care of you.'"

The audience booed, and Ellen was embarrassed to catch herself nodding vigorously. That's what she meant about Radcliffe. She wanted to study in an all-female environment, where the men didn't drown out what she and the other women had to say.

"Today at the workshops," Molly said, "you'll hear about issues that you can do something about, some things that are revolutionary acts: beginning to learn about our bodies, and taking control of our own health care, learning self-defense, especially judo and Tae Kwon Do – and by the way, we're offering classes two nights a week in Harvard Square for all who are interested. It's critical that women get stronger and know that you can defend yourself."

Defend yourself, Diane thought. She sat absolutely still. She started to drift back, but took several slow, deep breaths, forcing herself to stay present, right here, in this room, with these women, listening to the speaker. She told herself she was safe here; she could feel it.

"Another thing you can do," said Molly, "is to protest oppression where you find it. Restaurants and private clubs – like Locke-Ober in downtown Boston, which doesn't let women in except at certain hours and only if you go through a back door. Or look at the Playboy Club down the street a couple of miles – it makes money by exploiting women as objects."

Nina couldn't even look up. She was writing so fast that she was sweating with the effort, completely enthralled. She knew she had to get every word, because she couldn't write and process what she heard at the same time. Thinking about all this would have to come later.

"And another action you can take," urged Molly, who was now punctuating each point with a jab of her fist, "is to confront men on the street when they harass you. They can do these things because they believe you'll be too scared to call them on their piggy behavior and you'll put your head down and act all girly and take it – whatever disgusting names or comments they shout at you. NO MORE!" The room erupted with cheers.

Nina thought about how she felt walking past the empty construction site a couple of hours ago, braced for verbal attack. She'd been okay, even if the hardhats had been on the job, but she was tough; she'd grown up in Manhattan. She wondered about the others, but she didn't want to miss the speaker's next words.

"Only confront them when there're lots of other people around," Molly cautioned, "not when you're alone or on a deserted street, so you don't put yourself in danger. Tell them that you will be spoken to with respect!"

Someone in the back stood and belted out, "R-E-S-P-E-C-T..." but Molly held up her hand for her to stop. "I'm serious, sister!"

She said, "Think about re-naming yourself with something other than the name you got from the patriarchy."

Diane looked around to see if anyone else was as mystified as she, but everyone seemed to be nodding their heads in agreement.

"And look at our self-image, especially as it relates to using cosmetics and so-called fashion, which is shoved down our throats by Madison Avenue. Right now, we're a large population that's being exploited for profit – the new lipstick, the newest model boots, even the best kind of jeans. Are you making a free choice of what to wear, or were you sold a way to make yourself look sexy and fashionable and good-looking to men?"

Laurie and some of the other women squirmed uncomfortably. Others looked confused.

"Today in the workshops," said Molly, "You'll hear about class divisions in our so-called 'classless nation,' and about racism too. You'll hear from our Black sisters about what they're doing to take more power in their struggle. You may remember our sister Ruby Doris Smith-Robinson, who unfortunately passed away a couple of years ago at the age of only twenty-five, who was a moving force in the Student Non-Violent Coordinating Committee. In 1964, she contributed to a brilliant paper called *The Position of Women in SNCC*, which criticized the treatment of women civil rights workers at a SNCC staff meeting. Stokely Carmichael responded to the paper: 'The only position for women in SNCC is prone.'" She paused, waiting for all the boos and hisses to die down.

"Look, sisters," Molly said. "Men run the Movement. They're not going to give up their power voluntarily – why should they? To be nice? Nowhere in history do we see masters relinquishing their power to slaves or subordinates. The slaves have to rise up and take control. And that, my sisters, is what we've been – slaves. Slaves to our husbands, slaves to our fathers, slaves to our bosses and our professors, slaves to the capitalist system that tells us what to wear, how to look, what to do with our time."

Ellen thought of her father's admonishment right before she left Vermont. "Don't go getting any highfalutin ideas down there in the city, Ellen. You're a good girl, and me and your mother, we want you to stay that way. You're our little girl and you belong here with us until you get married."

Molly said, "Look here. Radical men may talk about the need for revolution, but sisters, let me tell you that unless we take matters into our own hands, guess who's gonna be cooking the celebration dinner the night we overthrow the system? Men will not give up their power. We have to take it from them."

"Right on, sister!" someone shouted from up near the podium, as many women clapped.

Molly paced around as she spoke. "We are slaves to men's ideas of sex, as evidenced by who gets to be on top, whose pleasure we're talking about in bed. How many of you in this room have never had an orgasm? Okay, you don't have to raise your hands right now. How many of you have faked an orgasm?" She pointed into the audience.

Nervous laughter, as lots and lots of hands were raised.

"And for what reason? So you can stroke the ego of your man? What about saying, 'Hey, buster, where's mine?' You'll find a workshop on sexuality, and you'll hear from a remarkable work in progress by Anne Koedt from New York, that she's calling *The Myth of The Vaginal Orgasm*."

Nina looked up and stared at the speaker. She'd heard about Anne Koedt at work, though she'd never met her. This sounded like some pretty radical stuff.

Molly walked back behind the podium as she began to conclude. "We also want you to talk to us and talk to each other, about the issues that are important to you in your own process of liberation. Our ultimate goal is the destruction of the caste system, and the posts that hold it up – the family, private property, the government, and the machinations that keep these going – capitalism, racism, imperialism, class divisions, and now sexism and misogyny."

"Go to your workshops now – you'll find the list on the papers at your seat, and if you don't have one, there are signs on the classroom doors. And talk to each other. Talk out loud and tell the truth. Sisters, I'm telling you, speak your truth and, like the poet Muriel Rukeyser told us, the whole world as we know it will blow apart!"

To Sisterhood!

The room exploded into stunning applause. Nina stopped writing and looked around. Women were standing up – some even standing on their chairs – and cheering and yelling and raising their voices with the kind of energy she'd heard last month at the anti-war rally in Central Park, only that was half a million people, not 500 women.

Ellen's face shone with the excitement of it all. Laurie was busy, trying to organize the four of them so they each could go to a different session and compare notes later.

Diane was the only one who was quiet. She didn't understand a lot of what Molly had said. It seemed like most of the women here were middle-class, college-educated, white women. What would her colleagues on the line at the candy factory think of this meeting? As far as Diane knew, no one there thought or talked like this speaker. No one at work seemed to know anything about this stuff. Most of the women she worked with had brothers or boyfriends or husbands or sons who were serving in Vietnam. *What did all this have to do with us?*

✳ **Three** ✳

As the women gathered their bags, and all the pamphlets and papers they'd picked up at the conference, Laurie proposed that they walk back across the river to Harvard Square. "It's not that far," she urged. "It's such a gorgeous day. And we have *so* much to talk about."

Ellen hesitated. "I'm not sure I can walk that far…" she began, but Diane looped her arm through Ellen's.

"C'mon, we can take it slow," she said. Only Diane had noticed Ellen's slight limp. "Or if you get tired, we can always hop on the T in Central Square."

Nina looked down at her favorite work boots, which already had a couple of New York miles and a few Boston miles on them today. "I'm in," she said, hoisting her knapsack over both shoulders. "Let's go!"

Nearly an hour later, they arrived in the center of the Square – hot, sweaty, and thirsty from talking nonstop about what they saw and heard all afternoon.

Ellen was excited about the workshop on Marriage as an Oppressive Institution. Nina was at the health group briefly, and learned about women taking control of their own bodies. Then the room got too hot and crowded, so she slipped in next door, where Laurie, mesmerized by the self-defense demonstration, was watching two women from the collective smash boards with their bare hands. Diane went to the community organizing group, and learned about class division, as well as racism and sexism in the workplace, and about how Harvard was trying to buy up her neighborhood. She knew something about that.

The property at the end of her block was vacant and she'd heard rumors about a new research building. It was a lot for her to take in at once. She listened to the excited talk of the others, not sure that she was feeling what they all seemed to be experiencing.

Diane shouted: "Anyone for ice cream?" and she and Laurie engaged in a brief debate on the merits of Brigham's versus Bailey's, considering both taste and price.

They decided to splurge, and headed around the corner to Bailey's. They ordered hot fudge sundaes all around, except Nina, who got black coffee and a cream cheese on date-nut bread sandwich.

"I, um, forgot to eat lunch," she confessed. "I was in a hurry getting off the train and finding Emmanuel."

The others groaned with delight as the server pushed the gooey sundaes toward them over the counter. Carefully carrying their treats and a glass of water each, they made their way to a round marble table, and settled down in the cast iron chairs to continue the conversation.

"This conference – all of today – was so far out!" Laurie said. "Of course, I was part of the strike at Harvard last month – I mean, I didn't occupy the building or anything, but I was part of the boycott, and the demonstrations. But this – this Movement is *ours*! Women unite!" Several people at the counter turned around to look at her. Laurie grinned, and flashed them a peace sign.

Nina liked Laurie's enthusiasm. "What impresses me," she said, "is how many radical women were in one place. I'm going to have to spend some time reading over my notes. And I hope I got down all the important points. I never thought in such clear terms about how screwed up the Movement is, with the men getting to make all the decisions." She leaned forward on her elbows, eyes shining.

"I wouldn't know much about that." Ellen popped a fudge-covered maraschino cherry into her mouth. "I'm thinking that at least we can choose who we wish to marry. The speaker in the workshop I went to said that for much of recorded history, women were chattel, to be passed from father's house to husband's house. Of course, I know that from reading the Old Testament, but –"

"I'm never getting married," Diane said. "I guess I haven't seen it work all that well." She knew too many couples who stayed together "for the sake of the children," when, Diane thought, the children would have been much better off without either of them, no matter what the Church said. She pictured her parents' constant battles, her mother screaming and her father getting quiet and leaving the house.

"That's kind of extreme," Laurie said. "My parents have a great marriage. My father teaches psychiatry at Harvard Med School and has a private practice. He works long hours and I know it can't be fun for my mom. But they have a good social life, lots of friends. They take a vacation each season, and we all go to our house on the Cape every summer. My mother doesn't work, but she's involved in about every Jewish charity on the Eastern seaboard."

"Sounds like work to me," said Nina. "My parents – or rather, I should say, my father and my stepmother – have a weird relationship. She married him for his money, but she didn't get it ahead of time that he doesn't *have* any money. He just lives like he does. It's all show. She's pissed at him that she didn't figure it out, and she takes every opportunity to snipe about him behind his back. But he thinks she married him because he's so talented – he's a writer, but he works as an editor. They each think I don't know the story. They're all lovey-dovey with each other in front of me."

"Wow," said Laurie. Ellen adjusted her glasses and leaned forward. Diane waited for Nina to go on.

"My mother died when I was thirteen," Nina said. "She and I were close. She'd been sick for a long time. One of the last things she asked me was to look after my father when she was gone. Kind of a strange request, don't you think, to ask a kid? My father completely fell apart without her. And only a year after she was gone, he married Muriel. That bitch. She hates me." Nina sat up straighter and paused to collect herself. She couldn't believe she was telling this to a group of women she hardly knew.

"Why would she hate you?" Laurie frowned.

"I don't know. Except she knows that my father loves me – and his work – better than he loves her. But I'm his daughter. He's supposed to love me." Nina gave a small shrug.

"What about you, Ellen?" Laurie asked. "Do your parents get along?"

"Oh, yes." Ellen was quick to reply. "But even if they have disagreements, I wouldn't know about it. Everything is talked about behind their bedroom door. My father rules the house and my mother does everything he says. Except she doesn't." Ellen stifled a giggle.

"When she wants something, she knows how to get around him. Like last month, we needed a new living room sofa. The old one was ratty, chewed on by the dogs and everything. The one she wanted cost a lot more than she knew my father would agree to. She went to the store up in Burlington, where they don't know our family. She put 25% down on layaway, then came home and told Father she'd ordered the sofa, and showed him a picture of it she'd cut out of the catalog and the receipt for the deposit. He grunted, 'hmm, expensive, but if it's what you want, I guess it's worth it.' He didn't get that the receipt was only for the deposit; he thought it was for the whole thing. Mother thanked him warmly. She paid for the rest of the sofa by selling her grandmother's brooch, which she seldom wore. He never knew it cost four times what he thought."

"Whew," Diane whistled. "Now *that* was sharp of her."

"Feminine wiles," Nina replied. "Sounds like woman-power to me. Good work, Ellen's mom!" Ellen smiled.

"Sounds like you have a pretty smart mother, Ellen. Did she go to college?" Laurie wanted to know.

"No," said Ellen quietly. "In our family, college is only for boys. You cannot *believe* how much I had to beg to get them to let me go to the junior college in our county. 'An education is wasted on a girl,' I heard all my life. 'Why spend the money when you're going to get married and raise children?'"

"Maybe because you want to learn about your world," Laurie said. "Religion, history, literature, mathematics, science, philosophy…"

To Sisterhood!

"I know, I know," Ellen's eyes were shining. "I want to come to Radcliffe *so* much. To get the best education. No distractions. No guys raising their hands and having the teacher call on them first. I want to study with and learn from women. My aunt went to Radcliffe, and going there has been my dream ever since I first read *The Little Locksmith* in junior high school."

"What's that?" Diane asked. She'd polished off her sundae, and sat back in her chair, listening carefully.

"It's a book, a memoir, by Katharine Butler Hathaway. She lived in Maine, she was an invalid as a child, confined to bed, and *her* dreams were to be able to pursue her writing, and to be independent, and to find someone to love. Her doctors and her family told her she was deformed, and no one would ever love her. When she was healthy enough to leave home, she came to Radcliffe, and met several fantastic women who took her under their wings, and her whole world opened up. Listen to this…"

Ellen took a breath, closed her eyes, and recited, *"If you let your fear of consequence prevent you from following your deepest instinct, then your life will be safe, expedient and thin."*

"Wow," said Laurie. "She wrote that?"

"Yes," said Ellen. "I've read *The Little Locksmith* probably forty times. It's a wonderful book. Then she says –"

"Wait!" Laurie stopped her. "Don't ruin it for us. I'll get a copy at the library."

Ellen laughed. "What's *your* dream, Laurie?"

"Me? I'm not sure. But I know it *will* have something to do with repairing the world. Look at the mess it's in – the war, the street people, kids going to bed at night hungry, all because the greedy military industrial complex rules the country. I don't know yet. But that's why I'm doing liberal arts. I want to learn a lot about a lot of things. And then I'll figure out how I can be most useful. Probably I'll get married and have kids someday. But not until I've had a chance to see the world, and do something valuable and important!"

Ellen reached over and squeezed Laurie's hand. She turned to Nina.

"What about you, Nina? Did you go to college?" Ellen asked.

"One year," said Nina. "Sarah Lawrence. Then I dropped out to go to work and live on my own. I was the big disappointment in my family, especially to my grandparents. They had high hopes for me. Me, I wanted to get out into the real world and try to become a writer like my father, only I want to write about things that matter, about what's happening in the world, things the straight press doesn't cover. I guess I want to be the best journalist the alternative press has ever seen! Right now, I'm still an intern at RNB. But I think," she said calmly, though her heart was beating fast. "I think, if this story about today's conference is good enough, I could get a real job there, as part of the collective. That's what I want. And it will make Muriel just shit." Ellen flinched at Nina's language, but didn't say anything.

"Cool," Laurie said. "Your turn, Diane. Are you in school?" And when Diane shook her head, Laurie asked her, "What's your dream?"

To Sisterhood!

"You know," Diane spoke softly. "I'm going to have to give that some thought and get back to you. I have some things I like to do, but not anything you'd call a grand passion. I get up every day, go to work, help out at home…" She sat up straight with a start.

"Oh, my gosh!" she said, pushing back her chair. "This, you all, it's been wonderful, but I've got to go. I promised my sister I'd be home by six. It's her birthday today. I'm so full. I don't know how I'm going to eat a bite at the party. But really, we all should keep in touch." She tore a napkin in pieces and wrote her phone number three times.

"Thanks, Diane," Ellen said. "Nina, write to us from New York, will you? Please send us a copy of your story when it's published. Here's my address," she said, writing on another napkin. "When do you think it will come out?"

"Of course I will," Nina said, "not sure yet when it will be in print. And someday," she said, "you'll see my byline in a cool paper, like the *Village Voice*."

As they got up to leave, Laurie said, "Can you imagine this conversation happening if we'd been a group of men? We'd have been sitting here for two hours talking about the Red Sox!"

Nina, Ellen, and Diane all laughed.

Laurie raised her nearly empty water glass. "Nina, here's to your success," Laurie said. "And to all of ours. Here's to sisterhood!"

"To sisterhood!" the others chimed in, clinking their glasses together and beaming at their new friends.

※ ※ ※ ※

Nina waited until the others had left Bailey's. She finished her now-cold coffee, picked up her knapsack and walked out, smack into a grubby-looking boy with long blond hair. He stood right in front of the door with his guitar, offering passersby a lusty, off-key rendition of *Daydream Believer*.

"Sorry," he mouthed.

Nina glared at him. She had no tolerance for bad music. She turned left, stopped for a minute to grab today's paper at Nini's Corner, then walked past the theater, the church graveyard, and on down Garden Street, to the Sheraton Commander Hotel.

"Reservation for Rosen," she told the clerk.

"Of course, Miss Rosen," he said. "Welcome to the Sheraton. Here you are." Nina took the key and went up to her room. It was so-so compared to the places she'd stayed with her parents, but a whole lot nicer than her East Village walk-up. She double locked the door, dumped her knapsack on the floor, then ran a hot bath.

Two hours later, she woke up freezing in cold water. "Oh, crap," she said to no one, and then stood up and took a hot shower to warm herself. She washed her hair, using the whole mini bottle of shampoo, and dried it using all the towels, which she left in a heap on the floor.

Nina flipped through the few local TV channels, hoping to see some coverage of the women's conference on the evening news, but what seemed to be happening was that yesterday, the Celtics won Game 6 of the NBA Finals, and were headed to Los Angeles to play Game 7

To Sisterhood!

tomorrow. All she knew about either team is that Wilt Chamberlain once tried to pick her up on Lexington Avenue. She turned him down. He was pretty cute, but too tall.

Bored and disgusted, she turned off the TV and crawled under the covers. She fell asleep right away in spite of her long nap in the tub.

※ ※ ※ ※

Diane rushed down the stairs into the T station. If she weren't already late, she could have walked home easily. She'd promised her sister she'd be there by 6:00 and it was almost 5:30. Who knew what state her mother would be in?

"*Oh, please, God,*" Diane prayed. "*Let her please not have started with the vodka already. Theresa deserves a good party.*" "*Hurry, hurry, hurry,*" she said to the train. She tapped her fingers against her pocketbook impatiently, and walked over to toss a dime into the guitar case of a boy singing *Hey, Jude,* accompanied by a strung-out-looking girl strumming an autoharp.

Finally, the train. Diane got a seat, and for the first time all day, she let herself relax. So much of what she'd seen and heard at the conference was strange. She thought about what the keynote speaker had said about women taking control of their own bodies, how childbirth was controlled by men, and the importance of learning how to protect yourself with karate. In the few minutes before the train reached Central Square, Diane closed her eyes. The past few years might have been different if she'd known about this stuff, especially about how to defend yourself. Maybe this Women's Liberation movement has something for her. She thought back to the last time she was completely happy, and she couldn't remember, just that everything changed when she realized she was the only one who could take care of her sister.

Every morning, ten-year-old Diane made them breakfast, usually corn flakes with bananas, while their mother slept in. Diane washed herself and helped her sister, because Theresa wasn't too good at it, and the nuns always checked for clean fingernails and a fresh handkerchief. Diane made them both lunch. She took out the Wonder Bread, slathered on the mayonnaise, the way Theresa liked it, then added exactly one leaf of lettuce and three pieces of bologna, being careful to remove the cellophane string from the edges. She put mustard on her own sandwich, never on Theresa's. Into the brown paper sacks went the sandwiches, and one apple each.

Every morning, Diane walked her sister to Sacred Heart School, ate with her in the lunchroom to keep the other girls from teasing her, and walked her home. When they got home, she hung up her school uniform, and Theresa's, and made them both a snack. She helped Theresa with her arithmetic problems, because she had a hard time with homework, and then while her sister watched Howdy Doody, *Diane went upstairs to do her own homework.*

Around 5:30, Diane prepared dinner, carefully scrubbing potatoes to bake, or starting a pot of rice. Theresa helped by setting the table. Only then – minutes before their father was due – would they go upstairs to wake their mother. Most of the time, she managed to get up and throw some hamburgers into a pan, and make an iceberg lettuce salad with Russian dressing, or macaroni with marinara. But not always. On those nights, Diane cooked the rest of the dinner too.

After the meal, she washed and Theresa dried the dishes, while their father opened a six-pack and their mother enjoyed another cocktail. Then they all watched TV. Mostly, it was quiet, except when John had too many beers, and got angry with his wife for not keeping the house cleaner, or for forgetting to call his mother on her birthday, or something that Diane couldn't get to or didn't remember.

Then there was shouting and fighting, and Diane took Theresa upstairs. She read to her, and told her stories of how someday, Diane was going to take her to Rome to see the Pope. Diane imagined how glorious it would be to have an audience with the Pope, and to see all the Cardinals in their cassocks, with the Pope all in white.

Theresa said she was going to ask the Pope to make Mother and Daddy stop fighting, and to help Mother not be tired all the time. When they got to Rome, everything would be better.

Diane's thoughts were interrupted by the slowing train. When it reached Central Square, she got off, climbed the stairs, and exited onto Mass. Ave. As she walked the few blocks toward home, she tried to understand all that had happened to her – to make sense of it in the context of what she heard today. She wondered if she was what those organizers would call an oppressed woman, and about all the ways she'd been screwed over.

As she walked up the front steps exactly at 6:00, Diane squared her shoulders. Tonight, she would start to talk to her sister about getting their own apartment. Diane couldn't stay here much longer. And she had to get Theresa out too. Now, no one could stop them.

Even though she had a headache and was exhausted by the long, confusing day, Diane was happier than she'd been in a long time. Though she was still working on a plan, she felt powerful like never before. She was not alone. She had her sister, and now, in a way, she had three new sisters too.

Diane opened the door. She saw her mother first – all dressed up, tipsy, but still okay. Diane could tell that even from across the room.

"Yoo hoo," her mother waved gaily. "Glad you're here. Did you have a good day?" She had no idea where Diane had been. Why was she being so pleasant?

"Fine. Where's Theresa?" Diane asked.

"Upstairs getting dressed. She is so excited. I have a surprise for you," Magda trilled in a little-girl sing-song voice. "Guess who's here?"

Diane turned toward the living room, and her full stomach gave a lurch. Her throat went dry and her heart started beating double time.

Leaning against the doorframe, with his arms spread wide, was a leaner, much darker-tanned Tony. He wore a big smirk, pretty much how she remembered him.

"Hey there, Dee," he said.

Diane didn't say a word. She couldn't open her mouth, or she'd vomit.

Dad came in now, behind Tony. "Hey, how do you greet a returning veteran? Where are your manners, Diane? Come give Tony a big hug."

To Sisterhood!

Diane felt her body go toward him, but her mind was outside her body, watching herself cross the room slowly, like moving through water. She was not going to spoil Theresa's day. Tony reached out toward her. She ducked his hand, gave him a nod, and quickly ran up the stairs.

Theresa wore her light blue party dress, with white vinyl go-go boots.

"That's quite an outfit." Diane smiled with pleasure at her sister, hiding her revulsion at seeing that man. She took her sister's hand.

"How was Paragon Park?" she said. "Did you have a good time?"

"Oh, yes! I did go on the carousel," Theresa said, "and my teacher sat with me on the horse so I wouldn't be afraid. But I wasn't afraid anyway! And then Daddy picked me up and Uncle Tony came too, and now we're home and it's time for my party!"

"I'm glad you're having a good birthday so far." Diane willed herself to sound cheerful. "You go downstairs now. There's a big cake waiting for you. I need a few minutes up here to get ready."

As Theresa trotted happily down the stairs, Diane sank to the floor and started to cry. Memories of the last time she'd seen Tony were too painful. Why did he have to show up tonight? How was she going to keep it together for Theresa's party with that awful man here? She remembered when she used to look up to him, when he was wonderful.

Diane laughed as she reached over the side of the rowboat, scooped up some water, and playfully splashed her sister.

"You're making me all wet!" eight-year-old Theresa squealed, and Uncle Tony, who was rowing, said in his silly imitation pirate voice, "Ahoy, me buckos! If you keep wriggling around in this jollyboat, you're both gonna end up in the drink."

"The Drink" was the Charles River, not far from where Diane and her sister lived with their parents, half a mile away from the service station where Uncle Tony – who was not their real uncle, but that's what Theresa called him – pumped gas after school for their father, John.

"Hey, now," Uncle Tony said in his regular voice, "it's about time to head back to the dock. I promised your mom I'd have you back by four." Both girls grumbled, and begged for more time on the water – it was so hot and muggy! – but he rowed back, helped the girls step out, threw each a towel, and bundled them into his pride and joy – the 1950 Pontiac he'd lovingly restored with John's help, even before he'd gotten his license a few months ago.

As Uncle Tony pulled into the narrow driveway between her house and the neighbors', Diane knew something was wrong. They could all hear the shouts, though that wasn't new – her parents yelled all the time. But when the shouts were followed by the sound of crashing glass and then a big thud, Theresa's eyes grew wide, and Diane was afraid, even though Uncle Tony was with them.

"You both stay here a minute." Uncle Tony tried to sound casual as he jumped from the car. Diane put her arm around Theresa's shoulders and pulled her close. "Sshhh, it's all right, honey," Diane whispered as Theresa snuggled closer. "It's gonna be all right."

A few minutes later, Uncle Tony appeared in the doorway and motioned for them to come in.

"All clear," he said. "Everything's okay."

Diane knew it was not okay, not in this house. It hadn't been okay for some time now.

"Your mom tripped and fell," Uncle Tony said. "She's not hurt. You can go in."

Holding Theresa by the hand, Diane walked up the front steps onto the porch, and pushed the door open wider. She could smell the liquor. She saw shards of broken glass on the floor, even though her father was tucking away the broom he'd used to try to sweep up the mess.

"There's my two lovely girls," he said with a joviality Diane knew was forced. "Your mother is upstairs resting now. She's had a fall."

"Why is your forehead bleeding?" Theresa squinted up at her father.

"Oh, it's nothing," John said, smiling. "I fell down too, trying to catch your mother. I'll go get a bandage. It'll be as good as new!"

No, it won't, Diane thought. Not anymore. Usually, her mother went to sleep and when she woke the next day, didn't remember anything. Now it seems she'd been throwing bottles – or was it a glass? – at Dad. Why didn't he see that something was wrong? Why didn't he call Dr. Mackenzie for help, like when Theresa had one of her stomach aches or when they both got chicken pox? Why couldn't her father make her mother stop yelling all the time? Theresa was scared a lot of the time, and Diane was pretty sure that she was the only one who could take good care of her. She loved her sister so much.

Magda's insistent shout brought Diane back to the present, to her sister's 18th birthday party. She wiped her eyes, and pulled herself together, for Theresa's sake.

Somehow, she managed to go downstairs. But seeing Tony sitting across from her, grinning, was so nauseating that she could hardly eat or say a word.

Fortunately, Theresa didn't seem to notice Diane's discomfort. She was excited by her party and the presents, and by her day at Paragon Park, which she talked about nonstop, and about having her favorite Uncle Tony come for her birthday, and about her high school graduation in two weeks.

Well, Diane thought, *at least Theresa's having a wonderful time, and that's important.* Diane's head was throbbing. She had to try to figure out how to avoid Tony now that he was back in Cambridge.

❉ **Four** ❉

Ellen had to take two buses from Harvard Square to get to Charlie's apartment, and she was exhausted by the time she got there. When she'd called her high school boyfriend last month to see if she could stay with him, he'd agreed right away. He also promised not to mention her stay to his parents, so it wouldn't get back to Ellen's.

"That's cool," he'd said. He knew as well as she that news travelled fast in their community. Ellen's parents would've made a big fuss about it not being proper. But not everything was their business.

Charlie opened the door wide and reached out to greet her with a big grin and an even bigger hug.

"Hey, babe," he said as he grabbed her two suitcases. "You sure are a sight for sore eyes."

"Hey, yourself, fresh guy," Ellen retorted. "Look at you!" Charlie had grown a scraggly beard and his hair was down to his collar. "What do your folks think of your new look?"

"Haven't been home since Christmas. Don't you think I would've come to visit you?"

"I guess, sure. Still, your father's going to hit the roof. I'll bet you a buck you're clean-shaven within an hour of crossing their front door, or you'll be sleeping in the woodshed. Your father would never stand to have a hippie in his house." Ellen shook her head, smiling.

"Yeah, you're probably right." Charlie said. "Tell me all about you, Ellen. How was your weekend? What did you do here in the Hub? And how the hell have you been?" He took her bags, and motioned her in.

"Great, excellent, too much to tell now. Charlie, I'm pooped. If you don't mind, can we catch up in the morning?"

Charlie patted his belly, which was much more ample than the last time Ellen had seen him. "I'm okay with that. I've already had dinner. Can I get you something to eat?"

"No, thanks," she said. "I'd rather get to bed. My bus isn't until noon, so let me take you out for breakfast, and we'll talk then, all right?"

"Or we can talk some in bed." He winked, and reached for her. She stepped back.

"Pardon me?" Having known Charlie nearly all her life, Ellen was used to his teasing, but he didn't sound like he was kidding now.

"Bed." he said. "What you just said you wanted to do." He took her hand eagerly, and led her into the next room, where the single bed was made up with what looked like clean sheets. *Uh, oh*, she thought.

"Thanks, Charlie," she said, yawning. "This is kind of you. Where are you going to sleep?"

"Here, of course," he said, starting to unbuckle his belt.

"Hold it right there, mister!" Ellen's loud voice startled him. He'd never heard her raise her voice, not in ordinary conversation.

"What's the matter?"

She spoke quietly now. "If we didn't sleep together when we were dating, what makes you think I would sleep with you now?"

He shrugged. "Well, you're a college woman now. I figured –"

"Forget it." Ellen's eyes were that darker shade of blue they turned when she got angry. He'd seen that look before. She was not going to change her mind.

"This is the only bed," he said petulantly, his eager anticipation fading to annoyance and disappointment.

"I am *not* sharing your bed." Ellen folded her arms and waited. She was good at waiting silently, he knew all too well.

"Where *are* you going to sleep then, huh? The couch is too small and it smells like cat piss. C'mon, you can sleep here with me. I won't try anything. Friends?"

"Friends," Ellen agreed. "But I am *not* sharing a bed with you. I'll sleep on the floor. Just give me a blanket and a pillow. I'm too exhausted to argue."

"Look," Charlie said. "Why don't you go sleep in Green's room? He has a big mattress on the floor, and he won't be home tonight. He's with his girlfriend."

"Who?"

"Green. Sam Green. My roommate."

Charlie led Ellen to the room at the end of the hall. Posters of Janis Joplin and The Mothers of Invention adorned the walls. A king-sized mattress, covered with a light blanket, took up most of the floor space. Beside the bed was a plain oak chair, a clock-radio, and an upside-down milk crate, which held two neatly folded pairs of jeans, and a few colored tees.

"Thanks, Charlie. See you in the morning."

He gave her a brotherly kiss on the forehead. She smiled and closed the door after him. There was no lock, she noticed, but Charlie wouldn't bother her. Ellen took off her skirt and her new blouse, hung them in the closet, unfolded her clean tee shirt, and stuffed one of the pillows into it. Then she pulled on her nightgown, crawled under the blanket, and fell asleep immediately.

Ellen didn't hear the door opening, but the sudden light from the naked bulb overhead jarred her from sleep. She opened her eyes and found herself staring at the glow-in-the-dark alarm clock, which read 2:08 am.

"WHAT???" she half-yelled, half-rasped, sitting up with the blanket around her. If that wasn't Charlie sneaking in, he'd never hear her yell. He'd joked many times about being able to sleep through a fire alarm.

"Who the hell are *you*? What are you doing here?" A tall, skinny, sandy-haired bearded guy stood in the doorway. Ellen gasped, thinking *Eddy?* but of course, that couldn't be. The guy looked harmless enough, she thought, but he could be crazy.

To Sisterhood!

"I'm Ellen. Who are you?" She hugged the blanket up under her chin so he couldn't see her quivering.

"Hey, Ellen. Charlie's girl, right? The one from up north?" Too startled to correct him, Ellen nodded.

"Hi, I'm Sam," he said, rubbing his chin. "This is my room." He gestured around the sparsely furnished space with the other hand. "And this," he continued, "this is my bed. I'm really tired and I've had a crappy day and an even worse night. I just want to go to sleep, so would you please leave and go back and sleep in Charlie's room?"

Ellen calmed herself, apologized, and tried to explain that she and Charlie had had a misunderstanding, and that he was the one who told her to sleep here because Sam wouldn't be home.

Sam nodded kindly, but said, "I *am* home and I would like my bed back, please."

Ellen's eyes filled with tears. She wiped them with the satin edge of the blanket, which made Sam smile.

"Oh, c'mon, don't cry," he said. "Here, look, the bed is plenty big. You roll over there and go to sleep. I'll sleep way over here." And just like that, Sam turned his back, stripped down to his briefs, crawled in, and fell asleep instantly, snoring loudly. *Could this day get any stranger?* Ellen thought, as she, too, drifted off for the second time that night.

Five hours later, Ellen woke to find Sam staring at her intently.

"Hey, Charlie's girl – you're beautiful," he said.

"Oh, I bet you say that to all your roommates' ex-girlfriends." Ellen rubbed her eyes sleepily and smiled.

"No, I mean it. Charlie used to tell me how pretty you are, but I thought it was his…you know, talking."

Ellen winced. "You don't need to be crude," she said. "We never slept together, did he tell you that?" *Ellen!* She chided herself. *Why are you telling such personal things to a stranger? But he doesn't feel like a stranger*, she thought, and then she heard Eddy's voice: *It's okay, Sis. He's a good guy.*

Sam looked at her strangely, and said, "We didn't get into it."

"Why are you here?" Ellen was surprised at her boldness.

"It *is* my room, remember?"

"Oh, right." Ellen said, playfully slapping her forehead.

"I was at my friend's house," Sam said. "We had a hassle. I got annoyed and came home."

"And look what you found in your bed!" Ellen knew she was flirting now. It was Monday morning, her last day in Boston. She was in the bed of a strange man, and having fun.

"Maybe we can do something about that." Sam reached toward her, and playfully tucked her straight hair behind one ear. "Tell me something you've never told anyone else."

To Sisterhood!

"Really?" Ellen looked directly into his eyes to see if he was teasing her. What she saw was calm, peacefulness, depth. *I can trust this man*, she thought. *I feel like I've known him before, somehow.*

"Really, truly," he said. "You might think this is kind of freaky, but I feel a strong connection with you. I want to know you better. I want to know all about you."

"OK." Ellen smiled again. "But can I have a bathroom break first, please?"

"Sure." He got up, went to the closet, pulled out a well-worn light flannel robe, and tossed it to her. "You get decent. I'll run down the hall first."

Sam came back in a minute. "We're in luck," he said, as Ellen brushed the hair out of her eyes and stood up in his much-too-long-for-her robe. "Looks like ol' Charlie got called out to drive an early shift. He left a note for you on the kitchen table. Says he's sorry and to have a good trip home." He thrust it at her.

Ellen didn't read it; she had to pee too badly. "I'll be right back." She dashed out to the bathroom. She'd managed to tuck her toothbrush under the sleeve of the robe. After washing up and brushing her teeth, she looked in the mirror. *What on earth are you doing, Ellen?* And then she heard Eddy again: *I said he's okay. You gotta trust me.* She took a breath and returned to the bedroom.

"Where were we?" Sam was back under the covers, reaching for her hand to pull her down to him. "Ah, I know. I want to hear your secret."

"For real?" Ellen was amazed. No one had ever asked her anything like this before.

"For real." Sam's warm eyes were kind and attentive.

Ellen paused. "Sometimes I can see things other people can't."

"What do you mean?" Sam looked at her curiously.

"Well, every so often I see things before they happen, and I can sort of see what's right there in front of everyone, but it's not visible to others." Ellen held her breath, hoping he wouldn't laugh or freak out.

"Far out," Sam said.

"You can't tell anyone." Ellen exhaled and twirled a piece of her hair, like she always did when she was nervous.

"Of course not, who would I tell?"

"I tried to tell my mother once but it was a disaster." She went on. "The first time it happened, I was almost nine. It was right after my great-aunt's funeral. I saw some women there, friends of hers I guess, who I felt I belonged with, somehow, though they didn't even talk to me. I thought that they would understand me, in a way no one else did. The next night…I don't know quite how to describe it. I tried to explain to my mother that I was having what I now think is called an out-of-body experience."

"What happened?" Sam's voice was soft. He took another piece of hair that had fallen in front of Ellen's face, and gently tucked it behind her other ear.

"There," he said, "now I can see you," and gave her a big grin. Ellen didn't know what to make of this tall stranger. Somehow…she didn't know what, except that she'd never felt it before.

"I think I said something like, 'Mother, I feel kind of strange.' She said, 'What's wrong, Ellen?' She was preparing dinner. She's pretty calm, not too much fazes her. I said, 'I can hear you talking to me and I can see you and know what you're saying but I feel like I'm up here kind of looking down at us talking.'"

Ellen paused, carefully searching Sam's face for any kind of ridicule. Finding none, she went on with her story.

"'Ellen,' she said. 'Have you been reading those silly science fiction books again? It's been a difficult week for us, with Martha's funeral and all. Now, go to your room and lie down until dinner. If your head hurts, wring out a cool washrag and put it on your brow.'"

"So," Ellen said, "I figured out pretty quickly that this was not something to talk about."

Sam waited.

"I told her: 'No, my head is fine, Mother. I guess I'm tired. I think I *will* lie down, if you don't need my help here.' And I never told my mother anything of importance again."

Sam was quiet for a long moment.

"Ellen. I don't think that's strange," he said. "I mean, I don't think you wigged out or anything. I've had those kinds of things happen to me. Not exactly. But I can think of someone I care about, and I dream about them, and the next time we speak, I find out that they were dreaming about me too. It's like we can communicate on another plane."

Ellen smiled. *What a relief.*

"Sam," she said, trying out his name. "You're the only person I've ever told this to." *Well, the only person besides Eddy, and that was long after...* "Thank you for not laughing."

"Ellen, I'd never laugh at you. And that's a promise. If it's important to you, it matters to me."

"Thank you." Ellen couldn't believe how comfortable she was with this man she'd just met. It's like he knew her, somehow.

Sam reached out to touch her again. Ellen didn't move.

"I want you." Sam held her face in both of his big hands, and kissed her, very, very gently.

Ellen leaned into him, allowing herself to be kissed and caressed. Sam's touch made her feel precious, not at all awkward or damaged.

He wrapped her in his arms, and held her close, breathing into her hair.

One part of her thought, *I shouldn't be doing this*. But Sam felt so good, and he was making her feel wanted. She was, after all, a liberated woman. She could do what she wished. It was her body.

Sam maneuvered her down to the mattress again and rolled on top of her, carefully not putting his full weight on her. His breathing was rough, and Ellen could feel him hard against her.

"Is it feasible…I mean, do you want to?" he asked in a husky voice.

"Um, no," said Ellen, as she struggled to get control of herself. She was *so* juicy. This was nothing like when Nick kissed her. This was…this was…exciting! Sam seemed to know something about her broken body, some secret that even she didn't know yet. Maybe if she let him touch her, she'd understand. But that would be wrong. A wrong thing to do to Nick, and wrong for their future together. But, oh, my God, Nick didn't feel like this. How could so much pleasure be wrong? Reluctantly, she squirmed out from under Sam and sat up.

"No? Are you sure?" Sam asked.

She nodded, pulling the blanket up to her neck. "I'm a virgin," she said primly. "*And* I have a steady boyfriend."

"Lucky him," said Sam, and turned away from her. He stretched once, got up, walked over to the chair where he'd left his jeans, and pulled them on. *He's taking this rather well*, Ellen thought. *Shouldn't he have blue balls or whatever it is the girls say happens to a guy you refuse?*

Instead, Sam seemed amused.

"My sweet little innocent farm girl. Elly. Elly May." He fingered his bushy mustache. "Yes, I do believe that's what I'll call you. Elly May, like Elly May Clampett. So gorgeous with all that blonde hair, and the best part of her charm is that she doesn't have an inkling of how gorgeous she is." He looked directly into Ellen's eyes. She stared back at him. Her face was bright pink from embarrassment and desire.

"I don't look anything like Elly May Clampett," she protested. "For one thing, her hair is all wavy, and she's got…" She pantomimed a large bust. Ellen glanced down at her own slender frame.

"You are sweet, you are innocent, you are gorgeous," Sam said firmly. "Trust me." He held her gaze as he spoke in a low voice. "I can wait. I have time. We have all the time in the world."

Ellen couldn't speak. She was appalled to find tears running down her cheeks. She wiped them away with the back of her arm.

"Hey, what're you crying for? I'm not *that* bad looking," Sam said. "And you're getting my bathrobe all wet." He held out his hand to help her up from the mattress. "C'mon, gorgeous Miss Elly May, let's get some breakfast and then I'll give you a lift to the terminal. You've got a bus to catch pretty soon, am I right?"

✳ **Five** ✳

Nina woke up and looked at the bedside clock. 10:00 am. *I must've been really pooped.* But what she had to do today quickly propelled her from bed. She pulled on a clean pair of underpants and socks, a black tee shirt, and yesterday's jeans. Her stomach growled.

Nina realized she'd forgotten to eat dinner last night, and now she was starving. She checked out of the hotel and walked back to the Square. She followed her nose to the Hayes-Bickford Cafeteria, which appeared to be populated by loud preppy guys about her age.

She ordered an omelet with toast and a black coffee, then turned and saw someone sitting in the back, with a coffee cup on her table.

"Laurie?" The woman looked up.

"Nina?" Laurie said. "You're still in town?"

Nina picked up her plate and sat down at Laurie's table. "Hey, Laurie."

"Wasn't that amazing yesterday?" Laurie looked bedraggled and awfully tired.

"Have you been here all night?" Nina dug into her breakfast.

"No, I went back to my dorm but I couldn't sleep so I read and then got up with the sun. I can't stop thinking about everything everyone said yesterday. It's like I had a whole shift in my thinking. I mean, now I'm wondering what's the point of going to school? There's a whole revolution out there…"

Nina smiled. "Yeah, and it's run by guys."

"There's so much work to do," Laurie said. "Can you tell me more about the Women's Bodies group?"

"I only went to the first half, then I went to the one you were in – the karate demonstration. I was standing behind you. Wasn't it incredible when that woman put her hand through a brick?"

"Imagine what that kind of strength could do if you had it!" Laurie's eyes were bright. "You wouldn't have to be afraid to walk through the Square alone at night. You could walk through Boston Common if you wanted to. If you can defend yourself, you're safe anywhere."

"At least on the streets," Nina said. "Karate chopping doesn't do much against imperialism or racism."

"But it's a good start," Laurie insisted. "Why am I studying the molecular structure of a cat when I could be learning how to defend myself – and maybe teaching other women too?"

"Go get 'em, sister," Nina said, wiping her mouth after taking a last sip of her coffee. "Hey, I've got to catch the train back to my office or my supervisor will chop my head off with his bare hands."

"Let's keep in touch." Laurie's smile was shy. "I know people always say stuff like that but I mean it. I like you, Nina."

"Sure thing." Nina stiffened slightly as Laurie stood to hug her. "OK. I've got your phone number at the dorm. And you have my address and number at the office – that's the best place to reach me. I practically sleep there anyway," Nina laughed.

Later, on the train, Nina closed her eyes. As she began to doze, she thought about how this story could get her started on a real career in alternative journalism. When she opened her eyes again, the conductor was calling "Providence."

That's fortuitous. Maybe it's a sign. She walked down to the food car, where she ordered another black coffee – *who knows what they call regular on the Penn Central?* – and a tuna salad sandwich, which she ate quickly back at her seat. Nina took a big slug of her coffee. She spread out her notes and got out her pen. Laurie wasn't wrong; this was pretty fantastic stuff:

"Liberation means creating one's own identity and lifestyle."

"We must come to terms with our bodies and learn to control them before we can be liberated women."

"We've been told…that we're successful as women if we're 'beautiful,' no matter how much it costs or how much disguise of the real self it entails."

Nina thought about that last one a lot.

She was eight years old, in third grade at the Dalton School, a private school not too far from her home. She was a chubby kid, not fat but not skinny like most of her classmates. Teasing wasn't allowed at Dalton, but it went on anyway. Nina learned early to raise her chin, toss her hair, and come up with a quick putdown of the girls who tried to torment her. And by the time she was ten, well, that was the year her mother got sick, so there wasn't a lot of time to stop after school for a can of soda and a bag of chips. She came straight home every day, and did her homework sitting on her mother's bed. She saw her gorgeous mother get paler and thinner by the week. Sometimes they even joked about it, when Nina got too sad.

"Just think, Nina," her mother would say, "I've spent my whole life counting calories, and now without any effort at all, I'll be at my ideal weight sometime between now and when I die."

Nina knew that her mother was dying. She'd never lied to her, and she told Nina the truth now, in her usual calm, loving way. They spent the long afternoons together, and when Nina's homework was finished, Nina read aloud the stories she'd composed for the school paper.

Her mom was an appreciative audience, even clapping at the end, and sometimes offering gentle suggestions for improvement.

"You keep writing, my love," she said. "You have a talent, a knack for seeing things that others don't see. You always seem to be able to find the story inside the story." Her mother often told Nina to focus on the things she was good at, and let go of the rest.

"You don't have to be good at everything," she said. "Just your one special talent."

Holding onto the power of her mother's love gave Nina the strength to get through the last sad weeks of her mother's illness, the grieving, and her father falling apart.

Bernadette, the housekeeper who'd been with them since Herb and Belle married in 1947, was the backbone of the family during that tough time. Without her, no one would've eaten or had clean clothes to wear. Even a year later, when Herb married the dreadful Muriel, Nina continued to wear her mother's protection like a magic cloak, warding off her new stepmother's jealousy and rudeness, with Bernadette to turn to for hugs and soup. Bernadette had loved Belle deeply too, and Nina could talk to her about her mother any time she was sad.

When the train stopped at New Haven, Nina snapped out of her reverie. She picked up her notebook and began to read again:

"Areas in which women are oppressed: Families. Childcare, working for men, child bearing, jobs outside home. Medical control of their bodies. Sexual control: abortion and birth control, sex education by men, state laws, male-dominated legislatures. Beauty, advertising. Physiology. Childbirth (Lamaze method.)"

OK, we have a story here. And she began to write as fast as she could.

※ ※ ※ ※

At 5:00 pm on Monday when Nina finally made it uptown to the office, Rod was waiting for her.

"Damn it, Nina, where have you been?" Rod said. "I thought you'd have taken the early train back. You missed the staff meeting at noon."

"Stuff it, Rod. Even though he was supervising her internship, she was not intimidated by him. "I've got a great story for you."

"Yeah, like the dykes are gonna take over the Movement, right?" He leaned back in his chair, crossing his arms over his chest.

"Something like that." Nina grinned.

God, Nina thought, *for a politically active guy, Rod could be such a pig. Most of the guys here were pigs most of the time. They dominated the staff meetings, ignoring or making fun of the few women who were brave enough to open their mouths. They made rude comments behind their backs, and sometimes right to their faces.*

Nina also considered the way most of the guys in the office talked about women. Before, she'd thought *that's just the way guys talk*. Now that she'd had some time to reflect on what she heard yesterday, their talking didn't sound quite so harmless. *It's a caste system, and women are not at the top. Of course, neither are Black people – men or women – or poor people. I know something about the oppression of those masses, but what about us?*

Nina banged so hard on her Remington typewriter that the keys stuck. She pried them loose, then got back to work on her story about those strong, brave women in Boston, until everyone else had left the office. She was alone in the near dark.

As she reached up to switch on her desk lamp, Nina was startled to hear someone behind her.

"Rod! You scared the crap out of me!" She turned around and glared. With his slicked-back long, black hair, narrow eyes, and pointy nose, Nina realized that he looked a lot like a weasel.

To Sisterhood!

"Hey, Nina baby," Rod said. "Looks like we're all alone now." He reached out his big hairy hands to rub her back.

"Knock it off, Rod. Want me to tell Kate you're trying to put the make on me again?"

"Aw, she's home with the kid. She never has time for me anymore."

"Oh, boo-hoo. You think I should feel sorry for you? Quit whining and go home to your family, Rod, and let me finish my story." Nina continued to pound on the typewriter.

"Can't blame a guy for trying," he said, shrugging his shoulders and turning to leave.

"Grow up, will you?" Nina muttered, as Rod walked out, slamming the office's front door.

※ ※ ※ ※

Nina awoke, surprised to hear footsteps and to smell fresh coffee. *Oh, crap, I fell asleep at the desk again.* The sunlight was already shining in from the windows, and it lit up the dust in the air above the whole newsroom. Nina stood and stretched, brushed her hair quickly, then reached over and pulled out the last page of her story.

"Damn, I'm good!" she said aloud. Her pages danced with the energy and excitement of Sunday's conference. She took her story over to the battered old Xerox machine, kicked it, and turned the key. As she left to go home and clean up, she dropped the original on Rod's desk with a satisfied thump. *Take a look at that, you creep!*

Grubby from sleeping in her clothes, Nina didn't feel like going all the way back downtown to her apartment to shower and change. She went outside and hailed a taxi, which dropped her off at her parents' building on Central Park South.

"Good morning, Miss Nina." The doorman was solicitous. "Just to let you know, your parents were at the Museum gala until the wee hours."

"Thanks, Patrick." Nina smiled warmly at him. "I'll be quiet."

The elevator opened directly into the foyer of the apartment. Looking out over Central Park to the north, the rooms were spacious, bright, and, since Muriel moved in, over-decorated. Nina went to her room – the only one Muriel hadn't touched, and that was because Nina had threatened never to come home again – and read the copy of her story again before bathing and crawling into her big, comfy bed.

Several hours later, Nina was awakened by a gentle tap on her door.

"Nina, love, may I come in?" It was Bernadette, holding a tea tray.

"Hey, Bernie," Nina smiled and reached up for a hug. "You won't believe what I've been up to!"

"Tell me all about it, darling. Just please eat something first." Bernadette set the tray on the bed, and adjusted the covers and pillows to make Nina more comfortable. Then she sat on the rocking chair near the bed to watch over her while she ate.

Nina slathered raspberry jam on the warm, buttery muffin and stuffed it hungrily into her mouth. Then she picked up the mug of steaming

To Sisterhood!

coffee and took a big sip. She told Bernadette all about the conference and what she'd learned, and about meeting Diane, Ellen, and Laurie.

"Well," said Bernadette, "if a woman is going to be in charge of the world someday, darlin', I'm sure it will be you!"

"I love you, Bernie." Nina reached over the tray to hug her childhood nanny and friend.

"And Lord knows I love you too, Nina."

Among Nina's first memories were playing cards and drinking cocoa with Bernadette, while Nina's beautiful, sweet-smelling mother, dressed up to chair yet another charity event, left for the evening with Nina's handsome, tuxedoed father.

"I'll bet Mom could've run the country," Nina mused. "She was the most organized, energetic person I've ever known."

"She was a fine woman, God rest her soul," Bernadette said, briefly closing her eyes.

Nina snuggled back into the comfy bed, missing her mother. She was grateful for Bernadette, and for her grandparents, Ben and Malka, who'd moved into the apartment after Mother died.

They had stayed to help raise Nina, until a year later, when Nina's dad Herb informed them that he was going to marry the decorator, a woman named Muriel. Both grandparents, still heartbroken by the loss of their daughter and now stunned by this news, had disliked Muriel on sight. Even after her grandmother died six months later, Nina had stayed close to her grandfather. She'd spent a lot of time with Ben at his home in Scarsdale on her school vacations and on weekends.

Nina had enrolled at Sarah Lawrence College ("not too far away" her grandfather had said happily) in 1966. The summer after her freshman year, she took a job as a clerk at a button and bumper sticker store on East 4th Street. She wanted her own digs.

Grandpa Ben was furious. "We got off the boat, and that is where we lived – the Lower East Side. I work hard all my life so you can go back to the tenements?"

"It's all right, Zadie," Nina had soothed him, "it's only for the summer. I need to try living on my own, I'm almost nineteen now."

"Promise me you won't go off with those long-haired beatnik bums."

"I promise, Zadie." Nina had kept her crossed fingers hidden behind her back. She respected her grandfather but there were some things he didn't have to know.

Nina's new pad in the East Village was a funky fifth-floor walk-up over a street-level record store which also sold posters, bumper stickers, buttons, and the like. She never invited her grandfather to come and visit – Nina knew he'd think it was crummy. She loved this part of the city, but when she wasn't at work, she mostly hung out on the west side, over at the Hip Bagel, and at the Bitter End, where more was happening.

Her sometimes-lover Zack was a walking ad for the store. His denim jacket, which he wore all the time, was adorned with what must have

To Sisterhood!

been a hundred slogan buttons: "Peanut Butter is Better Than Pot," "Peace Now," "Frodo Lives!" and Nina's favorite, "It Sucks."

One night, when she and Zack went to see the Fugs at Café Wha?, Nina could only imagine what her grandfather would say about their lyrics and onstage antics: "What do you want with some filthy no-good-niks who can't get a regular job and should have their mouths washed out with soap – feh!"

Soon after, Zack pretty much moved in with her, bringing his guitar, a duffel bag full of clothes, and his books. He didn't take up too much room. Nina wasn't in love with him, but he was good company most of the time. And he knew someone on the staff at *EVO* – the *East Village Other* – and was willing to make an introduction. Nina had loved her work at the underground paper so much, she'd applied for and was granted a leave of absence from Sarah Lawrence to "develop a career path." She never went back.

Several months later, she'd heard from one of the *EVO* staffers that Revolution News Bureau had relocated to New York, up near Columbia University. Nina brought in her portfolio of stories, met with the collective, and by agreeing to work for no pay, like most of the staff, managed to get an informal internship at RNB, almost ten miles uptown. She still had the pad in the East Village, though both the charm of sharing the cramped space with Zack and the long commute to work meant she'd stayed at her father's more often than downtown.

※ ※ ※ ※

The next morning, Nina dressed and headed back to the office, ready to receive kudos for her excellent story. Rod was on the phone. He motioned for her to sit while he finished his call.

While she waited, she thought about last month, when Rod had praised her to the whole staff.

"Nina," he'd said at that meeting. "I have your notes here on the rally. Is it all right with you if I read them to the staff? You did a good job, given that the pigs cut the mikes on and off. I think you got the meat of what they were saying."

So, on April 5th, at the age of twenty, Nina made her first real mark in Movement journalism, reporting on the GI-Civilian Anti-War Parade and Rally, a march up Sixth Avenue from Bryant Park to a rally in Central Park:

"Listen to this, people," Rod had crowed. "Listen up, all you pricks. Listen to what this new chick intern here has done!" I sent her to cover the Central Park March and Rally and listen to what she came back with. I'm gonna read her excellent notes out loud to everybody so you can learn how I want you to cover a story, and then you, Kazin, and you, Baldelli, you guys can show her how to write this up into something we can send out."

"Here goes, verbatim," Rod had announced:

"Jerry Rubin, leader of the Youth International Party: (trouble with microphones)[...] there's gonna be 5,000 Black Panthers in Chicago when the trial begins[...] to Chicago on Wednesday – we're gonna have to restrict travel cause they get us every time we move, for conspiracy[...] the Establishment is having the final dying gasp of a dying empire [...] the way to free ourselves is by bringing the high schools and the colleges to a close – the schools of Munich went on

To Sisterhood!

when they gassed the Jews – United States schools WON'T go on! (huge cheers from the crowd). He introduced Abbie:

Abbie Hoffman, leader of the Youth International Party. "Now there are two ground rules. 1. I disapprove of rallies with barricades. 2. cops are not here for our protection – they should take off their clothes and join us. Right before he died, Ike said, "Don't mourn, organize" and then he went to that great golf course in the sky[...] This is an anti-war rally, the next will be a pro-war rally, for the battle has begun [...] we, the Conspiracy, are gonna dance on the grave of this system... (he begins chant, which the crowd takes up) "free the Panthers, brothers and sisters, free the Panthers..."

Rod had continued, reading Nina's notes on the other speakers and musicians: the Freedom Singers, Barbara Dane, and Phil Ochs.

"She even got down all the lyrics of his new, unreleased song, All Quiet on the Western Front.*"*

"Now," Rod had announced. "That's the way you cover a story."

"Nina." Rod had looked up from the paper. "Good job, kid."

Nina had beamed.

Two weeks later, when Nina had heard about a women's conference in Boston in May, Rod was pleased to give her the assignment and the train fare to go to Emmanuel College to cover the conference.

Now Rod was off the phone, holding her story and scowling.

"Nina." Rod did not look pleased. "What is this crap? Who is this chick Anne Koedt and what the hell is she talking about? What do you mean about 'taking a name different from the one you got from the patriarchy?' Are you fucking kidding me?" He crumpled up her story, slapped a single sheet of paper on her desk, and stormed out.

Nina picked up the sheet. She read it in disbelief. Her terrific, four-page story had been cut to two paragraphs. She gave herself a few minutes to cool off some, then she marched into Rod's office and pounded on his desk.

"C'mon kid, nobody wants to read about a bunch of chicks yapping to each other. I was only giving you a trip to Boston, a prize for the good work you did covering the rally last month."

Nina stared at him and didn't say one word. She turned and left the office. She walked all the way to Central Park South and went back to bed, pulling the covers over her head. She refused to answer Rod's calls, and there were several, because Bernadette told her he kept trying. She knew she should bring this up at the weekly collective meeting, but she was too weary and too discouraged.

She'd had it with Rod, with RNB, and with New York, at least for the time being. Boston was where it was at, as far as Movement women were concerned. In the morning, she phoned Zack and told him he could have her apartment for the rest of the summer, and that with the security deposit and last month's rent, it was all paid through August.

Then she packed a bag, said goodbye to Bernadette, left a note for her father, and took the next train up to Boston.

✱ **Six** ✱

Laurie couldn't sleep. For the past three days, she'd been dragging herself to her remaining classes. Otherwise, she knew she'd spend all day walking by the river, trying to make sense of what she'd heard and seen at the conference. Laurie wanted to talk with her mother, but she and Papa were down in Boca finishing the new house they were building. Laurie thought about what their permanent move to Florida, planned for the end of this summer, would mean. Winter vacations there were fun, but the big blue Victorian in West Newton where she and her brothers had grown up was home. Couldn't they keep the house until she graduated? But Papa planned to retire at the end of June, and he and Mom wanted to make the big move as soon as they were sure Laurie was happy and settled at Radcliffe.

Laurie wondered if her mother wanted to move. She hadn't said much about it, though she generally looked and sounded content. She almost always agreed with what Papa wanted, and tried hard to make family life run smoothly for them all. Did her mother feel like she'd been oppressed by the male patriarchy? After all, Papa was much older; he'd been Mom's professor during her senior year in 1944. They did not begin seeing one another socially until much later, when Mom was already teaching elementary school in nearby Watertown ("To do so sooner would not have been proper," Papa often firmly said). Not until Laurie was thirteen did she hear her father's story:

Jacob Goodman was an up-and-coming young doctor in Vienna, a student of one of Freud's closest disciples, and with his own growing private practice, when in 1939, he was asked to fill in for his ailing teacher, who was scheduled to present a lecture at Harvard Medical School on the newest developments in psychoanalysis. Eager to promote his career, he'd jumped at the chance and onto a ship. It was the last time he saw his family. The Nazis, already in Austria, would not permit his safe return.

Through the influence of a prominent and philanthropic Harvard alumnus, and remarkably, considering that he was a Jew, Jacob was given the position of Visiting Lecturer – with a small stipend – in Harvard's Psychology Department "for the duration."

Although rumors came from others who'd escaped to America, Jacob did not know for certain that he was the only remaining member of the Goodman family until he made the agonizing trip back to Vienna after the war. Everyone he knew and loved was gone. With no one and nothing to go home to, he returned to Cambridge and applied for and received a tenure-track position in his department.

A few months later, he was in the library doing research, when he recognized one of his former students, a shy, pretty, dark-haired girl named Ruth. Though he could not recall her last name, he did remember her bright mind and excellent work. He invited her for coffee at the Faculty Club, and a few weeks later, Ruth invited him home to meet her parents.

The Millers immediately liked this serious doctor, who though much older than their only daughter, was obviously devoted to her. Jacob seemed to relax and accept the affection and warmth the Millers showered upon him – enough, but not too much – and six months later, Ruth and Jacob were married. Two sons followed almost immediately, and while Ruth devoted herself to their young family, Jacob devoted himself to his career. He earned tenure in Psychiatry at Harvard Medical School in 1951, the year after their daughter Laurie was born.

Jacob did not have as much time for or interest in a girl as he did for his sons. Laurie was "Mommy's Girl," and Ruth enjoyed dressing up her daughter in pretty things and teaching her to read, as well as how to cook, sew, and other skills she would need to be a good wife and mother someday after she graduated from college.

Laurie understood now why her father would spend more time with the boys, but that didn't mean she thought it was fair. She had many things she'd like to ask Papa, but he was distant much of the time, and downright blue at others. Laurie greatly preferred spending time with her pretty, cheerful mother, and hoped that she would call her soon.

Feeling lonely as she finished her last class of the day, Laurie was pleased to see Diane Romano walking toward Harvard Square. Diane was with a slightly shorter girl who could have been her twin. It must be the sister who'd recently had a birthday, Laurie guessed.

"Hey, Diane!" Laurie called. "It's me, Laurie Goodman," she added, in case Diane didn't recognize her from across the street.

"Hi, Laurie!" Diane waved back. "Wait there. We'll be right over."

The three met up on the corner of Mass. Ave. and Boylston, in front of the Tasty, a narrow, one-room diner and sandwich shop.

"This is my sister, Theresa," Diane said.

"Hello, Theresa," Laurie said, and the younger girl smiled back shyly. Laurie looked at Diane. "Anyone for a double cheeseburger?"

Theresa's eyes grew wide and she looked at her sister. "Dee, is it okay if we go in? Do you have enough money?"

"Sure, sweetheart," Diane said, and they found three stools together in the back of the tiny diner.

As they happily munched their cheeseburgers and fries and sipped their root beers, Laurie turned to Diane.

"I can't stop thinking about all the ideas at the conference, can you?" Laurie asked. "I mean, I'm having a hard time seeing the point of going to school. You at least have a real job. That means something."

Diane inclined her head slightly toward Theresa, who was busily dipping her French fries into a big puddle of ketchup.

"Maybe we can get together this weekend and talk some more," Diane said. "Right now Theresa and I need to finish up, get over to the Coop to get our shopping done, and get home."

"Oh, sure," Laurie said slowly. "Right. I have a couple of papers to finish, but I'm happy to take a break. Why don't you call me when you're free? I'm up late almost every night."

Diane nodded, and reached over to wipe ketchup off her sister's mouth with a paper napkin. "Hey, cutie, looks like you had a ketchup mustache there."

Theresa laughed and made a funny face at her sister.

"By the way, Laurie," Diane said, "did you get a call from Nina?"

To Sisterhood!

When Laurie shook her head, Diane continued, "That's strange. She called the day before yesterday, saying she'd decided to move to Boston, and wanting to know if she could stay with me. I told her no because I live with my family. She said she was going to call you and asked if I still had your number at the dorm."

"I haven't checked for messages, but I'm on my way back there now. Let's get together soon, Diane. Good to meet you, Theresa!"

Theresa reached out to give Laurie a big hug. "You're nice. I like you a lot!" she said, which made Laurie smile.

※ ※ ※ ※

Sure enough, when Laurie got back to Comstock Hall, she saw a pink message slip under her door.

"Call Nina at the Sheraton Commander, Room 311." It was dated yesterday. She must have walked right over it earlier. She went to the phone booth and called. Nina answered right away.

"Hey, Laurie, it's great to hear from you. Thanks so much for calling."

"Sorry it took so long. What's up, Nina? I ran into Diane and she said you're moving to Boston."

"There's a lot to talk about. Can you meet me somewhere?"

"Sure," Laurie said. "I'm supposed to be finishing some work – I'd planned to pull an all-nighter and get it all done, but sure, I can meet you for dinner if that's okay. I just had lunch so probably on the later side. Where do you want to meet?"

At 7:00 pm, Laurie was already seated at Young and Yee in a red, tufted, vinyl booth facing the door. Soon, Nina rushed in and slid into the booth, opposite Laurie.

The food arrived and Laurie dug in, while Nina sipped her wonton soup and ate a few crispy noodles. She told Laurie how excited she was about her story, what happened when she got back to the city, and how she couldn't trust the men at RNB, especially Rod, to understand what this Female Liberation Conference meant.

Laurie nodded sympathetically. "I've been walking around for the past three days, trying to make sense of my life in the context of the conference. Everything I'm studying, everything I'm doing, seems to perpetuate the – oh, I don't know, what's the word I want…?"

"The male-dominated hierarchy?" suggested Nina. "The rule of the macho pig?"

"The reign of white prick power?" added Laurie, and both women laughed as the waiter brought them a fresh pot of tea.

After dinner and a deep and wide-ranging conversation that covered everything from last month's student strike at Harvard, and the war, to sharing more about their family backgrounds, to opportunities for women in the media, to Laurie considering a major in psychology, and back to the conference, Nina turned to Laurie. She played with the square-cut emerald ring on the fourth finger of her right hand.

"You know, there is one other thing I wanted to ask you."

"Shoot," said Laurie.

"I need a place to crash until I can find my own place," said Nina. "Do you have room in your dorm? Ellen stayed with you this weekend."

"I have twin beds, but Ellen's was an authorized college visit. I can't invite you to stay except for like one or two nights, and that's only if I can still get a guest pass this late in the semester."

Nina looked disappointed. "Thanks, I understand. I was hoping to be able to stay, but all the rentals start June 1st and I don't have enough to stay at the hotel for the next few weeks. That's okay, though."

Laurie was quiet for a minute. She touched the top of Nina's hand.

"Look, Nina, I know we don't know each other well, but I'm pretty sure I can trust you. Do you know how to drive a stick shift?"

"Yes," Nina said, not questioning this apparent non sequitur. "I know that's pretty unusual for a city girl, but my grandfather taught me that women need to know how to drive, and his car had a manual transmission. Why do you ask?"

"My parents are in Florida, furnishing their new house. They won't be back until the first week in June at the earliest, when we all go to the Cape. If you can drive my mother's car, we can stay at our house in Newton. You'd just have to drive me to class every day – well, I could drive myself of course, but you'd have to drive back – and then pick me up in the late afternoon. There is absolutely no good place here to park except over by the MTA bus yards and that's too far a walk in the morning. That way, you could have the car all day to look for apartments."

"And a job," Nina said, and Laurie nodded. "That's very generous of you, Laurie! Can we go there tomorrow?"

"Absolutely." Looking at her watch, Laurie added, "But I've got to get some writing done now."

"You're the best," Nina said, and the two new friends walked out of the restaurant together.

※ ※ ※ ※

After the conference, Ellen went back to school feeling as though her whole life had been turned upside-down. And even though it wasn't due for several months, she began working on her preliminary transfer application to Radcliffe, without telling anyone. She was used to her mother's disapproval of everything she did; she didn't see any point in upsetting her now.

Ellen's world – limited for so long – was beginning to bloom with new possibilities and hope. Mid-May was still chilly in Vermont, but as she looked at the dazzling display of spring bulbs and the trees starting to leaf, Ellen thought of the message in *Moby Dick* – "watch for the signs."

She felt more connected to the brand-new friends she'd met at the conference than she did to anyone at Ethan Allen State. At the library, she used one of the typewriters to write them a letter.

To Sisterhood!

May 12, 1969

Dear Nina, Diane, and Laurie,

Please excuse the carbon copies – I returned to school on Tuesday, and immediately started studying for finals. But I did want to drop you a line to say how great it was to meet you all last weekend. Laurie, thanks again for your kind hospitality, and for turning me on to the Conference! There is SO much to think about! I feel as though everything up to this point was preparation for what is yet to be – what I could be, who we all will become. And thank you all too for sharing your stories with me. Listening to you talk and learning about your lives was interesting and exciting. I hope we get the chance to meet again, and that you all will stay in touch. Even though I gave you my campus mailbox address, it would be best to write back to me at home, as the semester ends soon. (As you can see, the address and phone number are above.)

You're all welcome to come up here for a visit –Vermont is gorgeous in June, once mud season is over.

Your new "sister,"
Ellen MacDougall

Ellen pulled the copies out of the typewriter and sighed. She still had three finals ahead of her. Through the window, she could see a couple of girls from her American Lit class walking by, talking and laughing. Ellen wondered if they were discussing the right of a woman to marry whom she wished and the oppression of the nuclear family, or if they were thinking about getting pinned, or even engaged, before graduation. She knew the answer.

Tonight, Nick was coming by to keep her company while she studied. It'd been almost ten days since they were together, and Ellen couldn't wait to tell him all about her weekend. Well, not *all* about it. Some things she definitely was going to keep private. Ellen smiled, thinking about Sam's touch, and the gentle way he looked at her that made her feel lovely and whole.

In the four months that she and Nick had been together, she'd told him how she felt about her body, how angry she got sometimes that she couldn't do everything she'd like, how walking long distances was hard, and running through the pastures at Grandfather's farm – something she and Eddy had done for hours and hours almost every warm day – was impossible. Nick had said he understood. He touched Ellen like a piece of delicate glass, fragile and liable to break. She knew he was doing his best to be kind.

Nick arrived right after her parents left for a church social, looking handsome in a blue chambray work shirt and black jeans. His light brown hair was longer. Ellen guessed that because graduation was near, Academy standards were more lenient for seniors.

When she'd first seen Nick a year ago at the initial meeting of Central Vermont Citizens Against the War, he was wearing an L.L. Bean striped oxford shirt, pressed khakis, and the standard cadet crew cut. Ellen was quite taken with the handsome Academy student, and impressed with his impassioned speech, exhorting the group to join him and some of the others organizing a rally at the state capitol building in Montpelier later that month.

She'd attended the rally, standing out in the rain, holding a poster of a sunflower that read, "War is not healthy for children and other living things." But Nick didn't even notice her that day. He was too busy directing the crowd and answering questions from the *Times-Argus* reporter. Not until this past winter, at a meeting to discuss possible actions they could take at the draft board, did Ellen finally gather her courage to speak up. She'd raised her hand to ask a question which apparently had interested him, and he'd invited her for coffee later so they could talk more.

From that evening on, they'd been seeing each other as often as Nick could borrow a car or get a ride to Ethan Allen State. He and Ellen often sat by the lake and talked about their lives. Nick had grown up in Sonoma County, north of San Francisco. His mother was an elementary schoolteacher, and his father, a career military man, had attained the rank of Colonel before retirement. Colonel Williams made certain that his only son would attend his own alma mater.

Nick hadn't wanted a military career, but when he started at the Academy, graduation and Army service were a long four years away. Now he confided his unhappiness to Ellen, telling her he found it unconscionable to serve in the Army when the United States was engaged in an illegal war. He didn't see the point of trying to "liberate" people who only wanted to determine their own destiny.

Nick found a sympathetic listener in his gentle, intelligent, and thoughtful friend. Ellen knew a thing or two about being pushed to follow a path she did not choose. All her life, she'd felt like a misfit: a bright, curious, young woman from a family in which girls were not encouraged to get a higher education.

For the past four months, she'd been dividing her attention between school and Nick. For one thing, he was more interesting than most of her classmates, as far as she could tell. He had ideas – big ideas – and wanted to share them with her.

Ellen smiled as Nick walked in, holding a bunch of yellow tulips.

"Hey, Ellen," he said, scooping her up in a big hug, before planting her back down gently and taking a seat on one side of the sofa. "I missed you. Did you have a good time in the city?" Nick wasn't too happy when Ellen had told him she was going to be staying with Charlie for a night, but she reassured him they were just friends.

"Yes, it was great! Can I get you a drink? Water? Juice?" Nick shook his head. Ellen cut the stems and placed the tulips in a tall, narrow vase, then poured herself a large glass of orange juice. She sat at the table and told Nick all about her visit to Radcliffe, and gave him an overview of the conference.

Nick listened carefully as she talked about the different workshops, the radical new ideas, and the new friends she'd made.

"That sounds great!" he said, and Ellen thought he meant it. "I'm glad you had fun. It sounds like there's a lot to think about. I mean, I'm glad you didn't have *too* good of a time. Then you wouldn't have missed me." He patted the couch and Ellen went to sit next to him.

"Nick," Ellen was patient. "If you are at all worried about Charlie, the answer is 'no.' Yes, he had some hopes, but nothing happened between us." Inwardly, she cringed, knowing she wouldn't mention Sam.

Nick's shoulders relaxed. He wasn't going to ask, but Ellen could tell he wanted to know, all the same. "I trust you, Ellen," Nick smiled.

"And now I need to tell you some exciting news of my own. It might upset you though."

"What is it?" Ellen laid her hand gently on his arm.

"You won't believe this!" he practically shouted. "The brother of a guy in my class is a public school teacher in San Francisco. When he was here a few months ago, right before you and I met, we went out for a beer, and he told me all about his work, how badly they need teachers who know what's going down, and who can help the kids get a real education, not what the Man wants them to learn. Teaching is a way to help them make something of themselves, to get out of poverty and a life headed for drugs and stuff. He told me to send in a résumé and an application, and I did it – mostly to see what would happen." Nick got up from the sofa and started pacing around the room.

"Ellen," Nick paused to catch his breath, "I got it! I got a job offer to teach seventh and eighth grade history at a public school in the Mission District. I start in late August. It's gonna be a real challenge. A lot of these kids get to junior high and they still can't read. This could be my chance to do something that *means* something. It's what I want to do!"

"Wow!" Ellen smiled at Nick's enthusiasm. "That's absolutely terrific! You'll be a great teacher. But what about your commission?" As a cadet at the Academy, Nick would graduate as a Second Lieutenant, required to serve in the Army for two years.

"Honey, now that's the thing." Nick was still standing, shifting his stocky frame from foot to foot. "I – uh – well, I mean, with your per…I mean, if you agree, I'm thinking I'm going to do it. I'm going to resign my commission. Right before graduation."

"You don't need my permission." Ellen spoke calmly. "Of course I support your decision. But if you resign your commission, you could be drafted. You probably would be –"

Nick cut her off. "I know, I've considered that. I'll get to that in a minute. I know I can do this by myself. But I was hoping you would agree, because, Ellen, I'd like you to come with me to California."

"Oh, my goodness! That's a lot to think about, all of a sudden."

"I know. We can talk more about that later. Let me tell you my plan."

Ellen nodded. She sat back against the cushion, her full attention on Nick's next words.

"I'm thinking of applying for a CO."

Ellen looked dubious. "Conscientious objector? That's pretty radical. I mean, it's great, Nick. But how on earth could you convince your draft board that you are now opposed to violence of any sort when you just finished four years in a military academy?"

"While you were away, right after I finished my thesis, I went up to Burlington, to the law library at the University. They had a book called *Handbook for Conscientious Objectors*, and it tells you all about how to get an I-O or I-W status."

"How does that work?" Ellen asked. Nick came over to sit close to her.

"You have to meet certain criteria, and you're likely to be assigned to what's called "substitute civilian work" instead of serving in the

To Sisterhood!

military, or you serve in the military without handling weapons. You fill out SSS Form 150. You have to state that you are a conscientious objector 'by reason of religious training and belief' and that you are 'opposed to war in any form.'"

Nick seemed to be vibrating with excitement, jumping up again and pacing the living room in circles. Ellen sat patiently as he continued.

"The folks at the library told me that the meaning of these phrases, in part because of Supreme Court decisions for guys who've appealed all the way to the top, that the meaning can encompass a wide variety of moral, ethical, religious, and spiritual beliefs. It's not only Quakers and others who belong to traditional pacifist religions."

"I see." Ellen frowned slightly. "What do you have to do?"

"The first step is to find a good draft counselor. I'm going back up to Burlington right after graduation. They said it should take a few weeks to get my case organized. I know someone there I can stay with. But then I'm going to need some money. I'm thinking that after I send in the forms, I'm going to go to Boston, around the second week of July or so. One of my buddies just got out of the Army. He's working a construction job, and said they could use more help, even if I can work only for a month or so. He makes a ton of money, and I could too, and I could put some away for us."

Ellen thought fast. "I'd like to live in Boston this summer, too," she said. "If I look around, I probably could find a sublet. You know my folks won't approve, but if I can convince them that I live in a respectable place, they might give in. Of course, we can see each other when you're not too busy," she teased.

"I guess we have a lot to talk about," said Nick, walking back to the couch and reaching for her. "But first, come over here and show me how much you missed me."

※ ※ ※ ※

The next few days went by quickly for Ellen. First, she had one more final exam, then she had to figure out if she could get to Boston this summer, and if so, where she would live and where she could work. If she didn't make plans fast, she'd be stuck in King's Lake, working at her grandparents' general store.

She began to contact classmates, high school friends, and everyone else she could think to call.

The next day, Charlie returned Ellen's call, and told her to call a girl named Mavis, the friend of someone in Charlie's psychology class. Ellen wanted to ask Charlie about Sam, but didn't.

Ellen phoned Mavis, who told her that her roommate just got engaged and decided to move out with only one week's notice. She had a large, sunny bedroom, with shared bath and kitchen, in a three-story brick building in Allston, near Boston College, that Ellen could have for $75 a month, including utilities, for the last week in May, plus June, July, and August if she wanted. "The phone is free for you," she said, "as long as you agree to answer it and take messages for me."

"Certainly," said Ellen, puzzled.

"It's just that I'm hardly ever there," Mavis explained. "Actually," she chuckled, "I live with my boyfriend, and I only come back to the apartment about once a week to check my mail and pick up clothes and stuff. But my folks would kill me if they knew."

"Of course, I understand completely." Ellen was relieved. A safe place to live, affordable rent, and almost entirely all to herself! *And*, she allowed herself to think, but just for a minute, *only a few blocks from Charlie and Sam's place*. "You'll leave me a number there at your boyfriend's place so I can let you know when they call?"

"You got it. Just say I'm across the street doing the laundry, or out to pick up some milk, and then call me and I'll call them right back and they'll be satisfied." Mavis waited a beat, making sure that whoever was on the other end of the line wasn't going to be a goody-two-shoes and spoil her living arrangements. When she heard no protest, she asked, "When do you want to come over and see the place?"

"I'm in Vermont now," Ellen told her, "but I can come next weekend."

"Great! Bring $150 for the security deposit and first month's rent. I'll throw in the first week for free. I'm sure we'll get along fine." She gave Ellen the address and they set a time to meet.

Ellen was thrilled. She had enough savings, since her grandparents had insisted on paying for her help, after school and on Saturdays, over her parents' objections. "A girl has to have her own money," Grandmother always said. Ellen now gave a silent prayer for Grandmother.

The tough part was going to be talking to her parents. They liked Nick. Ellen had overheard Mother describing him on the phone to a friend as "a nice Christian boy from a respectable family, a cadet with short hair and pleasant manners."

But they were not going to be happy to find out she wanted to go to Boston if Nick were going to be there, even with separate apartments. After all, Ellen had never lived away from home. She couldn't wait!

Ellen heard her mother call from the kitchen.

"Telephone for you, Ellen. Long distance. It's a girl."

Ellen hurried down the stairs. "Thank you, Mother," she said, as she stretched the long cord around the kitchen door and into the pantry, and closed the door.

"Hello?" she said tentatively.

"Ellen? Is that you? It's Nina Rosen."

"Hey, Nina!"

"Ellen, I got your letter, well, it came to New York so I had Bernie read it to me because guess what? I'm living in Boston! I'm in Newton right now, with Laurie, but I'm going to get my own place soon." Nina told Ellen the whole story, from what happened when she went back to work, right up to the present.

Ellen listened, and then whispered in case her mother was nearby.

"I've got some news of my own. I can't believe the timing!" And she told Nina about Mavis and her plan to head down to the city soon.

"Oh, that's great!" said Nina. "Then you can come to my birthday party the first weekend of June. I've talked to Laurie and called Diane and I'm taking everyone away for a weekend. We're going to decide together where to go. You have to come; you have to!"

"I'd like that," Ellen said quietly. She hardly knew Nina – but she liked how she threw herself into life with such enthusiasm. Pick up and move to another city? It looked exactly like what Ellen herself was going to do.

"Do you want to come down sooner and crash with us?"

"Thanks for the offer," Ellen replied, curious as to how Nina could extend an invitation to someone else's house, "but I'll be down soon, and I'll meet you then." They exchanged Boston phone numbers and set a time to get together, after Ellen settled into her new place.

※ ※ ※ ※

Nick's parents, Colonel and Mrs. Williams, arrived from California to see their son graduate from the Academy. They were thoroughly charmed by Ellen, who sat with them at the ceremony, as well as at the celebratory dinner for new graduates and their families. However, she excused herself right after dinner and drove home, leaving Nick alone to break the news to his parents about his life-changing decision.

He drove them out to the Barre-Montpelier Airport for the last flight to Boston, where they'd stay overnight before flying back to San Francisco. Nick wanted the timing to be right. He and Ellen had discussed the best way to do this. Nick waited until they arrived at the top of the hill at the small regional airport. He stopped the car and said he had something important to tell them.

"We adore her," his mother squealed, certain that the news involved an announcement about the lovely young lady who seemed to be so fond of her son. "Congratulations, Nicholas!"

She reached her arms around his neck and tried to hug him from the back seat, but she was stopped by the Colonel.

"For Christ's sake, Harriet," he barked. "Let the boy talk." The Colonel seemed to sense that the news wasn't good. If Nick had an engagement to announce, he would have done so at dinner.

Nick had to speak quickly. The small piston airplane was landing, and it wouldn't be more than half an hour before it was cleaned and refueled and ready to take off again with them aboard. He plunged in, saying that he was going to resign his commission and was making plans to take a teaching job in San Francisco in the fall. His mother looked relieved, and she knew enough to keep quiet. The Colonel met Nick's eagerness with stony silence. Finally, he spoke.

"There has never been a coward in our family. My son is *not* going to be the first."

The Colonel opened the car door. "Let's go, Harriet."

And grabbing both suitcases, he turned on his heel and walked toward the terminal. Nick's mother gave him a quick hug.

"Don't worry, darling," she said. "I'll work on him. You do what's right for you, and take care of that sweet girl. We love you, you know that."

To Sisterhood!

"I love you, Mom," Nick said as she ran after her husband. "And you, too, Father," he said wistfully as he drove away, not waiting to watch them take off.

✻ Seven ✻

Diane needed a plan fast. She had to get out of that house now and take Theresa with her. But she hadn't saved up enough money yet. Maybe Theresa could get a job.

Diane thought her sister would be great at taking care of small kids. Or she could get a job with Diane at the candy factory. Anyway, they both could work and live together, away from this sad house with their angry mother and unhappy father.

Tony being back in town after all this time changed everything. Diane had hoped never to see him again. And though Theresa was now eighteen and could legally move anywhere, Diane wasn't going to rush into a situation that would leave them broke, with no place to live. She needed time to plan. It would all have been different, if not for Tony.

It was a beautiful Sunday afternoon in late May, 1966. Magda had managed to cook a pretty good roast beef before passing out on the couch. John and Tony were sitting in the living room watching the Red Sox. Theresa was upstairs with another stomachache. Diane was in the kitchen doing dishes, when Tony popped his head in.

"Hey, Dee," he said, "It's too gorgeous outside for you to be stuck in the kitchen. The Sox are gonna bomb again. I can't stand to look. Wanna go for a ride?"

Diane's eyes sparkled as she threw him a towel. "If you dry, I'll be done in a jiffy."

To Sisterhood!

Tony gamely accepted the dishtowel, swiped a few plates, and set them on the kitchen table. He asked where she'd like to go. Diane said she didn't care. But first she went to check on her sister.

Diane came back downstairs in a few minutes, her new cranberry cotton sweater tied around her shoulders.

"She's asleep," she told Tony. "I didn't want to wake her."

"Let's go then," he said, and they climbed into his white Valiant with the blue racing stripes. Tony said he had to make one stop. He pulled into the parking lot of a big package store. Diane waited in the car, listening to The Beach Boys sing Sloop John B *until Tony came back and placed a brown paper sack on the back seat.*

"What'cha got there?" asked Diane.

"You're sixteen," Tony said. "It's time you learned to have fun."

Diane was puzzled; they always had fun. She leaned her head back, rolled down the window, and enjoyed the wind blowing her hair. When she and Theresa were with Tony, it was the only time she felt free.

They parked at the Point and spread out a blanket. No one else was up there. Everybody must've been down at the Memorial Day boat races. Tony turned on the transistor radio, and When a Man Loves a Woman *came on. He sang along as he got out a church key and flipped the cap off a beer.*

"There now, ain't this nice? Here, try some." He held out the bottle.

"What, are you kidding? My folks would kill me."

"Aw, a sip isn't going to hurt you."

"I don't think so." Diane shook her head.

"OK, suit yourself," Tony said. "If you want to be a baby..."

"Give me that." Diane took the bottle, then threw her head back and took a big swig.

"Not so bad, is it?"

Diane thought it tasted like paint thinner smelled but didn't say so. She was not a baby.

Tony was looking intently at her. He didn't look the same way he usually did, but she couldn't figure out what was wrong, except that he wasn't smiling now.

"What?" she said.

"Nothing."

"You were looking at me," Diane said.

"So what? Lookin's free, ain't it?"

"You were looking at me different."

To Sisterhood!

"You're getting to be quite a looker, Diane," Tony said. "I've been thinking about you a lot lately."

"So?" Diane shifted away, pulling her sweater across her chest. What happened to regular old Tony, with his easy laugh and fun things to do? He was acting like those boys at school, the ones who called to her in the halls, and looked at her when she walked home alone.

"Diane." Tony leaned closer to her. She smelled the beer and his hair tonic and the roast he had for Sunday dinner.

"What?" She was nervous but didn't know why.

"What if I told you I have a problem only you can solve?" His voice was low and urgent.

Ah, Diane thought. Something was wrong, and Tony wanted to confide in me. That explained the strange look in his eye.

"Come over here and sit close to me."

"Why?"

"I want to show you something," he said.

Cautiously, Diane moved across the blanket.

"C'mere." Tony reached out and took hold of her arm.

"Hey, wait a minute," Diane said. But she wasn't fast enough. Tony was kissing her, pressing his mouth on hers, insistently at first, and then more roughly.

"Whoa! Stop that!" Diane sat up and wiped her mouth on the sleeve of her sweater. "What did you do that for? Don't be a jerk!"

"I forgot to give it to you for your birthday," Tony said. "You were still a little girl back in December, but you're all grown up now."

"You're acting weird." Diane stood up quickly, wanting to leave. But how would she get home? Was this a joke? Tony wasn't laughing.

"OK, you're scared. I scared you. I'm sorry, honey." Tony looked sheepish. "But I can't stop thinking about you. I think about you every night before I go to sleep. I think about you when I'm working on the cars. I know you're still a kid, but I think about you like a man thinks about a woman. I want to make you happy."

He reached for Diane, but she sat completely still.

"I want to get you and Theresa out of that crazy house and take care of you. I do. I have plans – big plans. I'm not gonna work at the station forever. I'm going to start my own business. I want to have my own garage, work on foreign cars. There's real money in that. And I want you there with me when I make it to the top. C'mon Dee, you must've figured out by now that I love you."

Diane held her breath. Tony. The one person in the world besides Theresa she truly loved. He was telling her that he – that he loved her *too. But kissing him had to be a sin. He was a grown man. Grown men don't want only kisses. Even she knew that.*

"Let me kiss you for real, just once," he said. "And if you don't like it, we'll leave right away."

"Promise?" Mostly Diane was curious. After all, this was Tony. He would never hurt her.

Tony reached over and gently touched her cheek.

"Cross my heart, hope to die," he said, and pulled her close.

※ ※ ※ ※

Diane thought about calling Patty – the one person who'd always been there for her – but she hadn't seen much of her lately outside of work. After Patty didn't show up at the Conference, Diane learned Patty had met a new guy named Jimmy, and she seemed to have lost interest in community organizing, at least for now. As far as Diane could tell, Patty had lost interest in everything not related to Jimmy. Still, Patty was her oldest friend, and Diane needed help.

She picked up the phone, then put it down. Not for the first time, she lied to the girl who had been her best friend since elementary school.

"It's Magda again," Diane told Patty. "She's drinking more and passing out and then not remembering anything the next morning."

"What else is new?" Patty was sympathetic and not surprised.

"Theresa's going to be graduating in two weeks and then she'll be around the house all day. I want to get her out – I want both of us to get out. But I still don't have enough for our own place. I've been saving and I know I can do it by September 1st, what with all the overtime they've promised me. But I don't know what to do now…"

"Meet me at Brigham's in an hour," Patty said. "You know a peppermint stick cone will help you think. We'll figure it out."

Later, as she munched the jimmies off the top of the cone, Diane said, "Patty, you're the best!"

Patty smiled at her friend, then got serious. "Okay, let's lay out the facts. You can't stay at home. You've got to get Theresa out of that hellhole. You don't have enough money, but you will in a few months. You two have nowhere to go. You want to be with Theresa to take care of her and help her find a job she can handle. But that can't happen until you move."

"Yeah," Diane said dejectedly. "It's kinda hopeless."

"No, not hopeless. Like my mom always says, 'when you seem to have an unsolvable problem, you have to move the immovable.'"

Diane looked puzzled. "What do you mean, 'move the immovable?'"

"In this case, it's that you and Theresa are together for the summer. What if you weren't? What if someone else could look after her?"

"Who would do that?" Diane asked. "And where would I go?"

To Sisterhood!

"You're the easy part. You come and stay with me." Diane gave her friend a questioning glance.

"Yeah," Patty continued. "I know what you're thinking. Jimmy, you know, that groovy new guy I'm seeing, well, he stays over a few nights a week but it's not a problem. I have that alcove off the kitchen. We can just hang up a curtain and it's yours. We'd all have privacy – my bedroom is down the hall and besides, it's only for a couple of months. I don't even need you to pay any rent, just chip in for the groceries."

"Wow! That's so generous, Patty, but where would Theresa go?"

"Could she stay with your aunt in Brighton?"

Diane shook her head. "No, she's got a full house. Her daughter moved back in with her two-year-old."

"Your grandfather?"

Again, Diane said no. "He's getting too old to look after her. She'd be the one doing all the cooking and cleaning, I know it."

Diane finished her cone. Suddenly, she snapped her fingers.

"I've got an idea. Do you have any change with you?" Patty dug in her purse and handed over a bunch of coins.

Diane ran out to the phone booth on Mass. Ave. She was gone for a long time. When she came back into Brigham's, Patty was finishing a cup of coffee, and Diane was smiling broadly.

"What? What?" Patty all but shouted at her.

Diane sat down. She took a big drink of water and explained that she'd called the school on the Cape for handicapped kids that Theresa went to for a month last summer. It turned out that Mr. Lester, the teacher Theresa was so fond of, was now the headmaster. Diane described the situation at home and asked if there was any possibility that Theresa could go for the summer term.

Diane grinned. "Not only did he say 'yes' right away, but they have a job for her, working as an assistant with the younger kids, in exchange for tuition, plus a small stipend!"

"Wow! How did that happen?"

"One of the junior staff just quit, isn't that incredible?" Diane couldn't believe the timing. "Mr. Lester said they were thinking of dividing up the students into slightly larger classes, but now they could stick to the original plan. He was glad I phoned. He called it serendipity."

"You're the best big sister," Patty declared, reaching over the table to hug Diane.

"Thanks," she smiled. "And you know the best part? Theresa will get some work experience. That way, when we look for a job for her in the fall, probably in a nursery school or childcare center, she'll have something on her résumé. She might want to go to beauty school someday, but this would be great for now."

"It's a wonderful plan," Patty agreed. They worked out that Diane would tell her parents first that she was moving out, and that Theresa

To Sisterhood!

would be working at the school and they wouldn't have to pay tuition. She knew that Magda would not fight her, because she didn't want to have to deal with Theresa without Diane there.

"When can she go?" asked Patty.

"The summer term doesn't start until the day after Memorial Day. But Mr. Lester said she can come down any time. They'll be glad to have the extra help and of course, they'll supervise her work and look after her. I'll talk to her tonight. I know she'll be excited!"

※ ※ ※ ※

After celebrating Theresa's graduation the third week of May, Diane drove her down to Barnstable, so she could settle in a few days before the summer term started.

Theresa was cheerful about going back to the school and thrilled about having her first job. Diane reassured her that she would visit her often. She explained that since Theresa would be a staff member, she could have visitors whenever she wanted in her off-duty hours.

"You promise you'll come and visit me all the time, Dee?" Theresa asked, getting out of the car and waving to her old friends, who ran up to greet her.

"Absolutely, honey," Diane said, hugging her sister. "I promise I'll come see you next weekend, and then as much as I can." And after helping Theresa arrange all her things in her new room, Diane kissed her goodbye and headed happily back down Route 6 toward the Sagamore Bridge.

※ ※ ※ ※

The next weekend, after a terse goodbye from her mother, who most definitely did not approve of her summer plans, and a quick hug from her father, who slipped Ellen an envelope when his wife wasn't looking – "to tide you over until you find a job," he whispered – Ellen headed to Boston to her new apartment.

Ellen loved everything about the city. She spent most of the next couple of days walking around, trying to get a feel for the neighborhoods. She loved the stately trees on Commonwealth Avenue, now in full leaf. She walked through the park at the end of Comm. Ave., and quickly learned the differences between the Public Garden and Boston Common. She was especially fond of the swan boats and treated herself to a ride. She visited the lively stalls at Haymarket, buying her lunch from the open-air vendors, and she hung out in Harvard Square in the evenings, watching the street scene with curiosity and wonder.

On Monday, Ellen applied for and immediately got a job in the stationery department of the Harvard Cooperative Society, known as the Coop, starting the next day. She liked arranging the Radcliffe logo notebooks and colored pens, and she enjoyed waiting on the customers. Many of them were summer students; the rest were tourists. The other women in the department told her, "Wait till September if you want to see busy!" and Ellen laughed. She was earning her first paycheck that was not signed by a member of her family. Freedom! And she was counting the days until Nick arrived.

The next afternoon, as Ellen was preparing to go to lunch, she got a surprise. Nina walked into the department, looking for her.

"C'mon," she said, "I know a good Chinese place, right around the corner," and marched Ellen over to Young and Yee.

After they were seated, Nina told Ellen that she'd rented her own apartment on Inman Street in Cambridge, and was moving in this weekend. It was only about a mile to Central Square and the office of *Old Mole*, an easy walk. Nina said she hoped to hang out at the office of the underground paper until they gave her a story to cover, even though it wouldn't be for pay. She liked the folks there. Most of them were current or former Harvard students, but they seemed a whole lot hipper than the people at RNB. They had already sent her with one of the staff to cover a Cambridge City Council meeting.

Nina talked nonstop through lunch, only asking Ellen where she was living, and writing down her new address and phone number. Suddenly, Ellen looked at her watch.

"I can't be late from lunch on my second day!" she said, fishing in her bag for money to give Nina. "Sorry, Nina, I've got to go – now! Let's talk later," she called as she ran out the door.

"I'll call you tonight!" Nina shouted after her.

※ ※ ※ ※

Once the semester ended, Laurie spent her days helping her parents get ready for the move. There was so much to pack, and even more to give or throw away. Although the work was tedious, she was glad to finally get some time to spend with her mother.

Laurie carried a box of clothes for Goodwill to the kitchen, where her mom was wrapping each piece of china in newspaper.

"So much to do!" Ruth exclaimed. "And it's getting hot already," she said, wiping her forehead with the kerchief she'd tied in her hair. "Should we put on the air conditioner, do you think?"

"Sure, I'll do it," said Laurie, and she switched it on. Immediately, the quiet hum of the unit made a steady, comforting sound.

"Mom," Laurie began. "Can you take a break and listen?" Laurie picked up a stack of newspapers, cut in half to accommodate the smaller dishes, and began wrapping.

"Of course, dear. What's on your mind?" Ruth wiped her hands on her pedal pushers, went to the refrigerator, and took out a pitcher of juice. She poured two glasses over ice and handed one to her daughter.

Laurie began. "Something happened last month that I've been wanting to talk over with you."

Ruth immediately looked alarmed but her voice stayed calm as she sat at the table, looking directly at her daughter.

"You can tell me anything." Her voice was soothing.

And so Laurie did. She sat next to her mother, and started from the beginning, telling her about Ellen's visit, and how they happened to luck into going to the Female Liberation Conference, and all about the workshops, and what she'd been thinking and feeling since then, mostly that school was a waste of time and that she ought to be *doing* something, something important.

Ruth listened without speaking, then reached over to hug her daughter.

"My, my," was all she said, and Laurie burst into tears in her mother's comforting embrace.

"You know, Laurie," Ruth said after her daughter calmed down and took a drink of juice, "that's quite a lot to think about. But you're not like those other girls. For one, you have a family who loves you. And two, you don't work in a factory or attend a junior college up north that no one ever heard of. You go to Radcliffe! You are affiliated with the finest university in the world, like your brothers and your father…"

"And my mother," Laurie added proudly.

"Well, yes," Ruth said modestly. "And I can understand that some discontented girls might want to stir things up, but Laurie, that isn't who you are. You have so much promise. You're a hard worker, and you'll make a fine nurse – or doctor if that's what you decide – or whatever you want. Plus, you'll be a wonderful wife and mother."

"That's it," Laurie said. "I don't know what I want to be, or if I want to have a career and a family. I mean, I think I can do both, but now I'm not sure what I want. Maybe I don't want to get married. Maybe I don't even want to go back to school in the fall…"

Ruth gasped. "Laurie, what are you telling me?"

Laurie shook her head. "I don't know, Mom. I guess I need to think about it some more. Maybe talk it over with Ellen, Nina, or Diane."

"What about Amy and Sophie?" her mother countered, naming Laurie's two high school friends. "Aren't they home this summer?"

"Nah, Amy stayed at Vassar to do a summer art course and Sophie loves Providence so much she got a job as a waitress near her school. I haven't heard from either of them. We've drifted apart."

"Oh, I can only imagine what her mother must think!" clucked Ruth. "Sophie, a waitress!"

"Mom," said Laurie, looking at her mother with new eyes. "Mommy, are you happy? Do you feel oppressed by Papa?"

"Why, Laurie!" Ruth exclaimed. "What on earth are you saying? You know that your Papa treats me with kindness and love. He provides this lovely home – and a vacation home – for us, and we can even afford to retire early. He is good to you children, and he lets me do whatever I want and buy whatever I need."

"Do you hear what you're saying!" Laurie jumped to her feet, practically shouting at her mother. "He 'lets me…' Why do you think you need his permission? Everything we do here revolves around Papa – *When your Papa gets home, Let's ask Papa what he thinks, That's for Papa to decide.* Who says he gets to be the boss of the rest of us?"

Laurie couldn't stop. "Why does Papa always have time for the boys and not for me? Why doesn't he have time to listen to me talk about my ideas, my friends, my school activities?"

Ruth reached out a hand to calm her daughter.

"Laurie, you know that isn't true. Of course, Papa has been much busier than usual this year, wrapping up his work and training his colleagues and closing his practice so he can retire –"

To Sisterhood!

"No! No! No!" Laurie screamed. "He never listens to me. He listens to Andy and David all the time. He asks them about their classes and their research, and even about their friends. All he ever asks me is which courses am I taking and am I working hard? Does he ever ask me if I *like* the work? Or what I'm learning and if it's relevant to my real life? Or if I'm *happy*? No, he does not. I'm a woman. Women don't count with Papa, unless they're his rich bitch patients."

Ruth took a slow, deep breath. "Those rich patients, as you call them," she said in a quiet voice, "pay your tuition. They paid for this house. I've heard enough now, Laurie. I think you should go outside and take a walk and pull yourself together."

"Gladly!" Laurie grabbed her tennis shoes and ran out the door, wondering if her mother knew her at all.

❋ **Eight** ❋

Laurie called Nina, and asked if she would meet her at the Cambridge Library. They found a quiet bench outside, and Laurie recounted her troubled conversation with her mother.

"Divide and conquer," Nina observed. "I see it all the time at home. 'You're special. You're not like those other girls. You come from privilege. You are a Machman' – well, that last part came from my grandfather, not my father. And I'm starting to see it in the Movement, too. 'You're not Black; you can't do the Black man's struggle.' 'You're not working class, so you need to get a job in a factory to relate to the working man.'"

"Wow," Laurie said. "You've given this a lot of thought."

Nina smiled ruefully. "Not really. But remember, I've been working for two years in the alternative press and I've heard a lot of people taking a lot of positions. Do you know what a White Paper is?"

Laurie shook her head.

"Anybody who has an opinion and access to a typewriter and a mimeograph machine can write up whatever it is they want to say – why Vietnam is a racist war, why the imperialist warmongers are in Southeast Asia for the oil, not to preserve democracy, how the CIA withheld critical evidence which makes the Warren Report useful only as toilet paper, that sort of thing. They write the paper and make copies, and then people pass them to their friends, and they get mailed across the country and sometimes, a White Paper will make it to the underground press."

To Sisterhood!

Nina stood up and stretched, then walked over to a nearby tree and looked at Laurie.

"For now, get this: as much as your mother may love you, she has *her* best interest at heart, not yours. She wants you to go down the straight path – college, marriage, a safe little career, something like her life but with a job you can fall back on so you can support yourself if your husband turns out to be a jerk, am I right?"

"Pretty much, I guess." Laurie nodded slowly. "I never thought about it before. It's like she loves me, I know that – I mean, she's always been my best friend and best supporter – but then, I've always done exactly what she wants. I guess I have to think about this."

"I get it. I told you my mother died when I was thirteen, so we never got into the mother/adolescent daughter thing. I never got a chance."

"Tell me about your mother," Laurie said gently, and Nina did. She sat back down on the bench. An hour later, when she got to the part about sitting on her mother's bed after school every day as she was dying, Nina started to get teary. Laurie moved closer and hugged Nina.

"I'm sorry," Nina said, reaching into her bag for a tissue, blowing her nose, and struggling to regain her composure. "I never talk about my mother with anyone. You're the first person I've told the whole story to. You're such a good listener, Laurie. You should be a counselor or something. You've got the knack."

Laurie blushed. "Thanks, Nina, and thank you for trusting me with your story. I can't imagine how difficult it must be for you, even now. You must miss her every day."

"I do," Nina said simply, and that began a fresh wave of tears. Laurie held her while she cried.

"I can't believe this," Nina said. "I *never* cry in front of anyone. At least I haven't until now."

"It's fine," Laurie reassured her. "You know," she said shyly, "I've always wanted a big sister."

Nina wiped her eyes again and smiled. "I've always liked being an only child. Most of my friends fight all the time with their siblings. But I like this, thanks," and Nina reached out to take Laurie's hand.

※ ※ ※ ※

With Laurie's enthusiastic help, Nina worked on organizing her grand 21st birthday weekend. Inviting Ellen and Diane to join them, they planned to stay at Laurie's family's vacation home in Wellfleet, hang out at the beach, and explore the lively street scene in Provincetown at the tip of the Cape.

Ellen said she was scheduled to work on Saturday but was pretty sure she could swap with someone. "Count me in!" she said happily.

Diane was surprised and pleased to hear from Laurie.

She said she didn't work weekends, though she was planning to go to Barnstable to visit her sister. She'd been down there this weekend, and everything seemed to be going fine, but Diane missed her and wanted to see her again.

To Sisterhood!

"That could work out!" Laurie said. She'd met Theresa and guessed how important it was for Diane to be with her. "We can drop you off in Barnstable for a couple of hours Sunday afternoon on our way back so you can visit her, and the rest of us can go tour Hyannis. Do you think that would work?"

Diane said yes, and the women agreed to meet in Central Square next Friday afternoon, shortly after Diane got off her shift.

※ ※ ※ ※

On Friday, Laurie picked up the others right on time in her mother's red Volvo wagon. Nina claimed the front passenger seat, and Diane and Ellen climbed into the back. After throwing everyone's gear into the cargo compartment, Laurie cranked up WRKO. They all sang along loudly to *Aquarius/Let the Sunshine In* as she headed toward the Southeast Expressway.

Everyone was in high spirits, listening to the top 40, and chatting excitedly about what they were going to do all weekend.

Laurie told the others about the art galleries in the East End, and the cool folk music place down in the West End, where she saw Arlo Guthrie perform *Alice's Restaurant* a couple of years ago, and where Eric Andersen, Maria Muldaur, and Dave Van Ronk played when they were in town.

Laurie's classmate Ginger was a summer apprentice at the Provincetown Playhouse-on-the-Wharf, off Gosnold Street. Laurie said she thought the season didn't open for another week, but the company would be in rehearsals and they definitely could go visit. She explained to Ellen, the only one who had never been to Provincetown, that it was a popular vacation destination for gays, both men and women. Some of the men could be "very flamboyant," especially on Saturday nights, she said, so Ellen should be prepared to see men dressed up like women, as movie stars and popular singers, and just about anything. "It's quite a show!" she laughed.

When they finally arrived in Wellfleet, Laurie pulled into the circular driveway made of crushed shells, with a cheerful, "Here we are!"

Diane and Ellen stared at the huge, grey-shingled, two-and-a-half story house, with white-trimmed windows and sloping roofs. The driveway surrounded a sandy garden with tall beach grass, and they could see a large body of water behind the house.

"Wow!" Diane said, as Laurie led them upstairs and showed them to their rooms. Laurie's room was on the top floor, all by itself. She invited them up to take a peek at her cozy retreat.

The others climbed the narrow staircase which opened into a room with dormers in both the front and the back. Crisp pink-and-white dotted Swiss curtains framed the small windows, and an old honeycomb quilt in pastels with a lot of pink and white covered the single bed. On the bed were a few well-loved stuffed animals, including a Steiff Teddy, and an orangutan.

"This is Jocko," Laurie said, picking up the orangutan and giving him a squeeze. He squeaked a return greeting. "He's my favorite."

Diane was surprised that Laurie didn't seem at all embarrassed about what essentially was a young girl's room. Her own room at home was decorated with pictures of her idol, Paul McCartney, and the Beach

Boys. Even Theresa had put up pictures of horses, and her favorite, Herman's Hermits.

Laurie gestured to the large bookcases lining both sides of the walls flanking the window seat, which had soft, plump pink cushions – just the spot to curl up and read on a rainy summer day.

"Cherry Ames, Nancy Drew, The Bobbsey Twins – they're all there," she said matter-of-factly. "*Mary Poppins. The Secret Garden.* All the Narnia books. I re-read my favorites when I'm up here. I like reverting to childhood."

Nina, who knew a thing or two about books thought: *if these are all first editions and in good shape, they're worth a bundle*, but talking about money was tacky, so she kept quiet.

"I know what you mean about re-reading your favorites," said Ellen, who did the exact same thing every chance she got. "It's so comforting. Laurie, this house is stunning."

Ellen was sitting on the window seat, looking out at the twinkling lights in the distance.

"It's like living in paradise." She reflected on how different this feminine room was from Laurie's sophisticated room in the dorm.

"Let's go downstairs. It's kind of crowded up here with everyone," Laurie said.

They all went into the big kitchen and sat around the butcher block farmhouse table.

"I've something to get us in a party mood." Nina reached into her bag and pulled out two joints.

Ellen's and Diane's eyes went wide. "Marijuana?" they said together, looking at one another.

"Please don't tell me you two have never smoked dope!" Nina exclaimed, while Laurie was already up and heading to the cabinet over the sink for the box of safety matches.

She handed the box to Nina, who lit one of the joints, took a deep drag, and passed it to Laurie. Laurie took a hit and passed it to Diane, who shook her head.

"I think I'll stick to beer. Is there any here, Laurie?"

Laurie blew out the smoke she'd been holding in and said, "no, but Nina can buy some tomorrow. In a couple of hours, she'll be legal!"

Diane accepted Laurie's offer of a Pepsi, while Ellen cautiously puffed on the joint, immediately coughing and sputtering and turning red.

"Yikes!" said Nina, and showed Ellen how to hold the joint, breathe it in, and hold in the smoke. Of course, Ellen had seen others smoking dope before, and had been eager to try it, but was afraid she'd be seen.

Shortly, all four women – even Diane, who seemed to have a contact high – were giggling. "I'm starving!" Laurie wailed, and they munched through their meager supplies, plus most of what was left in the cupboards – stale graham crackers, a jar of peanut butter, a new jar

To Sisterhood!

of beach plum jam, some chocolate bars, and a package of dried-up marshmallows, which Diane started to roast over the matches.

Laurie said, "come with me," and opened the back door off the kitchen, where five rocking chairs waited invitingly on the large deck, which overlooked Cape Cod Bay.

"Oh, what a view!" Ellen exclaimed. "This house is gorgeous, Laurie. You are so lucky!"

"How long has it been in your family?" Nina wanted to know.

"You should see it first thing in the morning," Laurie said to Ellen. And to Nina, "My parents bought the house when I was small. We've been coming down here as long as I can remember. Usually, Mom would take us all down here as soon as school got out, and Papa would come down Friday afternoon to Monday morning, and then for all of August. Sometimes, if we didn't go skiing over Christmas, we would come down here then too. It's wonderful in the winter too, quiet and peaceful."

Diane simply couldn't fathom that a family could go on vacation for an entire summer. *Laurie lives in another world*, she thought, but didn't say anything.

"Where does your family vacation?" Laurie asked the others.

"Hampton Beach, a couple of times," Diane said. Her family didn't do much together.

Nina told them that when her mother was alive, they'd travelled all over Europe, to the Bahamas in the winter, and a few other places she was too young to remember.

"I haven't done any travelling with my dad since he married Muriel, though. But there are still a lot of places I'd like to see."

Ellen said that her family – between helping her two sets of grandparents run the farm and the general store – didn't take vacations, although they had driven up to Lake Champlain once for the weekend, when her father had some sort of meeting there.

Ellen thought about the glorious few summers she and Eddy had spent on the farm. After the chickens were fed, and the new tomatoes picked – chores that made the four-year-olds feel important and needed, they were free for the rest of the day to explore the apple orchard, climb the trees, help the hands with the horses – how Eddy loved the horses! – and play Jim Bowie exploring the jungle, which really was a large meadow filled with wildflowers, some taller than the twins.

Ellen missed her brother so much. She talked to him all the time in her mind, and didn't think it strange when he answered her. She knew it was only her imagination, but couldn't help thinking that Eddy had grown up right beside her. She could imagine how handsome he would be now at almost nineteen – tall and blonde, with that same mischievous twinkle in his eye. But she was not at all ready to talk about her twin with these women, as much as she was growing to like them all. Not yet. And she'd told Nick only the bare details of the story: that when she'd just started kindergarten, she'd lost her twin brother in the accident that left her lame in one leg, that she missed him every day, and that she didn't want to discuss it. Nick, bless him, nodded

To Sisterhood!

solemnly and said he would respect her wish and that he'd always be available to listen if she ever had a change of heart.

Laurie told them that in addition to the Christmas vacation ski trips to Aspen or a week down here relaxing, they always went either to Boca Raton or Palm Beach for February break. And now her parents were retiring to Boca, she said with a sigh. "I mean, it's great to visit in February when it's cold in New England. But I can't understand why they'd want to live down there full-time," she complained. "Of course, they'll be up here all summer. At least they're not selling *this* house."

"It could have something to do with their tax situation," Nina offered. She'd heard plenty of this kind of conversation at home, but it always ended with Muriel furious that they couldn't afford to retire anywhere for a long time. But then, Nina's father was much younger than Laurie's, so they didn't have to think about it right now. "Why don't you ask your father?"

Laurie laughed at the idea. "He wouldn't talk to me about taxes, or money, or anything like that," she said. "But I can talk to my mother – if she's still speaking to me." She gave Ellen and Diane a brief overview of the loud disagreement with her mother.

"At least you can talk to your mother," Diane and Ellen said, pretty much at the same time.

Laurie shook her head. "I don't know. We used to talk about everything, but now I feel like she doesn't get me at all. I told her I didn't see the point of going back to school and she freaked."

"Laurie," Ellen said quietly, gently touching her friend's arm. "Let's talk about this tomorrow."

But Laurie continued. "It's that there's so much to do, what with the war, and poverty, and all the injustice in the world…and speaking of the world, there are many places I'd like to see – I want to see everything!"

"Speaking of seeing everything," Diane yawned. "I think my head would like to see a pillow right about now. I'm bushed."

"Yup, big day tomorrow," agreed Laurie. "But it's after midnight, so hey, Nina, happy birthday!"

"Happy birthday," the others chimed in. With a chorus of "good nights," they all went upstairs.

※ ※ ※ ※

Ellen was the first one awake. She went to the kitchen wearing a short robe over her pajamas. She poked through the cabinets, and found some coffee, which she brewed in the drip pot she first rinsed and dried. The coffee was stale and there was no milk, but she was grateful for the rush it gave her.

She toasted a couple of pieces of the bread Laurie brought, and ate them with a dollop of the jam they'd opened last night.

The others came downstairs not too long after. Diane, dressed in jeans and a yellow blouse, was cheerful and said she was "absolutely starving." Laurie had already washed her hair and was dressed in bib overalls with a red and purple tie-dyed tee shirt and brown leather

To Sisterhood!

sandals. When Ellen admired them, she told her she'd bought them in Provincetown the year before.

"You can get some too," she urged Ellen, who'd never worn custom-made anything in her life, unless you counted the Halloween costumes her mother sewed for her and Eddy. After he died, all of Ellen's costumes came from the general store.

Finally, Nina came down, looking bright and bouncy in a white piqué sundress with what looked like brand-new white tennis shoes.

"Here's the birthday girl!" Laurie shouted, and Nina said hopefully, "Coffee?"

"There's no milk," Ellen said, pouring her a cup, and Nina said, "It's fine. I take it black."

"Let's go into Provincetown for breakfast," Laurie suggested.

The women all piled into the Volvo. Laurie stopped on Route 6 to fill up the tank, and Nina pulled out her wallet.

"The whole weekend is on me" she reminded her friend. "Everything. You are kind enough to let us stay with you. My father is paying for the rest. Let's enjoy ourselves! Happy birthday to me!"

Laurie took the exit for 6A at Beach Point in North Truro.

"You have got to see this view," she told the others, as she drove more slowly down the residential road. As they crested the hill, Laurie told them to shush for a minute, then she rounded the bend. Cape Cod Bay and the town, with the tall granite Provincetown Monument right on the horizon, was a spectacular sight. This early in the morning, the sky was exactly the same grey-blue as the water, and the hazy light gave the town an almost surreal look.

"Wow!" they all said at once.

Even Nina was impressed. "I can see why artists talk about Provincetown as having the most incredible light. It's somewhat like the Mediterranean, only even more beautiful."

Soon, Laurie parked the car. "This is the East End of town," she explained. "This part is all residential, and as we walk up Commercial Street, soon you'll see the galleries. You all don't mind a short walk, do you?"

Diane slipped her arm through Ellen's. "Are you okay?" she asked quietly. "We can go slowly."

Ellen nodded gratefully. "Okay for now," she said. "It's harder when I'm tired, but I slept well, and I've got on my sturdy shoes."

As they walked, the four exclaimed over the charming cottages with the pretty gardens out front.

"It's gorgeous here," said Ellen. "I can't believe it. Who lives here year-round?"

"Artists and writers," Laurie said. "This used to be primarily a Portuguese fishing village. There are still a lot of fishermen and their families here. Silva, Costa, you see those names everywhere. And of

To Sisterhood!

course, as I said before, there's a large gay population too. Everyone seems to be tolerant of one another. There's very little crime. You can walk down Commercial Street pretty much any time of the night and feel safe. People look out for one another."

After breakfast at a sidewalk café and a chance to rest, they headed to the center of town.

"C'mon, everyone, I've got to show you the Playhouse!" Laurie said. She led them down Gosnold Street toward the water and in one short block, they saw a large old wharf building, with a smaller building attached. Between the two was a large wooden deck, where a group of young men and women were busy building sets.

"Where's Ginger?" she asked a cute guy, who gestured toward the box office.

Ginger came out and gave Laurie an enthusiastic hug. Laurie introduced her friends.

"Hello to all of you!" Ginger chirped. She said she didn't have much time but was happy to show them around the theater if they could do it quickly. She introduced them all to the crew and to some of the more junior actors who were building the set.

"Just tell me who that adorable guy with the great smile is," said Nina.

"Oh, that's Richard, Richard Gere. He goes to UMass, I think," she said. "And over there," she continued in a reverent tone, "is the incredible woman who started the company, Catharine Huntington. We call her Miss Catharine."

Laurie whispered quietly to Diane, "Huntington. As in Huntington Avenue, y'know?" Diane's eyes widened at the name of the famous Boston street.

At the sound of her name, the much older woman, who was wearing a summer dress printed with blue and yellow flowers, and a large, wide-brimmed hat to protect her fair skin from the sun, turned toward them.

"How do you do?" she said graciously in her lovely, lilting actress voice, which held a Boston Brahmin accent.

"Miss Catharine," said Ginger, "I would like you to meet my Radcliffe classmate, Laurie Goodman, and her friends, um…"

Laurie reached out a hand.

"It's such a pleasure to meet you," she said, for Laurie had been to the Playhouse performances many times and had seen the producer and director, instrumental in keeping Eugene O'Neill's work alive, also act in many plays. "This is Ellen, and Diane, and Nina."

Diane and Nina nodded politely, murmuring greetings, but Ellen stood staring at Miss Catharine, her mouth dropped open in surprise.

"Miss Catharine Huntington? Radcliffe Class of 1911?"

Miss Catharine smiled. "Why yes. Do I know you, my dear?" she asked, peering over the top of her tinted sunglasses with more interest.

"Well, no," stammered Ellen, now totally flushed with embarrassment. "I mean, no, I've read about you, of course. I mean, in *The Little*

Locksmith. You were a friend of Katharine Butler Hathaway when she was at Radcliffe. You were the one who was so helpful to her, and encouraged her, and..." Ellen realized she was babbling but she couldn't seem to stop.

"Oh, she was much too kind," Miss Catharine said with a modest chuckle. "But please do come in and have some iced tea. I must leave you now but Ginger will be delighted to serve you." With a flourish, the grand lady turned and went into the air-conditioned box office.

✳ ✳ ✳ ✳

"Holy Moley!" said Ellen when they got back to Commercial Street. "I mean, meeting Miss Catharine was incredible!"

"Far out!" Laurie agreed, glad that Ellen was pleased.

After lunch at the Lobster Pot and a visit to the 252-foot-high Pilgrim Monument, which Ellen and Diane declined to climb, waiting in the museum at the base, the women walked back to Commercial Street and browsed in the bookshop, the two candy shops, and what Laurie called "the tchotchke stores" full of Cape Cod souvenirs, tee shirts, post cards, and bumper stickers. They decided to rest their feet by having their portraits done in charcoal by a street artist. They laughed at the finished pictures, and agreed that he did a pretty good job.

It was almost dinner time, and they walked back toward the East End to Ciro and Sal's. They waited in the garden until it was time to have dinner in the iconic Italian restaurant. The pleasant host showed them down a couple of stone stairs to their table, in the cool basement with a low ceiling. Each table was illuminated by a hanging lamp made either from an old Chianti bottle or a cut-out tin cylinder. Nina ordered a glass of red wine and was thrilled when the waiter asked for identification.

"Happy birthday!" he said with a wink.

"Get whatever you like," Nina generously told the others. She ordered an iceberg lettuce salad and a pasta dish featuring the unlikely combination of anchovies, raisins, walnuts, and olive oil, which she pronounced, "Delicious!" Laurie and Ellen ordered fish, and Diane chose a spicy chicken dish. Laurie started her meal with oysters with pesto sauce. They munched on the plentiful, delicious fresh bread, and talked and talked.

After he cleared the dishes, their waiter brought out a miniature cake with a candle for Nina and the people at the surrounding tables joined Ellen, Diane, and Laurie in singing "Happy Birthday" to their friend, who basked in the attention.

※ ※ ※ ※

Late that night, the women sat on the back deck, looking up at the stars, and at the far lights of Provincetown across the water. Nina passed around a couple more joints, while Diane had a beer. The night was completely quiet and still, except for the peaceful sound of the waves on the bay.

Ellen spoke softly. "Remember the day we met last month and we talked about our wishes and dreams?"

The others said yes. "And Laurie, remember how last night you said you were thinking of leaving school? My newest dream, I think, is not only to get into Radcliffe, but to become a teacher. Maybe even a

To Sisterhood!

professor. I'd love to have a student like you, Laurie. I can't wait to learn so many new things, and then to be able to pass them along to someone else, someone bright and full of enthusiasm like you, who has such good ideas. It will be wonderful to see what you can do with your education, Laurie. We'll support you in whatever you decide, but for me…"

Ellen coughed, then cleared her throat. "For me, would you stay at Radcliffe for one more year? Until I see if I get in? I would love to be in class with you. I would love to learn with you."

"That would be junior year, then, by the time you start," said Laurie. "But, yes, I guess so. My parents would cut me off if I dropped out, anyway. And I would never hear the end of it from my big brothers. I guess I can think of myself as one of those lucky Americans."

Nina laughed and the others looked puzzled until Laurie explained. "You know, like Che Guevara said, 'you Americans are so lucky to live in the heart of the beast.' I guess there's still a lot I can do from inside the system." Laurie sighed deeply.

"Look at that!" Diane shouted suddenly, pointing straight up. "A shooting star!"

"Whoa!" said Ellen. "There's another! And another. It looks like a meteor shower!"

"Quick, everyone, make a wish!" Laurie said.

"You already know my wish. My byline in *The Village Voice* someday," Nina said immediately*." Or even *The New Yorker*." And I can get my trust fund now that I'm twenty-one. Yeah, baby!*

"I wish my mother would understand me," Laurie said wistfully. *And that Papa would love me.*

"Radcliffe," said Ellen, thinking of Eddy, and then, to her surprise, *Sam.*

"A great apartment for Theresa and me," said Diane, while she thought, *Valerie.*

✻ **Nine** ✻

On the last Saturday in July 1966, Diane sat in the break room of Johnnie's Foodmaster supermarket, where she worked as a cashier after school and Saturdays. She had only fifteen minutes for her break, and she hadn't eaten anything since last night, but she didn't want to waste any time. Patty sat next to her at the long Formica table, sneaking a cigarette and fanning the smoke out the window.

"Patty." Diane spoke quietly. "Patty, you've gotta help me. I'm in trouble." Diane was sitting up straight, not lounging back like she usually did at break. She looked grim.

Patty looked at her. "What is it? What's the matter, Diane?"

When Diane didn't answer, Patty said, "Oh, my God. You mean 'in trouble' kind of trouble? I hope you're kidding?"

Diane shook her head. "I wish I was, but no, I'm in a bad way, Patty."

"Shit." Patty put out the cigarette, and took Diane's hands in hers. "Whose is it?"

Diane turned and pulled her hands away.

"Dee, I'm your best friend. You can tell me." Patty's voice was low. She looked around the room, making sure it was still empty and no one could hear them.

Diane said nothing.

"You didn't even tell me you were dating anyone. Is it that guy Roger from St. John's? Or that big guy, what's his name, Billy? The one who has homeroom across from you?"

Diane still didn't answer. She hadn't thought this through. Dumb, dumb, dumb. Of course, it was the first thing anyone would ask. She had to think fast.

"You have to swear you won't tell," she said.

Patty nodded. "Cross my heart and hope to die. You know you can trust me, Dee."

Diane leaned her elbows on the table and whispered. "He's older. You don't know him. I met him at the church picnic this spring. And he, um, he kind of forced me. And I can't tell my parents. They would kill me. You know that."

"Will he marry you?"

"No. I haven't seen him again. That's the thing. My parents would find him and make him marry me. I don't want to get married, especially not to him." She grimaced. "I hate his guts!"

"Oh, honey." Patty dug in her purse for her calendar. "How far along are you?"

"About two months. I think the due date's around Valentine's Day. How's that for a laugh?"

To Sisterhood!

"Oh, my God!" said Patty. "You're gonna start showing soon. Right around when school starts. What are you going to do?"

"I was hoping you could help me come up with an answer." Diane had planned for, longed for, senior year ever since she started high school. Now it was all ruined. She wiped away tears.

"Did you go to confession?" Patty asked, and when Diane shook her head, added, "If he forced you, you should tell the police and he could go to jail and it wouldn't be a mortal sin."

"I don't want to see him again, Patty. I don't even know his last name." Diane started to cry. Patty held her friend tightly.

"You've got to tell your parents," she said softly. "Why would you want to protect him?"

"No, no, I can't," Diane cried. "I know what would happen." Covering her eyes with her hands, she started to sob in earnest.

"Sshhh," Patty said, gently rocking her. "You've got to stop. Someone will hear you. You've got to tell them. I'll come with you. I'll help you."

Diane managed a weak smile, and sat up straight. "Thanks, Patty, you're a real friend. But I've got to handle them on my own. The timing will be tricky. Could you go out and cover for me for a few minutes so I can fix my mascara?"

"Of course. I'll punch you back in. Go splash some water on your face, and for God's sake, put on some lipstick too. You look like hell."

That night, Diane didn't go straight home from work. Instead, she called her mother and said she had to work late, and she'd walk down to the garage and ride home with her dad.

"You'd better hurry," Magda said. "He's leaving early. It's his bowling night." Yes, Diane remembered. She'd worked it all out. She'd get there just a few minutes too late.

"Hey, babe." Tony looked happy to see her. "Long time." He hadn't come to dinner since that day on the Point. Magda had wondered where he was, but John told her he'd been putting in a lot of overtime since he got back from Guard duty last week. Plus Mrs. Giovanni had been complaining about her youngest son not coming to see her enough since he got his own place in East Cambridge.

Tony moved toward her to give her a hug, but Diane pulled away. She looked right at him.

"Where's Dad?" she asked, even though she knew.

"You just missed him," Tony said, wiping his greasy hands on his coveralls. "Bowling night."

"Right." Diane's stomach and head both hurt. She dreaded the next few minutes. But better to get it over with, and to know if he was going to help her. This was Tony, who'd been her friend since she was small. Maybe he'd been drunk, or he'd just lost his mind that day. Maybe he was sorry. Anyway, he had to help her. He simply had to.

Tony turned a chair around and straddled it. "Sit here for a couple of minutes," he said, indicating the beat-up sofa. "I'm almost done with

To Sisterhood!

putting the transmission back in this VW. Be about half an hour, tops. Then I'll give you a lift. Make yourself at home."

Diane's gaze went from the dirty fingerprints on the wall, to Miss July on the calendar, smiling like she knew a thing or two, to the Snap-on tool cabinet, a crushed soda can, and the remains of someone's sandwich that missed the wastebasket. She waited. She twisted her short curls around her finger, and when she tired of that, she went over to the gumball machine and put in a penny. She popped the gum in her mouth and chewed furiously.

Soon, Tony came back into the office whistling, wiping his hands on a red rag. He went to the register, took out the day's receipts, and put them into a burlap night deposit bag.

"Let's go," he said. "I've gotta drop this off at the bank."

Diane followed him out to his pride-and-joy Valiant.

"I just put in a new carburetor," he said. "She runs like a dream now."

Diane was silent. She clutched the clasp of her pocketbook with both hands. She would not cry.

"Hey, Diane, what's the matter? I haven't seen you in what, a couple of months?" He opened the passenger door. "Come on, get in here."

She climbed in and sat stiffly, straight up. At the next corner, Tony turned and pulled the car over to the side of the road.

"Hey, gorgeous, gimme a kiss." He reached over to try to pull her closer to him.

Diane pushed him away. "Don't!" she yelled. "Stop it!"

"Aren't you glad to see me? I thought of you every night while I was away on Guard duty, Dee." He smiled smugly. "I couldn't wait to get home."

"I'm pregnant." Her voice was flat.

Tony let out a long, low whistle. "Wow. That's tough. Who's the guy?"

Diane stared at him. She was prepared for his anger, his surprise, and maybe – if what he said that day was true – maybe he'd even be happy. She was not prepared for his denial.

"Whoa, wait a minute," he moaned, shutting off the engine and turning toward her again. "You don't think it's mine, do you?"

Diane started to cry.

"C'mon, there are all those guys at school," Tony sneered. "You must know at least one of them pretty good. I mean, when we were together you sure seemed like you knew what you were doing." He gripped the steering wheel and looked hard at her.

Diane shook her head. "Don't do this, Tony. You know it's yours. You know you're the only one." She sobbed, her nose running. She reached into her bag for a tissue.

To Sisterhood!

"You're sure?" His gaze softened and he looked at her with concern.

"Of course I'm sure," Diane sniffed.

"How far gone are you?"

"Almost two months already. I'll be showing by the beginning of school. It's due in the middle of February."

"Oh, man, oh, man," said Tony, his head in his hands. "This is tough. Look, Dee, I've got a buddy. His girlfriend had the same problem. She went to Baltimore. Got rid of it. Three hundred bucks. She came back, went right back to work. No one else knew."

"Are you saying – abortion?" Diane gasped.

"Yeah, it's not too late, though I'd hurry if I was you. Tell you what I'll do, honey. I'll pay for half of it." He smiled expectantly. He reached into the bag and counted out fifteen twenties.

"Here, look," he said, "there's enough for train fare and even a hotel room too. You'll probably need to stay over."

"That's my father's money," Diane said.

"You gonna tell him?" Tony gave her a big, slow grin.

Diane stared at him. She opened the car door and got out, but not before grabbing the cash. She slammed the door behind her. She walked all the way home. She'd think of something. She always did.

※ ※ ※ ※

Theresa met her at the door. "Hey, Dee! Look what I made today!"

"What is it, Theresa?" Diane forced her voice to be calm.

"I made an apple cake. An upside-down one."

"Wow, I can't wait for dessert! I'll bet it's yummy."

"And my group leader said I could bake blueberry muffins tomorrow." Theresa looked so happy.

"That's great, honey," Diane said. "Yours will be even better than the ones at Jordan Marsh."

Both girls looked up at the sudden clatter from the other room. It was Magda, coming down the stairs unsteadily.

"Nice of you to show up, Missy." Her mother now stood in the doorway, furious.

"I missed Dad," Diane said. "I walked home."

"Why didn't Tony give you a ride?" Magda glared at her accusingly.

"He offered," said Diane, "but he had to do some errands first, so I figured walking would be quicker. Look, you must be hungry, Mother. I'll have dinner ready in a few minutes. Why don't you go relax? It's almost time for The Lucy Show.*"*

"Oh, is it 8:30 already?"

"I'll bring you dinner on a tray," Diane said. *"Go and sit down."*

Oh, great, Diane thought. They can't function without me. What if I leave? Who will take care of Theresa if I'm not here?

Diane waited until after Sunday dinner, when Theresa went upstairs to take a nap. When Diane broke her news, Magda yelled and moved toward her, but John got in between them. Oddly, Diane thought, they took some time to get around to asking who the father was. Mostly, it was Magda shrieking about what this was going to mean to her and the family's reputation, and how would she ever be able to hold up her head at Sacred Heart?

When John finally asked Diane who was responsible, she refused to tell. She knew that all hell would break loose if she told the truth. She didn't think Mother would believe her anyway. It didn't matter, because what Magda said, after she'd had a few slugs directly from the bottle was:

"You leave this house at once, you filthy tramp!" And then she slapped her. John roused himself from the sofa, grabbed Magda, and yelled at her not to touch their daughter, couldn't she see that Diane was in enough pain? John went over to the phone and called the priest.

Before long, Magda, now on her best behavior, greeted Father Ryan at the door. She served him leftover ham and gravy, which he pronounced, "Excellent." John broke out the bottle of Jameson, and together, the three adults arranged for Diane to go to a home for unwed mothers in Maine, run by the nuns.

They would continue her education, so she could come back and graduate with her class. Diane was not consulted. John figured out that they could tell everyone that Diane had to go to Italy to help care for her grandmother, who would "die" at the end of the pregnancy.

Magda, who'd had quite a lot of the whiskey, slumped over on the chair while the priest patted her shoulder. John took Diane aside and said he still loved her, but that she was wild like her mother, and the nuns would set her straight. Diane knew the law said they had to support her until age eighteen, and she also knew that Magda would never, ever kick her out of the house, because then who would take care of Theresa?

Diane forced herself to keep her head. She took advantage of the fact that Father Ryan was present to finally spring on her parents the idea of having Theresa go to the special school on Cape Cod where her summer camp counselor was on staff. As drunk as she was, Magda grasped right away that this was a good thing, but John said he couldn't afford the tuition.

"Don't worry," Diane told him. "I applied for a scholarship. All you have to pay for is the books, same as here at Sacred Heart, and drive her to Barnstable in September and pick her up at Christmas. You can visit her every weekend. It's all set."

"It sounds like that will be a great relief," Father Ryan said. "And who knows, with all this sorted out, Magda and John, maybe God will finally bless you with a son."

Magda got up and poured herself another shot.

On Labor Day, John and Diane drove Theresa to her new school on the Cape. Diane had worked hard to convince the director that Theresa needed to be there. She had to get her into that school, especially after she'd lied to her parents about already getting the scholarship. But there was no way Diane would let Theresa stay at home with them. Not without her there.

John drove Diane up to Portland the next day, leaving her in the care of the nuns. Diane was met by a kind-faced sister in modern dress. After briefing Diane on what she could expect during her stay, she took Diane over to Cape Elizabeth to the home sponsored by the Sisters of Mercy, who also ran the local hospital.

Although the other residents, as they were called, were pleasant, there was a shared understanding that they would not become friends. They all knew that when they went back to their "real lives," they would want to forget this place forever.

In addition to academic studies, morning walks, and evening prayers, each girl was assigned to a specific work area. Diane spent this time in the kitchen, under the tutelage of Sister Marie, the head cook. She liked Diane and taught her how to bake bread, how to make pastry, and many of the basics of cooking for a crowd. She even encouraged Diane to develop some recipes of her own. Diane was comfortable with the nuns. Cooking and studies took her mind off her troubles, at least most of the time.

Diane's baby girl was born on her due date, February 14th, 1967. The sisters thought it best that she be drugged for the labor, but Diane insisted on being awake. One of them taught her some breathing exercises, but when the pain got hard, the doctor offered to give her something "to ease things a bit," and that's all she remembered.

When Diane woke up – minutes or hours later, she didn't know which – the TV was on. The first thing she heard was the week's body count, the deaths of American soldiers in Vietnam, including the report of one only eighteen years old.

What kind of crazy world was this for a baby? The sister came in, quietly closing the door behind her. She did not have a baby in her arms. She told Diane that the baby was fine, a lovely, healthy girl with fuzzy black hair. Diane asked to see her daughter, and the sister told her gently that it was better not to see her, that it would make it more difficult later. But she could fill out the papers, and give her daughter a name.

Diane wanted desperately to hold her baby, even once, but the sister was adamant. Diane named her daughter Valerie, in honor of St. Valentine. She was exhausted, still groggy from the drugs, bitterly angry at Tony and her parents, and so, so sad.

After spending ten more days at the home to recuperate, Diane said goodbye to Sister Marie, and to a couple of the other girls. When she arrived home on Friday, her mother was not pleased, especially when Diane insisted that they drive her down to Barnstable to visit Theresa, who was overjoyed to see her. By Monday, Diane was back at school, on track to graduate with her class. No one believed the grandmother story. Everybody knew what had happened, but no one ever mentioned it, at least not in front of her. Mostly, her classmates left her alone.

Patty was the only one who went out of her way to be kind.

To Sisterhood!

Diane was relieved to learn from her father, who bemoaned his lack of help at the station, that Tony had enlisted in the Army more than two months ago.

"Isn't he brave?" cooed her mother.

"Coward," Diane thought. "Damn good thing he's halfway around the world."

✣ **Ten** ✣

Ellen was practical. She knew that now she and Nick would be living in the same city, sooner rather than later he would want to take their physical relationship to the next step. She was going to have to find some way to get protection.

She couldn't ask anyone from school or back home. She couldn't talk to Diane about it, she was Catholic and probably very sheltered. Ellen liked Laurie, but she had a big mouth, and Ellen didn't want everyone in the world knowing her private business.

That left Nina. She was probably the best choice anyway. She seemed to know what was what about stuff like this.

A few weeks after Nina's birthday, Ellen and Nina were hanging out, taking a walk around Harvard Square after work. Ellen told her that things were starting to get serious with her boyfriend.

"Meaning?" Nina slowed her pace.

Ellen blushed. "We're talking about having relations."

Nina raised one well-shaped eyebrow. "You're still a virgin?"

"I'm surmising by your question that you are not," Ellen shot back.

"Bingo."

"Here's the $64,000 question: where can I get birth control?"

"Oh, that's right," Nina chewed her fingernail. "It's not legal in this backwater state, is it?"

Ellen shook her head. "No, and I can't go anywhere in Vermont either. I'm sure every single pharmacist knows my grandparents."

"That's probably an exaggeration but I see your point. What about condoms? There isn't a guy in the world who doesn't carry one in his wallet."

Ellen looked at her. "With only eighty-five percent effectiveness?"

Nina laughed. Of course, careful Ellen would have researched this already. "You know, this is kind of heavy. Let's go grab a coffee."

They stopped at the next coffee shop, ordered to go, and sat on the front steps of the First Parish Church.

Nina blew on her hot coffee and took a big sip. "Sounds like a trip to New York is in order."

"You would take me? Where would we go? I wouldn't want to run into anyone."

"Don't worry. We'll go to Planned Parenthood up in Harlem. You won't meet anyone there who knows you," Nina said, trying not to sound sarcastic.

"Do you know how much I appreciate this?" Ellen set her cup down, started to reach over to hug Nina, seemed to think better of it, and dropped her arms by her sides.

"What's a friend for, if she can't help her friend get laid?" Nina smiled.

"I like the delicate way you put that. But seriously, thanks, Nina. I'll pay for your train ticket."

"Thanks, that's okay, I'm all set. Can you go this weekend? I'll get us a place to stay."

"That would be great. I'll be seeing Nick the next weekend, and…"

"I get the picture." Suddenly Nina looked up.

"Nick? You know, I don't think I've ever heard you mention his name before. First it was 'my beau,' then when we all made fun of you enough, 'my boyfriend.' So, he has a name. I knew a Nick once, he went to a military school up north somewhere. Cute guy, originally from the Bay area, I think. He was always talking about San Francisco."

"Really?" Ellen's eyes widened. "My Nick's from Northern California."

"Does he have a last name?"

"Williams."

Nina stared at Ellen, then started to laugh. "Oh, honey, I know him. Yup, that's the Nick I knew. Cute guy, not too tall, kind of solid, with a light brown crew cut?"

To Sisterhood!

Now it was Ellen's turn to stare. "You know my Nick? The crew cut is required by the Academy. His hair's longer now. But how did you meet him?"

"My first summer at RNB. He came down to the city to hang with my friend Roger, to find out about organizing and stuff. We hung out for the whole summer. Nice guy but…"

Nina kept looking at Ellen, who had turned completely red and was fidgeting nervously.

"What?" Ellen asked.

"Huh?" Nina countered.

"You said, 'nice guy *but*…'"

"Nothing." Nina drank the last of her coffee and crushed the cup.

"Come on, Nina. Is there anything I should know?" Ellen looked worried.

"No, nothing important." She shook her head. "Nick and you. You and Nick – you'd be perfect together. Forget it."

Ellen let it drop. She stood up and stretched. Nina stood too and tossed her empty cup into a nearby trash bin.

"I am *so* grateful to you. Is there anything to do ahead of time to see the doctor?" Ellen asked.

"I'm guessing you've never had a pelvic exam before?"

Ellen blushed again. "Dr. Rutherford is the doctor who delivered me. I couldn't go to him unless it was a pre-marital exam, and even then..."

"OK," Nina said. "We'll take care of it next weekend. Oh, wait, that's July 4th. Everything will be closed. Can you take off from work Thursday? We can go down early that morning, and then we can spend the whole weekend in the city."

Ellen nodded. "Yeah, I'll call in sick if I have to. It won't be busy right before the holiday."

"But you know, to answer your question, you definitely should do some reading about the exam beforehand, so you're ready and not too freaked out. It can be pretty weird the first time."

※ ※ ※ ※

A few days later, Ellen and Nina headed south on the Penn Central. Ellen had never been to New York before, and she was doing her best to act cool. Nina was uncharacteristically quiet for much of the trip, spending her time reading and taking notes.

Shortly after the train pulled away from the Stanford station, Nina cleared her throat.

"Hey, Ellen, listen," she said.

Ellen was reading a magazine – the same copy of *Life* from early May, which she'd found in her overnight bag. She was engrossed in the article about Bernadette Devlin. *If women could serve in Parliament*

To Sisterhood!

in Northern Ireland, Ellen thought, *maybe someday, a woman would run for President of the United States.*

"Ellen!" Nina said more loudly.

Startled, Ellen looked up.

"I have something to tell you," Nina said.

"About Nick?"

"No, no, nothing about that. That was – it was nothing at all." *He didn't seem to know all that much about women,* Nina thought wryly and decided it was better to keep that information to herself. "I definitely can see the two of you together, yeah."

"What is it then?" Ellen was curious to see that the usually unflappable Nina was fidgeting, and she was sympathetic. Could Nina and Nick possibly have been intimate? Ellen wouldn't dream of asking her. And she certainly wouldn't ask Nick. If it happened before she met him, it was none of her business.

"Well…" Nina hesitated.

"It's okay, Nina. You can trust me." Ellen touched her friend's arm lightly.

"It's just that – I tried to find us a place to crash with my friend in the East Village. It's um, my pad, but I told him he could use it for the rest of the summer and it seems it's full because he has guests for the holiday weekend. So, um, we're gonna stay at my house, okay? I mean, my family's – my dad and stepmother, actually, it was my mother's…"

Ellen waited. She'd never seen confident Nina flustered before.

"There's something I thought you should know before we get there. We're sort of well-off," Nina blurted. "I mean not super rich or anything. We don't have an airplane or a yacht or anything like that."

Ellen kept still.

Nina explained, "It was my grandfather, my mother's father, who made the money. Dry goods. Then, you know, I told you, my mother died when I was thirteen. Then only a year later, my father married a real bitch. Remember, I think I told you some of the story the first day we met? That's why I can't live at home, and I don't go there that often anymore. She'll probably be nice to you, though. She'll try to impress you with how big the apartment is and stuff like that. She wears all these ugly designer clothes and doesn't give a damn about politics or the war or anything that matters." Nina stopped to breathe.

"Muriel – that's her name – she's angry most of the time," Nina said. "Because when she married Herb – that's my father – she thought he was wealthy, because of the building we live in, and I was in private school, and we had a driver, and all. But she's a gold digger. What she didn't know was that he just has the apartment – that's a big deal in Manhattan, if you didn't know, I mean, to own an apartment that has as many rooms as ours – and that was my mother's, it was a gift from my grandfather Ben when they got married. Herb worked for a publishing company that my grandfather's friend owns, but when Herb married Muriel so soon, my grandfather was so angry, he got him fired.

To Sisterhood!

"Herb still gets a distribution from the trust fund my mother set up, barely enough to cover his expenses, and that's what they live on. I get one too, now that I've turned twenty-one – not enough to buy stuff, but enough so I don't have to do paid work if I'm careful."

"What's wrong with that?" Ellen asked.

"That kind of puts me in the lackey imperialist capitalist ruling class, doesn't it? Not so good for a revolutionary." Nina shook her head.

"I'm sure you'll use it well," Ellen said. "I mean, there are all sorts of good things you can do –"

Nina cut her off. "So now you know the worst thing about me," she said, grinning bravely. "Now you tell me a secret, so we're even."

"Well, you already know mine," said Ellen. "It's why we're going to New York City."

"You mean, it's why we're *in* New York City," Nina shouted, as the train pulled into Pennsylvania Station. "We're here! Welcome to my hometown!"

※ ※ ※ ※

When they got to the apartment on Central Park South, Nina proudly introduced Ellen to Bernadette, "our housekeeper and my best friend," who greeted Ellen warmly, then told Nina that her father and Muriel had decided to go away for the weekend, and sent their love.

Bernadette had prepared tuna sandwiches with potato chips, and homemade cream of tomato soup.

"My favorites," Nina said, reaching for a sandwich. "Thanks so much, Bernie." And then to Ellen: "What would you like to do first?" Nina was eager to show off her city.

"Actually," said Ellen. "I'm kind of nervous. I'd like to get the appointment taken care of first. I'd rather not wait until Monday. Are you sure you can just walk in?"

"It depends on how busy they are. Why don't we eat, then take a rest, and I'll give them a call."

Bernadette showed Ellen to the guest room. Ellen looked around in wonder at the huge room, which had red velvety wallpaper, a canopied four-poster bed, a chaise lounge covered in red and gold brocade, and plush gold carpeting. Heavy gold damask draperies framed a gorgeous view of Central Park. The carved mahogany dresser was empty and Ellen quickly put her underwear, socks, and nightgown into one of the drawers, which was lined with thin, lavender-scented paper. The room was too fancy for Ellen's taste, though she liked having a bathroom all to herself.

Ellen was hanging up her dress and slacks in the walk-in closet when Nina burst into the room.

"Yup, you were right, appointments-only today, but they have a cancellation at four. If you hurry, Patrick – he's the doorman – will get us a taxi and we can make it. And Ellen…" she hesitated for a minute. "Here. It was my grandmother's. You can borrow it."

Ellen smiled and slipped on the thin gold ring. It fit perfectly.

To Sisterhood!

They got to 125th Street by 3:55 pm.

The two women attracted stares in the mostly Black neighborhood. Ellen was surprised as she took in the lively, crowded street scene. This wasn't like Central Park South, and it sure wasn't King's Lake.

"Let's go." Nina tugged at Ellen's sleeve. "You don't want to be late."

They were greeted at Planned Parenthood by a sweet young woman. "Take a seat, please, ladies, the doctor will be right with you."

"Mrs. MacDougall," the receptionist called, a minute later. "Come right in."

Ellen went into the examination room. A nurse handed her a blue cotton gown.

"Everything off, you can keep your socks on, it ties in front," she said, and walked out.

Ellen was sitting on the table when the nurse came back, followed by a short, plump man about her grandfather's age.

"Hello, Mrs. ..." He consulted the chart. "MacDougall. What brings you here?" he asked kindly.

"She's come to be fitted for a diaphragm, Dr. Cohen," said the nurse.

"All right, missus, now lie back on the table, scoot down to the edge, that's it," he said.

"Feet in the stirrups. Now I am going to insert the speculum. I tried to warm it up but it might be a little cold."

"Ouch!" yelled Ellen.

"What?" said the doctor as the nurse whispered urgently, "Doctor, this girl is a virgin."

"Oy, I'm sorry," said the doctor, and to the nurse, "Go get me a smaller one then."

After that, the exam proceeded smoothly. The doctor palpated Ellen's breasts, listened to her breathing, looked at the blood pressure reading on the chart, and pronounced her "healthy as a horse."

He told her to dress and to meet him in his office when she was ready.

"Any questions?" he asked, scribbling on a pad. He handed her a prescription for a diaphragm. He winked. "Tell him the doctor said to be gentle with you, to go slowly. Sex is such a wonderful thing when you take the time to do it right."

Ellen's face and throat were red. She thanked the doctor and stumbled out of the office, holding the precious prescription.

Nina hailed a taxi. "We have some celebrating to do!" she cried. "And I'm gonna show you my part of the city!"

Nina led Ellen on a walking tour of Greenwich Village past her favorite clubs and coffeehouses – The Café Wha?, The Red Lion, The Village Gate, The Bitter End – where she'd seen Dylan, The Incredible

To Sisterhood!

String Band, The Fugs, Phil Ochs, and many others. When they got to the East Village, Nina pointed out her former apartment, near the Fillmore East.

"I saw The Who here last month. I took the train down, I think it must have been the week you were doing your exams. They were far out!"

"Wow!" Ellen said. "New York City is incredible – the energy, all the stuff you can do at any hour of the day or night. And all these restaurants!" Suddenly the pain in her leg reminded her that she'd been walking for more than an hour. Plus, she was starving.

"You're in luck!" Nina said. "Welcome to Ratner's!"

"You order for me," Ellen pleaded as she scanned the enormous menu of the kosher dairy deli. The delicious smells were making her hungrier. "I don't know what most of this stuff is."

Nina laughed and bantered with the waiter. "Hey, Solly, we've got a shiksa here from Vermont, never been to New York. What do you suggest?"

"Tell you what," said Solly. I'll bring her a sampler plate. A real Jewish pu pu platter."

"That would be great," Nina said. "And I'll have a side order of latkes with applesauce and sour cream both, please."

Solly soon returned from the kitchen, bringing Nina's latkes and a huge platter that he set in front of Ellen.

"OK, little lady. You got here a potato knish," he said, pointing proudly. "A side order of kasha varnishkes. One cheese blintz. One piece gefilte fish, and of course, some half-sour pickles and sour tomatoes."

Nina nodded and thanked him, and tucked into her plate. Ellen tasted everything, and didn't say a word until she'd finished nearly everything on the platter.

"I'm completely stuffed!"

"Your bubbe would be proud," Nina said.

"Bubbe?" Ellen asked, and Nina laughed and told her that it was Yiddish for Grandmother.

Ellen told Nina about her own grandmothers, the one who, with her husband, owned a dairy farm, and the one who owned a general store. Both were born and still lived in King's Lake.

Nina gave Ellen more of her family background, explaining how her grandparents came over from Russia and raised her mom in this neighborhood.

The two women mused about what their grandmothers' lives were like when they were their age, and calculated how young each woman was when she gave birth to the children who would become Ellen's and Nina's parents. They tried to imagine if their grandmothers had girlhood dreams that were set aside for the reality of taking care of husbands and children, and helping in the family business. Ellen and

To Sisterhood!

Nina agreed that their own lives offered many more opportunities than their grandmothers' could have provided.

On the way back to Central Park South, they again went through the Village. Nina pointed out the Stonewall Inn, a gay bar and dance club, at Sheridan Square and Christopher Street. She told Ellen about the raid last weekend – "the pigs came in smashing heads" – and how after years of this kind of oppression, finally, finally, the patrons fought back. Ellen wanted to know how Nina knew so much about this.

"I read the newspapers, don't you?" Nina asked, adding that the riot was the hot topic in the *Old Mole* office the day after it happened. They sent a staffer down to interview some of the men who'd been there.

"Yes, of course," Ellen bristled, "but not the New York papers."

"Sister," Nina said. "You've got to inform yourself. If you're going to work for the liberation of women, you need to read more, especially about other oppressed people. Have you read *The Autobiography of Malcolm X*? *Manchild in the Promised Land*?"

Ellen shook her head.

Nina laughed. "Okay, you can skip the last one. Claude Brown is brilliant, but the book's not too respectful of women."

How did I miss knowing about these books? Ellen wondered. She couldn't wait to get to a bookstore. Nina had opened the door to a whole new world.

※ ※ ※ ※

On Tuesday, Ellen was back at her job as a cashier at the Coop. Even though she'd told Nick she would think about going to California, talking with Nina about their grandmothers' lives made Ellen focus on what she wanted for herself, both now and long-term. And what she wanted was a shot at getting into the best women's college. How Laurie could even consider dropping out of Radcliffe was simply beyond her.

Ellen was sure that going to California was not the right thing to do. She would stay here for the summer, put in as many hours at work as she could to save money for tuition – no more weekends away! no more days off! – and then go back to complete her sophomore year. Then she'd apply to Radcliffe, get in, and graduate. Once she had her degree, she and Nick could make plans for their future together.

Nick had sublet a room in a two-bedroom apartment with his friend Peter, who'd been a senior when Nick was a freshman, and his bride, Amanda. The newlyweds were happy to have rent help, and Peter was able to get Nick a construction job with his company. Nick planned to arrive in Boston on Friday, and he and Ellen had been joking about all the fun things they could do with the money they'd save on their huge long-distance phone bills.

Before Nick arrived, though, Ellen planned to see Charlie, because she knew Nick would want her to spend her free time with him, not with her old friend. Ellen and Charlie had talked on the phone the first week Ellen arrived, but not since then.

It wasn't only Charlie who Ellen wanted to see. In a bold, or stupid, move – she couldn't tell which – without calling ahead, she walked over to Charlie and Sam's apartment, and knocked. She could hear

To Sisterhood!

Jimi Hendrix singing *Manic Depression,* and was completely surprised when a girl with long, stringy black hair, who smelled of pot, answered the door dressed only in a towel.

"Charlie's not here," she said. "He split about a week ago. He sublet the apartment to me and my old man. He'll be back later in the summer; I don't know when."

"What about the other guy who lives here?"

"I don't know. Charlie didn't say anything about a roommate." Ellen thanked her and turned to leave.

"You wanna buy a lid?" the girl called after her. "Good stuff, five bucks." When Ellen said no, she said, "Okay, that's cool. Ciao, man."

⌘ Eleven ⌘

Nina loved working at *Old Mole*. She was assigned to cover stories in the neighborhood and sometimes about actions going down in Boston. The guys on the staff didn't seem to be as piggy as the guys at RNB. They were actively trying to struggle with their white male privilege, or at least they said they were.

While the few other women were pleasant, they seemed to hang together and hadn't reached out to make friends. Nina didn't mind so much. Until a couple of months ago, she didn't have many women friends. There were some girls from school, but most of Nina's friends were guys.

She missed seeing Laurie, and the two had a few long phone conversations. Laurie said she'd been doing "as much nothing as she could" in Wellfleet, swimming every day, reading, and lounging in the hammock. She and her mother had called a truce, simply by not bringing up their last conversation. Laurie said she missed the company of someone who understood the struggles she was going through, and invited Nina to come visit whenever she wanted.

"When are your brothers going to be there?" Nina asked.

"Not until the end of July," Laurie laughed. "But I wouldn't get my hopes up, Nina. David's engaged. And they are both such tools. All they do is study all the time."

Nina reached out to Diane a couple of times, but the man who answered – she guessed it was Diane's father – always said she wasn't

To Sisterhood!

there. Nina knew Diane was putting in a lot of overtime, and that she'd been staying at her friend's on the weekends.

She'd catch up with her soon. Even though they didn't have much in common, Nina found a lot to admire in Diane. She was tough. She worked hard and seemed to have a good grasp of the real world, something Nina thought Laurie may never have. *Or me either*.

And Ellen? Ellen was a dreamer. Still, Nina enjoyed Ellen's bright mind and absolute belief in doing the right thing. Since Nick's arrival, Nina had been avoiding Ellen's calls by not answering her phone in the evening. Nina had no desire to see Nick again, and since he was going to be in town for only a month or so, she'd wait to see Ellen until he left. Or she'd go by Ellen's work at lunchtime one of these days.

Nina had a routine. Every day, before going across the street to work, she stopped at Brookline Lunch. If she ate a full breakfast, she could make it until dinnertime on a yogurt and coffee. The counterman already knew her and started her order when she walked in: two eggs over easy on toasted English muffins, a small glass of orange juice, and black coffee, lots of refills.

While she ate, she read the *Globe* to learn how the straight press covered mainstream news stories.

She missed reading the *Times* every morning, but she was getting a feel for Boston: the politics, the culture, the funny combination of liberal Irish Catholic Democrats running the place with an undercurrent of the strait-laced Puritan "we're not having fun until you're not having fun" ethic.

When Nina walked into work on Tuesday, she saw a poster on the main story idea bulletin board. She recognized the graphic: a black panther with its claws bared, ready to defend itself.

The poster read: "People's Rally, held by the Black Panther Party. Place: Malcolm X Memorial Park (Franklin Park). Date: July 27th, 1969, Sunday 2:00 pm. Topics: 1. Fascism. 2. Community Control of Politics. 3. Breakfast Program II. 4. Liberation School. 5. Medical Program for Community. All members of the Community Should Attend the Rally. All Power to the People. Boston Chapter. Black Panther Party," and a phone number in Boston. In the corner, Nina spied the logo of New England Free Press, which had printed the flyer.

"The story's yours if you want it," she heard Perry say behind her.

Nina turned around. "Cool!"

"The rest of us have assignments. And I thought you might be interested, New York White Girl."

Nina liked Perry. She knew he was teasing, and frankly, the idea of covering a Black Panther rally would be a challenge. Nina had long been fascinated by Black culture, and equated the struggle of the Panthers and other Black militants with the struggle of her own ancestors. In the liberal arena in which Nina had grown up, Black Power was chic. She wanted to get beyond the superficial rhetoric she'd read about in the progressive press and see first-hand what these brave brothers and sisters were doing for their people and their community.

To Sisterhood!

"Thanks, Perry. Now, where do I look for background on the Boston Panthers?"

Perry gestured to a file cabinet in the back of the room. "Try in there. I think we have some old issues of their newspaper here. And as you know, we get the RNB news about what the Panthers are doing in Oakland, Detroit, and Philadelphia. Hell, you should find pretty much everything you need in there. Or if not, you probably can take a trip over to their headquarters on Winthrop Street. It's in Roxbury, between Dudley and Warren."

For the next few days, Nina completely immersed herself in her research. She and everyone else she knew in the Movement were astonished by how much the Panthers had accomplished this year alone. The Free Breakfast Program, which they'd started at a Catholic church in Oakland last January, had been replicated in every major city in the country. Thousands of poor kids no longer went to school hungry, thanks to the Party.

And the fact that J. Edgar Hoover called the Breakfast Program a "huge threat to national security," meant the Panthers must have been doing something right. Nina remembered her mother's adage: "If no one opposes you, you're not going out far enough on a limb. Stretch further."

※ ※ ※ ※

Meanwhile, Ellen was completely engrossed in her work and in Nick, who was happy to be with her without the constraints of school, parents, and the lack of transportation. He could walk to her apartment and did so nearly every evening after work. Or she walked back with him to his place where they could see a TV show or visit with Nick's roommates. She liked the quiet couple, though they didn't have much in common.

On the night of the Moonwalk, Ellen, Nick, Peter, and Amanda huddled in front of the TV. It was late, but everyone who was able was up to witness the event that President Kennedy had promised would happen before the decade was over. The picture was grainy and hard to see. Nick reached over to hold Ellen's hand as Neil Armstrong took the first floating steps onto the lunar surface. Nick looked into her eyes and said, "Someday, we'll tell our grandchildren about this moment." Ellen thought *yikes*, but smiled at her boyfriend.

Later that week, Ellen's supervisor dropped a beat-up white envelope at her counter. It was addressed to: *Miss Ellen MacDougall, c/o The Harvard Cooperative Society, Cambridge, Massachusetts, 02138*. Puzzled, she opened it, and found a note on the stationery of the Dean of Students' office at Ethan Allen State.

"Dear Ellen," it read. "I sure hope this finds you. I asked all over the campus and finally I found someone who said you got a job in the Harvard Coop. It doesn't look like something I thought you would've wanted me to send to your parents' house. I hope you are well, and that I'll see you in class in the fall. Best regards, Janet King."

She'd signed her name with a tiny heart over the "i". Ellen tried to place her but could not. Maybe a student worker in the Dean's office?

Folded inside a plain piece of paper was a postcard with a picture of a meadow of purple flowers.

To Sisterhood!

"I've been dreaming about you," it read. "If you can, call me at home in Ohio. Here's the number. S."

Ellen smiled and tucked the card into her bag. She went through the rest of her workday humming softly to herself. *Sam!*

Before she got on the bus to go home that evening, Ellen walked a couple of blocks to find a phone booth on a quiet corner. She jiggled her pocketful of coins as she called the number.

"Hey," she said, when she heard Sam's voice.

"Elly May, hello! I guess you got my card? Where are you? I tried to find you. And I didn't want to ask Charlie about you. He doesn't even know we met."

"Well," said Ellen, speaking slowly so she could catch her breath. She was much more nervous than she thought she'd be. "Right now, I'm in Boston, living a few blocks from your place."

"No kidding?" Ellen could hear his excitement as he asked about her job. Sam told her about being home for the summer working at his dad's furniture store with his brother. They made small talk, and then the operator cut in, asking Ellen to deposit another seventy-five cents for the next three minutes.

"I'd better make this short," Sam said. "I've been dreaming about you every night."

"So you said on the card." Ellen forced herself to sound steady, but her heart was beating fast.

"Are you thinking about me?"

"Truth?" she asked.

"Truth," he said earnestly.

"I dream about you too," she said simply.

"Elly May, I want to see you. No, I *need* to see you."

"When are you coming back to Boston?"

"So," Sam said, "my brother and I got tickets for this music festival in New York in the middle of August – it sounds far out – there're some cool acts lined up. It's the weekend of the 15th. I'll be back in Boston a couple of days later. Tell me how to find you." Ellen gave him the phone number at the apartment, and let him know Nick was in town, living not too far away, and that she didn't know how to handle this.

"I knew something like this would happen," Ellen said, trying to keep her tone light.

"What?"

"I'm starting to figure out a plan for myself," she said. "I've got this great guy who apparently wants to make a life with me. And I'm following my dream and applying to school here in Cambridge. And now *you* show up to make a mess of everything."

"I don't have to call you," Sam said.

To Sisterhood!

"That would be hard, given what you've told me," Ellen said.

"You know what I mean, Elly May."

"I must be out of my mind," Ellen laughed.

"Let's take it one step at a time. I'll be there in a few weeks. Can you live that long without me?" Sam's voice was low and playful.

"I guess I'll find out."

"Elly May," Sam said seriously. "Ellen. This, I mean you, um, you mean something to me. I want to get to know you better. I don't want to mess up your life, but I want to be in it. However you want. I feel like I've known you before, like we have some karma to work out."

"Please deposit seventy-five cents," said the operator.

"Take care of yourself, Elly May," Sam said. "You're very important to me." And he hung up.

※ ※ ※ ※

Diane was putting in as many hours as she could, and had lots of time to think while working on the packing line. She'd been wondering if she should get more involved in community organizing actions; Harvard was building what looked like new housing at the end of her block. But when would she find the time? Plus, she had Theresa to think of. If she kept up this rate of overtime, she'd be able to start looking for an apartment for September.

Diane liked spending the weekends at Patty's, even though Jimmy was there most of the time, along with a bunch of his hard-drinking friends. She'd been going to see Theresa as often as she could – she missed her so much! Patty's mom was great about letting Diane borrow her car to drive to Barnstable, and Diane was always careful to fill the gas tank before returning it to her.

This Friday, the summer term break would start, and Diane planned to pick up Theresa and stay with her at their parents' house. Fortunately, Magda and John would be leaving for their anniversary trip to New Hampshire, so Diane would get to spend a few quiet days at home alone with her sister.

Since Jimmy had been stuck on the evening shift this month, Patty was happy to hang out with Diane. Sometimes they walked over to the new Orson Welles Cinema on Mass. Ave. Diane loved their films, even the foreign ones she didn't always understand. And whenever they could, the two friends drove out to the cool green woods around Walden Pond after their shift ended at 4:00 pm. One of the women working on the line had a son in 'Nam. She said they were always welcome to use his yellow VW Beetle, as long as they took good care of it; he would be happy that two such pretty girls were riding around in it.

They were glad to get out of the city on these muggy summer nights.

Even the noise of what must have been dozens of shouting children did not detract from the lovely oasis of Walden, where Henry David Thoreau had once made his home, to live simply and commune with nature. Patty set down her bag, stripped off the jeans and tee shirt she had on over her suit, and ran in, shrieking as the cold water hit her skin. A minute later, she was floating happily on her back, looking up at the cloudless sky surrounded by shade trees.

Diane slowly settled on her blanket. First, she covered herself head to toe with tanning oil, then lay with her head toward the pond. She must have dozed off, because the next thing she knew, Patty was standing over her, drying her hair with a towel.

"What a day!" Patty said, and Diane smiled.

Diane noticed a woman nearby trying to get two small children to eat their sandwiches. One boy, one girl. The girl was small and solid, about two years old, with dark curls a lot like her own. *Valerie?* Diane wondered, and shook her head.

Where is she? Is she healthy? Is she happy? Did the sisters place her with good people who will love and protect her?

Patty saw her staring at the toddler and spoke softly.

"Diane. You made the right decision for both of you. You did the best you could for her, even though I'm sure it's hard for you."

"Thanks, Patty," Diane said, wiping away a tear. *Please, God, let her grow up knowing that someone wanted her, even if I couldn't take care of her. Let her be happy, Sweet Mary, Mother of God, let her be happy and well.*

Diane tried to focus on the good parts of her life now. Theresa seemed content at school this summer. Work was going okay, and Diane was on track to having enough saved for their own place. She had Patty and a couple of other girls from high school she saw occasionally, plus the few new friends she'd met at the conference in May.

Ellen, for instance, had turned out to be a real sweetheart. Even though her background was a lot different from Diane's, the two women seemed to understand each other. Neither of them fit in with the lefties who ran the Boston female liberation movement, but each of them could grasp some of the ideas and what the radical women were trying to accomplish.

"Their hearts seemed to be in the right place," Diane had remarked to Patty, "though most of them can't relate that well to working people."

"They're trying," Patty had said generously, "and they must be smart, because they all go to college."

Diane agreed for the most part. She liked Nina, even though she was a puzzle – a sharp girl from New York whose family could afford to send her to college, but she'd dropped out. Still, Nina didn't seem to be afraid to get her hands dirty, and she could talk to all kinds of people: radical women, women who worked in Diane's factory, young, old, everyone. Nina was like that.

And Laurie? Diane didn't know what she thought of Laurie. True, she was energetic, exuberant, and a lot of fun. Spending time with her at Nina's birthday weekend, and the few times they'd met for coffee was interesting, but Diane didn't get what made Laurie tick. She seemed discontented with what to Diane looked like a pretty darn good life.

She hadn't seen Laurie since she'd left for the Cape. Laurie was generous about inviting them all to come down and visit her any time, not seeming to realize that Ellen hadn't yet earned any days off from her job, and Diane only had five vacation days for this half of the year, and it would take most of two of them to drive all the way to Wellfleet and back, what with the traffic. *People like Laurie don't need to think about earned vacation days*, she guessed.

After a good, bracing swim to the other side of the pond, their hunger got the best of them, so Diane and Patty packed up to leave.

※ ※ ※ ※

Laurie toweled off after a refreshing swim in Gull Pond, a popular Wellfleet swimming spot featured in Thoreau's account of his travels on Cape Cod. Laurie was lonely, and for the first time ever, she was not having a great time at the Cape. For one thing, the easy give-and-take with her mom was gone. Laurie sensed that she had to be careful about everything she said. She didn't want to upset her mother, but she also knew that her mother didn't understand her. All her life, the two had been so close.

And in a few weeks, Laurie's parents would be moving. The house in Newton had sold after only a week on the market, and the new house was completely furnished, thanks to the decorator Ruth had hired. Jacob had cleared out his office at Harvard. He would have the title of Professor Emeritus, which, as best as Laurie could figure, meant he'd retain privileges at the Faculty Club, have to write letters of recommendation for graduate students, and perhaps get called back to give a lecture or two each year.

Their plan was for Laurie to come down to Florida on her winter break, where she'd see the new house. This would be the first time Laurie wouldn't be with her family for the High Holidays, and her mother was worried.

"If you want, I can call some of our friends in Newton," Ruth fussed. "I know they'd all be happy to invite you."

"That's okay, Mom, thanks, I have friends too, you know," she laughed. "I won't be alone. And yes, I'll go to services on Rosh Hashanah and Yom Kippur. Don't worry about me, I'll be fine."

Laurie couldn't wait for her brothers to arrive. Usually she could talk to Andy, and she had so much she wanted to tell him. Laurie finally understood what Ellen had meant about not dropping out of school – and she couldn't imagine how she would support herself if she did – but she wanted to talk to her brother about it all.

Andy was on a straight career path – Harvard undergrad, Harvard Med School, choosing a specialty, private practice, maybe after a couple of years of working in the inner city. He'd always had a soft spot for the less fortunate. And David's life was all mapped out too. He'd be graduating in a couple of years, and had plans to move to upstate New York to go into practice with his fiancée Roberta's father, a successful obstetrician, who'd delivered two generations of babies so far.

But when her brothers showed up on Friday, Andy surprised them all by bringing a guest, a classmate he introduced as "my study partner and best friend," a small, blonde woman named Susan. David had come alone, since Roberta was living with her parents for the summer.

Ruth and Laurie greeted Susan warmly, and Jacob shook her hand formally, inquiring about her studies ("same classes as Andy, yes, one

To Sisterhood!

of the few women admitted to Harvard Med School in this class") and then about her parents ("a pharmacist and a housewife") and where she was from ("a small town outside of Scranton, Pennsylvania"). Ruth hurried to set another place at the table, and then asked Laurie to light the Sabbath candles. Ruth always made plenty of food, so there was enough chicken noodle soup, brisket, roasted potatoes, and vegetables to go around. Laurie did her best to be friendly, but now she probably wouldn't get the time alone with Andy that she desperately craved.

So the next day, when Andy and David invited her to come along on the whale watch expedition they'd promised Susan, Laurie, feeling even more lonely and misunderstood, turned them down.

"But you can drop me in town," she said. "I've got some things to do."

"Have fun!" Ruth called after her children.

When she got to town, Laurie found a phone booth. She deposited four quarters and called Nina.

"Any chance you'll be able to make it down here this week?" she asked when Nina answered. She told Nina to forget about meeting Andy, that he'd brought a girlfriend.

"Too bad for me," Nina laughed. "I was going to call you later. I got a lead on a new story, and I'm going to be pretty busy for the next couple of weeks. Then I'm planning to go down to New York for a few days. But I'll call you when I get back and we'll make time to get together. Have a good week, Laurie!"

Laurie hung up the phone, dejected. She walked down to the Provincetown Playhouse to find Ginger wearing a tool belt, with nails sticking out of her mouth, working hard on building a set for next week's performance.

"Hey, Laurie!" she said, replacing the nails into her belt and wiping her forehead with a bandana she'd stuck in her back pocket. "It's great to see you again! But I can only take a short break. We've got to finish up here and I'm on duty in the box office right after lunch."

"Can you walk over to Adams for a frappe?" Laurie asked. Ginger checked the time, dropped her tool belt, and called out to one of the other crew members that she'd be back in twenty minutes.

"Sure!" she grinned.

Perched on the red leather stools, and sipping the thick shakes, the two women caught up. Ginger told Laurie all about the season's productions, and how excited she was to have a small part in next week's show.

"I hope you'll come and see my stage debut," she said.

"Of course I will," Laurie told her. "That is, if I'm still in town. I was thinking of going back to Cambridge early if I can get into the dorm. There's nothing happening for me here." She explained that her parents were moving, her mother was preoccupied, and she was ready – more than ready – for some new energy in her life.

"Oh, my God! Then you've *got* to go see Desirée!" Ginger pulled a pen from her overalls pocket and wrote an address on a napkin. "She's

To Sisterhood!

this amazing, completely fucking amazing, psychic down in the West End. She's done readings for the whole junior company at the Playhouse, and even some of the actors too. She'll blow your mind!"

"Wow!" And before Laurie could even ask a single question, Ginger jumped off the stool and raced for the door.

"Gotta go. Hope you can make it next week. I'm gonna be a star!"

Laurie watched her classmate run out to Commercial Street. She picked up the check, paid it, and put the napkin into her pocket. She had nothing else to do this afternoon, so she walked down toward the West End to find the woman who was about to alter the course of her life.

✣ Twelve ✣

Diane was looking forward to spending a whole week with her sister. She was not at all prepared for how thin Theresa was when she picked her up in Barnstable late Thursday afternoon. She looked like she'd lost at least ten pounds since Diane saw her, less than two weeks ago.

"Hey honey, how're you doing?" Theresa's normally rosy cheeks were white, and she looked drained and haggard, even though her bright smile was the same.

"Dee!" Theresa threw herself into her sister's arms. "I'm glad to see you! I missed you so much." She chattered happily about school, and her job helping to take care of the younger kids, and how she'd won the ring toss game at the end-of-term celebration last night.

"Do you feel okay?" Diane tried to keep her tone light. "You look thin."

"Well, my stomach has been hurting a little. Some mornings I throw up my breakfast. But I can eat my lunch fine!"

"Did the counselors ask you what was the matter? Did they send you to the nurse?" Diane was concerned.

"No, I didn't tell them. I always feel better by lunchtime, but I'm tired all the time. I take a nap in the afternoon, when they have crafts."

As Theresa talked, Diane started to shiver. She rolled down the car windows. She took the next exit off Route 3, and stopped the car in the first empty parking lot, at a church.

To Sisterhood!

"Why are we stopping here, Dee?" Theresa asked.

"Oh, honey, I'm tired of driving," Diane said calmly. "Just gonna take a break for a few minutes, is that all right?" When Theresa nodded yes, Diane paused. Then, gently, she asked Theresa if she was still getting her "friend." Theresa was quiet as she thought back to her last period. Diane, usually so patient with her sister, couldn't let her anxiety show. She made herself keep still.

No, Theresa told her, the last time was right after her birthday in May.

"Did I do a wrong thing?" she asked. "It didn't come in the middle of June and not in July either, so I didn't have anything to mark down on the calendar like you showed me."

Diane went absolutely cold. Her throat got dry. She had to force herself to breathe, to say something that wouldn't scare Theresa. Could she be pregnant? How could that possibly be?

"It's okay," Diane heard herself say. "It's probably just the excitement from going away to school again. Everything is fine."

Theresa smiled, and Diane started the car to head back to the highway. She didn't trust herself to talk, so she switched on the radio.

"Hey," she made herself say brightly. "Have you heard this tune yet?" and hummed along about a bad moon on the rise. Theresa smiled, and dreamily dozed off in her seat as Diane drove north.

It couldn't be true. Not Theresa. Who could be so callous and careless to take advantage of her sister like that? A staff member? A student?

Surely not. Mr. Lester had promised to take good care of Theresa and was eager for her to be part of the staff. Could they have left her unsupervised long enough for someone to attack her? And why wouldn't she have told Diane?

She can't go through what I did, thought Diane. *She wouldn't understand the changes in her body. She could not deal with it emotionally.* Diane didn't know what she was going to do, but she'd figure it out. She always did.

After a sleepless night, in which she tried to think of all her options, Diane knew for certain that there was only one way out. And that was a mortal sin. And, she would have to arrange it so that her parents never found out.

Fortunately, when they got home, neither of them seemed to notice how awful their younger daughter looked. Diane suspected that Theresa didn't even know how she got pregnant, if in fact that's what was happening, which she was pretty sure was the case. And Diane couldn't even imagine how to ask Theresa who did this to her. She knew that she had to get her sister some help, and quickly. Theresa needed a blood test.

Diane knew of a walk-in clinic in Quincy, about 15 miles south, where some of the girls at work had gone for things they wouldn't want their family doctor, or their parents, to know about. She told her parents that she and Theresa were going out for the afternoon, and on Saturday, they headed down to Quincy Center. She explained to Theresa that she was concerned about her throwing up, and that Dr. Mac was away on vacation so they were going to a different doctor. Theresa said okay

To Sisterhood!

and was happy when Diane told her they could go ride on the carousel after the appointment.

The lady at the clinic said Diane could call the next day for results, even though it was a Sunday. Diane was stunned, but not surprised, when she called the next morning. She knew exactly what she'd looked and felt like in the first two months.

Sunday afternoon, when everyone else was preparing to stay up late to watch the Apollo 11 Moonwalk, Diane had to figure out how to explain the situation to Theresa and find out who got her pregnant. She assumed Theresa had a boyfriend at school. If anyone had hurt her, she definitely would have told Diane, and probably Mr. Lester too. Unless…no. Diane couldn't think about that. He was such a good man, with a wife and children who lived right on campus.

Diane found a quiet time later that afternoon while her parents were napping.

"I guess a pretty girl like you must have a boyfriend, huh?" Theresa blushed and shook her head. Diane thought it had to be one of the other junior staff members, or God help him, one of the senior staff. Diane would kill him with her bare hands.

But Theresa didn't seem particularly upset by Diane's questions.

"Did you go someplace private with any of the boys at school?" Diane was patient with her sister, but she needed to know.

Theresa looked embarrassed. "No. I like George, but he likes Ruthanne, and I don't think he likes me much."

Diane took a breath and tried again. "Theresa. You have to tell me this. Did some boy or teacher from the school get you alone and take your pants off?" Theresa shook her head.

Diane had to leave it alone for now. The important thing was to get help for Theresa. She couldn't carry a pregnancy to term. And labor? No way was she going to go through that.

On her morning break the next day, Diane called their family doctor, Harry Mackenzie, who'd delivered both her and Theresa, to ask for his help.

"I've got to be able to trust you," she said, when the nurse put her through. "You can't tell my parents."

"You've always been able to trust me before," Dr. Mac said kindly. "What is it, dear?"

"It's Theresa. She's pregnant. You have *got* to help us, Dr. Mac. She can't have the baby. She cannot – I will not let her – go through what I went through!"

There was a long silence. When he finally spoke, Dr. Mac sounded weary. "I'm so sorry, Diane. There are laws in Massachusetts, and even then, there is Church law. Your parents –"

"My parents don't know and they aren't going to find out. If you won't help us, I'll find someone who will!" She slammed down the phone, angrier than she'd ever been in her life.

To Sisterhood!

Diane didn't know who to call. It was a sin; she couldn't go to the priest. She couldn't tell anyone, not even her new friends, not even Ellen. But that gave her an idea. She still had the literature from the conference.

When she got home that night, she found a referral sheet for medical concerns. There was a Women's Tour to England, or at least that's what they called it, with the destination a fancy women's clinic, and accommodations at a nice hotel. Diane did not have the money to take Theresa to England.

There was also a Clergy for Choice hot line. She waited until John took Theresa out for ice cream and Magda was passed out on the couch before she called. A kind woman spoke to her soothingly and gave her a local phone number.

After several tries, she got through to a woman, who handed the phone to a man. He said he could help her, and that he needed $500 in cash. Diane had the $400 she'd saved for the apartment hidden in her sock drawer. As soon as she cashed her paycheck, she'd have enough. She told him okay. He said to meet him in an apartment in Boston on Beacon Hill Tuesday at 10:00 am and gave Diane the address.

"Could you make it Wednesday morning instead?" she asked. That was the day her parents were to leave for New Hampshire. *That would work*, Diane thought with some relief. By the time they returned on Sunday, Theresa should be fine and able to go back to school that evening. Diane would have to call in sick to work for a few days, but she'd had such good attendance she knew she could pull it off.

"OK. Wednesday at 9:00 am. Don't eat anything before the procedure," he said. "Water is fine."

"It's not for me, it's for my sister. She's slow. She can't have this baby. Can you help us?"

"You got the five hundred bucks, I can help you, honeybunch."

Diane put down the phone and sobbed until she fell asleep.

On Tuesday evening, after their parents had gone to bed, Diane explained to Theresa that she was going to take her to a special doctor in the morning, one who would help her feel better. She gave her sister a brief explanation of a pelvic exam. Theresa's eyes grew wide, but she nodded when Diane told her that she had this same exam, and that was what girls did once they turned eighteen. Diane felt awful about lying to her sister and betraying her trust, but she simply didn't see any alternative. She promised Theresa that she'd bring her ice cream when the appointment was over, and that Theresa could rest in bed for a day or two if she wanted.

Theresa wanted to know if Diane would talk to her about going to see the Pope in Rome if she got scared, and Diane promised she would. Diane had even made up a song about it.

"Someday, I'll take you there for real," she reminded her sister.

On Wednesday morning, Diane took her sister to a third-floor walk-up on the back slope of Beacon Hill, the side facing away from the Public Garden. The side with the rats. The apartment was dark and untidy, and she was dismayed to see the dark oily hair and scraggly

To Sisterhood!

beard on the guy who greeted them. At least, Diane noted, the white sheet on the kitchen table looked clean.

"You are going to do it here?" Diane asked, alarmed.

"What did you expect?" He was impatient but not unkind. He looked at Theresa. "Relax, honey. I've done this a lot. You'll be fine. Hop up onto the table now."

Diane turned to her sister, who looked frightened. "Theresa, this man is like a doctor. He's going to help you. Now lie back and hold my hand." Diane reminded her about the rest of the procedure. Again, Theresa's eyes opened wide in alarm.

"I'm afraid, Dee," she said. "I don't want him to hurt me. I don't want to take off my pants in front of this man." She started to cry.

"Give us a minute, will you?" Diane said.

He rolled his eyes. "I don't got all day, I got another appointment in an hour."

"Just a couple of minutes, okay?" He shrugged and left the room.

"Theresa," Diane spoke gently. "I know you're scared, honey, but it will be all right. I will sit right beside you. I love you, Theresa."

Fortunately, the procedure went quickly. Diane held her sister's hand throughout and willed herself not to look. She kept reminding herself that this was far, far better for Theresa than having to carry a baby for nine months and then having her child taken away by the nuns. That

Diane wished she'd had an abortion. But then she wouldn't have had Valerie. And abortion was a sin. Murder. Diane was terrified but kept calm for her sister's sake.

Diane took Theresa home in a taxi right after the procedure. She asked the driver to stop briefly while she ran into the store to get ice cream, like she'd promised. Theresa seemed to be all right, as she ate her ice cream happily, though she was drowsy from the pill the man had given her. *Thank God their parents were away*, Diane thought. *A man walked on the moon this week, and I helped my sister kill her baby. And as soon as Theresa was well enough to go back to school, I'm going after the bastard who did this to her.*

While she tucked her sister into bed, Diane tried one more time.

"Theresa, you know how the doctor touched you there in your private parts?" Theresa nodded sleepily. He'd given her a strong painkiller, something that would help her sleep, and a few more to take if she needed them tomorrow.

"He hurt me."

"Yes, honey, I know. I'm sorry about that, but it's all done now. No more hurting. Just some bleeding, like when you get your friend every month. In a few days, you'll be good as new. But Theresa, honey, you have to tell me. Who else did that to you? Who else touched you in your private parts?"

Theresa shook her head. "I'm tired, Dee. I want to go to sleep now. No more talking."

Diane looked at her sister lying there, pale and quiet. *She's been through enough today. I'll try again tomorrow.*

Diane crawled into bed with her sister and held her all night. In the morning, Theresa still didn't want to talk, and when Diane brought her breakfast, she told Diane that her stomach hurt a lot.

Oh no, Diane thought. *What a lousy time for Theresa to get one of her bad stomach aches. Not on top of this, not now.*

"OK, honey," she said, removing the tray of bacon and eggs. "I'll get you some broth. Do you think you can eat that?"

Theresa shook her head. "I don't feel good, Dee. My head hurts too. I kinda hurt all over."

Diane reached over and put a hand on her sister's forehead. Definitely warm. Maybe she was getting sick. What bad timing. She ran downstairs for a minute and came back with some warm chicken broth.

"See if you can take a sip, honey."

Theresa took a few spoonsful of the broth and immediately threw up. Diane helped her get cleaned up and told her to rest.

"All right, honey. It's gonna be okay. Probably a bug or something. Go to sleep now." And Theresa did, falling right to sleep and sleeping until late afternoon.

Later, she sat up and was able to drink some water and some broth. Diane helped her change the sanitary pad again, and told her to rest some more and that she'd feel better in the morning. She brought up a deck of cards, and they played a few games of Go Fish before Theresa said she needed to sleep. Diane knew she should let her sister rest. But before turning out the light, she tried one more time to find out who did this to her.

Now Theresa seemed to understand Diane's questions. She told Diane about her visitor, who'd come to see her every Saturday afternoon since the first week she'd arrived. He took her out for rides, and told her she was pretty, and that she was special to him. Every Saturday, he took her to a cabin near the camp, and he touched her in a way to make her feel good. He told her not to tell anyone at all – not even Diane – no, especially not Diane – she would be jealous and mad. *This is our secret*, Uncle Tony had said.

Diane's mouth went dry. Her heart felt like it would fly out of her chest, and at the same time her legs started to shake. But she forced her voice to stay steady.

"No, it's right that you told me, sweetheart. That was a wrong thing for Uncle Tony to do."

"He made me feel good, Dee. He said it might hurt the first time but it didn't. He made me feel pretty."

Diane took a deep breath. She dug her fingernails into her palms. Her voice was calm. "I know, Theresa. You are so good and so pretty. Now try to go back to sleep, all right? You'll feel better in the morning, I know it."

Diane turned out the light and just made it to her own room before the horror turned into violent rage. She was going to kill him. She definitely was going to do it this time. No wonder he hadn't been around Cambridge on the weekends. He'd been screwing her sister, her little sister who couldn't understand, for weeks now. She was going to strangle him with her own hands.

All was calm in Theresa's room overnight. Diane checked on her a few times, then went back to her own room to try to read. Before turning out her light, she checked on Theresa again. She still had a fever, but was sleeping peacefully.

In the morning, Diane heard her go into the bathroom. Diane drifted back to sleep, only to be awakened by Theresa's feeble call.

Diane rushed in. Theresa was leaning against the sink, clutching her stomach and crying.

"Oh, my God, Theresa." Theresa was pale and clammy. Diane felt her head. It was burning. She helped Theresa back to her bed.

"Hold still. Lay down." She returned to the bathroom, wet a towel with cool water, and placed it gently on her sister's head. Then she brought her some aspirin and a glass of water. Theresa was too weak to sit up, and Diane helped her get the medicine down.

"Good girl," she said. "I'll be right back. I'm gonna call the doctor."

"No more doctors! Dee, I hurt! I hurt all over." Theresa's voice was almost a whisper now.

"No, the real doctor. Dr. Mac. You hang on, baby."

Diane rushed to the phone. "Dr. Mac," she panted. "You have to help us. Theresa is in a lot of pain. Fever. Clammy. Achy all over. Something went wrong."

"My God! What happened? Diane, what did you do? Where are you? Where are your parents?"

Diane gave him the grim brief version.

"I'm on my way. Keep her comfortable, talk to her."

Diane returned to her sister, who was lying on her back, not moving.

"Come on, baby. You're gonna be fine. I love you, Theresa." All the color had left Theresa's face. She was as white as the sheets.

"I love you too, Dee," she breathed. Diane sat on the bed right next to Theresa, willing her sister to be all right.

"C'mon honey. Let's think about going to Rome to see the Pope." Diane sang the song they made up together: "We're going to Rome to see the Pope, Pope Paul, Pope Paul. Going to Rome, going home, he's the best Pope of them all…"

Theresa managed a faint smile.

"Sing our special song, Dee."

Diane picked up her sister's limp hand and started to sing. "Who's my little best girl?"

"Me," Theresa sang weakly.

"And who do I love?"

"Me."

"Who's my little darling?'

"Me." This time it was a whisper.

"And who am I thinking of?"

By the time Dr. Mac rushed in ten minutes later, Theresa lay completely still. Diane touched her gently, trying to get some response, any response.

Dr. Mac took one look at Theresa. "Oh, Heavenly Father, Diane. Why didn't you tell me?" He was white-faced and angry.

"I *did* tell you. You wouldn't help!" Diane shouted. "Help her! Help!"

Dr. Mac went to the bed and picked up Theresa's other hand. He got out his stethoscope to listen for a pulse, then shook his head sadly.

"She's gone," he said.

"NO!" Diane shouted. "No! No! Do something! Help her! You've got to help her!" She grabbed the doctor's arm, pushing him toward the satchel he always carried.

"It's too late," he said, tears welling up. "I couldn't do anything when you called, Diane, but I'll help you now. What son of a bitch did this to her?"

Diane stared at him. She couldn't move. Then she threw herself on her sister, yelling at her to wake up, please wake up, she was so sorry.

She looked wildly at Dr. Mac.

"She couldn't go through what I did. I couldn't let her. I asked you. I did. You wouldn't help me. You wouldn't help her." Diane couldn't talk anymore. She was sobbing so hard that her whole body shook. She tried to grab the doctor and then flung herself into his arms.

"Please," she cried, "Help me, please, please, do something for Theresa, make her okay."

"Diane," he said, "we'll talk later. Give me a minute here with Theresa." Diane clutched her sister's hand, begging her to wake up. She couldn't let go.

Dr. Mac gently pulled her away. "Diane, where's the phone?"

Diane was sobbing. Snot ran down her chin and she wiped it off with her sleeve. Her shirt was soaked with sweat and she couldn't catch her breath.

To Sisterhood!

"Pleeease!" she wailed now.

"Listen to me, Diane. I could lose my medical license. You could go to jail. And so could I. You have to trust me now."

He turned and walked into the hall, then went to the master bedroom and picked up the phone.

"Father Ryan, please," he cleared his throat several times during the pause. Diane could hear only part of what he said. "Yes, to the Romanos'. No, the younger one. Ruptured appendix. No, I got here too late. She's gone."

And then he made a second call, to the funeral home. Fortunately, Diane couldn't hear much of what he said.

Father Ryan let himself in and immediately came upstairs to offer prayers for Theresa. He murmured a few words to the doctor and nodded sympathetically to Diane.

When he finished, he spoke to Diane. "I am very sorry for your loss, my child. Your dear sister will go to God in a state of grace." He looked sad, but continued, "She is at peace now."

Diane felt dizzy. Dr. Mac came back into the room with a clean bed sheet and covered Theresa. Behind him, the attendants from the funeral home waited.

Diane shrieked, "Noooo!" and then her legs gave out from under her and she slowly melted to the floor.

When she came to, she saw that Father Ryan and Dr. Mac were still in the room, standing over her, talking softly. The bed was empty.

"You've had quite a shock, young lady," Dr. Mac told her. "Just rest now. Your parents are on their way. Father Ryan will stay with you until they arrive. I'll come back this afternoon and speak with them." He reached out to embrace Diane but she turned away.

"Be strong, my dear," he said, and walked slowly down the stairs.

Magda and John arrived an hour later to find Diane sitting on the sofa, staring straight ahead. Father Ryan rose to greet them. Magda turned to Diane in a rage.

"Why didn't you call the doctor sooner?" she demanded. Father Ryan rested his hand gently on Magda's arm. Diane just cried. She couldn't answer; she couldn't even look at her parents.

When Dr. Mac came back later, Father Ryan took his leave. Magda turned to the doctor and let loose with the full force of her fury.

"You killed my baby girl!" she screamed. "You knew she had all those stomach aches. You should have taken out that rotten appendix years ago!"

"Magda." Dr. Mac looked old and gaunt. He glanced pleadingly at John. "Magda. We can't do surgery because of a few stomach aches. The appendix is over here" – he showed her on his own torso – "and Theresa's pains sometimes were in her intestines. Probably due to chronic constipation."

To Sisterhood!

"My baby's dead and you're telling me it's because she didn't take a crap?"

John tried to hold Magda, but she pushed him away. Her eyes were black with anger.

"Magda," he said gently. "It's no one's fault. It's a terrible thing our girl is gone, but it's not Dr. Mac's fault. He came right when Diane first noticed she had a fever. But by then it was too late."

Diane sat still, wanting to scream, weeping quietly for her sister, because it was her fault, it was totally her fault. If she hadn't taken her to that horrible man in Boston…

If she hadn't taken her to that man, Theresa would be pregnant with Tony's child.

Tony! Diane had forgotten him in her grief. She wondered where he was and how soon she could find him and slit his throat.

Would he dare to show up at the wake? Of course he'd come – he didn't know he had anything to do with Theresa's death. He didn't know she was pregnant. But he was going to find out, by God. Diane was going to tell him right before she killed him. Diane couldn't listen to any more of Magda's shrieking. She looked imploringly at her father, who, she realized with sudden clarity, wasn't going to do anything at all. Just like he hadn't done anything in the past to protect her, to keep her safe. Or Theresa.

Dr. Mac gave Magda a sedative and told John to put her to bed.

Like she'd done all her life, Diane realized that she was the one who had to cope, even though her heart was breaking and her own rage might kill her from the inside out.

Around six that evening, the doorbell rang. Diane opened it to find a neighbor holding a casserole.

"You have our condolences, my dear." It was Mrs. Fannelli from across the street. "I brought some dinner so your poor mother won't have to cook. I won't come in now, I'll leave you be."

Diane managed a weak, "thank you," and accepted the warm dish from her neighbor. *So your mother won't have to cook, my ass*, she thought, *like Magda ever cooked.*

Whatever it was smelled good. Diane realized that she hadn't eaten anything since last night. She got a fork out of the sink, ran some hot water over it, and sat down at the kitchen table. Soon, the chicken-and-rice casserole was half gone.

When the doorbell rang again, Diane was in the bathroom vomiting her dinner. She wiped her mouth and staggered to the door. There on the stoop was a large basket of pink and white flowers. Diane wanted to lie down right there and go to sleep, and not get up until the wake and the funeral were over. Maybe never. The last thing she wanted was to be around people. All those people were going to look at her. They would know that she killed her baby sister. Her gentle, sweet sister.

✳ **Thirteen** ✳

Nina found the Boston headquarters of the Black Panther Party on a busy street. As she knocked, the door was opened by a solidly built man about her height and age. He was wearing a green tee shirt and blue jeans, not the black leather jacket and wool beret she was expecting. But then, it was a hot Saturday afternoon in July. *C'mon Nina,* she thought. *Get past your expectations and do this with an open mind.* The guy was pretty cute, and Nina was always a sucker for a good-looking man.

The man stuck out his hand. "Dennis Burton, Acting Minister of Information, Boston Black Panther Party," he said, without a trace of a smile.

Nina took his hand and immediately felt all tingly. *Uh oh,* she thought. "Nina Rosen, *Old Mole.*"

He nodded curtly.

Nina told him she'd been sent by the paper to cover the rally at Franklin Park tomorrow and asked if he would give her some background information about it.

Still leaning against the door, he said that the Party had renamed the park "Malcolm X Memorial Park."

"You can come if you want, to see our Party in action." He motioned for her to enter.

"Far out," Nina said, and followed him inside.

Dennis offered Nina a cup of coffee and politely pulled out a chair for her, taking a seat near her. He outlined some of the work the Party was doing in Boston and across the country. He said that recently, there had been a schism in the Party, and the leadership had changed hands. The Panthers who remained in Boston were committed to a working-class revolution, not only for the Black community, but for all oppressed people.

"What caused the schism?" Nina asked, pausing her pen.

Dennis frowned and told her it was internal Party politics, not something he wanted to discuss on record.

"Of course, capitalism is the real enemy," he added solemnly.

Nina nodded. "I understand."

Dennis relaxed his rigid posture as he explained that the Boston chapter followed the Ten Point Plan laid down by National, which included, "free health care, full employment for our people, housing we can live in, and Black people exempt from the military that doesn't serve us."

He added that an important part of their work is PE, or Political Education, and that they studied and read every day. He reached into his back pocket and handed her a copy of Mao's *Little Red Book*. Of course, she already had her own copy back at the office, but she didn't tell Dennis that. She thanked him and continued writing as fast as she could, trying to capture both his words and his strong emotion.

To Sisterhood!

"Complacency is the enemy of study," he quoted, eyes closed, leaning back in his chair. "We cannot learn anything until we rid ourselves of complacency. Our attitude towards ourselves should be 'to be insatiable in learning' and towards others 'to be tireless in teaching.'"

※ ※ ※ ※

The rally the next day was everything Nina expected and more. She was blown away by the energy and commitment of the speakers, and mesmerized by the dynamic, handsome Dennis. She hung on his every word, watching him more than she took notes.

Dennis spoke passionately about organizing a health center, which the Party hoped to have up and running by next spring.

"We need to serve our people with free medical care," he shouted with a raised fist, and the crowd replied with cries of "Right On!" and "All Power to the People!"

After the rally, Nina waited until the crowd thinned out around Dennis. Hoping to look cool and professional, she tried to stay relaxed. She asked if she might come back soon to interview him for a follow-up feature about the Peoples' Free Health Center. Dennis agreed on the condition that he could read the article before it went to press. For the first time in her short journalism career, Nina decided to make an exception. She said yes.

"You can come tomorrow then," he said.

The next morning, Nina got up early. She dressed with extra care, choosing a crisp, sleeveless, pink cotton shirt with white embroidery along the hem, so she could wear it untucked over a short, denim skirt with her favorite sandals. She pinned her hair up into a loose topknot. It was so hot outside and the subways weren't air-conditioned. Nina would have greatly preferred to take a taxi, but she didn't want anyone at Party headquarters to see her getting out of a cab.

Dennis was all business. He led her into a large, bustling office and introduced her briefly to the few other Party members, explaining why she was there. They didn't seem particularly interested. As Acting Minister of Information, Dennis's job was to handle the reporter from the white underground press. The others nodded politely to Nina and left the room.

Dennis showed her to a soft, comfortable sofa, and Nina sunk in, trying to sit up straight and keep her skirt from riding up on her thighs. Dennis sat opposite her behind a desk.

Nina took out her spiral bound steno pad and began to write as Dennis told her in more detail about the work the Party was doing. He emphasized the extraordinary discipline they followed.

He looked directly at Nina as he recited a list of Party rules, the 8 Points of Attention, which were drawn from Chairman Mao's *Little Red Book*: "1. Speak politely. 2. Pay fairly for what you buy. 3. Return everything you borrow. 4. Pay for anything you damage. 5. Do not hit or swear at people. 6. Do not damage property or crops of the poor, oppressed masses. 7. Do not take liberties with women. 8. If we ever have to take captives do not ill-treat them."

Nina wrote as fast as she could.

To Sisterhood!

Dennis continued, "and then there are the 3 Main Rules of Discipline: 1. Obey orders in all your actions. 2. Do not take a single needle or piece of thread from the poor and oppressed masses. 3. Turn in everything captured from the attacking enemy."

Nina asked Dennis about the health center: how was it going to be organized and run, where would it be, and how would it be funded?

Dennis described the plans, although he let her know upfront that some of the details needed to be kept private for security reasons.

"Of course, I understand," Nina said, hoping she didn't sound like she was gushing. She was captivated by this attractive, committed revolutionary. He and the Party were doing things – real things! exciting things! – to make the Black community a better place. Nina wanted to get involved, maybe do more than write about it. But this was not her struggle.

She especially wanted to see Dennis again. She thanked him and told him she was going to need more information for her story closer to the opening of the health center, and that she'd bring a camera with her next time. He nodded solemnly and told her that would be fine.

"One last question. Are you allowed to, um, you know, hang out with women who aren't Party members?" Nina tried to sound calm.

Dennis answered her respectfully. "The Black Panther Party does not fight racism with racism. As our Chairman Bobby Seale says, 'We fight racism with solidarity.'"

He continued seriously. "There are no white people in the Black Panther Party. But we do form alliances with white radical student organizations who are standing up against this racist, imperialist war."

"So you can form alliances?" Nina asked. Dennis looked at her and suddenly seemed to grasp her meaning. He smiled, a slow, spreading grin that made Nina tingle deep in her groin.

"Oh, we surely can do that, sister," he said, taking Nina's hand as he led her from the Party headquarters office and out the door.

※ ※ ※ ※

Upon hearing the sad news from Diane, Ellen had tried several times without success to reach Nina, and then she called Laurie, who was shocked to hear about Theresa. Crying, Laurie told Ellen that she couldn't make it down for the wake but she'd be there for the funeral on Tuesday. She offered to pick up Ellen and Nick.

"I'm looking forward to meeting Nick," Laurie sniffed. "Too bad it'll be at such a sad occasion."

"I know. What a tragedy! It's so scary. It could've been any of us. Appendix. Just like that. We don't need a ride though, thanks. Nick can borrow a car. We'll meet you there," and Ellen gave Laurie the address of the funeral home.

As Diane walked into the church with her parents and grandfather, Ellen was the first person she saw. Ellen stood next to a sturdy-looking, sandy-haired man dressed in a dark blue suit, who held Ellen by the arm. As Ellen and the man walked up to her, Magda, who was right behind Diane, started to wail. Diane thought that her mother cared more about her ruined vacation than she did about Theresa. *Why should Magda cry?* Diane thought bitterly. *Magda is now free.*

Ellen stepped up to Diane and touched her lightly on the arm. "Diane, I am so sorry for your loss. This is my friend, Nick Williams."

Nick murmured, "My condolences, Diane," and the couple slid into the nearest pew.

Laurie arrived a few minutes later, looking disheveled and out of breath. She rushed up to Diane and gave her a big hug.

"Oh, Diane, I'm so sad about your sister. She was such a sweet girl." Diane started to cry. Of all three of Diane's new friends, Laurie was the only one who'd met Theresa, so her words meant a lot. Laurie went to sit next to Ellen and Nick, and smiled briefly at Nick as the organ began to play.

Diane took her place in the front row. She nodded to Patty, who was sitting across the aisle with her whole family. Diane couldn't grasp it all. She bowed her head and could envision Theresa dressed in white, ready to receive her First Communion.

She remembered how excited Theresa had been when their aunt gave her rosary beads that day, the same beads Theresa now clutched in her lifeless hands over her white dress. Diane recalled other celebrations, Christmases, and Easters, and her own and Theresa's Confirmations, held right here in this sanctuary.

Magda kept crying all the way to the front of the church, as she was led to the pew by her sister and brother-in-law, Theresa's godparents.

John and his father trailed behind. John looked uncomfortable in his Sunday suit, which was at least one size too small. The last time he wore it was probably for Theresa's Confirmation.

As soon as Magda saw the coffin, she began to howl again.

"For the love of Jesus, Magda," John whispered fiercely. "Pull yourself together."

Diane's head snapped up. Her father's voice, barely audible above the organ music, brought her back to the present. Her father's voice – silent for so long – sounded like it was muffled in a cloud of grief. He loved Theresa, Diane knew, even if he didn't do much to protect her.

But in that moment, Diane could see how her father wanted to protect his wife. She wasn't annoying him with her caterwauling; he wanted to spare her the public embarrassment of making such a spectacle of herself. Of course, mothers cry at funerals. But Diane guessed that her father didn't want people talking about "poor Magda" for years.

John moved closer to Magda's side, but she pushed him away.

"My baby, my baby, my sweet girl!" she wailed.

Yeah, Diane thought. *Then how come you didn't protect your sweet girl, Mother? Both of your girls, for that matter.*

Diane looked up, then behind her, then wildly around the room. *Where was Tony? That scumbag. Why wasn't he here? He was practically family himself. Is family*, Diane thought wryly. *Yeah, the father of my child, also my sister's child's father. How was that for family?* Diane

To Sisterhood!

wanted to stand up and scream, but she stifled herself by biting her fingernails, tearing them off one at a time.

And now she started tearing into herself. Why, why did she protect him? What would have happened if she had named him as the father when they sent her away? Then they all would have known and Theresa would not be lying there in that fancy brown box with all those nasty, smelly flowers. Theresa, her darling. Her shoulders heaved with sobs, but she didn't make a sound.

Diane had thought at the time that Tony was in love with her, and that she was special.

Special.

That was what she was now. A special teenage mother with a dead sister. All because of her. Stupid, stupid, stupid.

Without Diane being aware, somehow the service was over and Patty was guiding her by the elbow so she could walk behind the coffin.

"Hang in there, Diane," Patty whispered. "I'll be right behind you. I'll meet you at the cemetery," and she went off to ride with her parents.

Diane didn't have to wait long to find out where Tony was.

As she stood near the hearse watching the coffin being loaded into the back, Diane heard someone call her. She looked up as Mrs. Giovanni hobbled toward her, supported by two young men – Tony's brothers.

The older woman made the sign of the cross. "May God bless you and comfort you, child. I'm Mrs. Giovanni. I don't know if you remember me. My youngest son Anthony used to bring you girls over to the house sometimes when you were little."

"I know who you are." Diane was not rude, but she wouldn't be deferential either.

Standing before her was the grandmother of her daughter, a grandmother who didn't know and would never know about Valerie. Standing before her was the woman who gave birth to a man who'd molested her and her sister. But her need to stay in control won out over her strong revulsion.

"Thank you for coming," Diane said shortly, and with a wave of her arm indicated all three of them. She looked at each of the men. They looked like Tony. Uncles to her daughter. Family.

Mrs. Giovanni gave a sharp cough.

"My Anthony also wishes to pay his respects. Poor boy was so broke up over that little retarded girl's death that he cried for a whole day and night. In the morning, he was gone. Disappeared." She started to weep with deep, wracking sobs.

The taller of the two men reached into his pocket and handed her a handkerchief.

"Aw, Ma, he's gonna be all right. He did fine before. He'll come back all in one piece."

She blew her nose loudly and waved the handkerchief in his direction. He took it from her and pocketed it.

"It's my brother," the shorter one said to Diane. "We got a telegram this morning. Re-upped."

Diane looked confused.

"He went back to 'Nam. Another tour."

That rat bastard, thought Diane. *He's run away. He knew. He must've known.* Diane was puzzled. *But he couldn't have known*, she reasoned, *when Theresa could barely explain to her what happened. Theresa could not have said anything to Tony. Then why? Was he too much of a chicken to face Diane and her parents?*

The limo driver motioned for Diane to get into the car behind the hearse. Her parents were in the car. She got in, facing the rear, which she knew was going to make her sick. *It can't possibly get any worse*, she thought on the way to bury her only sister. The one she killed.

Back at the house, the neighbors had left enough food to feed all of Cambridgeport. Diane got out of the car, looking up at the window in the room that wasn't Theresa's anymore.

There's nothing left here for me, she thought as she opened the door to the house that would never again feel like home.

Inside, Diane found neighbors who'd come over to bring even more food. She nodded at the expressions of sympathy, thinking, *these people didn't love Theresa, they didn't even know her.*

She was going to smack the next jerk who said, "It's all part of God's plan, dear," or "the Lord works in mysterious ways," or even that fat Mrs. Tortello across the street who had the nerve to say to Diane, "In a way it was all for the best."

"It was fucking not *for the best,"* she wanted to scream, but that seemed to be Magda's job today. Theresa was Diane's darling, her love. Theresa was the only person she cared about in this whole stinking world. Then it hit her. Theresa wasn't coming home. Diane's knees buckled and she collapsed. Someone helped her up, gave her a glass of water, and told her, "sit right there."

She heard people murmuring, "It's the shock, poor thing." "How sad to lose your only sibling."

Diane heard them in a blur. She'd only now realized why that coward ran away. He figured out they'd examine Theresa's body after her death and would find out she wasn't a virgin. Since he showed up at the school every week, and he was the only man she was ever alone with, it wouldn't be too hard to figure it out. And then Tony finally would have to face John, who'd been his role model, friend, and boss for more than ten years.

Diane knew that Tony was a lot safer in Vietnam right now than he'd be if he were here. She hoped he rotted in the jungle somewhere.

A few minutes later, Ellen found Diane and did not leave her side for the rest of the afternoon. Ellen's leg was hurting a lot, especially in these new heels. Nick was not there for her to lean on. He'd had to go back to work and dropped her at Diane's so she could help out.

Ellen tried to get more comfortable by shifting her weight onto her good leg when she could, and she kept close to Diane. She listened to all the comments, comforting and stupid, and tried to intercept the people who might upset Diane. Ellen made sure that Diane's grandfather, who was much older and feebler than her own, had a cold beverage and a comfortable place to sit. He looked like he didn't understand what was going on. Ellen wondered if he even knew his granddaughter was dead. After some time, Diane's aunt and uncle came to take him home.

As soon as her sister left, Magda turned up the volume. She wailed, she screamed, she threw herself on the sofa, yelling loudly that it was all her fault, she never should have left Theresa with that stupid girl, by which she meant Diane. Fortunately, not many people could understand her drunken ranting.

Most did understand, however, that it was time to leave. John managed to get Magda upstairs, and didn't return. Eventually, Laurie and Nina and even the nosiest of the neighbors went home.

"This has been a heck of a day," Ellen said. "Give me a minute or two in the kitchen, to put some of the perishables in the refrigerator. The rest can wait until tomorrow. Go get your toothbrush and a nightgown and some clean underwear, Diane. I'm taking you home with me."

Diane stared at Ellen, in gratitude and relief. She heard Ellen on the phone. A few minutes later, a taxi pulled up in front of the house.

Ellen led Diane outside. "C'mon. Sleep will help. Let's go home."

Soon, they arrived at Ellen's apartment.

"You can sleep in my bed with me. It's a double. There's plenty of room." Ellen pulled back the light blanket, Diane got in, and Ellen held her close until she fell asleep.

Then Ellen phoned Nina again, this time reaching her to tell her the sad news. Having spent the day with Dennis, Nina hadn't been answering her phone. She told Ellen how sorry she was and asked what she could do to help. Could she speak with Diane? Ellen said she was sleeping, and she'd convey Nina's condolences.

Diane did not wake until early the next afternoon. When she opened her eyes, Ellen was by her side, holding a small tray with a cup of tea and a fresh cinnamon muffin.

"Nick came by this morning. He stopped at Pewter Pot," Ellen said. Diane nodded gratefully.

"Diane." Ellen paused to clear her throat. "I can't know how you feel and I'm not going to pretend to. But I do know that mostly you need to rest. I called the factory first thing this morning and told them that you wouldn't be in for the rest of the week, possibly next week too. Your boss said he understood and that Patty and the others have already divided up your shifts and they'll cover them."

Diane managed a weak, "thank you." She gave Ellen a wan smile.

"What good friends you have at work. They all send you their sympathy and love," Ellen said.

Diane smiled again. She didn't trust herself to say anything more.

To Sisterhood!

"All you have to do right now is lie down," Ellen said. "Take a shower or bath later when you feel like it. I'll bring you food when you're hungry, if you want me to. I can hold you when you cry, or leave you alone if that's what you need. I'll do whatever I can to help you feel at least a bit better."

Diane stared at her friend. Then she started to sob, burying her face in her hands.

"Ellen, you're so kind. I don't deserve this. You're better to me than my own mother," Diane sniffed. "That's not saying much. But how do you know what to do?"

Ellen looked at Diane for a brief moment. She seemed to be deciding something. Then she said quietly, "I lost a sibling, too. A brother. Long ago. I'll tell you about it another time."

Diane started to speak, but Ellen stopped her. "Right now, how about if I run a bath for you? Nick left a couple of tee shirts that should fit, and I've got a peasant skirt you can wear for now. I'll go over to your house later and get you some clothes and whatever else you need."

Diane nodded. "I need my diary. It's in my desk drawer. That's the only thing I don't want my mother to get her hands on."

"I'll go right now. You go get cleaned up, and I'll be back in no time. Do you need me to stop at Patty's? Did you leave anything there?"

Diane shook her head. "No, I bring a bag. Nothing's there."

For the second time in two days, Ellen called a taxi. She asked the driver to please wait while she went inside. Diane's father let her in.

"I'm very sorry about your daughter, Mr. Romano. We met briefly yesterday. I'm Ellen MacDougall, Diane's friend. I've come for some of Diane's clothes. She's going to stay with me for now, if that's all right with you." She glanced meaningfully at Magda, asleep – or passed out – on the sofa.

He reached out to shake Ellen's hand. "Thanks, Ellen. Diane's room is upstairs. I'll show you."

When Ellen got back to her apartment, Diane was sitting at the kitchen table with a towel around her wet hair, sipping tea.

"Hey, Diane. I've got your things. Your father said to call him, and can you come to the house tomorrow? The priest will be there and…"

"I'll go." Diane stared into the mug. "I guess I have to do what they expect me to do. This is all my fault."

Ellen shook her head no, but didn't try to argue. She knew that grief had its own ways, and that Diane was going to feel guilty for not calling the doctor sooner, even though there was no way she could've known that Theresa's appendix was going to rupture.

Ellen spent the rest of the day with Diane, quietly urging her to lie down when she was sleepy, and feeding her a simple supper of soup and rye bread from the deli around the corner.

To Sisterhood!

She tucked Diane in, telling her that she was going over to Nick's. Ellen didn't want to leave Diane alone, but Nick had called, saying he needed to see her, and that he'd pick her up at 9:00 pm. He could drive her back later, so she shouldn't be gone for more than an hour or so.

Nick didn't say much on the short ride to his place. He helped Ellen out of the car, opened the front door, then offered Ellen a drink. She shook her head.

Nick grabbed a beer and sat at the table, head down, staring at his glass like it was going to tell him what to say. Something was wrong but Ellen couldn't guess what. She went around to his side of the table, and he stood up and held out his arms. Ellen leaned into his solid, hard chest for a few minutes. She could hear his heart beating rapidly.

"You're okay?" he said, half-question, half-statement.

"It's so sad." Ellen leaned away from him, twisting her hair, the way she always did when she was worried or upset. Nick kissed her forehead lightly.

"I know, babe," he said.

Ellen sat down next to him.

"Ellen." Nick's sudden urgency made her look up. She saw his caring, concerned look, and she saw something else – something that wasn't just sympathy.

"What is it, Nick?"

"Look, Ellen." He hesitated. "I'm so sorry this happened to your friend. But I wanted to talk to you soon, about us."

"What about us?" Ellen was drained. *I don't want to talk at all, never mind about the rest of my life.*

"Ellen," Nick began again. "I was hoping you'd be in a better head space before we had this talk. I'm sorry the timing is lousy. It's about, well, our future. Our future together."

Ellen waited. There wasn't anything to do. He wasn't going to stop.

"You know I'll be leaving for San Francisco soon," Nick said. "School doesn't start until September, but I need to find a place to live. I've got enough saved for the tuition, and about a month's rent and security deposit for a halfway decent place. But Ellen…" He took a big breath. "It wouldn't be the same without you there. Will you come with me?"

Ellen's first thought was, *See, Mother, someone does indeed want me.* Then for an instant: *Sam, oh Sam.* And then she thought about Diane, asleep in her bed, grieving for her only sibling. Nick was so, well, stable, and he had a promising future, as long as he didn't get drafted. *Eddy. Eddy, tell me what to do. Here is this gentle, kind man, who cares for me and wants me.*

After a few moments, Ellen spoke.

"No."

"No?" Nick's shoulders slumped.

"You know I care for you. But it wouldn't be the right thing to do."

Nick turned away sharply, trying not to look like a little boy whose kite got loose and swirled away on a puff of wind. He was trying not to cry. After a long pause, he cleared his throat and repeated Ellen's words, "It wouldn't be the right thing to do."

She slowly let out her breath. She hadn't even realized she'd been holding it. *He's all right with it, he doesn't hate me, I didn't hurt him.*

"No, you're right, Ellen," he said. "It wouldn't be right. Not that way. I'm sorry. Please let me try this again. I should have asked you this differently." He paused. Then he reached over and took her hand. His face lit up as he smiled broadly at her.

"Ellen Patricia MacDougall, will you do me the great honor of becoming my wife?"

There's only one thing you can say that won't ruin everything, she heard Eddy say, *and you know what that is.* Ellen breathed in and made herself speak calmly.

"Nick, I'm the one who is honored. Thank you, thank you so much. Marriage is such a big step. Will you give me time to think about it?"

"You're not saying no?" He beamed.

"I'm not saying no." She smiled too.

Nick reached out and pulled her close. Then he got up, lifted her out of her chair, and spun her around. "You're my girl," he crowed.

I'm my own girl, Ellen thought, but she kept on smiling.

Nick kissed her gently, this time full on the lips. "Thank you, my dear," he said. "I'll always do my best to make you happy."

Still holding her in his arms, Nick walked into the bedroom and gently placed her on the bed. He stroked her hair and held her. Ellen wanted only one thing and that was to sleep. But this meant a lot to Nick. She pulled him close and kissed him back. Slowly, he unbuttoned her blouse and eased it off, placing it neatly on the chair next to the bed. He took off his own clothes, and then kissing and stroking, removed the rest of Ellen's. They lay there together naked, looking at the moon, seemingly caught in the branches of the oak tree outside the window. Nick did not press for more. He held Ellen as she dozed.

When the first light of dawn came in through the curtains, Nick was awake, looking at her.

"Think about what I asked you last night, Ellen," he said. "I want you to be really, truly mine."

She nodded. "I will. I promise. And now I have got to get back to my place. I want to be there when Diane wakes up. I told her last night I'd be gone only a couple of hours."

"I'll drive you." Nick jumped up and dressed quickly.

They rode in silence. They both had a lot on their minds.

❉ Fourteen ❉

Nina hadn't heard from Dennis. She'd finished her story on the Rally, and got the go-ahead to do a follow up for *Old Mole* on the progress of the People's Free Health Center. But she'd been avoiding that assignment because she felt awkward about calling Dennis, even though it was for work. She certainly wasn't going to pursue him. If he didn't want to see her again after the wonderful time they'd spent together, well, his tough luck.

Ellen had called a few times, urging Nina to come over to her place to see Diane, but Nina had been avoiding that too. She wanted to spend time with Diane, but didn't want to take the chance of running into Nick. While she was sure that what she and Nick might have had was over soon after it started, she didn't know how Nick felt about her now. She wouldn't risk messing up things for Ellen, or even complicating them. Ellen had told her that Nick would be leaving town soon. Nina could wait until then to see her friends.

Except that Nina didn't know anyone else here other than a few staff members. But Boston was a small city. And one day, while she was doing research at the Boston Public Library, Nina was surprised to hear someone softly call her name.

She looked up.

"Hey, stranger," she said, willing herself to act calmer than she felt.

"Hey, yourself." Dennis stood there, looking uncomfortable. He couldn't quite meet her gaze.

"You never called." Nina was direct. And she wanted to know what had happened.

"Sshhh!" the librarian at the desk whispered in their direction.

"Let's take a walk," Dennis said, so Nina gathered her papers and stuffed them into her knapsack. They went outside and sat by the fountain in Copley Square.

"You didn't phone me," Nina repeated. Even if their relationship – if that's what it was – started out too intensely too soon, Nina was used to being the one to call the shots. She wasn't sure how to play this. *Act like you don't care.* But she did care. She was deeply attracted to this man, who was so obviously passionate about his desire to defend and improve his community, and to help create justice for his people. Nina was blown away by how eloquently he'd spoken at the rally last month, though right now he seemed to be grasping for words.

"No, um, that's right, I didn't," Dennis stammered.

"I thought we had a pretty good time," Nina said softly.

"Me too."

Dennis was quiet. After a long pause he said, "Look, Nina. I like you. I do." He started to reach out to take her hand, then seemed to think better of it and rested his hand on his muscled thigh.

"I kinda like you too," Nina said, smiling.

To Sisterhood!

Dennis returned her smile with a frown. "Here's the thing. It's that some of the folks in the Party, especially the sisters, were ticked off about the possibility of me seeing a white girl. And there aren't too many places we could be seen together. At least not in Boston…"

"Oh," said Nina, suddenly aware of her surroundings. She sat up and set the knapsack in the space between them. She angled her body until she was facing Dennis but was not close enough to touch him.

"The sisters see it as a betrayal of Black Womanhood." He looked sad but determined.

Nina didn't speak. But she realized that Dennis wasn't wrong about it being dangerous for him to be seen with her. This wasn't New York.

Dennis explained that his absence the day after the rally was noticed. He was called in by the other Party leaders and asked to account for his whereabouts. Of course, he told them the truth. He was told to break it off with her immediately.

"So you see," he said regretfully, "even though I do like you a lot, I can't see you anymore."

Nina immediately switched to what Perry and the other guys at *Old Mole* teasingly called her "Lois Lane, Girl Reporter" persona. She said she understood and asked if it would still be all right to do the additional interview about the health center. Dennis said that would be fine, as long as their relationship stayed on a work-only basis.

"Thanks," Nina said, tossing her hair. "I'll call you at Headquarters to make an appointment. As for the rest – your loss!" She picked up her bag and walked quickly down Boylston Street, away from him.

⌘ ⌘ ⌘ ⌘

That evening Nina called Laurie in Wellfleet and told her everything about Dennis, from the rally to today's chance meeting.

"So *that* explains why you missed Diane's sister's funeral?" Laurie was fascinated with Nina's story.

"Um, yes. I feel pretty bad about that. Ellen got on my case about it."

"Yeah, Ellen can be kinda uptight at times, don't you think?" Laurie was careful not to be too critical.

"Priggish is more like it," Nina said, laughing. "God, that girl needs to get laid. I hope she's getting it on with that Army guy."

"I met him at the funeral. Nick. He seems like a pretty nice guy."

"Nice he is," Nina said dryly.

"How did you meet him?"

"I knew him a couple of years ago in New York. He's okay. Just right for Ellen. But enough about her. What do you think about this Black women's struggle thing? Do you think it's an excuse for Dennis not to see me anymore?"

"It's hard to say," Laurie said thoughtfully. "It sounds like he truly does like you. I think, though, that Black women today have to choose between the Black struggle and their struggle as women. It's my opinion that they would identify more with being Black. I mean, the civil rights movement is much older, and thinking about women's subjugation is still pretty new. What a tough choice it would make for Black women. Being doubly oppressed."

"I get it," Nina said.

"So," said Laurie, "we can sit here and try to analyze this from our privileged white point of view, but we can't pretend to know what's in our Black sisters' heads."

"I guess not. I'm thinking I could ask one of my Black friends from home what she thinks. But I don't want the whole world to know about my relationship with Dennis. Or non-relationship, I guess it is now." Nina paused. "Call you in a few days, Laurie. I know things are rough for you right now with your mom and all. But you'll be back here soon and we'll tear up the town!"

"Groovy," said Laurie, laughing as she hung up.

※ ※ ※ ※

Diane stayed in Ellen's room, while Ellen moved into Mavis's room on the nights she wasn't there. Mavis was fine with the arrangement, and Ellen certainly didn't mind having a real roommate. She'd grown fond of Diane in such a short time. The only thing that worried Ellen was that Diane was drinking every evening. First, it was only the beer Nick brought over. But now she'd moved on to harder stuff. Ellen didn't want to confront her grieving friend, but she was curious about where she was getting the liquor, as she wasn't yet twenty-one.

"Oh, that package store over on Brighton Ave.," Diane said airily. "The brother of someone I went to high school with has the day shift. He never cards me."

"I see," Ellen said uneasily. "I guess if you're not driving…"

Diane looked at her friend sharply.

"Don't worry about me. I'm not going to end up like my mother. Right now, it helps to take the edge off. I can stop any time."

Ellen nodded, and reached over to hug her friend. "I'm sure that's true. And you must have such a lot of pain. Diane leaned into her embrace but she didn't let herself cry.

The next day, Diane asked Ellen if she would go over to the factory with her to give her notice. Even though she needed the money, Diane couldn't deal with any of it right now – not her co-workers' sympathy, or having to do her job on the days she couldn't manage to get going in the morning. She needed time.

Ellen was happy to help and even walked into the building with her. When Diane came back downstairs, she was smiling. The lady in the personnel office had said she could take an unpaid leave of absence and come back anytime she wanted. But they couldn't promise her the same shift or any overtime. Diane said she understood and thanked her, both for her kindness, and for the beautiful flowers they'd sent to the funeral home.

To Sisterhood!

Ellen and Diane walked to the bus arm-in-arm in silence. When they got back to the apartment, Diane confessed that though she had no idea what to do next, she knew she didn't want to be a burden to Ellen any longer. Ellen reassured her that she was glad to have her, and laughingly told her it was because Diane was cooking real meals.

Diane was a wonderful cook. Ellen came home each evening to fabulous aromas and a delicious dinner. Diane made lasagna with a marinara sauce that was out of this world, succulent spaghetti and meatballs, and a huge pot of minestrone that lasted for three days, with plenty for the freezer.

One night, right before Nick was scheduled to leave for California, Diane had a surprise. She'd planned a romantic dinner, to let Nick and Ellen say a proper goodbye.

Ellen returned from work to find the table set for two, laid with a red-and-white checkered tablecloth, and topped with a candle in a Chianti bottle.

Ellen smiled. "This is lovely Diane. Thank you so much. Where did you find the cloth?"

"At Goodwill, for fifty cents. But don't worry, I washed it and hung it over the balcony railing to dry in the sun. I'm pretty sure it's sanitary."

When Nick arrived, bearing a large bouquet of daisies, he greeted Ellen with a quick kiss and Diane with an awkward hug.

"I'm going to serve dinner, and then go out and leave you two alone." Diane smiled at the couple, glad to be able to do something for her friend. Ellen was worried about Diane. She figured she'd go over to Patty's and they'd spend the evening drinking with Jimmy and his buddies. But Diane was a big girl, and there wasn't anything Ellen could do to stop her. At least Diane wouldn't be driving. She'd take the bus home.

After a tasty meal, Nick and Ellen cuddled on the blanket they kept out on the small balcony to escape the heat in the apartment. She had an idea she'd been thinking about for a few days now.

"You know that I care for you," Ellen said. "I do. It's just that I need to go back to Vermont and finish next year and apply to Radcliffe. I don't want to jeopardize my education."

"Yeah," Nick said with a big sigh. "I figured that was going to be your final answer."

"But when I graduate, why, then, we can start to make some plans for us," Ellen hoped she sounded enthusiastic.

"I'm disappointed, but I understand. I thought you could transfer to a school out west –"

Ellen interrupted him. "Nick, I want to ask you to do something for me. Will you take Diane with you? If she wants to go?"

Nick looked confused.

She continued, "I mean, to share the driving. You're so good with people – you know when to keep quiet, when to be cheerful – and I think a change of scenery would do her a world of good. She's been drinking a lot since her sister died, and I think, well…"

Nick assumed his "I'm thinking about it" look that Ellen had come to know, the one that said, "Don't say anything else, I'm considering what you said and I don't want to be interrupted with more information." She twisted her hair around one finger, then another, while she waited. After what seemed like a long time, Nick spoke.

"Yes, I think that could work. The thing is, I was planning to crash with some of my school buddies and a cousin or two along the way. Seems like our family has relatives in every state. My mother is so over the moon that I'm coming home that she wrote to every one of them. I guess if I let her know, she can get the word out that I'm bringing a friend. Not the friend I'd *like* to be bringing, mind you. And how would she get back?"

Ellen started to speak, but Nick was already planning the trip.

"I guess I can get her a plane ticket," he said, more to himself than to Ellen. "Yeah, maybe it would help her get her head back together some. Okay, yes. Good idea."

"Oh, that's great, Nick. Thank you. You're wonderful!" Ellen threw her arms around him.

"I think we have to celebrate my second-to-last night in town," Nick said. "I'm not sure we'll get another chance to be alone. I think tonight's the night, if that's all right with you?"

Ellen smiled again.

"Give me a few minutes." She climbed over the window ledge and went into the bathroom. After a while, she called to him, "Ready!"

Nick came in too. "Um, are you positive you're comfortable with this?" He looked unsure.

"Yes, Nick," Ellen said. "I would love to make love with you." She lit the pink candle next to the bed, then looked through the stack of records on the floor.

"Joni's new album, okay?" When he nodded, she put on *Clouds*. Joni Mitchell's sweet soprano seemed to cool the hot, sticky room. Ellen unbuttoned her light cotton dress and hung it in the closet. She turned down the sheet, set her glasses on the nightstand, climbed into the bed, and motioned for Nick to join her. She wished she had another fan. It was such a hot night.

Nick sat on the bed and took off his sandals. He pulled his shirt over his head, folded his pants, and draped them over the desk chair. He slid in next to Ellen, still wearing his briefs.

"Are you alright?" Nick sounded calm. He didn't want to frighten her.

Ellen didn't say anything. She reached out and pulled Nick to her. He kissed her gently at first, then with an intensity that surprised her. He touched her carefully, running his hand down her back, down her behind, down her legs. He held her close to him so she could feel how hard he was through his briefs.

"Ellen," he said, "you know I love you and respect you."

Get on with it already, Ellen thought, but said, "I love you too, Nick."

Nick carefully removed her bra and panties, and caressed her gently. In less than five minutes, he was inside her, pumping, stopping every so often to look at her.

"You are so lovely," he gasped. Ellen closed her eyes. She felt him tense up, then stiffen and shudder. He collapsed on her in a big heap.

So that's what all the fuss was about.

Nick roused himself, went into the bathroom, and came out with a warm washcloth.

"Here," he said, handing it to Ellen. "I guess it's kind of messy."

Ellen looked at him and grinned. "So, we did it, huh?"

"Well," Nick said, blushing. "It gets better with practice."

Ellen hadn't expected fireworks. She knew that it didn't always feel wonderful at first. Nick was a kind man, not selfish. It could get better.

They lay together, resting comfortably. Nick stroked her hair, telling her how beautiful she was.

"Boy, you sure look like you're in a good mood," she teased.

"I know it wasn't that great for you," Nick said seriously. "We can keep trying until we get it right!"

Ellen hoped so. This wasn't the first time her body had let her down. More often than not, the physical things she tried to do – from riding a bike to learning how to skate, even to walking more than a couple of miles, had been too taxing for her. Only in the water, swimming for pleasure in King's Lake, or doing laps at a friend's pool, did she feel connected to her body.

And now here was Nick – sweet, kind, gentle Nick, who sang off-key along with Joni, which made Ellen laugh. And then the record ended and they fell asleep, holding each other tightly.

When Diane came home late that night, Nick heard her close the door. He disentangled himself carefully from the still-sleeping Ellen, pulled on his pants and shirt, and went into the kitchen.

"Diane," he said. "First of all, thank you for that fantastic dinner. You are one hell of a cook."

Diane beamed.

"Oh, it's no big deal," she said. "I wanted you and Ellen to have something special."

Nick interrupted her. "Which is why I feel greedy asking you to do me a favor right now."

"What is it?" Diane was unsteady on her feet, as she made her way to the table and sat down.

As Nick outlined the plan, Ellen stumbled into the kitchen and put the kettle on for tea. Nick explained to Diane the route he was going to

To Sisterhood!

take, said he needed an extra driver, and that he hadn't thought too carefully about how long it would take to drive across the country all by himself, so would she please help him out?

After glancing at Ellen and getting an enthusiastic nod of approval, Diane immediately agreed.

"Getting out of here would be great. Not that you haven't been wonderful to me, both of you."

Nick cleared his throat. "Just one thing, Diane. No drinking on the job. Only when we stop for the night. Do we have a deal?"

"You got it, boss." Diane grinned, and then somewhat drunkenly, saluted Nick. It was good to have someone need her again, even if it was only as a back-up driver. An adventure right about now sounded terrific.

✹ **Fifteen** ✹

The long drive across the country in Nick's 1964 VW bug was hot, but not unpleasant. *Thankfully*, Diane thought, *Nick wasn't much of a talker.* He didn't ask questions. They listened to whatever rock music station was playing as they drove.

Nick seemed to have a classmate or cousin in every city. His relatives were uniformly kind and not at all intrusive with Diane. His friends welcomed her as a friend and offered the travelers a beer or a joint – sometimes both – and a place to crash for the night.

A week after they left Boston, Nick and Diane headed down Route 80 toward the Bay Bridge. Nick insisted on making a detour into North Berkeley, so they could stop at Peets Coffee, which Nick proclaimed, "the absolute best coffee in the world!" Diane agreed, and quickly downed a second and then a third espresso, which made her drive a tad too fast for Nick's taste.

Plus, Nick wanted to give Diane a grand tour of the whole city, so he took the wheel. Diane looked with wonder at the new sights: the colorful Victorian houses; the steep hills with stone steps cut right into the sidewalks; the cable cars, which seemed to run up and down those streets by magic; and all the unfamiliar flowers and trees. She gazed at Alcatraz Island dotting the sparkling bay. She liked the people they met, who all looked different from the stuffy uptight Easterners she'd known all her life. *Theresa will love this*, she thought, and stopped cold. As beautiful as the days were, the nights were tough. Diane frequently dreamed about her sister, mostly nightmares that woke her, sweating and gasping for air.

As Nick drove through the Haight, Diane gawked at the head shops and colorful street people, and at the tiny music and used clothing shops everywhere. Then he took her down through the Mission District, with its ratty housing and funky storefront businesses and small parks, some with statues of Catholic saints. When they could find a parking space, they stopped for coffee, and Diane quickly developed a serious espresso habit.

I could be happy here, she thought. *Or happier, maybe*, she amended.

She was mesmerized by the smells and noise of Chinatown, and wanted to stop at every food shop to look at the unfamiliar kitchen utensils – giant cleavers, woks, and bamboo steamers.

That evening, Nick took Diane to a vegetarian café named Sun Sprouts. Diane tentatively tasted a few bites of her unfamiliar-looking dinner. She recognized the greens and the radishes in the salad, of course, but not the crunchy celery-like cubes she learned were called jicama. She ordered sautéed tofu on brown rice and a vegetable medley, which included what looked like minuscule brown worms, but which, when she asked the friendly waiter, turned out to be seaweed. Diane sipped her glass of wheat grass juice.

"I feel healthier already," she laughed.

Spearing a stalk of crisp asparagus, Nick laughed. "Welcome to California!"

I could cook like this, Diane mused, but only in passing. She didn't allow herself to have too many pleasant thoughts these days. How could she, still guilty and grieving, when her sister was lying in the ground and it was all her fault?

※ ※ ※ ※

The next afternoon, Nick and Diane drove up through the cool green shade of the Presidio, and over the Golden Gate Bridge, up the 101, north to Petaluma. They arrived at the Williams' home right before dinnertime.

Nick's mother was warm and friendly; his father was cordial but more stand-offish. Diane thought there would've been a lot more to say if she weren't there.

When they sat down to dinner, Diane sensed the tension. Used to a troubled family life, she didn't see evidence of anyone drinking too much. It must have been something else. Clearly, something was not right with Colonel and Mrs. Williams.

Their only son had moved back – at least he'd be only an hour away – and the dinner table talk was as superficial as with a roomful of strangers. Why weren't they thrilled to have Nick home?

After dinner, Diane insisted on doing the dishes, over Mrs. Williams's protests. Nick rolled up his sleeves and started clearing the table. Diane waited until his parents went upstairs before speaking.

"Is it just me being here, or do I sense that your father is pissed off about something?"

To Sisterhood!

"Yeah, you got that right. I'm a class-A failure in his view. College grad, gonna be a teacher, not a second lieutenant, following him into the service. Big fucking disappointment."

Diane knew all too well how it felt to not be accepted by your own parent. She patted Nick's arm. "Then you'd better be the best fucking teacher you can be!"

Nick smiled and smacked her playfully with the dishtowel.

"Your mother seems crazy about you," Diane said. "I get the feeling she'll support you no matter what you do."

"They're both all right. It's that now the Colonel can't hold his head up at the country club. Most of his buddies' sons are in 'Nam, or finished their tour and they're back, in law school, med school, business school. Some of them already have families and are making a good living. And then there's Colonel Williams, with the no-good, peacenik, draft-dodger, hippie bum of a son. Ah, screw it all." Nick dried the last plate and stacked it none-too-gently in the cupboard.

"Let's call it a night," he said. "I'm whipped."

Diane woke early the next morning, even though she'd had a couple of days to adjust to Pacific time. She stayed in bed until she heard movement in the kitchen. She threw on her sweatshirt and pants, and quietly went downstairs.

Nick's mother was sitting at the kitchen table by herself, drinking coffee from a large, red mug and looking out her backyard window at the bird feeder, where two blue birds with rust-and-white breasts nibbled at the seeds.

"Western Bluebirds," said Mrs. Williams, answering Diane's unasked question. "They often come here in pairs."

"Coffee?" she added, motioning for Diane to sit.

Diane nodded.

"You are Ellen's good friend," she said, pouring a cup for Diane.

"Yes. We've only known each other a few months but we've become close. Ellen's been so helpful to me since my sister died. And Nick too," Diane added loyally.

Mrs. Williams looked thoughtful. "I had the pleasure of meeting Ellen only that once at Nick's graduation, and she *is* a lovely girl. Nick talks about her all the time, at least to me. But I get the feeling that Ellen is not as devoted to Nick as Nick is to her. Now I don't want to put you on the spot…" her voice trailed off.

Diane smiled. "Well, Mrs. Williams, I don't know what to say. Ellen seems to care for Nick a lot, but it's hard to tell what's in someone else's head, don't you think?"

"Harriet. Please call me Harriet." Lost in thought, she didn't appear to have heard Diane.

But then she said, "I think that's the basis for a good marriage. In every relationship, there is a lover and a beloved. When it's the woman who is the beloved, it seems to work better."

Diane stared at her. She hadn't seen marriage work particularly well, still, she kind of knew what Mrs. Williams – Harriet – meant. If her own father didn't adore Magda, there was no way they'd still be together, Church or no Church. She wasn't sure exactly what her father saw in her mother. But clearly, he was crazy about her, and most of the time, Magda acted like she couldn't care less. Maybe there was truth to this theory.

"I wonder why that is." Diane sipped her coffee.

"I think it has to do with the balance of power. In our culture, women are the people pleasers. Men seem to think it's their God-given right to be taken care of, nurtured, listened to. What they want and need counts. What we want and need is secondary. When it's the other way around, when the man loves his partner more than she seems to love him, it makes him work harder to please her. Kind of evens things out, don't you think?" she laughed, then sighed. "I've always wished I'd had a daughter. I could teach her so much."

What did we need a women's conference for? We could all just listen to Harriet. Diane wrapped her arms around herself and thought about her daughter Valerie, now two-and-a-half. What would she learn, what would she see while she was growing up? How would she learn to be a strong woman, without Diane there to help her? And for the millionth time, it seemed, Diane bitterly regretted giving up her daughter.

"Well," Diane said. "If all goes according to Nick's plan, it looks like you may have a daughter before too long."

❋ ❋ ❋ ❋

With Diane in California, Ellen was alone in the city. Laurie had called a few times from Wellfleet, chattering excitedly about a surprising adventure she'd explain to Ellen when she returned at the end of the month. Nina had left for New York after meeting Ellen once for lunch, and it'd be a week before Diane would fly back. Sam had called to say he'd be arriving late Wednesday, after driving his brother home to Ohio, then flying back to Boston.

So when he knocked at the apartment door, Ellen was eager, happy, and just plain scared. She wore a new blue sundress printed with silver stars, one she'd bought yesterday at the Coop. It matched her eyes.

Wearing baggy jeans and a black tee shirt, Sam looked travel-worn but as handsome and sexy as she remembered. Ellen's heart was beating so hard she had to hold onto the door for support.

"Come on in, stranger," she laughed, opening the door wide. Sam reached down and gave her a big hug.

"Hi there, Elly May. You look great. Better than in my dreams."

Ellen blushed and gestured for him to sit down. "Can I get you a drink?" she asked.

"A beer would be great if you have one. Otherwise, anything cold." He immediately made himself at home on the sofa.

To Sisterhood!

Ellen went to the refrigerator and grabbed one of Diane's beers.

"Here you go," she said, handing Sam the bottle and then sitting at the table with her own glass of iced tea. "How was the concert?"

"It was totally far out. You wouldn't believe who played there! Richie Havens, Creedence Clearwater, Country Joe, The Who, The Band… I mean, it was totally outasight! Johnny and Edgar Winter, even Joan Baez. Santana was awesome, but we left right before Jimi Hendrix played last thing Monday morning."

Sam went on to describe the scene in Bethel, NY: the rain, the mud, the traffic, the crowds, the way people helped each other and shared food and rain gear and dope from August 15th until the 18th. Ellen's attention was totally on Sam's stories from the festival.

"Well now," he said, after finishing the beer and shifting his position on the sofa. "I've been talking your ears off. What's with you?"

Ellen laughed, then grew quiet. *Can I trust him?* she wondered, and heard Eddy say *I told you he's okay, Sis.* Ellen took a breath and told him about her plan to transfer to Radcliffe. He asked Ellen thoughtful questions, listened intently, and told her to follow her dream.

Sam excitedly told Ellen *his* dream: he'd been accepted to join the Venceremos Brigade and would petition the dean to get credit for a semester abroad. If that didn't work, he'd take a leave of absence from school for the fall and maybe for spring semester too.

"By the time my draft board catches up with me, I'll be back at school. And pretty much undesirable for the U.S. Army."

"Wait, slow down a minute," Ellen laughed. "What is *Venceremos*?"

"*Venceremos* means 'We shall overcome.'" Sam said he and a group of other Movement folks – mostly from SDS, SNCC, the Chicano Communications Center, and Weathermen – would be going to Cuba at the end of November for three months "to help our Cuban comrades" with the sugar harvest.

"Cuba has set a goal to harvest 10 million tons – that's like two and a half million more tons than they've ever done before," he explained. "We'll be showing solidarity with the Cuban revolutionaries and working together with them, learning to appreciate their struggle, eating their food, and learning their music and culture. It's a way of sticking it to the U.S. fascist government and its piggy economic blockade on our brothers." He clenched both fists together excitedly and stood and stretched.

"But isn't there a ban on travel to Cuba?"

"Yes," Sam said. "That's why we have to go through Mexico and Canada. I think we're going to get in by flying from Mexico City or Montreal, and coming back by freighter to St. John. I volunteered to go down right away to help with the travel plans."

"How many people are going?" Ellen was curious to know more.

"Right now," Sam said, "there are more than a hundred and fifty signed up. I think they're trying to get two hundred."

"So I'll be up in Vermont studying and making snowmen for fun," Ellen said, "and you'll be cutting sugar cane? That's food for thought."

She got up and refilled her glass, gestured to the refrigerator to offer Sam another beer, but he shook his head.

"Speaking of food," Sam deadpanned, "I hear the tomato ice cream in Cuba is something else!"

"Eeeww!" The granddaughter of dairy farmers, Ellen winced at the thought.

"The visit will help us in our struggle here at home," he said. "While we're there, we're going to visit hospitals, schools, co-ops, and other systems Fidel has put into place, to see how Socialism can be successful."

Ellen listened carefully, resting her chin on her hand, as he sat back down on the sofa and leaned toward her.

"Elly May," Sam said. "I know I don't have the right to ask you this, seeing as how you are with What's-His-Name and all that –"

"Nick."

"Right." He paused. "But I was hoping, I mean, I hope that you'll be here when I get back."

"I'm not planning on going anywhere yet – except to Radcliffe, *if* I'm lucky enough to get in for next September. So I would say 'yes,' I plan to be right here in New England when you return. Only a couple of hours north."

"I didn't mean here, here." Sam said. "I mean, I know it's soon and all, but Elly, I feel a connection with you. I want you to be *with* me…"

"Oh, Sam," she said, her voice small.

"Elly May, can you see how much I want you?" he asked. "Can't you tell?" He held out his arms and opened them wide. "Come here to me, beautiful. I won't do anything you don't want."

Ellen didn't move. Sam got up and walked around the table to where she was sitting, looking up at him. He put his hands under her arms and lifted her, so she was standing close to him.

Slowly, and without saying anything, Sam lifted the dress over her head. He stood behind her, and holding her hair up, blew on her neck.

Ellen shivered from the sudden shock of cool air. Sam nibbled softly and then kissed her on the back of her neck.

"You're so hot," he said. Sam laughed and started to sing a few lines from Dylan's hit new single, "*Lay, Lady, Lay.*" He twirled Ellen around so she was in his arms. He dipped her and they danced around the room.

Ellen loved his deep, rich voice. Her skin was alive all over. Sam bent down and kissed her once. His lips were tender, full and soft. Ellen wanted more kisses, faster and harder, and she wanted them slower and gentler too. She sighed deeply. Sam kissed her again, full on the mouth, then his kisses moved to her neck, to her shoulders.

Gently, very gently, Sam guided her into the other room and down on the bed.

"Okay?" he breathed.

"Yes, oh yes," Ellen answered, as his fingers made slow circles on her breasts. Her nipples were hard. He kissed her there, letting his tongue trace where his fingers had just outlined. He licked and kissed her skin, moving slowly down her belly, pushing aside and then carefully removing her underpants. Ellen's breath came in short gasps, as Sam moved down between her legs, positioning himself to give her the most pleasure. He circled gently with his tongue, lightly, now fast, now slower and more tantalizing.

"You *like* this?" Ellen managed to gasp in astonishment.

He looked up at her, smiling. "Oh, yes," he mumbled, and resumed his gentle touch, now bringing her to the edge of delight, then softly holding back, so she had a chance to breathe.

How does he seem to know exactly what I need to feel? Ellen wondered, but only for a moment. Suddenly, she couldn't hold back. She felt the circles, closer and closer, now building like a force inside her she didn't know was there, a strength she didn't know was hers. She opened her eyes for a second and saw dear Sam, giving her so much pleasure.

She was trembling all over, shaky and hot. Sam slid up next to her, and covered her all over with his body. "There, yes, dear, my dear Elly. That's it, come for me, come for me, come…"

"AAAHHH!" she screamed. "Oh my God! Oh my God!"

All the tension melted out of her and away. She breathed and breathed again – full, deep exhalations. "Oh, God," she moaned. "Was that it?"

"Yes, I surely do think so, Miss Elly May. Again?" And before she could reply, Sam slid right back down. This time, when she came, Ellen grabbed the pillow and held it over her face. She didn't want to wake the neighbors, she said, right after she'd caught her breath.

"Screw the neighbors," he said. "You are so gorgeous, girl."

"Um, wow. Thank you?"

"Not at all," he grinned, "Wanna do it again?"

"Will I wear out?"

"Don't think so. Should we find out?"

"Um, yes, yes."

A few minutes later, Ellen said, "I want to make you happy too, Sam."

"Oh, believe me, you are."

"No, I mean…" she said.

"I know what you mean. This time's for you."

"I appreciate that, but it's not quite fair." She reached down to touch him, and he moaned loudly.

And it was precisely at that moment that Ellen remembered Nick, her sort-of-almost-fiancé, sweet, good-natured Nick, who was on the other side of the country, planning their future together. She thought of Nick and a lifetime of pleasant but probably ordinary sex. Not like this. This wasn't just making love with Sam. This was healing, healing a part of her she thought would always be damaged.

"Come here, you," she said, astonished at her lack of shyness. "I want you inside me."

"Is it safe?" he said.

"Let me get up for a minute." Ellen went into the bathroom, where, with shaking hands, she managed to get her diaphragm into place.

She hurried back to the bed, to find Sam lying on his back, looking out the window at the stars.

"Elly May, I don't want to complicate your life. Should we wait and see if this is a good idea?"

"I think it's a great idea." Ellen reached for him. "Right now, right here, Sam. This is you and me, and I definitely do want you."

"Then let's stop talking," Sam said, kissing her again. In what seemed like one smooth motion, he was naked. He pulled Ellen on top of him.

"What are you doing?" she asked.

"You'll get more pleasure this way," he said.

How does he know all this stuff? Ellen thought, but not for too long. She was sitting on top, riding him, her small breasts free and bouncing. Sam had one hand on her behind, holding her steady, the other hand was playing with her in a most sensitive place she hadn't even known was there until tonight.

"Oh, my God!" Ellen moaned, at the same time Sam yelled, "Here it comes!" She collapsed onto his chest and they lay together, sweaty and panting.

"Oh my, is it always like this?" Ellen asked, when she was finally able to speak.

"Some people just fit together well," he said with a smile.

Ellen snuggled into his chest.

"You're my sweetie, Elly May."

"Yes, I guess I sure am," Ellen said, and fell into a drowsy trance.

This was nothing like what she'd experienced with Nick. Sam was a skilled and enthusiastic lover, and he happily taught Ellen all sorts of things she didn't know she could feel. Ellen called in sick to the Coop, and she and Sam shared four magical days together.

Before she knew it, it was Sunday. This was the last time they'd be able to spend the night together, at least for now.

Sam was going back to Ohio, to tell his parents about Cuba, and that he wanted to do organizing work in the community after graduation instead of going on to business school.

Ellen, the girl who'd never planned a future with anyone, was now thinking of how wonderful it would be when Sam returned.

✵ **Sixteen** ✵

When she returned to the office on Monday, Nina heard Perry call to her from the back room.

"You had a visitor last week," Perry said as he came to her desk. He seemed pretty bummed that you weren't here, kiddo."

Nina arched one eyebrow. "He?"

"Panther brother. Name Dennis."

Nina kept cool. "Yes, he's the one I interviewed in July about the free health program. Did he say what he wanted?"

"No, but if I had to put money on it, I'd say he wanted you."

Nina shrugged. "Oh, doesn't everyone," she laughed, her voice steady and light.

"Yeah, he left his new phone number, in case you need to follow up with an article on the progress of the center opening."

When Nina got home that evening, Dennis was sitting on her front steps, chin resting in his hand, cap pulled over his eyes.

"Have you been waiting here for two weeks?" Nina tried to sound nonchalant.

"Nope," Dennis said, standing up to greet her. "Just got here half an hour ago. I was going to wait a little longer and then leave you a note.

To Sisterhood!

I figured you might be out of town when you didn't answer your phone all week."

"You've been calling me for a week?" Nina asked. "What's up? Wait, don't answer yet. I want to put my stuff down. Come on in." She held out her hand and Dennis took it as she led him into the apartment. She dumped her bag on the kitchen table, and gestured for him to take a seat in the living room.

"Explain to me why you're here," she said, handing him a beer. "Wait a minute, you *are* over twenty-one, aren't you?"

Dennis laughed. "I'm twenty-three. Lifelong resident of Boston, recent graduate of Northeastern, major in Political Science. Youngest of three brothers. My dad works for the MTA, and my mom works part-time in the children's room of the local branch of the library. You need to know anything else?" he said, a teasing challenge in his voice.

Nina grinned at him. "Sounds normal to me. But why are you here? Did you get dispensation or whatever from the Party to visit me?"

Dennis grew quiet. "No, they don't know I'm here."

"Well, then." Nina sat down on her new grey corduroy sofa.

"Nina," he said. "Look, I want us to be friends. Would that be okay?"

"Yes, I guess so," she said, suddenly unsure of her feelings for him.

Dennis started to talk, telling her about some of the recent events at national Party headquarters, and about his dream to organize the new health center. He used to want to be a doctor, he told her, but he wasn't sure he could make it in medical school, such a white-dominated, Establishment institution.

Nina listened sympathetically, while he went on and on. She was attracted to him, for sure, but mostly she admired his work and commitment. Usually, she didn't give a damn what people thought of her. But Dennis…well, she wanted him to think she was cool. She wanted to be "good enough" – at least politically – in his eyes.

Dennis turned to her. "I guess I've been talking a lot," he said somewhat apologetically. "It's that you're really easy to talk to, Nina."

She smiled.

"I'd really like to get to know you better," he continued. "What you want to do with your life, what you hope for, all that."

"It's getting late," Nina yawned, and got up to stretch. "I don't mind telling you that it's been interesting talking with you."

"If you can call a monologue interesting," Dennis said. "Can I come back? Next time, I'll listen."

"Sure," she said, and reached out a hand.

He took it in both of his, looked deeply into her eyes, and said, "Yeah, don't worry. I'll be back," as he headed to the door.

※ ※ ※ ※

To Sisterhood!

Every time she thought about Sam, Ellen was amazed at how much pleasure she'd experienced. Her body, always a source of difficulty and stress, had opened in ways she could not have imagined. *Healing*, she thought again.

You've gotten yourself into a mess. She'd agreed to wait for Sam, even though Nick was still hoping she'd give up her plans and join him in San Francisco. But Ellen was not the kind of girl who could be with two men at once. Right before they'd said goodbye, she told Sam she couldn't sleep with him again until she'd broken it off with Nick.

"I get it," he said. "Take your time. We have all the time in the world."

So Ellen was faced with saying goodbye to Nick, who'd been nothing but good to her, via long-distance telephone, or worse, by a letter.

When Diane flew home a couple of days later, she was full of excitement about her trip and singing Nick's praises, as well as his mother's. She sensed that something had happened to Ellen. But Ellen wasn't talking.

Ellen didn't want to burden Diane, who seemed to be doing much better. It wasn't fair to keep Nick dangling. She put in for a station-to-station call, and waited two hours for the long-distance operator to call her back with a connection.

Nick answered the phone with a tentative, "Hello?"

"Hello, Nick," she began, and took a breath, ready to plunge in.

"Ellen, I am *so* glad to hear your voice, honey. I have some bad news."

"Are you okay?" He didn't sound right.

"Ellen, the Colonel had a heart attack early this morning. I just got off the phone with my mother. She'd been trying to reach me all day, but I've been over at the school at a faculty meeting. They took him to the local hospital, but I think they're going to transfer him down to UC Medical Center when he's more stable. They don't know yet. They're not even sure he's going to make it. My mother is beside herself. I'm going over there now. I was going to call you from the waiting room, but I knew that you knew somehow. Oh, Ellen, this is hard! I wish you were with me now. I love you, Ellen." Nick choked back a sob.

Ellen thought, *Oh, geez*, but she said, "I'm here, Nick. You can talk to me. Is there anything I can do? Anyone I can call for you?"

"Can you come out here to be with me?"

"Um, I can't miss my last two days of work. I'm leaving for home Monday – school starts next Tuesday. But you can call me tomorrow night, and we can talk it all through. And please tell your mother that my good wishes and prayers are with her, and your father, of course."

"Thanks, Ellen. I don't know what I'd do without you in my life."

"Talk to you later, Nick."

"Goodbye, dear," he said, and hung up.

That didn't go as planned, Ellen thought. *Poor Nick.* Still, Sam wasn't coming back until the beginning of January. She had time. She hadn't heard from him, except for one brief call right after he arrived in Ohio.

He'd told her he'd try to call once he got to Mexico, and left her the contact number in Mexico City where he'd be crashing with the Cuba trip organizers, but she knew not to bother him there. He'd call or write when he could.

Nick called the next night to say his father was still in critical condition, and said, "Please let's talk about anything else."

Ellen chatted about work, and Nick told her that he'd found a comfortable room in a shared house near a park and a bus line that would take him straight to work.

Ellen asked about the status of his CO application.

"I haven't heard anything yet. But that's not unusual. They have to call me in for an interview before they make a decision, so I guess no news is good news."

"Fingers crossed," Ellen said.

The next afternoon, as Ellen was packing, she got a call from Laurie, who'd returned from Wellfleet. Laurie suggested they get together for dinner.

"I have so much to tell you!" she chirped. Her enthusiasm made Ellen smile.

"Find Diane and Nina and meet me at Young and Yee at 7:00 pm, okay? I want them to hear all about my adventure too."

"Okay," Ellen said. She wasn't even sure if Nina was back yet from New York, but when she phoned her, Nina answered. She said she'd join them, and would be happy to see Diane.

Laurie was already waiting for the others when they arrived a few minutes before 7:00 pm.

Laurie turned first to Diane. "How're you doing, babe? Did you go back to work yet? It must be so hard for you –"

Diane cut her off. "I'm okay. I got home a few days ago. No, I'm still on leave, but I've gotta start earning a paycheck again soon. I'd like to do something different; I don't know what yet."

Diane said she'd felt good while she was driving cross country with Nick – he was such a terrific guy, Ellen was lucky – but that as soon as she went back to her parents' house, the huge shock and sadness of her sister's death hit her again hard. She needed to get her own place; she couldn't keep staying at her friend's, but now she didn't have enough money saved up.

Laurie nodded. "I wish I could help..." she began, as the waiter brought over the menus and they all took a minute to decide. "If you need a loan or something, say the word."

Diane nodded her thanks.

"I appreciate you coming to meet me," Laurie continued, "especially you, Ellen, what with your trip home tomorrow and all. I promise it won't be long. But after what happened recently, I feel like everything has changed."

To Sisterhood!

"What happened?" Ellen asked.

"More to the point," Nina said dryly, "who did you meet?"

"That's the good part!" Laurie squirmed with excitement. "I know, I know, you all think it's a guy, but it wasn't. I mean, she isn't."

"You met a woman?" Nina raised one eyebrow.

"No, not like that," Laurie continued. "If you'd all keep still for a minute, I'll tell you."

"What's that smell?" Ellen wrinkled her nose. "Who's wearing new perfume?"

Nina sniffed the inside of her wrist. "Estée," she said, holding her wrist under Ellen's nose.

"No, that's not it," Ellen shook her head. "This is kind of…stinky."

"Oh," laughed Laurie, "you're probably smelling my patchouli oil. Now if you'll all please shut up and let me talk –"

"As if we could stop you," Nina teased, as the waiter brought several large platters of food, and everyone dug in.

After finishing everything on her plate, Laurie put down her chopsticks and looked at her friends.

"So listen. I went into town and I went over to see Ginger at the Playhouse – remember, you all met her on your birthday, Nina – but she was too busy working to hang out and she told me to go see a woman who's from New Orleans who does readings in a storefront in the West End. I went into her shop, and she'd done it all up to look like something on Bourbon Street, like a voodoo shop – I mean it, it was the real deal – with candles and dolls and skulls, and all kinds of charms and books about spells and stuff."

"Yeah," said Nina, "sounds like a real deal tourist trap."

"You can laugh if you want," Laurie replied. "But she was this lovely old lady, with the softest hands and the kindest smile. Her name is Desirée, and she said that she'd tell me my future. I went into the back room, and she gave me a mug of tea. Then she looked into my eyes, and she took my hands in hers, and she told me that I was destined to be a healer. She said she didn't know how that would manifest, that I had to find my own path to healing, but that I had the gift and that's what I should do with my life."

Ellen listened intently. "Did she tell you where to start looking?"

"No, you see that's the thing," Laurie explained. "She didn't. She said that the world is in great need of healing, and this was my purpose, and that anything I did would be good. She gave me a prayer and told me to say it every morning, first thing, when I get up. It didn't sound like voodoo to me, but I have been following her advice, and I –"

"Wait a minute." Nina the reporter wanted facts. "Can you tell us what this so-called prayer is? Can you do that or will it break the spell?"

"Don't laugh at me." Laurie looked at Nina. "Just because you all can't see it doesn't mean it isn't real. Please let me finish, will you?"

To Sisterhood!

Nina sat back in her chair and kept quiet. Diane signaled the waiter for another pot of tea. She needed a drink, and she couldn't wait to get over to Patty's, where she knew a party would be going on, especially if Jimmy and his friends were there. Laurie continued.

"Every morning, when I get up, I say this: 'I am a healer. Everything I do or say brings me or someone else closer to harmony.'"

"That's it?" Nina sounded even more skeptical than before. "Just say 'I'm a healer?'"

"I'm not done." Laurie looked miffed. "Will you *please* let me finish, Nina?"

Ellen turned to Nina. "I understand what Laurie means. Even our political work can be construed as healing, if you use that definition."

"Exactly." Laurie flashed Ellen a grateful look. "As soon as I walked out of the shop, everything around me seemed to be different. I mean, I could see that I shouldn't step on an ant on the sidewalk because that would not be a healing thing to do. I smiled at a baby in a carriage, and he gave me a great big toothless grin. Maybe that was healing. And yes, Ellen, I can see that being in a demonstration against the war, even if it's only holding up a sign, that's good too."

"By that definition, what isn't healing?" asked Diane. *Unless you're murdering someone*, she thought. She'd finished her tea and now sat tapping her fingers one by one on the sticky table.

"I'm still trying to figure that out," Laurie said. "But I feel like ever since I met Desirée, I'm more – *aware*, I guess you'd call it. Of everything. Of how everything is all connected. Of how even a bee on a flower is part of the same universe I live in."

"Are you sure she didn't put any mushrooms in that tea?" Nina snorted. "Sounds like a peyote trip to me."

"You can laugh," Laurie shot back. "But I feel it, Nina, I do. I know what she meant and everything's changed for me. I *am* going back to school next week, but why should I stay? What's the point of learning about literature by dead white men? There's a whole world to heal!"

"Laurie," Ellen said gently. "I can see that you feel you have a direction, and Lord knows, we all could use one. But remember what we talked about before? Don't leave school. That's how you better your life. Education is the one thing no one – no one – can take away from you, ever. And you're at what is arguably the finest university anywhere in the world. You don't know how lucky you are to be there. I'd swap places with you in an instant."

"I know I've been fortunate," Laurie said. "But there's much more to do outside the walls of academia." She spread her arms wide, nearly knocking into the waiter, who was approaching with the check.

Diane started to fidget in her seat. "I understand what you're saying, Laurie. But what good is healing if it can't take the pain away?"

"Maybe it can," Laurie said, reaching for her purse. She grabbed a few bills and threw them on the table. "Oh, you all sound like my mother! I'm just getting started on this new path, and I'd hoped that my new friends would support me. I guess I was too optimistic." She pushed her chair back from the table and got up.

To Sisterhood!

Ellen grabbed her hand. "Laurie, we care for you. Don't do anything precipitous, okay?" She stood up too. "I've got a bus to catch in the morning. Diane, ride home with me?"

"Well, I was going to go over to Patty's," Diane began.

"Before we all go," Laurie interrupted. "I wanted to tell you – especially you, Diane – that I saw a notice for Tae Kwon Do classes offered by the women who organized the conference. I'm planning to go, Diane, and I thought you could come with me? That might be a healing thing for both of us, do you think?"

"Thanks, Laurie," Diane said. "I'll think about it and get back to you. In the meantime, I've got some people to meet. G'night, all."

✡ **Seventeen** ✡

Having finally decided that her best option was to stay in school, Laurie started her sophomore year full of hope, and briefly toyed with switching to pre-med. But that would mean many more years of school and training. She'd be in her late twenties before her real life began.

She considered what Desirée had said, but with a full course load, she didn't have time to focus on much else. Laurie missed her parents more than she'd expected. They'd invited her to come for Rosh Hashanah – "it's on the weekend, after all" – but her biology class didn't get out until 3:00 pm Friday, and the holiday started at sundown that night.

When Friday afternoon rolled around, Laurie washed her hair, fixed it loose with a headband, put on her best dress and a pair of heels, and headed over to the new Hillel center on Bryant Street.

She walked in feeling shy, and was immediately greeted by a soft-spoken rabbi and a couple of students. They introduced her around, and as she headed into the main room, she recognized a few people from her classes. She immediately felt at home, even in this large group.

"The kitchen is too small to prepare dinner for a crowd this size," the rabbi explained, "so some of the Board members kindly cooked food at their homes and brought it in."

The rabbi made Sabbath and New Year blessings over the wine and the round challah with raisins, then everyone dipped apples into honey to help ensure a sweet new year.

To Sisterhood!

After the brief service and a lot of singing, a delicious dinner of roasted chicken, potato kugel, and green bean casserole was served. Laurie ate more than she'd intended.

The conversation was lively and noisy. Some of the graduate students were headed to Mississippi to help with relief efforts after the devastation left by the recent hurricane. There was mention of Paul Newman's new movie with Katherine Ross, due to be released soon. Mostly, there was pleasant chatter about classes, baseball, and the weather.

"What do you hope for the New Year?" Laurie was surprised to hear a familiar voice behind her. She turned to see Joel Mandel, a tall, handsome guy from her biology class.

"Hey, Joel, Happy New Year."

"L'shanah tova, and Shabbat Shalom to you, Laurie. Do you have a special intention for 5730?" he asked, naming the new Hebrew year.

"I haven't given it much thought. Mostly I've been wondering how to get my homework done, since the holiday lasts all weekend."

Joel laughed. "I know. It's going to be a long Sunday night. Would you like to come to services with me tomorrow morning? I haven't seen you here before. The rabbi is pretty good."

Laurie paused, then said, "Sure, why not?"

Joel beamed. "May I walk you back to your dorm?"

Laurie took his arm and thought, *Nice guy. My parents would like him.*

✼ ✼ ✼ ✼

Keeping herself busy with work, Nina had done as much as she could on the Black Panther story. The health center was still in the planning stages, at least until they raised more money.

One of the other *Old Mole* staff members was working on a story on the Venceremos Brigade, and Nina helped by interviewing a couple of the Boston folks who were headed to Mexico City in November. She'd flirted with the idea of going to Cuba herself, but decided that she wanted to stay here in Boston. Even though the city was small and quiet compared to Manhattan, Nina felt a sense of belonging here she hadn't experienced before. And there was her growing friendship – that's how they'd firmly agreed to leave it – with Dennis.

Dennis came by her apartment in the evenings when he could, which was not nearly often enough for Nina. They talked about politics, their plans for the future, what each one might be doing in five years, and what was going to happen after the Revolution. Nina was pleased to find that they shared a love of jazz, as well as some of the same rock groups.

Dennis was impressed that she'd seen so many live performances, and she promised to take him to New York sometime. The Who was scheduled to play at the Fillmore the third week of October and Dennis said he'd love to figure out a way to go, but it was doubtful. He didn't like having secrets from the other Party members.

Nina shrugged. While she was still attracted to Dennis, she did not like waiting. She wasn't one to sit home for a man, any man. She frequently went out to hear live music – sometimes by herself, sometimes with Diane – at one of the clubs in Kenmore Square, or at a local Inman

To Sisterhood!

Square bar. Nina liked her neighborhood, a mix of working-class folks, students, and those who, like her, were from someplace else.

※ ※ ※ ※

Ten days later, Nick called Ellen in tears to say his father had passed away. "It was peaceful at least," he said. "The funeral is Sunday."

Sad for Nick and feeling more than a little guilty, Ellen decided she could do one thing right. In the morning, she booked a student standby ticket to San Francisco for Saturday.

When Ellen's plane landed, Nick was waiting for her at the gate. They were quiet on the drive up to Petaluma. It was nearly 10:00 pm when they arrived at the Williams' house, and Ellen was so exhausted she went straight to bed.

When she woke the next morning, Nick was already up making coffee.

"The car is coming for us at 9:30 am. Can I get you anything?"

"Just some tea, and maybe some toast. Let me get it." Ellen got up and found the bread and butter. Anything to keep moving.

Ellen was surprised to see how many people showed up for the funeral. *That should bring some comfort to Nick and his mother.* Ellen guessed that Nick would mourn not only his father, but the fact that they never made peace, and how his father had died disappointed in his only son.

Mrs. Williams was so sweet. Even though she was grieving the loss of her husband of more than a quarter of a century, she made an effort to reach out to Ellen, her son's beloved.

"We're grateful you could come out here," she said. "I know it means so much to Nick. And his father was happy he found the right girl."

"Thank you, Mrs. Williams. And I'm sorry that we had to meet again under these sad circumstances."

Mrs. Williams hugged her. "Please call me Harriet. Or Mom, if you'd rather."

How can I break up with Nick right now? It would break this sweet lady's heart. Ellen smiled warmly and said, "Thank you, Harriet. I'm glad I can be of some comfort to you. Is there anything I can help with?"

"No, dear, we're all set. The kind folks from church are taking care of food and such. I'm just glad you're here," she repeated. Harriet dabbed at her eyes with a handkerchief edged with lace, Ellen noted. Like the ones her own mother and grandmother used at funerals, christenings, and weddings.

Nick came up beside them. "Hey, my two favorite ladies," he said, trying to project calm and cheerfulness he didn't feel. He put his arm around Ellen's waist and with his other hand, he stroked his mother's shoulder. "How are you holding up, Mom?"

"I'm okay, dear," she said quietly, "but I surely will be glad to get this day behind us."

What a nice family, Ellen thought. Her own family liked Nick. Her mother wasn't happy when she told them she was flying to the funeral, but when Ellen explained she would be staying at Mrs. Williams' home, and that she would be chaperoned, Ellen's mother said it was all right.

Not that I need her permission anymore. Not like her hovering and her strict rules did any good. And then she thought of Sam and again was flooded with guilt.

Ellen sat with Nick and his mother in the front pew. Several of the Colonel's friends and colleagues spoke, and Nick's uncle spoke on behalf of the family. After the service, the family filed out to the gravesite behind the church, where the Colonel was laid to rest. The military guard folded the American flag that had draped his coffin and presented it to his widow. Soon, it was all over, the guests greeted and thanked in the church hall, and the three were on their way back to the house.

Ellen and Nick spent the rest of the day looking at photo albums his mother brought out, taking a walk around the neighborhood, and sitting in the backyard, not saying much. No one felt like eating, but Harriet insisted they needed to "keep their strength up," and she reheated one of the many casseroles brought by kind neighbors.

After a fretful night's sleep and a quick shower, Ellen went downstairs early to find Nick and Harriet seated at the kitchen table reading the newspaper.

"Good morning, dear," Nick said, rising from his chair. "Can I get you some tea? Toast?"

Harriet rose too, but Nick said, "You sit, Mom. I'll get this."

Ellen walked over and bent down to give Harriet a hug. She gave Ellen a brave smile.

"I guess it's going to take some time to get used to," she said. "I'm grateful he's out of pain. He wouldn't have wanted to linger like that."

"I'm sure," Ellen said. "And I'm sorry. I do wish I could stay here with you, Harriet, at least for a few more days. But I'm already missing school today and –"

"Of course, dear," Harriet said. "You know you're always welcome to come back."

Nick put down a mug of tea and a small spinach omelet with whole grain toast in front of Ellen.

"Don't want to rush you, but I don't know what the traffic will be like, so we need to get a move on." Ellen's flight was at 11:00 am. It would get into Boston in time for her to make the last connecting flight to Barre-Montpelier, if all ran smoothly.

Nick dropped Ellen off at the airport in plenty of time. She arrived at the gate, only to discover that her flight had been delayed, with no estimated time of departure.

"*It figures*," she thought. She called home collect and told her father that she'd miss her connection from Boston, and would call him with an update, and see him in the morning.

"Take good care of yourself, girl," her father said. "You've had a tough couple of days, I'm sure."

"Love you, Father," Ellen said.

To Sisterhood!

After a stroll around the terminal – with no update on her flight – Ellen passed a bank of phone booths. She still had the phone number in Mexico City Sam had given her. It'd been more than a month with no word. She didn't want to chase him, but she was getting concerned. She checked the time there, dug out the credit card her father had given her for emergencies, and placed the call. It wasn't long before the international operator called her back with an open line.

"I'm looking for Sam Green," Ellen said, when a man answered.

"Who?"

"Sam Green."

"Sorry, don't know him," and he passed the phone to someone else who didn't understand English. Finally, an angry-sounding guy picked up and told her that Sam "was here only for a few weeks before he split for Canada with some broad," and that no one had heard from them since. He hung up.

That couldn't be right. Just a short time and Sam went off with another girl? Ellen tried calling back, though it cost a fortune, and she wasn't sure how she was going to explain the charges to her father. This time she spoke with a woman who told her pretty much the same thing.

"They took most of our travel budget and were supposed to bring it to Montreal. But our contact there said they never showed up. They must've taken the money and split."

"Did anyone look for them? Call the authorities?"

The woman snorted. "Yeah, like the cops would help us find them. We're going around the law here to get to Havana, remember?"

Ellen had no idea what to do or say. She realized with shock that she didn't know Sam that well, or for that long. Did something bad happen to him? Should she try to contact his parents? Or maybe she'd completely misread what happened between them. Did she mean so little to Sam?

Confused, hurt, scared, and angry, Ellen decided there was nothing she could do, unless she heard from him. *Our whole time together was probably a big mistake.*

"Look," the woman said, "when you hear from him, tell him we're all looking for him and that chick. They took all the money for our airfare to Havana. We are seriously pissed at them and we can't leave here because he has all the bread. What an asshole!" She slammed down the phone.

Oh, Sam. And then, *Oh, Ellen, how could you have been this stupid?*

As she often did when she needed comfort, Ellen turned to Katharine Butler Hathaway. She pulled out her well-worn copy of *The Little Locksmith*, opened it to a page at random, and read: "*A person needs at intervals to separate himself from family and companions and go to new places. He must go without his familiars in order to be open to influences, to change.*"

Ellen closed her eyes. She definitely needed a change.

She must have dozed off, because the next thing she heard was the announcement that her flight had been cancelled, and that travelers should proceed to the gate to make alternate arrangements.

Apparently, she'd meant nothing more to Sam than a brief fling. Nick was sad and seemed to need her, and he obviously cared for her. Another semester at Ethan Allen State would be more of the same tedium. Her application to Radcliffe wasn't due until December, and she wouldn't hear from them until next spring.

Why not stay here?

California colleges didn't start until the end of September or even the first week of October, Ellen knew. If she moved fast, she could enroll at San Francisco State and pick up more credits. She could get references from her current teachers before they forgot all about her.

For the second time that summer – and just the second time in her life – Ellen did something totally impulsive. *Maybe this time will balance out the first.*

She went back to the phone booth and called Nick, who happily agreed to come pick her up. And then, with a great deal of apprehension, Ellen phoned her parents to tell them she was not coming home until Christmas. As she anticipated, they were not pleased.

"We expect better from you, Ellen," said her mother, and hung up.

The next morning, Ellen and Nick headed back to the city. Ellen phoned her grandmother, who agreed to pack up some of Ellen's clothes and books and ship them to her once she was settled.

"Don't worry, dear," she told a tearful Ellen. "Your parents will come around."

A few days later, after sending for her transcripts, Ellen enrolled as a transfer student at San Francisco State College. Things had calmed down on the campus, after the demonstrations of the previous year. Ellen heard all about it from the girl in the Admissions Office, who'd been assigned to give her a tour. Ellen was surprised to hear how the students had defied the administration and that President S. I. Hayakawa had taken a firm stance rather than let the students rule.

She was thrilled to see the Olympic-sized swimming pool at the Athletic Center. At least she could exercise again. Swimming made her feel free, and helped clear her head. And she needed a clear head. She had a lot to consider.

☼ Eighteen ☼

After nearly three months bereavement leave, and unable to find another job that suited her, Diane went back to work at the candy factory. She'd also moved in with Patty, who had a new two-bedroom apartment in Central Square, Cambridge, that she couldn't afford by herself. Patty was happy for the company, especially because Diane volunteered to do all the cooking. Most evenings, they hung out with a group from work at The Plough and Stars, a new bar already popular with neighborhood folks. Near the apartment, it was an easy walk home even when Diane drank too much, which was often.

While nights were for forgetting, during the days Diane was brokenhearted. The reality of what she'd done deeply distressed her, and she began to eat for comfort, putting on some extra pounds. She wore her grief like a shawl, which she pulled over her head when she wanted to keep everyone away. No one could talk to her, except about superficial things. She refused to discuss Theresa's death. She wouldn't return calls from her father. Her mother didn't even bother to call. Diane put on a pleasant smile to go to work, then came home, turned on the television, and grabbed a beer. Then she'd head over to the Plough with Patty, or alone.

Nina and her friends from *Old Mole* hung out at the Plough a couple of nights a week. Nina did her best to try to help Diane by inviting her to do things that didn't involve drinking. Diane usually said no, but she did go with Nina to the movies a couple of times. And sometimes Laurie stopped by on the nights she wasn't taking Tarot card reading lessons or going to Tae Kwon Do.

After a few pleasant dates with Joel, the guy from Hillel, who she dumped for being "too straight," though she didn't tell him that, and a brief flirtation with a young teaching assistant, Laurie was looking around again. She liked one of the regular musicians at the Plough. His name was Marvin, and he played guitar like Jeff Beck. But after going out with him a couple of times, though never on weekends, Laurie found out there was a Mrs. Marvin. *It figures*, she thought. *I always go for the wrong guys.*

Nina teased her about it. "If he's married, gay, weird, or likes to wear women's underwear, Laurie will find him," she said.

Diane spent most nights with her new group at the Plough, drinking and listening to music until closing time or they ran out of money. Then Diane would stumble home, fall into bed, and lie awake until the alarm rang a few hours later.

On the nights she was able to fall asleep, she had violent nightmares. After several weeks of restless sleep or none at all, she'd get up in the morning not knowing how or when she got home.

Diane was aware that she had to do something to help herself. But no doctors. She wasn't nuts. She was grieving. Finally, after much urging from Laurie, she agreed to go with her to the Tae Kwon Do lessons the women from the collective gave on Mondays, Wednesdays, and Thursdays in Harvard Square.

Diane walked into the first class scared and walked out an hour later feeling more confident. She started going to the lessons all three nights and found she liked the discipline, the way she could lose herself in the rhythm of the moves, and the feeling of control. She worked hard, and for the first time since Theresa died, she had a goal: to earn her yellow belt. She made herself practice every day. But she was still in pain. And she was still drinking.

※ ※ ※ ※

Nick's room was too small for the two of them, so Ellen checked the bulletin board in the Student Center and found several promising possibilities. On the 3rd of October, after putting down the first and last month's rent, they moved into a larger house near the college, which already had five people living there. Nick was overjoyed to have Ellen with him. He felt bad that their decision to live together had caused a serious rift with her parents, but she seemed to be at peace with it.

Nick's grief for his father was tempered by his enthusiasm for teaching. Ellen liked listening to him tell stories about the kids. She was drawn into the picture he painted of their lives: what they brought for lunch, how they played stick ball with entirely different rules than the ones he'd grown up with, how he could determine the social hierarchy among the girls by watching them jump rope. Ellen considered that she, too, might like to teach one day. But not 7th and 8th graders. Too much energy. They were like hormones on feet. Maybe older students.

Ellen and Nick did as many pick-up jobs as they could on the weekends. From the student employment board, Ellen found them work as helpers to a fancy caterer, putting parsley on canapés for rich folks up on Russian Hill. Her new housemates, Ed and Susan, who were on staff at Draft Help, got Ellen an internship as a draft counselor three mornings a week, helping young men find legal ways to avoid the service. It didn't pay much, but she could ride the bus to work with Nick. She signed up for classes that met in the afternoon: two sociology courses and statistics. She was so busy she barely had time to breathe.

And every night when he wasn't correcting papers, Nick was at the college at anti-war meetings. Even though he was no longer a student, his experience as an organizer back east was appreciated by the group. They listened to what he had to say – at least some of the time.

They were working on planning actions in San Francisco for the first Moratorium Against the War on October 15th. Part of a national anti-Vietnam War protest, a war that was never declared by Congress, thus violating the Constitution, the Moratorium was going to manifest in different ways all over the country. Local marches and rallies, workers calling in "sick of war" and staying home, silent vigils by Mothers for Peace, sit-ins at draft boards, and closures of schools and colleges, all to show Nixon that he could not continue this illegal war.

Nick was preoccupied, and didn't notice that Ellen's body seemed to be changing. But she did. She wondered if she'd gained weight. She didn't feel different, except her breasts seemed to have swelled some.

Ellen counted back. She realized with alarm that she never got her period last month. The last one was – when? Back in August, not too long before Nick left for California. It had crossed her mind that her period might be late, but she'd blamed the stress of moving, the tension between her and her parents, Sam deserting her, and even the unsettledness of having to wait so long to hear from Radcliffe. She'd never been all that regular. One more way she couldn't depend on her body. But here it was, nearly mid-October, time for her period after missing September's. She couldn't possibly be pregnant – could she?

To Sisterhood!

As Grandmother would say, "Before you try to solve a problem, first determine if there really *is* a problem." Ellen needed to find out.

The next day, after a discreet inquiry, Ellen learned from one of the women at Draft Help that there was a free clinic in the Haight. She decided to go on the day Nick – and everyone else she knew – would be at the Moratorium. Draft Help was going to close, at least for part of the day, while the whole staff went over to Oakland to sit-in at the Induction Center. It was a perfect time for Ellen to take the bus up to Clayton Street. If anyone asked, she could tell her work colleagues she was going to the demonstration with Nick, and she could tell Nick she was going to Oakland. No one would miss her.

On the morning of October 15th, the streets were jammed with protesters, both young and older, all concerned about the illegal war, the troop escalations, and the innocent women and children being blown up by the American military. Not that she didn't care about the war, she certainly did, but today, Ellen had only one thing on her mind.

She found the Free Clinic in a big Victorian house. The sign on the door pictured a dove, and read: "Please – NO Dealing, Holding, or Using." Ellen shuddered and walked in.

A soft-spoken woman not much older than Ellen took her name, then explained that she was one of the counselors. She led Ellen into an examination room, and asked her a few questions. Ellen twirled a bit of her hair as she struggled to recall the exact date of her last period in early August. All she could remember was that it was finished shortly before Nick left. She was embarrassed to realize that only a week later, she had been with Sam – right in the middle of her cycle.

She'd never been regular, she told the counselor, but she was pretty sure that if she were pregnant, she'd conceived around the 21st of August. She wondered aloud how she possibly could have become pregnant, because she was careful to use her diaphragm. The counselor asked if she'd used more spermicidal jelly every time they got it on. Ellen thought back to those four wonderful days with Sam, and she couldn't help smiling. But she stopped smiling when she realized she didn't replace the jelly every time.

"I guess I don't understand," Ellen said unhappily. "The directions said to wait six hours before removing the diaphragm, and, well, we didn't always wait six hours before we, um..."

The counselor nodded, knowingly. "The diaphragm is only about 90% effective. Accidents can happen, even when you think you're being careful. With the diaphragm, if you're really active, you can kind of push it out of place. And you need to insert more jelly, because after two hours, it loses its effectiveness. You don't have to take the diaphragm out, in fact, you're right, you need to leave it in for six hours. What you do is insert more jelly with that little plunger that comes with it."

"Ooooh," Ellen said, feeling stupid. "I didn't see any plunger."

"Then you probably bought a box that had just the jelly, not the whole kit." The counselor was kind. "A lot of women make that mistake, especially when they're starting to use the diaphragm. So, yes, it's possible that you are pregnant. Let's take a look and see what we can find out."

To Sisterhood!

A few minutes later, Ellen got dressed and joined the counselor in a sitting room with a rocking chair and posters on the wall, mostly of flowers and children with great big eyes.

The counselor told her that she could do a blood test, but between her bluish-looking cervix, and how her uterus felt when she palpated it, she was pretty sure that Ellen was almost two months pregnant. She started to talk about abortion, but Ellen immediately stopped her.

"No!" Ellen surprised herself with how loud her voice sounded. "I want this baby!" This baby was proof of her body's strength and how much healing she'd experienced making love with Sam, but she didn't say that. *And it might be the only part of Sam I get to keep.*

The counselor smiled. "We don't hear too much of that. Especially when the woman isn't married. Good luck to you. Let's talk instead about due dates and prenatal care, all right?"

By the counselor's best estimate, Ellen's baby would be due on May 13th. She walked out of the clinic, with an instruction sheet of what to eat, what vitamins to take, and what to avoid. Across the street, a little girl, with sandy brown hair like Sam's, was roller skating down the hill in the warm sunshine. Ellen smiled and continued walking on Clayton, over to Haight. There, upstairs over a record shop, she saw a sign: "Psychic Readings."

Impulsively, she decided to go in. Maybe she'd have an experience like Laurie's. She surely could use some guidance right about now.

The woman who answered Ellen's tentative knock was not at all who she expected. Instead of a young hippie wearing tattered jeans and an embroidered peasant blouse, Ellen was greeted by a lovely older woman, in a pretty yellow sun dress. Her long, silver hair parted in the middle, was done up in the same braids that Ellen's grandmother did before arthritis knotted her hands. And like her grandmother's, Ellen saw in this woman's face the same patient lines that spoke of long life, silent suffering, and the wisdom of the joys and challenges of a woman's body and psyche.

"Sit down." She gestured to a tall, upholstered chair. The soothing, faint smell of rose incense permeated the room.

Her voice was clear and strong. Ellen was not afraid, though she had the same feeling at the back of her neck – a kind of tingling – that she got when Eddy spoke to her. She trusted this woman. This must have been what Laurie was talking about. *Wise women have a lot to offer.*

The psychic told her immediately that she sensed a new life, and that the man she was with would be a wonderful father. She didn't say "your husband" or "your old man," Ellen noted. She said, "the man you are with."

Ellen tried to ask her a question, but the woman put a gentle, restraining hand on Ellen's arm. She closed her eyes briefly, then opened them and looked straight into Ellen's.

"Your baby will be born healthy, a girl – and she will be a blessing to you always. Take good care of yourself, of your health, my dear. You are stronger than you could have imagined. You are going to be the mother of many – perhaps not on this plane, but in another. Maybe a teacher, yes, that's it." She paused for a few moments, and was quiet

To Sisterhood!

for so long that Ellen wondered if the reading was over. Finally, the woman continued:

"It is important that you be honest and straightforward with your man," she said. "Doing otherwise will cause you great pain. He loves you and he will always be good to you and to your baby. That's all I can see." She paused for a sip of tea. "But it is enough."

She sat back, breathed deeply, and smiled.

"Your freewill offering of five dollars or more will help to support the work we do here."

Ellen dug into her wallet and handed the woman a bill.

"I understand and I – well, thank you."

"Blessings to you and to your daughter, my dear."

Ellen walked out into the bright sunlight. She felt dizzy and realized she hadn't eaten since breakfast. She found a luncheonette on the next block. She took a booth, and ordered a bowl of vegetable soup. What an eventful day this had turned out to be! Pregnant!

She thought about what the psychic had said about being honest. She took her words as a sign that she should tell Nick about Sam, and that she was pregnant with Sam's baby. If he couldn't handle the truth, and she had every reason to expect he'd be angry and hurt, then she would leave him and – she'd figure out a plan. She had all the way until May. Nick absolutely deserved to know the truth, even if it was painful. One thing she knew for sure was that she would *not* see Sam again. If he was irresponsible enough not to call her after what they had – or what she thought they had – together, she surely wasn't going to tell him that he had a child on the way. Lord only knows how he might react.

As she walked toward the Market Street bus, the whole street seemed to be filled with dazzling pregnant women and small children. An attractive Black woman wearing a colorful caftan caught Ellen looking at her round belly and smiled at her over the heads of the two adorable toddlers she held by their hands. She looked at Ellen, then at her flat belly, then back at Ellen.

"Just got the news, is that right?"

Ellen was surprised. "How…" she began. "How could you tell?"

The woman threw back her head and laughed loudly.

"Oh, honey, when you're having your fourth, you know these things! You're gonna be fine, sister. God bless you."

"Thank you so much," Ellen replied, as the woman walked slowly up the street, holding her children's hands and swaying gracefully.

She called me sister. I'm going to be part of the sisterhood of mothers.

"Thank you so much," Ellen repeated in a whisper, standing in the sun with both hands on her belly, as tears rolled down her cheeks. *Hey, Sis,* Eddy echoed, *you're gonna be fine.*

⌘ **Nineteen** ⌘

Nick came home from the Moratorium Wednesday evening all fired up about the Movement.

"You should have been with us!" he told Ellen. "There were so many people in the streets. We *are* going to stop Nixon's evil war!" He was practically shouting at her as he paced energetically around the room.

"And we have to see the news tonight. People *everywhere* stayed home from work in protest – there were demonstrations all over the country. And next month – a month from today, in fact, on November 15th, there's going to be a huge demonstration in DC, organized by the Vietnam Moratorium Committee. And they're even talking about having two demonstrations that day, one right here in the city."

Ellen smiled at his fervor. She waited patiently for him to finish. Finally, he noticed.

"How did you do today, honey?" he asked. "Did you close down the Induction Center?"

"Oh, everything was fine," she said, getting up. "But I'm awfully tired. I'll tell you all about it later. Now, what would you like for dinner – spaghetti with tomato sauce, or spaghetti with garlic and butter sauce?"

She grinned at their daily joke. They were almost always broke. Nick's salary covered their share of the rent and utilities, and an occasional ice cream cone at Baskin-Robbins, but not too much else. To economize, Ellen alternated spaghetti nights with brown-rice-and-bean nights.

Not only was she getting bored with this diet, she now realized she was going to have to figure out a more nutritious meal than spaghetti, so she and the baby could be healthy and strong. She'd deal with that later this week. She drank some orange juice and wondered how they'd afford the vitamins the clinician suggested she take.

On Friday, Nick returned from work with some scary news. He didn't want to upset Ellen, but she'd hear it soon enough. It was in the paper today and would be on the news tonight.

"Um, Ellen?" he began. "You know that taxi driver, the student from State, who was killed last Saturday by that, that – the one who called himself Zodiac?"

"Oh, no! Did he strike again?" At least two murders had been linked to this guy already.

"No," Nick said, "but he claims his next target is going to be schoolchildren – that he's gonna shoot out the tires of a school bus and then shoot the kids as they leave the bus."

"Oh, my God!" Ellen put her hand to her mouth and slumped onto the sofa. Nick sat down and took her into his arms.

"The police were out in full force today," he said. "They escorted every single bus. Some of the kids got home hours late because we kept them inside until a patrol car was available. It was a mess."

"How long will this go on?" Ellen cried, resting her head on his shoulder. "I sure hope they catch this guy."

Fortunately, Zodiac did not strike out against children, and there was no news of him again in October. Nick still spent most evenings grading papers, or at teacher meetings, or attending Movement meetings in support of upcoming actions.

"You guys are working too hard," roommate Nancy announced late on November 1st. "Guess what? I scored some organic mescaline. Come on, it's Saturday. You all need a break from this organizing shit." She opened a bottle of diet root beer and downed a sparkly purple capsule.

"Hey, I'm in!" Phil delicately held a capsule between his thumb and index finger. "Here's to Nirvana!" he said, and swallowed it dry. He immediately began to gag, and Ellen rushed over to give him water.

Everyone but Ellen dropped the mescaline. She grabbed a cap and while no one was looking, opened it into the bathroom sink and ran the hot water until it dissolved. Nick knew she didn't do drugs. She could pretend with the others. It was easier than trying to explain it to them right now. Once they got off, no one would know the difference.

A few hours later, when everyone had gone to their rooms to experience their own particular form of bliss, Ellen and Nick lay on their bed, looking at the swirls in the ceiling paint. They talked softly about who they thought truly understood how the universe worked. Nick described how good this trip was, feeling the warmth of the radiant love of everyone they knew and everyone whose art tapped into this spiritual experience.

"The Beatles," Nick said. "They totally get it. Donovan, Phil Ochs, and Dylan, for sure…" He went on, with a long list of musicians, and their friends, and other public figures, both present and past, he'd include in that elite circle. Ellen sighed happily.

Nick hummed softly to himself. Suddenly, he sat up and pulled Ellen to him. They made love gently, and Ellen felt connected to Nick in a way that surprised and pleased her. She knew that Nick would be a much better father than Sam could ever be. For one thing, he was here.

※ ※ ※ ※

Ellen had been awake for hours. No one else was in the kitchen yet, and she started a soft dough for cinnamon rolls. While she waited for the dough to rise, she walked down to Albertson's. She bought beef cubes, carrots, potatoes, onions, and some milk, butter, and eggs, plus a half gallon of orange juice.

Starting dinner for tomorrow night, she spent the morning dredging the beef cubes in flour sprinkled with salt and pepper, then browning them in oil. She cut up the vegetables and added them to the pot with the beef. She covered the pot and looked at the wall clock. Noon. No one else had budged. *Must have been some strong stuff.*

After the second rising, Ellen kneaded the dough and rolled out flat rounds, which she spread with softened butter and chopped walnuts and cinnamon. Then she shaped the rolls, twisting them into place, and put them in the oven to bake.

Over the next hour, Nancy, Phil, and Margie dragged themselves into the kitchen, where the luscious smells welcomed them.

"Coffee," croaked Nancy. "Please."

To Sisterhood!

"Make that two." Phil took down the mugs.

Ellen grinned. She'd started the Peets brewing as soon as she'd heard the toilet flush and the shower running.

"Morning, all. Some trip, huh?" Margie rubbed her eyes with her fists and yawned. Nancy looked at Ellen. "What time did *you* get up?"

"Oh, I've been up for a while. I feel good." Ellen serenely brushed her floury hands on the kitchen towel she'd tucked into her jeans.

"You know," said Margie, "I think I'm done with this stuff for a while. It takes a lot out of you."

Nick came in and kissed Ellen's cheek. "Hey, babe."

"Hey yourself, sleepyhead."

Nick and Phil each took three rolls.

"Help yourself, everyone," said Ellen, a bit after the fact. "And hey, please be on time tomorrow night. It's my turn to do dinner. We're having beef stew at six, right before our house meeting. Nixon's giving a speech, remember?"

At dinner the next evening, they turned on the TV. President Nixon was talking about his decision to keep U.S. forces in Vietnam.

He attempted to explain why peace negotiations had failed so far.

"Bullshit," said Nick.

"Tricky Dick lies again," said Phil.

The front door slammed and Ed and Susan came in, looking weary.

"Sorry we're back late," Susan said. "We had two Navy kids jump ship. They're over at Henry's. We stayed there last night."

"Ellen, I told them you might be able to talk with them tomorrow," Ed added. "But I wanted to see how you felt about it first. They've got the Military Police looking for them. After 24 hours, they're AWOL."

Ellen nodded. "Send them over, sure. You'll have to help me, though. I don't know the procedure. I'd like to learn."

"Sshhh," Nancy said. "We'll talk about it after the speech."

"Did you eat?" Ellen asked. "There's some beef stew in –"

"SSHHH!" Nancy and Nick said in unison.

"And so tonight – to you, the great Silent Majority of my fellow Americans," the President said, looking sincere, "I ask for your support. I pledged in my campaign for the presidency to end the war in a way that we could win the peace. I have initiated a plan of action which will enable me to keep that pledge."

"Horse manure!" said Ed, as Nick said, "What a load of crap."

"Yup, a total load of BS," Nancy echoed.

To Sisterhood!

"Silent Majority, my ass," Margie mimicked. "More like the great mass of brain-dead middle Americans who wouldn't know an ARVN from an armpit."

"I think we should all be in Washington on the 15th." Ed was enthusiastic. "We're doing a lot of organizing. It should be the biggest demonstration ever!"

"Why should we go to Washington when there's gonna be a march here too?" Margie asked.

"Marching on the Capitol will be much more fun!" Ed liked to make things exciting. And figuring out how to find the money to get them all across the country sure would be a big project.

"Darn!" said Nick. "I've got to give exams that Monday. But I'll see what I can do. It would be good to go there. But if there's a demonstration here too, we probably should support it."

"I've got some money left from my waitress job this summer," Nancy said. "And my next paycheck should cover at least two of the airfares."

"Do you think Draft Help could help pay for me to go?" Ellen asked, but she was thinking: *Mass demonstration? Risk getting beat up – or worse? No way, not now.*

"We have got to talk about these two kids who jumped ship," Susan brought the discussion back to the immediate situation.

"Why did they split?" Margie was curious.

"Oh," said Susan wryly. "The ship is leaving tomorrow for Southeast Asia. Guess they didn't want to go."

At Draft Help the next day, Joey and Rick came in, having ditched their uniforms and looking like they'd walked out of a straight person's vision of life on the streets of the Haight. Torn bell bottoms, fringed suede vests over tee shirts. Joey wore a bandana, Rick, a beaded headband. They looked eagerly at Ellen, who'd had a quick training session earlier from the more experienced staff. She invited them to sit down and discuss how they might get landed immigrant status once they arrived in Canada.

"Joey, Rick. Now, your hair – that will grow. But for now, you have *got* to get some different footwear." They looked down at their Navy-issued shoes.

"Oh, man," Joey said.

"Oops," said Rick.

Ellen tried hard to hold back a laugh. It wasn't funny. She was aiding and abetting criminals. This wasn't like counseling boys to avoid the draft. She could be prosecuted. She had to give them some direction and get them out of here, fast.

"Look," she said, "this is serious. You are wanted men. The Navy is out looking for you now, and this is one of the first places they'll look. Let's talk quickly and get you on your way north."

They both nodded, giddy with their sudden freedom but understanding it could be taken from them in an instant if they weren't careful.

To Sisterhood!

"When you leave here, first go and get some sandals," Ellen said, looking at the checklist on her desk. "You have ten points for speaking English. Either of you know French?"

"Mais oui," Rick replied. "Je parle le Français un peu."

"Um, I think you have to be fluent. Let's try something else." Ellen walked them through the checklist that could enable them to stay and work in Canada. She knew that as deserters, they would have a more difficult time than the guys the American government called "draft dodgers."

Ellen called ahead to a safe house up north in Humboldt County, to let them know to expect two men AWOL from the Navy.

She gave the phone number of the safe house to Joey and Rick and told them to call when they arrived in Arcata. Someone would meet them at the bus and take them to the house. They would be given food and shelter, and an introduction to the next safe house in West Linn, Oregon. From there they would travel up to the Seattle area – Ellen couldn't tell them where, exactly, because she didn't know – and on into Vancouver.

There, the Vancouver Committee to Aid American War Objectors would help them find temporary housing, counsel them further on how to obtain landed immigrant status, and provide a safe haven to hang out with other Americans avoiding the draft or deserting service.

Joey and Rick thanked Ellen profusely, and after getting directions to the bus station on Market, they left Draft Help, flashing the peace sign.

Ellen shook her head. They were so young. She gave them about a one-in-five chance that they'd make it over the border without being captured and thrown in the brig.

Ellen was getting weary in the evenings now. When she got home, she found her housemates involved in a serious discussion about organizing for the demonstrations on November 15th. *Not another tedious house meeting.* She was still trying to figure out how to get out of going to the demonstration without revealing her pregnancy. For one thing, she couldn't count on finding an available rest room and it seemed she had to pee every twenty minutes. For another, she would not put herself in front of cops with billy clubs. Trina, a friend at work, got clubbed in the stomach during the last march when she was six months pregnant. The cops did it on purpose, Trina said, and thank God her baby was fine, or she would have sued their asses. At the end of the discussion, fortunately for Ellen, they all decided to stay home and focus on the demonstration here in San Francisco.

Pretty soon, Ellen was going to start showing. It was well past time to tell Nick. But each day she put it off, Ellen was less sure of what to say and how he might react, and what she would do if he got angry – furious even! – and kicked her out. He had every right to hate her. And she really didn't want him to.

Still, the psychic told her to be honest and straightforward. Nick deserved no less. She resolved to tell him tomorrow.

That night Ellen dreamed about Eddy. They were running together in the meadow at their grandparents' farm, and Eddy was holding her hand. He looked at her, and she heard him say, *Sis, something's coming and you have to do whatever it takes to care for yourself.*

To Sisterhood!

As it happened, in the next day's mail there was a package from Harriet. Ellen handed it to Nick when he got home that afternoon. He turned pale as he tore open one letter, then another.

"It's from the draft board," he said dejectedly. He read more. "Oh, sweet Jesus. It's Monday. This coming Monday! They want me to report for my induction physical at the Oakland induction center." He read the rest. He'd been reclassified as I-A.

"Those bastards turned down my application for CO status."

"How can that be?" asked Ellen, "You didn't even get a chance to appear in person."

"Yeah. Harvey is on the draft board – you know, my dad's golf buddy. Those guys can do pretty much anything they want. Harvey's pissed because I resigned my commission and probably thinks he'll be honoring the Colonel's memory by sending me to Vietnam. And they rushed it through! They did this right before the lottery starts next month, so I don't even get to take my chances with everyone else."

Ellen knew that once Nick showed up for his induction physical and passed it, which she had every reason to believe he would, he'd be on the bus. In the army. With no commission, just a private on his way to basic training then, likely, to Vietnam.

She would be completely on her own with her baby, with no one to help or support her, a job that didn't pay enough to live on, and an unfinished degree. She couldn't go home to her parents. Unmarried and pregnant? Unthinkable in King's Lake. No, she had to make up her mind right now. Surely Nick had a right to know the baby was not his. Still, even if he accepted her and forgave her, what would their life be like in the months ahead? Would he use the fact that she'd been unfaithful to him and throw it back at her every time he got angry with her? What would it be like for her child?

By the time they got ready for bed that night, Ellen had made her decision. She was sitting on the bed, smiling. Nick looked miserable.

"What's up?" he asked, his shoulders slumping.

"I think I know how you can get out of going."

"No way. They wouldn't even look at my CO application. I don't have time or money for a lawyer to appeal it. I don't have chronic bronchitis. I'm not color blind. I'm not gay. Nothing is going to work for me." He sagged down in the chair, looking as if he were about to cry.

"Oh, you'd be surprised." Ellen was smiling more broadly now. She was holding a copy of Tatum and Tuchinsky's *Guide to the Draft*, which she'd been using with great success as her bible at work. She'd found a lot of legal loopholes for a lot of men. She pointed to the place on the page she was reading:

III-A
Registrant with a child or children; registrant deferred by reason of extreme hardship to dependents.

Nick looked at the passage, not understanding. Then he looked up at Ellen's beaming face.

It took him a minute, but then he got it.

To Sisterhood!

"But, I mean, wow…you mean you're…we're gonna have a baby?" Nick sounded ecstatic. He picked Ellen up and hugged her gently.

Now he started to cry. He looked radiant, and Ellen could see that no matter what the cost, she'd made the right choice. Nick held her tenderly, and told her he loved her and that he would do everything possible to do right by her and their child.

Ellen knew her only job was to protect her child, and give her a good home and a loving father. And if her pregnancy meant that Nick could avoid the draft and support them, she'd keep her secret. Nick really loved her. That much was obvious, from his shining eyes.

The next morning, they went to get their marriage license. Nick called his mother to tell her the news, and Harriet, with a new hairdo, met them at City Hall the next day. They decided not to call Ellen's parents until later that afternoon. Ellen wore a pink pantsuit that was a little tight in the waist. She held a nosegay of sweetheart roses Nick bought from the neighborhood florist.

Nick took Ellen's hand as the City Clerk had them repeat the standard marriage vows and sign the certificate. As the Clerk said, "I now pronounce you man and wife," Nick leaned over to kiss his bride. He promised to take good care of her and their baby. Harriet wiped away tears. Ellen teared up too as Nick said, "I love you so much," but Ellen's tears were not for him.

✳ Twenty ✳

One month after covering the October 15th Moratorium in Boston, at which both Senators George McGovern and Ted Kennedy spoke, and which had the largest turnout of any city in the national protest – more than 100,000, even by the conservative estimate of the straight press – Nina headed to Washington.

The demonstration on November 15th was mostly peaceful. Tens of thousands of protesters marched in silence up Pennsylvania Avenue to the White House. There, each called out the name of a soldier killed in the war. Nina saw not only students, but many her dad's age and even older, who looked like ordinary working folks, making their opposition to the war known.

Late in the day, over at Dupont Circle, a skirmish broke out. It seemed to be some kind of Yippie action, and the police responded by tear gassing the entire crowd. Nina saw people run from the gas, coughing, their eyes streaming with tears. She was far enough away so that she wasn't hurt, but her eyes were stinging.

As she walked quickly back to her hotel, away from the chaos, she hummed the new John Lennon song that Pete Seeger had led the crowd in singing that morning at the main rally.

I wonder if we really can give peace a chance, Nina thought. *Not much of a chance, as long as Tricky Dick was still in office.*

As she headed back to Cambridge on the train the next day, Nina wrote her story. Recently, she'd spent most of her time focused on her work, and on learning about the historical roots of the Black struggle, so she could better understand what Dennis was doing. She hadn't seen him often. He seemed to be involved in some sort of power struggle at the Party. *Oh, well.* She had other things to do.

※ ※ ※ ※

Feeling healthy and strong, Ellen started thinking a lot more about the future. Her favorite course was "The Sociology of Women and the Family," which, along with another social theory course and statistics, stimulated and challenged her. Ellen decided that when she got into Radcliffe, she'd declare as a sociology major.

Gina, a young graduate student who was teaching the Women and Family class, made it lively and fun. She told her students, all but one of whom were female, that she was active in something called the Women's Caucus of the American Sociological Association, which had met in September in San Francisco. The Women's Caucus, Gina explained, was concerned with promoting the careers of women in the field. With one or two exceptions, women who were hired as faculty were given positions as lecturers, part-timers, and assistant professors, most without a tenure track. While most sociology programs were actively recruiting Black men for their departments, these women, being neither male nor Black, faced a double whammy.

Mid-November brought a slight chill to the San Francisco air. Ellen was homesick for the changing seasons. Although she enjoyed the misty mornings, she missed the gorgeous autumn leaves. She tried to visualize the large maple outside her bedroom window. She closed her eyes and saw that flaming red tree, even which section had changed color first.

She missed her parents and wished they could understand her life. Dutifully, she wrote them a letter each week, but so far all she'd received in return was a crayon drawing from her little brother Ronald and a check from her grandmother with a note that urged Ellen to "give them time" to accept her choice. Now that she was married, her grandmother said, they were beginning to soften.

Ellen was still lost in her autumn-in-Vermont reverie, when she heard the front door slam.

"Did you hear what happened today at Alcatraz?" Margie took off her poncho and tossed it on the floor.

"Um, the Birdman escaped?" Ellen adjusted her glasses and poured Margie a cup of peppermint tea from the pot she'd just made.

"I am ignoring your pathetic attempt at humor." Margie was practically hopping with excitement. "No, the Indians took it over!"

"What!" Ellen put the teapot back on the counter and sat down.

"Indian activists – not only students, but families with children, even, are reclaiming Alcatraz as Indian land. They have a list of demands, including respect for the Indian people. They're protesting the government's neglect."

Ellen listened thoughtfully.

"I've read some about the Indian struggles," she said. "I know that the United States has repeatedly failed to honor treaties and hasn't allowed

To Sisterhood!

the tribes to govern themselves as agreed." "And there are more than 550 American Indian nations in the country, if I remember correctly."

"All power to the Indians!" Margie gave the Black Power fist-in-the-air salute. "I wonder if it's on the news yet." She went over and turned on the TV, but all she could find were soap operas.

Ellen exhaled. "What is it?" asked Margie. "Do you feel all right?"

"It's nothing. Hearing about the Indian struggle reminds me a lot of my friends back home. You all are great, but sometimes, I miss them."

"Why don't you call them?"

"I would but it's so expensive. I did call them all to tell them about the wedding and the baby, but Nick and I don't have much money and –"

Margie cut her off. "Are you kidding me? You mean to tell me that you pay for telephone calls? Don't you know how to make a free credit card call?"

As Ellen shook her head, Margie explained. "OK, I'll lay it out for you, but you have to promise never to call from this line, because if anything goes wrong, they can trace it, and it's my name on the bill. Give me a minute while I go dig up the letter from my cousin. You go get a pencil."

"All right," Margie said when they were both back at the table. "My cousin Carl – he's a student at MIT – sent me instructions. He calls me all the time. Okay, from the top."

"A credit card number is composed of the person's phone number, plus a three-digit city code (not the same as the area code), plus a code letter corresponding to the sixth digit of the whole deal. So, if my phone number is 782-7431, my credit card number would be 782-7431-001-E. The 001 is the city code for Boston and the E corresponds to the number 3, which is the sixth digit. Call the operator and say, 'Operator, this is a credit card call. My number is 782-7431-001-E, and the number I'm calling is 415-555-5555.' Speak slowly, distinctly, and with confidence. The first time can be scary, but after a while, you'll never pay for a call again."

"Slow down a minute, will you?" Ellen said. "I can't write this fast!"

Margie chuckled and continued to give Ellen explicit instructions on how to circumvent the phone company, including a warning to always call from a pay phone and, obviously, never call person-to-person.

Both women were laughing as Margie put down the letter.

"Now you should send a note to all your friends back home and tell them you're gonna call soon. Make sure to let them know that if the phone company calls them later to trace your call not to let on that they know anyone in San Francisco, or they gotcha, babe."

※ ※ ※ ※

Diane was still on the phone with Ellen when Patty knocked on her bedroom door.

"Diane, look, I need some help," Patty pleaded. "Jimmy's here, he's real sick, and I can't miss another work shift. Can you take care of him, please, just for tonight?"

Diane nodded and held up one finger, gesturing to the phone. "Ellen, I have to go now. But let's talk again soon. Or write. Or something. I miss you. And say 'hi' to Nick for me."

Diane was glad to have something useful to do, happy that someone needed her. She walked into Patty's room, where Jimmy was lying on the bed under a pile of blankets.

"Hey, Jimmy." She smiled at him. He was sweating and shaking.

"Hey, Diane. I'm really cold, man. Can you get me another blanket?"

Diane didn't see how he could be cold with the heat turned up high and all those blankets, but she got the quilt from her own bed. Then she went to the kitchen and heated up some tomato soup. He sat up and took a few sips, then fell back onto the bed.

"What is it?" she asked gently. "A virus or something?" His head didn't feel warm, and he was shivering.

"I dunno."

"Can you try to sleep?" Diane spoke softly. "I can stay right here if you want me to. You should probably try to drink something though."

"Got any beer?" Jimmy asked.

She brought him a large glass of ice water and his hands shook as he tried to drink it. She tucked the blankets around him and touched his brow again. She thought of Theresa, shivering and burning up with fever, and had to will herself to stop remembering.

"Shush now, sleep," Diane told him.

The next day, when Jimmy got up, he looked better. Patty was grateful.

"Can you give him something to eat, Diane, before you leave for work? I've got to do a double shift today." It was Christmas Eve, and Diane was glad she didn't have to spend it with her parents. Without Theresa.

After Patty left for work, Diane was surprised that Jimmy wanted to talk. Usually, he joked around, and she couldn't remember the two of them ever having a serious conversation. He told her that recently, he got a full scholarship to Brandeis. His high school guidance counselor put him up for it and didn't tell him until it was time to write a personal essay.

"I guess it worked," he said dryly. He would start a special college prep course next month, then do some remedial work in the summer term, and start as a freshman in the fall.

"No kidding, wow, Jimmy, that's fantastic!" Diane enthused. She hadn't known Jimmy was that bright, but then, all she'd ever seen him do was hang out with his buddies, partying and carrying on.

"I guess they figure they'd bring in a poor kid from East Cambridge along with all those rich kids."

"I've heard it's a good school. What are you gonna major in?"

"Politics, I guess. When I finish, I can come back here and help with community organizing. Maybe run for City Council. Maybe even go to Washington someday!" *He looked happy*, Diane realized. *That's what having a dream can do for someone.*

To Sisterhood!

"Sounds good to me." Diane squeezed Jimmy's hand. "Let's get you comfortable and then you can go back to bed and sleep some more."

As Diane got ready for her last shift before the factory closed for a week, she heard some young carolers warming up. It was going to be a long week. Patty and Jimmy were going home to their folks. Laurie was skiing with her family somewhere up north. Ellen and Nick had asked her to meet them in Vermont – an invitation she'd declined – where Ellen's parents, who'd finally come around, were hosting a delayed wedding reception. And Nina, well, who knew where Nina was these days?

Diane was alone. She had a large bottle of vodka, and Patty's cat for company. She'd be fine.

She got through the holidays in a haze. She didn't even go outside until the day after Christmas. A light snow had fallen, the kind that melted as soon as the sun shone. Diane walked to Harvard Square. She put a quarter in the Salvation Army kettle, and gave a dollar to the disheveled-looking mother and kids sitting on the sidewalk outside the Coop.

Diane was grateful. She'd made it through her first Christmas without Theresa. For the first time in her life, she did not go to Midnight Mass, and she didn't decorate the big tree, though she and Patty had a little potted tree on their coffee table. She didn't shop, open gifts, or sing "O Holy Night" with her sister by her side. But she'd survived. Things would be okay. Sort of.

She went back to work after the first of the year, determined to stay focused on doing a good job, earning money, and putting it away so she could get her own place eventually. She went back to her Tae Kwon Do lessons three nights a week, getting stronger every day. She passed the test for her yellow belt, happy and proud, and starting to feel good, for the first time in months.

※ ※ ※ ※

Ellen was back in San Francisco, after the brief Christmas visit home, which went surprisingly well. She'd signed up for five courses this term, so she'd be on track to finish her sophomore year on time. Finals were scheduled for the same week as her due date. She'd already spoken to her professors about the possibility of an extension for final papers and exams if necessary. All but her Statistics II professor – who Ellen thought was a jerk – had already given their okay.

Nick was talking about going back for a master's degree in education, once Ellen finished school. Ellen was counting the days until she heard from Radcliffe. Letters of acceptance to transfer students were due to go out on April 15th, not too much longer now.

She wasn't exactly sure how she'd be able to juggle a baby and two more years of coursework, especially with Nick working full-time. And then, of course, she'd have to convince Nick to move back east. She'd figure it out. *How hard can it be to take care of one tiny baby?*

※ ※ ※ ※

Late one afternoon in mid-February, Patty ran up the stairs and burst into the apartment.

"That fucking Jimmy Palmer..." she gasped. Tears choked her.

"What is it honey?" Diane said, jumping up and putting her arms around Patty. "What did he do to you? Are you okay?"

To Sisterhood!

"No, I am not fucking okay. He didn't do anything to me. That fucking Jimmy Palmer – he's dead!"

"*What!?*" Diane held Patty tightly then helped her into the nearest chair. She ran to get a glass of water and handed it to her friend.

"He's dead, man. Just when it was turning around for him, for us."

"Oh, honey, what happened to him?" Diane stroked Patty's hair.

"Those junkie friends of his. Those pigs. He went to say goodbye. He got an apartment near Brandeis and a job, and he was moving out this weekend. Those scumbags probably couldn't stand it – here he was, clean for weeks now, I'll bet they were jealous. And you know what they did? Those fucking junkies stole his bicycle."

"I'm not following you…" *Junkies? Clean?* Diane thought back to the week before Christmas. *How stupid of me. I thought he was sick. He must have been kicking. Oh, shit.*

"He went to say goodbye and they probably said, 'Oh, come on man, once more for old time's sake.' Then he shot up. It must've been some pretty strong stuff. They found him dead in the bathtub. Overdosed. And then they stole his bicycle and left him there."

Patty's brother Will suddenly appeared at their door. "Oh baby, I'm sorry, I just heard." He held her and she sobbed against his shoulder.

"I'll stay with her," Will said. "Diane, can you go over to my house and get my brother and sister? They're probably home by now…"

Diane ran all the way down to the river, where Patty's family lived.

She banged on the door, and Patty's older brother opened it right away.

"Jimmy," she panted. "Palmer. Dead. OD. Last night." Patty's brother ran all the way back with her – a mile and a half – at top speed. Together they all tried to comfort Patty.

Later that week at the funeral, Diane kept looking around to see which of Jimmy's sleazy, junkie friends had the guts to show up. Jimmy looked handsome in his dark blue suit, with almost a smile on his face.

You are too gentle a soul for this world, mused Diane, and then, *Oh, God, how corny.* Still, her tears were genuine, as real as last summer when Theresa died, and she remembered Jimmy's sweet, low voice, and how grateful he was when she'd nursed him back to health. All so he could end up in a funeral home in Cambridge. Diane saw Jimmy's mother – so young and sad, yet somehow resigned.

Patty's two brothers and her sister Elena sat with Diane. Elena, who believed in reincarnation, said solemnly: "Jimmy won't come back until drugs are not the problem they are now." *We could be waiting a long time*, Diane thought.

On the way home from the funeral, Diane went to the cemetery where her sister was buried. She didn't even feel the cold as she sat next to the grave for a long, long time.

Hey, Theresa, it's been more than six months since you died. You're not here, but I still am. And even though I couldn't protect you and I couldn't protect myself, I'm starting to learn how with Tae Kwon Do.

I'm getting stronger. And I'm gonna get straight and I will get tough and I will go find those bastards – both of them – who did this to us, and they'll be sorry they were ever born. I'm gonna do this for you, and for Valerie too.

And then Diane started to cry. She cried for her murdered sister, and for her daughter who turned three today, not even knowing that she had a mother who'd wanted her so much. Then she cried for herself, finally, for little Diane who didn't have a mother who'd loved or nurtured her, for the father who couldn't protect her, for all the years she spent taking care of Theresa, which ultimately amounted to nothing, because her sister was dead. And somehow, Diane realized, she'd made it past her teens without ever – *ever* – having one carefree day in her whole life, and what a stinking mess she was in.

Diane cried until she had no more tears. And then, for the first time in nearly four years, she prayed.

"Holy Mary, Mother of God, pray for us sinners, now and at the hour of our death. Amen."

Sobbing, she struggled to get to her feet. As she stood on Theresa's grave in the biting cold, Diane thought: *fornication, murder, despair, lying, cheating, dishonoring my parents. I guess I can't be any worse of a sinner than that.*

Oddly, this thought cheered her a bit, and she started walking home, suddenly aware that she was freezing, hungry, and exhausted. Her feet hurt from the heels she'd worn with her good dress.

Diane stopped at the first church on her way. She entered and walked quietly to the confessional booth, when she saw the light was on.

"In the Name of the Father, and of the Son, and of the Holy Spirit. Amen. Bless me, Father, for I have sinned. My last Confession was more than three years ago. These are my sins. I have dishonored my parents. I have lied and cheated. I have given in to despair. I've had impure thoughts. I have done fornication. I have…"

Diane began to cry again, thinking *Theresa, Theresa, Theresa, I killed you! I can't tell anyone about doing murder*. She ran out of the booth.

The priest called after her: "Say the Act of Contrition, my child, and come back when you are ready. God is waiting…"

Diane ran awkwardly in her heels, her coat flapping behind her. The rhythm of her heartbeat pounded in her ears. *Oh. My. God. I. Am. Heartily. Sorry. For. Having. Offended. Thee. And. I. Detest. All. My. Sins. And. I. Detest…Tony. And that butcher. And I detest You, too, God. Where were you when that pig put his hands all over me and Theresa? If You are so powerful and so merciful, why did You let him hurt Theresa? Why didn't You let him die instead of my darling baby sister? I hate him and I hate my bitch of a mother and my dad for not stopping him. They knew, they had to have known, it was him. I hate those nuns. I hate the Church. And I hate, hate, hate myself. No one can make me better. I don't deserve forgiveness. I am a murderer, I am a horrible, horrible sinner.*

Diane was panting and soaking wet by the time she got home. The heel of one shoe had broken off and she was limping. She wanted a drink so badly she was shaking. She looked around the apartment. Patty wasn't back yet.

Diane went into the kitchen and took down the fifth of vodka. She picked it up, started to tip it into her mouth, and as she did, she saw her reflection in the hall mirror. Behind her in the mirror was a bright light. Startled, Diane turned around and saw a figure – it was definitely female – peaceful and kind.

The last thing Diane wanted now was kindness. She was furious. She spit out the vodka, and turned and threw the bottle at the mirror, which shattered and fell. She wanted to kill the light being. Diane bent over and picked up one of the shards. She held it to her wrist. *God, give me one good reason...give me one sign.* She turned around and the shimmering figure was gone.

Across the hall, the neighbor's door slammed shut, and the radio came on. Diane heard Art Garfunkel's plaintive voice, singing *Bridge Over Troubled Water*, offering her comfort in the darkness and pain.

She sat down in the mess. She didn't get to die. Not yet. Death was too easy. Drinking was too easy. No one could take away her guilt. Nothing could take away her anguish. She would have to learn to live with it.

Diane went to the bedroom, wrapped herself tightly in the blanket, and pulled the bedspread all the way up to her head. She was utterly depleted. She was only twenty years old.

✳ **Twenty-One** ✳

Diane didn't wake until noon the next day. Her head hurt so much she could hardly move. But she made herself get out of bed, and she stumbled into the kitchen. The mess was gone. She tried to figure out what had happened – what she'd seen, and what she'd thought she'd seen. What she almost did.

She made a pot of coffee and sat at the kitchen table. As she did, she saw a note propped up against the sugar bowl:

"Diane, I can't hack it here right now. I waited for you as long as I could, but you're not awake yet. I wanted to say goodbye in person, but I've got to go. I gave notice at work. My parents are taking me with them to my aunt's place in Florida. I'll send you my share of next month's rent. Will call soon. Take care of yourself. Love, Patty. PS Thanks so much for everything."

Oh, great, Diane thought. *Now I'm responsible for the whole rent and utilities and everything else. Patty is blessed to have good parents. Mine are useless. I have to get strong like I promised Theresa and Valerie and take care of myself from now on.*

She sat up straighter. She *would* get herself together, starting right this minute. In spite of her pain. If what she thought she saw last night was real, she'd have some help from the Universe.

The first thing to do, she decided, after she finished the pot of coffee, had a shower, and took some aspirin, was to get a better job, one that could cover all the rent. Diane went out into the hall to get the *Globe*. Ignoring the news, she turned to the classified ad section.

To Sisterhood!

Help Wanted – Female
"Adventure Weekends is a dynamic, independent company specializing in weekend and longer trips for the discerning traveler. We are currently looking for a highly motivated and persuasive individual to work with our extremely enthusiastic team. The right girl must be able to work a variety of shifts, including some evenings and weekends. This is an excellent opportunity for someone looking to work full-time hours in an exciting environment.
Duties: Conduct telephone screening with potential and existing customers. Complete customer records and type forms in a thorough and timely fashion. Help trace customers who have moved or changed location. Qualifications: Excellent communication and interpersonal skills. Pleasant telephone manner, and good typing skills (45 wpm or more). Previous work in customer service. Understanding of, or a willingness to learn, the travel industry from the ground up. High school diploma and at least two years of work experience and/or training or equivalent combination of education and experience."

"OK," Diane said aloud. "How hard can this be? I can type. I can talk nicely on the telephone."

She dialed.

"Adventure Weekends," answered a cheerful voice, "where our customers are always leaving…"

Oh, spare me, Diane thought.

"Hello," she said. "I'm calling about your ad in the paper."

※ ※ ※ ※

One week later, Diane was watching the clock nearing five and hoping the phone didn't ring, when Polly stopped by her desk.

"*Perky Polly*," Diane silently called her.

"Boss wants you," she said, jerking with her thumb up to the glass-walled office that overlooked the sales floor.

"Me? Are you sure he said me?" *Why would the big boss want to talk to her?*

"You're the new girl, aren't you?" Polly asked with a shrug.

Diane sneaked a peek in her compact, ran a comb through her curls, and headed for the stairs.

"Hello, Diane, please sit down." Mr. Bachman smiled at her. "I was wondering if you were free after work for a few moments?" He leaned back in his chair, running his fingers through his thinning hair.

Diane wondered, *is this a request or an order?* She said, "Certainly, sir. What can I do for you?"

"Diane, I'd like to give you a proper welcome to Adventure Weekends. There's a lounge across the street where many of the staff go to unwind after work. The Red Bar. Why don't we take a stroll over there and get to know each other?" He stood up and got his jacket.

Again, Diane thought, *Oh, crap. Can I refuse this guy and keep my job? Probably not.*

Ten minutes later, she was seated across from Mr. Bachman in a red leather booth. He faced the mirror and she could see him sneaking a glance at himself, checking out his reflection.

"What can I get you to drink?" he asked.

"A ginger ale, please." Her look said, *no nonsense, mister.*

"The usual for me," he told the waitress.

"Teetotaler?" he asked Diane. She wanted a drink. But she was done with all that.

"Not always," she lied. "I have class tonight."

"What are you studying?"

"No, teaching. Tae Kwon Do. The White Belt class." *Don't get any funny ideas, mister.*

"That sounds like quite an undertaking for a little lady like you." The waitress appeared with their drinks. He gave her a broad smile, then turned back to Diane.

"Tell me about yourself, your family. Any brothers or sisters?" He leaned across the table and looked intently at Diane, making her the focus of his attention.

Diane stared at him. She could not, would not, break down in front of this asshole.

She forced herself to speak. "One sister. She died."

"Oh, I'm sorry," Mr. Bachman said. As he leaned back, a sorrowful look replaced the smile. "Accident or illness?"

"You could say that." Diane picked up her glass. She was not going to answer any more of his stupid questions if she could help it.

Fortunately, at that moment, several other women from the calling desks came into the Red Bar, laughing and talking. They took the booth directly across from Diane. Behind Mr. Bachman's back, Diane saw them looking her way and pointing. One of them jerked her thumb toward Mr. Bachman and made a gagging motion. Another rolled her eyes exaggeratedly. Diane nodded slightly. They smiled back. *Sisters.*

"We're happy you've joined the Adventure Weekends team," Mr. Bachman said brightly. "Many of our girls go on to supervisor positions. Of course, along with the extra opportunity that entails, there are extra duty hours."

"Naturally," Diane said. The fingers of her right hand were beating out a rhythm on her knee. *How long until I can get out of here?*

"Let me tell you more about what we expect from our girls…"

Diane kept smiling and started making a mental list of the things she needed at the Foodmaster. She nodded slightly every few minutes, as he went on and on about customer relations, the duties of the supervisory team, and the opportunity for travel from time to time.

To Sisterhood!

"For example, next weekend," he said, "we need someone who can fill in for my secretary. She'll be out on medical leave. Would you like to come with the management team to Rome?"

This got Diane's attention. "Excuse me. Rome? As in Italy?"

"One of the perks of working here."

Diane could almost see him patting himself on the back. *What a jerk.*

"I've always wanted to go to Rome." Diane couldn't help herself. This was the trip she and Theresa had always talked about, the one she'd been saving for.

"Come with me," he said, "I'll tell you all about it on the way home."

"Home?" Diane looked wary.

"Yes, I live only a few miles from you, on Brattle Street. I'll give you a lift in my Rolls."

He signaled the waitress for the check and patted her on the arm as she dropped it on the table.

The next day at work, Diane was beside herself with excitement. Sure, Mr. Bachman was a sleazeball, but he'd behaved like a gentleman on the ride yesterday. She could handle herself. All she had to do was answer the phone and type a few letters – and she got to go to Rome! She called Laurie to tell her.

"Your boss sounds like a real piece of work," said Laurie. "Seriously, how well do you know this guy?"

"He's the goddam boss. How bad could it be?"

"Just keep your guard up. Did you warn him your hands are a deadly weapon?"

※ ※ ※ ※

Mr. Bachman and Diane were seated in first class, where the stewardesses fawned all over them, bringing them blankets, and drinks, which Diane refused. The attention from these women her own age made her uncomfortable, and she was embarrassed that they might think this creep was her boyfriend, not her boss. He got louder with each Scotch and soda, and patted the behind of the stewardess who served their dinner. She pretended not to notice.

Diane tried to hide behind the in-flight magazine. It hadn't occurred to her to bring something to read, and she was bored. But she was on her way to Rome – the Rome she and Theresa had dreamed about, and sang about, for all those years.

When they landed, they were met at the airport by a chauffeured car. Mr. Bachman spoke in rapid Italian to the driver. Diane understood some of what he said, and she was not pleased. When she heard him refer to her as *il mio compagno bella,* she began to suspect that this trip might not be all business.

As they checked into the hotel, Diane looked up in amazement at the gorgeous late 19th century building, the spacious lobby, the huge

To Sisterhood!

crystal chandeliers, and the stained-glass skylights. Her heart ached because Theresa was not here to see it too.

Mr. Bachman handed one of the keys to Diane. The valet carried their bags upstairs, opening the door to a suite so luxurious and plush, Diane had never seen anything like it, even in the movies. Three brocade sofas surrounded a glass-topped table, which held a huge fruit basket and a bottle of sparkling wine cooling in a silver bucket. Tall, oak bookcases flanked a large, marble fireplace, over which was a painting of Saint Peter's Basilica. Through the large picture windows, Diane could see the dome of the real Saint Peter's.

"This is lovely," said Diane. "But I'm wiped out. Can you please show me to my room? And what time will you need me in the morning?"

Mr. Bachman smiled as he uncorked the wine and filled two flutes. "Diane, Diane. What a silly little thing you are. Did you think I would bring you all the way to Rome just to type a few letters?"

"Um, yes. That's my job, isn't it?" Her breathing was getting shallow and her fists were clenched at her sides. *Stay cool*, she told herself.

He laughed and reached for her. She backed away, nearly knocking over the brass lamp on the credenza. He leaned forward, grabbing her upper arms in his big hands.

"Don't do that, Mr. Bachman."

She twisted away, trying to free herself from his grip.

"Oh, Diane," he groaned. "It's all your fault. Look what you've done to me." He grabbed her hand and put it on his swollen crotch. "I want to screw you right here, right now."

Diane didn't take time to think. Up came her knee to his groin, followed swiftly by a palm strike to his face. She heard the bone in his nose break. She grabbed her bag, and left Mr. Bachman moaning in pain as she slammed the door behind her.

On her way out the revolving door, Diane told the concierge, "You have an accident, um, *un incidente,* up in the *Suite Presidenziale.* You might want to check on him." She whistled for a taxi and told the driver, "*Mi porti all'aeroporto, per favore.*"

Two hours later, having explained the situation to the sympathetic, young female ticket agent who re-booked her first-class return ticket for one in coach and some cash, Diane set out to explore Rome. She found a room in a much smaller hotel. She did not go to see the Pope.

When she arrived back in Boston on Monday, she called Ellen.

"I'm out of work."

"What! Already? What on earth happened?"

Diane gave her the short version. Ellen was laughing so hard that she snorted, "You did *what?*"

"Yeah, so I'm out of a job again. And I won't go back to the bar scene. I am sober for good. I want to deal with my life, not keep hiding."

To Sisterhood!

"Why don't you come out here?" Ellen suggested. "We're moving to our own place in two weeks. We're on the waiting list for student family housing, a two-bedroom. The baby won't need her own room for a while. It's yours until you get back on your feet."

"Her?" Diane smiled.

"I definitely think so, Nick is sure it's going to be a boy, but that's guys for you…"

"Ellen, you're such a good friend to me, but I don't want to impose on you and Nick." Diane was saying all the right things, while she was already thinking how much she'd love to go back to San Francisco.

"Diane." Ellen's voice was firm. "I'd love to have you here. I truly would. And Nick likes you too. It will be fine."

"If you're sure…"

"I'm sure."

"Let me get my things organized here," Diane said, "and I'll call you back tomorrow. California is great, and a change of scene would be good. You know, I do have two weeks' pay coming, unless Mr. Jerko decides to keep it."

"He wouldn't do that," Ellen said. "He can't do that."

"Sure he can. It's his word against mine. I'm insubordinate, he fires me. He can do anything he wants. There's no law against it."

So Diane packed, paid the last month's rent from her meager savings, and flew out west.

※ ※ ※ ※

A few weeks after Valentine's Day, Laurie heard the sad news that three Weathermen, members of the radical leftist group, were killed by a pipe bomb in a townhouse in Greenwich Village. She immediately phoned Nina.

Nina answered with, "Oh, my God, Laurie. Did you hear about the townhouse?"

"I know. What a shame. Did you know any of them?"

"No, not really," Nina said, "though I met a few Weathermen at the RNB office a while back. I don't think it was any of the folks who were killed."

According to news reports, Diana Oughton and Terry Robbins apparently had been working on constructing a bomb, which killed them and Ted Gold. Gold had just entered the house owned by the family of Cathy Wilkerson. She survived the blast and escaped the building along with her friend Kathy Boudin.

"That's horrible," Laurie said. "I mean, I support their goals and all that, but I don't see how blowing up stuff is the way to go."

"Sometimes you have to speak the language of the imperialist, racist warmongers to get their attention," Nina countered.

"I guess. But there has to be a better way than to stoop to their level."

To Sisterhood!

As she thought about it, the more Laurie realized there were two ways to heal the world. You could work *against* the bad, or you could work *for* the good. The Weathermen and others on the radical left clearly belonged to the first category. The U.S. government was waging an illegal war, and maybe violent action was all that could stop it.

The call ended and Laurie walked back down the hall to her room. She put on James Taylor's new album, a gentle counterpoint to all the scary news. Swaying in time to his sweet singing, she thought that surely there had to be another way. What should she do? Clearly, it wasn't in her nature to be a violent protester. But if she – and millions like her – didn't show up in the streets when it counted, the government would keep on with its killing.

Once again, Laurie thought about continuing on to medical school. Becoming a doctor like Papa and her brothers would bring healing to those in need and in pain. But for now, she was reluctant to think about two more years of undergrad work, followed by four years of medical training, an internship, and a residency in whatever specialty she might choose. Perhaps her plan to major in psychology, with a lot of extra science courses, would be her best course of action.

※ ※ ※ ※

By mid-March, almost five months since Nina had last heard from Dennis, she figured he'd moved on. She'd been asked to cover the opening of the Panthers' Free Clothing Program back in January, but she'd traded stories with another staffer so she didn't have to run into him. The program had opened just in time for winter, so children and adults in the community could have warm coats, hats, mittens, and boots, as well as other necessities.

The story said that while the United States was the richest country in the world, spending billions of dollars on defense, it failed to meet even the most basic needs of many of its people. And that Black people, at the bottom of society, were routinely ignored, and according to the program's coordinator, had the "right and the power to take care of ourselves." Programs that provided free clothing, food, and healthcare, he said, had two basic goals: "to meet fundamental material needs of our people, and to raise the consciousness of our people."

Nina now wished that she'd taken the assignment. She asked that she be allowed to cover the opening of the Free Health Center late in the spring, thinking she might see Dennis then.

She didn't have to wait that long. On the first of April, Dennis surprised her by showing up on her front steps. She immediately felt that same tingle she got whenever he was near. She grinned, and held out her hand, but he didn't take it.

"April Fool's," he said, but his smile didn't reach his eyes. He was a bit stooped, and Nina thought he seemed sad.

"Hey. What's up?" Determined to stay cool, and not show him how much she'd missed him, Nina held the door open and waved him in.

"I'm sorry I didn't call before I left." Dennis walked in slowly, his energy and bravado seeming to have disappeared. "I probably should have told you I'd be away for a while but I wasn't sure where the Party was going to send me, and I couldn't tell you anyway." He sprawled out on the sofa, leaning back and resting his hands above his neck.

Nina folded her arms across her chest and nodded.

To Sisterhood!

"How are you?" he asked. "Are you working on any good stories?"

Nina told him that she'd been covering the Cambridge City Council and the changes in the community, but that she hoped to be assigned to cover the opening of the People's Free Health Center. She walked to the kitchen and grabbed two sodas, handing one to him.

"Yeah, that," said Dennis, taking a sip, and perking up as he spoke. "I'm working on raising money for that right now. We've lined up a whole cadre of volunteers – doctors and nurses and technicians – and I think we know where it's going to be located, but I can't talk about that yet. And we need a lot of bread."

"How much?" Nina asked. She sat next to him on the sofa.

"It depends," he explained. "If we rent a storefront, that's not going to be as much as what we're hoping to do, which is to get a large trailer. If we can get a used trailer, possibly 25 thousand for the first year, including the purchase. Otherwise, if we have to buy a new trailer, it could be like 50 thou. We've done some fundraising in the community, and folks are being generous, but that kind of money isn't going to come out of thin air." He shrugged, and let his head drop into his hands. Nina patted his knee.

"I'm kind of down right now, that's all," he said. "I guess I'm not good company. There's a lot of shit going on. Political stuff. I don't know who to trust anymore, even Wayne, a brother who joined us a few months ago. But I figure I can trust you."

Nina smiled. "Is there anything you want to say?" she asked quietly.

"To be perfectly honest, Nina, I wish there could be more between us. But it's too risky." He took her hand and gave her a look that said what he couldn't express in words. "We need to continue to stay just friends. At least for now."

She sensed that he was waiting for her to say something.

"For now," she said solemnly, and reached over to give him a hug.

✵ Twenty-Two ✵

The waitlist for married student housing was so long that Ellen and Nick decided to go out on their own. They found a small, two-story apartment in a house on a quiet street, a short walk from the college, and they happily made room for Diane.

Diane was glad to be living with friends on a peaceful, pretty street. She spent the first couple of weeks exploring the neighborhood and its many corner grocery shops, where she picked up exotic ingredients for the dinners she made almost every night. Ellen and Nick were grateful, as they were busy and often too tired to cook.

In addition to teaching, Nick had taken on the job of advisor to the school chess club. His students were entered in the citywide tournament, and he said these kids, who'd never had a win of any kind in their young lives, had a decent shot at first place. Ellen was thrilled that Nick had found his avocation. The happier he was with their new life, the more relieved she felt.

She often thought about Sam, more so now that the birth of their child was imminent. She wondered whether he'd deserted her, or if he were in some kind of trouble. But she couldn't dwell on that. She had to make preparations for the new life she was bringing into the world.

The weeks passed quickly, and on the morning of May 1st, Ellen tore off the old calendar page.

"You know what I'm thinking?" she asked Diane. "We should have a little celebration Monday night. It'll be May 4th and the one-year anniversary of the day we met."

"That sounds like fun," Diane said. It also would have been Theresa's 19th birthday, but Diane didn't remind Ellen.

So on Monday, with Ellen at class and Nick at work, Diane decided to tackle a Sacher-Torte for the celebration. She had the chocolate layers cooling on racks on the countertop, she'd strained the apricot jam, and she was already on her second batch of ganache – it wasn't working – when she heard the door slam. Ellen burst in. It wasn't even noon.

"Did you hear the news? Is it on yet?" Ellen ran to the radio and switched it on. She couldn't seem to find what she was looking for.

"What happened?" Diane asked. "What's going on?"

"It's at a school in Ohio." Ellen was panting with the effort of having run up the stairs. "I was at the college's newspaper office, and it just came over the AP wire. It was a couple of hours ago." She paused to wipe her forehead. Diane handed her a glass of water.

"Slow down a minute," Diane said calmly. "Why don't you sit? Tell me what happened."

"The National Guard shot and killed a whole bunch of kids out at a little college in Ohio. Someplace called Kent State." Diane's hands flew up in shock, then she stood and helped Ellen into a chair.

Ellen gave the news to Diane as she'd heard it, that a protest against Nixon's invasion of Cambodia got out of control, students started throwing rocks, and the National Guard started to gas the crowd. The students lobbed the tear gas canisters back at the soldiers, who then

To Sisterhood!

fired into the crowd. At least four kids were dead, and many others were wounded. Diane gasped, and reached for Ellen's free hand.

Ellen gulped the water. "The first report said that a Guardsman was dead too, but the next report said he was only wounded. We don't know yet." She fiddled with the radio again, snapped it off in frustration, then went into the living room with Diane and turned on the TV. There was a breaking news report from Kent.

The two women watched the images in horror.

"The government is shooting us!" Diane cried. "This can't happen in America!"

Ellen cradled her abdomen, as if to protect her baby from the madness.

Neither of them felt much like a celebration that evening. They held each other and cried, and lit a candle for the four dead students: Allison Krause and Jeffrey Miller, who were in the protest, but hundreds of yards away from the troops who fired on them; William Schroeder, who was a member of campus ROTC; and Sandra Lee Scheuer, who was walking from one class to another when she was shot in the throat. She died a few minutes later from loss of blood.

Her death seemed to move Ellen more than the others. Not that any of them deserved to be killed. But a woman, walking with her friend, not part of the protest, who was merely in the wrong place at the wrong time. Ellen held that image and thought about her baby.

"Sandra," she mused. "Such a pretty name." Ellen turned to Diane. "Oh, Diane – it's your sister's birthday, too, isn't it?" Diane nodded.

Both women began to weep again, which is how Nick found them when he came home. It looked like he'd been crying too.

In the days that followed, 900 colleges and universities across the United States, including San Francisco State, shut down in protest. Ellen's classes and finals were cancelled – so much for having to make up her exams in case of an early delivery. She skipped the teach-ins and demonstrations on campus, and spent the time at home to prepare for her baby.

Ellen's due date came and went. On the evening of May 14th, Diane, Nick, and Ellen sat down in front of the television to relax. Instead, they saw more shocking news: two students at Jackson State College, James Earl Green and Phillip Gibbs, who were participating in a protest over the events at Kent State, were shot and killed by police. What was not a shock was what happened next: almost nothing. Four white students at Kent State were killed, sparking a nationwide strike by four million students. The killing of two Black students in Mississippi seemed to be only a tragic afterthought.

Nick wanted to stay home, but the chess tournament was going on as planned over the weekend, and he wouldn't let his students down. The public schools stayed open on Friday, and they did a small teach-in at the regular assembly, so the kids could talk about their feelings about the killings. Many of them had brothers or cousins in Vietnam. Most expressed support for the National Guard. Tempering his own political views, Nick tried to listen carefully to his students.

The chess team was psyched up and ready for the tournament Saturday afternoon at the Civic Center. Every junior high school in the city and surrounding counties would send a team. Nick was reluctant to leave

Ellen alone, but her doctor had assured them that first babies were often a week or more late.

"Go," she told him. "It's only a few hours, and if anything exciting happens, Diane's here with me. It's probably not going to be until sometime next week. Or next year. Look how fat I am."

She spoke softly to her belly: "You're in no hurry to get here, are you, Baby?"

"If you need me," Nick said, "call the Civic Center and leave a message with the security people, and they'll find me. Okay, honey?"

"We'll be fine," Ellen reassured him. "You go and win that trophy!"

Early Saturday morning, Ellen could feel her labor beginning. These were little contractions, not much stronger than the practice ones she'd been having on and off for the past few weeks. She didn't want to tell Nick. Mostly, she wanted to be alone.

She went downstairs into the kitchen, careful not to wake the others. She boiled water for tea. Sitting in the rocker Nick had found in a dumpster, and then sanded and painted so she could nurse the baby in comfort, Ellen held a mug of tea and listened to the birds in the backyard. She remembered her own childhood and thought about Eddy, and her mother, and what she must have experienced bringing twins into the world. *How hard could it be?* Ellen knew the answer now: *hard.* It could be extremely hard to be a mother.

Ellen rocked and sipped. She was keenly aware that this might be the last time she was going to be truly and absolutely alone. From now on, she would be somebody's mother, responsible for a new life. No more thinking only of herself, not that she'd done that lately, but this was it.

A contraction a bit stronger than the others caught her, and when the next one came, she began to time them. After about an hour of puttering around the kitchen in the early morning light, Ellen figured they were now about ten minutes apart. No need for alarm. No need to tell Nick, who was now awake and showering.

After a few minutes, Nick came into the kitchen smiling, grabbed a cup of coffee, ate some cereal, and was out the door with a big hug for Ellen and a reminder to call him if she felt anything – anything! – starting to happen. He came back seconds later, tossing her the car keys "just in case." He'd take the bus, he said.

When Diane came downstairs, she took one look at Ellen, who was in the throes of a medium-strength contraction, and whistled.

Ellen nodded.

"Wow!" Diane grinned "This is it? Not Braxton-Hicks contractions?"

"I'm pretty sure. I was just going to call the doctor." Ellen got up and began to clear the breakfast dishes.

"Let me do that," Diane said, taking the cereal bowl from her hand. "You probably should go upstairs and get your things together."

"All packed," Ellen said, and then another contraction began.

To Sisterhood!

"Um, Diane," she said after a bit, "maybe you should call. And you might want to tell him the last couple were about five minutes apart."

"Do you want me to get hold of Nick?" Diane sounded concerned.

Ellen shook her head.

"You know, he left us the car keys. They're here somewhere." She found them on top of the newspaper and handed them to Diane. "You can drive his car, right? I don't think I'm quite up to it."

"Sure. But should I leave a message at the Civic Center?"

"Let's wait and see what the doctor says. I wouldn't want Nick to have to let down his team for a false alarm." Ellen's voice was calm, but she was beginning to sweat. She left the dishes and headed upstairs. Diane heard her pause on the stairs, and she reached for the phone.

"They said come right in!" she called up to Ellen.

Less than ten minutes later, they were in the car, driving straight uphill to California Street. Diane was terrified, and she didn't want to frighten Ellen. It had been a long time since she'd driven a stick shift, and she had to use the emergency brake at every corner. *These hills are so steep we're gonna tip over backwards*, she thought, but she said to Ellen, "Try to take slow, deep breaths. We'll be there in no time."

Good thing she'd checked the map Nick bought last week so she knew how to get to the hospital. Diane switched on the radio. She sang along with Three Dog Night, knowing this would be a day to celebrate.

"Diane, do you mind?" Ellen was hunched over, holding her belly. She loved Diane but the slightly off-key singing was driving her crazy.

"We're almost there, honey. Hang on. Breathe!"

Diane pulled up to the emergency entrance and told Ellen to get out.

"I'll be right behind you," Diane assured her.

Ellen waited for the current contraction to subside, then walked into the Emergency Room and told the desk clerk she was in active labor. She gave the woman her insurance card, signed some papers, and waited while the woman called up to the Labor and Delivery floor. Someone arrived shortly with a wheelchair.

"I'm fine," Ellen protested, "I can walk." She wasn't sick; she didn't want to be treated like a patient. But the orderly insisted it was "regulations," so Ellen allowed herself to be helped into the chair, brought upstairs, tucked into a narrow bed, and told to "wait here for the doctor," who would be in soon. Like she'd be going anyplace else.

The doctor arrived fifteen minutes later, with Diane at his heels. He introduced himself to Ellen and asked Diane to step outside while he did an internal exam.

"Four centimeters dilated," he pronounced. "And everything looks fine. How far apart are the contractions, dear?"

Ellen frowned at the "dear," but didn't say anything. She realized that she had not had a single contraction since she left the car. Embarrassed, she told this to the doctor.

To Sisterhood!

"We'll check you again in a little while," he said. "And if you're still not making any progress, we'll help you along. Now be a good girl and let's get things going in there again." He patted her arm, turned, and strode out of the room.

A cheerful nurse with a rolling Irish brogue came in immediately. "Now, don't you worry about him one bit," she told Ellen. "It's not at all unusual for your labor to stop when you first get here. You've got to feel safe, that's all. Have you ever seen an animal give birth?"

Ellen laughed. "I grew up on a farm," she said, feeling a little self-conscious. "I should have thought of that. The dogs would always go into the closet or under the bed when they were delivering their litters."

"That's right," said the nurse encouragingly. "Now, let me check your vital signs. Your friend can stay here with you if you want."

Ellen looked at Diane, who nodded.

"That would be great," Ellen said.

Again, Diane asked, "Do you want me to try to find Nick?"

Ellen shook her head. "Not until things actually start happening. It could be hours. Let him finish the tournament. What time is it?" She was getting restless.

"A little after eleven." Diane pulled the one chair in the tiny room close to the bed. She reached over and started to massage Ellen's feet.

"Mmm. You give the best foot rubs. Thanks a million for being with me, Diane. It means a lot."

Diane smiled but didn't answer.

"Hey, did you grab any breakfast before we left?" When Diane shook her head, Ellen continued.

"You must be hungry. Why don't you go get something? There should be a cafeteria or a coffee shop here somewhere."

"OK, I guess so," Diane said, "if you're sure you'll be all right. I could use some coffee." She stopped at the nurse's station to tell them that Ellen was alone.

A minute after Diane left, Ellen's water broke, flooding the bed. Immediately, a tremendous contraction literally took her breath away. She was soaked in sweat, and soaked underneath. She grabbed for the cord to ring the nurse, but she couldn't reach it.

Another contraction followed almost immediately, then another, then another. Ellen thought of Pearl, her golden retriever, and remembered her delivering her puppies. Ellen started to pant, with her tongue up against the roof of her mouth. *Help me, Eddy!*

By the time Diane came back, the nurse was next to Ellen, who was panting with all her might.

"Here comes another one," said the nurse, and when it was over, she slipped a dry pad under Ellen. "Oh, good, you're back," she said to

To Sisterhood!

Diane. "I'm going to get the doctor. I think this young lady has progressed rapidly!"

Diane sat on the bed and held Ellen's hand. "We probably should try to find Nick," Ellen said, "but I don't want you to leave me."

"I'm right here, honey. Just hang on."

"I'm so scared," Ellen said, in the thirty seconds she had between contractions, which felt like they were about to lift her off the bed.

The nurse returned, exuding calm and confidence.

"Look at me, Ellen," she said. She put her own face close to Ellen's.

"Breathe with me, like this: 'Huh, huh, huh,'" she panted, quickly and rhythmically. "That's it, you're doing fine."

Ellen was panting as hard as she could. She yelled for a blanket, said she was freezing, but Diane saw she was sweating. Ellen's thighs started to tremble. Diane wanted to help, but she didn't know what to do. She wished the doctor would hurry up.

Ellen, gentle Ellen, always-in-control Ellen, was yelling things Diane didn't quite catch, but the gist seemed to be, "Where are you?" and "damn, damn, oh damn," or was it "Sam?" – Diane couldn't tell and that didn't make any sense, then she heard, "Where the fuck are you, anyway?" Ellen never swore, ever.

The nurse turned to Diane.

"Sounds like transition," she said. "Not much longer until she can push." Sure enough, with the next contraction, they both heard the telltale throaty "uunh, uunh" in the middle of the panting.

"OK, honey," the nurse told Ellen. "You've got to wait for the doctor. He'll be here in a minute."

"Can't wait," Ellen moaned, "gotta push…NOW!" She gave one big guttural moan, her face turned bright red, and the nurse said, "Hang in there. Now listen to me. When the next contraction comes, you take three deep breaths, and then go with what your body tells you…"

The doctor strolled in, took one look at Ellen, and said, "OK, now Ellen, I don't want you to push, while I check you." Ellen ignored him, took a big breath, held it, gave one more big grunt, and pushed her daughter out into the surprised doctor's waiting hands.

※ ※ ※ ※

An hour later, Nick burst into the room, holding a trophy. He started to apologize, then stopped when he saw the little bundle. Back from the nursery, weighed, measured, and wiped clean, Sandra Edie Martha Williams slept contentedly in her proud, radiant mother's arms.

Nick sat down on the bed, took Ellen's hand, and started to cry. "Wow, look at her," he said. "She's so beautiful, just like her mama."

"Do you want to hold her?" Ellen smiled and handed the baby to her husband, who immediately started to sing her a wordless tune.

"She's a miracle," Nick said. "Ellen, you're a miracle. Thank you, honey." He rocked Sandra gently, and gingerly touched her hair. "I'm

To Sisterhood!

so sorry I wasn't here with you. Tell me all about the labor. It must have been fast…"

Ellen gave him the short version. "I'm exhausted now," she said. "If you'd like to hold Sandra, I think I'll try to doze for a bit."

"My two girls," Nick said proudly. "Look at them," he said to Diane, who'd come back into the room, after slipping out to give the new family some time alone. "Aren't they the best?"

※ ※ ※ ※

The next couple of days were a blur for Ellen. Harriet arrived to coo over her granddaughter. Ellen's parents sent flowers and got through to the nurse's station to send their congratulations.

Ellen was glad to get home. She was exhausted. Trying to sleep in the hospital, with its bright lights and constant noise, was difficult. In the morning, Nick picked up the baby, allowing Ellen a few minutes to take a shower and wash her hair. Wrapped in a robe, she settled back into bed and brushed out her long hair.

Must do something about this, she thought. *Time for a shorter cut.* She lifted Sandra for her feeding and told Nick to take a nap. He'd been up much of the night, diapering the baby before turning her over to Ellen. Nick gratefully went into the living room to snooze on the sofa.

Ellen finished the feeding, then burped Sandra and put her down in the bassinet. She walked around to the nightstand next to her side of the bed, where she saw a large manila Special Delivery envelope postmarked King's Lake.

She opened it, smiling at the card from her parents, "Welcome, baby girl!" There was a note in her father's hand, and one from her mother, saying how happy they were, and how they couldn't wait to meet their granddaughter. A check fluttered out and fell on the floor. Ellen picked it up, and was surprised and delighted to see the generous amount.

"For layette, etc.," the memo line read. This would come in handy.

She dug into the envelope again and fished out a card from her grandmother, also with a big check. Ellen considered all the things she could do with it for Sandra. As she set the package on the nightstand, another envelope fell out.

Ellen reached over and picked it up. When she saw the return address logo and the April 15th postmark, she gasped, then sat back on the bed, her still-damp hair brushing against the letter as she opened it and read:

"Dear Miss MacDougall, The President and Fellows of Harvard University are very pleased to inform you that you have been accepted for admission as a transfer student into the Radcliffe College Class of 1972. Please read this letter carefully, as the following information will help as you..."

Ellen dropped the letter on the floor and began to sob.

※ ※ ※ ※

A week later, as the books predicted, Sandra had her ten-day growth spurt. Ellen was worn out but happy. She knew what to expect, and that was to sit still and stay hydrated and nurse the baby. Diane was right there, bringing her water and juice and even a beer whenever Ellen's nipples got sore.

To Sisterhood!

Diane sat by as Ellen nursed Sandra. Ellen was in the rocking chair by a window, the sun beaming down on mother and baby. *A regular Madonna*, Diane thought. She tried hard to focus on this baby girl and how happy she was for Ellen and Nick. She thought about Valerie and how impossible it would have been to keep her. She knew she did the best thing for her daughter – and for herself – but that knowledge did not take away her pain.

"Diane," Ellen detached Sandra from one nipple, burped her, and shifted her to the other side. She latched on immediately. "I've been meaning to ask you something."

"Sure. Ask away."

"How is it that you knew so much about what it was like for me to be pregnant? Did you read some of my books?"

Diane stared, and didn't say a word. Ellen waited, rocking the baby and cooing to her. She looked up expectantly. Finally, Diane spoke.

"Who's Sam?"

Now it was Ellen's turn to stare. She realized she was shaking, because Sandra started to fret.

Ellen took a breath, then patted her baby gently on her back.

"Oh, honey," she told Diane. "I guess we have a lot of talking to do."

When Nick came home at five o'clock, he found Ellen on the day bed with Sandra asleep, tucked beside her. Diane was sprawled out on the

Rya rug, a pillow from the couch under her head, with Ellen's comforter covering her.

"How're all my ladies?" he asked cheerfully.

Ellen roused first. "Hi, Nick. We're all simply exhausted. Do you mind heating up some soup or something?"

"You need more than soup. Let me go get a pizza." He turned around and walked out, whistling.

With Nick gone, and Sandra nursing peacefully, Diane got up and went into the kitchen. Without asking, she brewed Ellen a cup of chamomile tea and set it on the table next to the rocking chair. She sat beside Ellen on the sofa. Ellen looked at her and the tears came again. There was nothing more to say. They now knew one another's most precious secrets, told in the way that women do so well: an even exchange of hearts. Trust is at the core of the deepest friendships. Both women knew that from here on, they'd always be tender with one another. Each one's life depended upon it.

❉ Twenty-Three ❉

When the end of May finally rolled around, Nina was immersed in researching several stories at once – one having to do with Harvard's expansion into the Riverside neighborhood, a short distance from the office of *Old Mole*. As Diane had explained to her the day they met, residents had been trying to get Harvard to acknowledge and stop its real estate expansion. The university, they said, continued to buy up properties, displacing long-time residents from their homes, and building student and rental housing in their place.

Nina followed the story closely and interviewed several of the most active leaders. She wanted to help their cause, but felt powerless against Harvard's machinations. Writing about and calling attention to these issues was good, but Nina wanted to do more. She had an idea.

She phoned the Black Panther headquarters and left a message asking Dennis to call her about a follow-up story.

That night, he was waiting on her front steps when she got home.

"What's up?" he asked. At least this time, Nina could see that he was more relaxed and smiling than when she'd seen him last month.

"C'mon in," Nina said. "I need to rustle up some dinner. Join me?"

He nodded and Nina went into the kitchen and pulled out a pot of brown rice she'd cooked the night before, and cut up some vegetables for a stir fry. She added some tofu, liberally sprinkled the whole dish with tamari and toasted sesame seeds, and divided it into two bowls.

She set out two pairs of chopsticks and gestured toward the table.

As they ate, Dennis told her what was going on with the Party.

It hadn't been even a year since the founders of the Boston branch of the Party were ousted by the national leaders. The Boston faction believed that both class and race caused the oppression in their community. They were doing everything they could to help the people, and their latest project, the health center, was no exception. They'd finally chosen the location: a large trailer at the corner of Columbus Avenue and Whittier Street. That land had been taken by the Boston Redevelopment Authority to build a giant connector highway, straight through the middle of their neighborhood, dividing it into pieces. The Black United Front, an umbrella organization for a coalition of activist groups, was putting up the money for the Panthers so they could locate the health center right at the construction site.

"That's what I wanted to talk to you about," Nina said. "I want to contribute to the project."

Dennis nodded.

"Thank you, Nina," he smiled warmly at her. "We sure can use whatever you're willing to give."

She went into her bedroom and came out with her checkbook. "Who should I make the check to? The Black United Front or the Black Panther Party?"

"The Black Panther Party, Boston Chapter," he said. "It's good of you to support us. Even a little bit will help."

To Sisterhood!

Nina tore out the check, got an envelope out of her desk, and put the check inside, wrapped in a single sheet of plain paper.

"Open it when you get back," she said.

Dennis thanked her again, got up from the table, and said he'd better get going. "You're a righteous woman, Nina Rosen. I'll see you soon."

Nina waved. "Bye, and take good care." And to herself, *I really care about you.*

Nina didn't see Dennis again until she was sent to cover the opening of the Franklin Lynch People's Free Health Center on May 31st. They'd named the center after a promising young soul singer, who was shot and killed by a Boston Police officer on duty at Boston City Hospital when Lynch was a patient there.

Dennis was surrounded by both the press and other members of the Party, so Nina didn't get to talk to him alone. As the crowd began to thin out, he did come over to say a quick hello. He introduced Nina to Wayne, a tall, dark man with the biggest Afro Nina had ever seen.

"Hello," Wayne said, taking Nina's hand in both of his, "so you're the little lady we have to thank for the generous gift?"

Dennis excused himself, but not before signaling to Nina, by putting his hand over his heart and mouthing, "thanks again, so much."

Nina hoped with all her heart that her gift of $5,000 – a substantial portion of her trust fund distribution this year – would help a lot of Black folks stay healthy.

❋ ❋ ❋ ❋

On Sunday of the July 4th weekend, Nina picked up the phone to hear an unfamiliar voice.

"You want a story?" the young man on the line asked. "Get down here to the People's Free Health Center trailer. We've been shot!"

Nina immediately thought of Dennis. *Was he okay?* She grabbed her notebook and ran up Inman Street over to City Hospital, where she found a waiting taxi.

"Columbus Ave.," she told the driver, "corner of Whittier."

He shook his head. "I'm not going over to that neighborhood, lady."

"What!"

"I got a family here to support."

"Oh, for God's sake!" Nina jumped out of the taxi. She hailed another, and this one sped into Boston.

When she got to the health center, Dennis was nowhere to be found, but plenty of folks were milling around, talking excitedly. One of the Party members, a guy whose name Nina couldn't remember, recognized her.

"Dennis is fine," he said, before she could ask. "He's not even in town this weekend. C'mon, let me show you what the pigs did to us."

He walked over to the trailer, Nina following behind him.

To Sisterhood!

"Look at this," he said in disgust. "Thirteen shots. Sometime between midnight last night when we did the last security check and noon today before we opened."

He led Nina inside the trailer. A young boy was getting his hand bandaged – playing with fireworks, Nina guessed – and he grinned at her bravely as she squeezed past him.

"One bullet hole in the lab. One in the patient examining room. One near the receptionist's desk. Thirteen in all, as best as we can tell, all done with a .38 special, the same kind Mayor White's finest use – but there's no hard evidence to prove it was them. But who else would use the cover of fireworks to hide the sound of the shots?"

Nina nodded. She was writing as fast as she could.

"Are you going to stay open?" she asked.

"Of course we are," said the brother, who told Nina that he was called Little Joe. His hands were clenched as he spoke. "We've got a great program here. We have two doctors, two nurses, a lab tech, a dietitian, and two patient advocates, all serving the people. We're even planning to expand our services and the present facilities into something more permanent. The pigs can't scare us off. You write that, miss. All Power to the People!" He gave the raised fist salute and Nina nodded.

As she took out her camera to get some photos for her story, Little Joe touched her respectfully on the arm. He looked around, and whispered, "And thank you. We appreciate what you did for the people."

Nina filed the story with *Old Mole*. She also submitted a different, more mainstream version to the *Boston Globe*. The *Globe* did not print her story, but ran one of its own – one paragraph in the back of the city section, saying that the Black Panther Party Health Center was the target of an unknown assailant, probably "rowdy youth from the neighborhood," according to the police lieutenant the *Globe* reporter interviewed.

✣ **Twenty-Four** ✣

With Sandra now a few months old, the small apartment was getting even more crowded. Sandra was still sleeping in a bassinet next to her parents' bed, but it wouldn't be long before they'd have to move her into the nursery, where Diane was staying.

Ellen and Nick discussed how they were going to manage in the fall. Nick had been offered extra work as the wrestling coach, and he could continue to coach the chess team. They needed the income from the small stipends both jobs paid.

Ellen cut back at Draft Help to one morning a week, so she could continue to work toward her degree, but only if she took all her classes on the two days a week when Harriet could babysit.

Harriet was thrilled to be able to help out, and the young couple realized there was no feasible way they could do this without her. *As for Radcliffe,* Ellen told herself, *at least I got accepted. And I can finish my degree here.*

When she felt disappointed, she looked at her beautiful little girl, who was starting to smile. Ellen breathed in her luscious scent, a mixture of baby powder, sweet milky breath, and violets.

When Ellen got back from class that afternoon, toting Sandra in a red Snugli™, Diane was preparing dinner. After hearing about Ellen's efforts to attend classes with a nursing baby, Diane grew more serious.

"Ellen?" Diane looked up from chopping vegetables. Ellen sat in the rocking chair nursing Sandra. "I've been thinking a lot about our talk the other day."

"Me too." Ellen was quiet.

Diane continued. "I first thought this on Theresa's birthday, but that wasn't the right time. Remember after her funeral, you said you had lost a sibling too? Would you tell me about it?"

Ellen burped Sandra, who was now almost asleep, then walked into the living room, where she put her into the bassinet, patting her until she was completely asleep.

Ellen came back and picked up a knife to help Diane slice carrots.

"Yes, I lost a sibling," Ellen said softly. "My twin. Eddy. His name was Eddy." Just thinking about him made Ellen start to cry. *Eddy and Ellen. Ellen and Eddy.*

"Oh, how terrible for you." Diane put her arms around Ellen while she cried. Words from a Psalm came to her; she didn't know why. It had been a long time since she'd been to a regular Church service. Still, Diane knew, in hearing a story like the one Ellen was about to tell, she had to leave room between the words. *"To You, silence is praise."*

"It was right after our fifth birthday," Ellen dried her eyes on her sleeve and sniffled. "It was an accident with the horses. Well, just one horse, the one our grandfather specifically told us to stay away from. She was only a two-year-old. He'd just bought her from a place down the road.

Not trained yet, not broken. Eddy was such a rambunctious boy." Ellen smiled bravely.

"He dared me to come with him to give the horse some sugar. When we got out to the corral, Eddy gave me the sugar, then he climbed the fence and tried to mount her. He managed to get one leg over her back as he grabbed for her mane. The horse got spooked, turned, and reared up, trying to shake him off. Eddy got thrown and knocked me down, and landed hard on his head. I watched him fall, then I screamed and went for help. We rushed Eddy to the hospital up in Burlington. He had suffered traumatic head injuries. No one paid much attention to me because they were all concerned about him. They didn't even realize that my leg was fractured until the next day when I refused to walk on it. I made it. Eddy did not." Ellen's eyes were wet.

"I miss him every single day, even now. Especially now." She glanced over to the living room where her baby girl slept. "You were the only one who noticed my limp, the first day we met."

Diane nodded. "Yes, but I never imagined…"

"No, how could you?" Ellen said. "And my mother never let me forget that the wrong twin had died. Then when I got to adolescence, she let me know how unattractive I was with the brace – I still wore a leg brace then – and the limp, and that no boy would ever want me. I think that's why she was annoyed when I met Nick. Not that she doesn't love me, of course, and now she even likes Nick. It's that she couldn't stand to be wrong, she still can't. Someone *did* like me." Ellen stood up, grabbed a tissue, and wiped her eyes.

"For a long time, she tried to have another child and could not get pregnant. Then, she had two miscarriages. I wasn't supposed to know any of this but I overheard my grandmother telling it all to her sister. Then, when I was twelve, they adopted an infant, my brother Ronald."

Diane sat quietly, leaning forward, elbows on her knees.

"Eddy and me," Ellen said. "We were so close, the way twins often are. We had our own special language. Most of the time, though, we didn't even need to talk. We could just look at one another. He could get into all kinds of mischief, and of course, being my parents' favorite, he could get away with anything."

"Oh, Ellen," Diane reached over and took her friend's hand.

"Yeah, that's the thing," Ellen said. "Sometimes you wake up in the morning and it looks like a perfectly good day, and you just don't know, do you?"

Diane's eyes filled with tears too. *At least I had Theresa for eighteen years."* She wanted to tell Ellen. She *needed* to tell someone what she did to her sister. She'd never gotten to that part of the story the other day when she'd told Ellen about Tony. She wasn't sure she could tell it now, but she had to try.

"Ellen. I am so, so sorry for your loss. I can't even imagine what it would've been like to be that young and to suffer like that. At least I was older. Ellen…" she broke off, afraid to continue.

"Ellen, now I have to tell you something." Diane started to sob in earnest. "I killed my sister."

To Sisterhood!

Ellen was crying again too. "No, no, honey, you didn't. You did everything you could to save her. She was sick, you called the doctor. He didn't get there in time." She got up and reached out to Diane. They held one another tightly.

"No, you don't understand," Diane let go of Ellen and stood up, suddenly realizing that she might have to hold the full truth of her story by herself forever. "And there's nothing – no one – for me at home. I don't want to go back there."

"You can stay here for as long as you want," Ellen smiled and gently took Diane's hand. "At least until you feel stronger. Then you can figure out something else. You can think about it later. Right now, let's both try to get some rest while Sandra's asleep. Dinner can wait."

※ ※ ※ ※

Laurie sat at the table in Wellfleet, helping her mother prepare lunch. Ruth had been extra careful with her – a truce after their fight last fall. Laurie was kinder to her mother too. For one thing, she'd missed her.

And Jacob, now retired for almost a year, seemed to be more mellow. He spent his afternoons on the deck, reading scholarly journals and papers "so I can keep up with the young whippersnappers."

Laurie wondered if her parents were happy with each other, or if they were happy at all. Ruth was cheerful enough most of the time, though sometimes it looked to Laurie like she was trying too hard. But Jacob seemed to carry a deep sadness. Laurie knew that he'd lost his parents and siblings in the Holocaust, but that was such a long time ago. She wished she could heal his pain. Then maybe he'd care more about her.

She was doing her best to be a good daughter, helping Ruth with hostess duties for the many weekend guests, mostly new friends of her parents who'd come north to avoid the sultry South Florida summer. To hear them talk, one wouldn't even know a war was going on.

As relaxing as it was to hang around the house reading and sunbathing, Laurie was getting restless. So on a sunny Saturday morning, she asked to borrow the car and drove to Provincetown, leaving early enough to beat what was sure to be horrendous traffic. It was "changeover day": all the week-long rentals went from Saturday to Saturday.

Laurie found a parking space on the street in the East End. She loved this time of day, before the town woke up. No one was out except two middle-aged men walking their poodle.

As she headed into town on Commercial Street, she paused to peek in the windows of the many galleries, and promised herself to come back later when they opened. A pretty watercolor at the Tirca Karlis gallery, across from the Chrysler Museum, caught her eye.

Her classmate Ginger wasn't here this summer, having fled the wild life of Provincetown for a more staid summer stock job at the Dorset Playhouse in Vermont. Laurie didn't know a soul in town except for some of the long-time shopkeepers. Still, since she'd woken up this morning, she'd had a feeling that this was going to be an extraordinarily special day.

※ ※ ※ ※

After a leisurely lunch at The Lobster Pot – a bowl of creamy clam chowder and a salad, followed by her favorite dessert – warm Indian pudding with a tiny scoop of vanilla ice cream – Laurie walked past

Town Hall and its ever-present sidewalk show. Today, a teenager dressed in rainbow colors strummed a guitar and sang a folksong, *Copper Kettle*, as a monkey danced on her shoulder. Laurie tossed a quarter in her guitar case and got a grateful smile in return.

Eventually, she reached the Provincetown Bookshop and went to the poetry section in the back. She picked up a volume by e.e. cummings, one she didn't already own, and flipped through it. She was startled to hear a deep male voice behind her, quoting one of the poems.

Turning around, Laurie looked up into warm brown eyes. They belonged to a man about her age, dressed in a blue chambray work shirt and khakis, and sandals that looked handmade. His light brown hair was a little long, the way she liked it, and he was smiling.

"Actually," she said, "that's one of my favorites."

"Mine as well. Although I also like the one about Buffalo Bill, and that one about the little Christmas tree."

"Oh, me too!" Laurie exclaimed.

"So, now that I know you have good taste, may I introduce myself? I'm Matthew Jonas Becker. My friends call me Matt."

"Hello, Matt." Laurie reached out to shake his hand. "Laurie Goodman."

"Lovely Laurie, hello," he replied with a sexy grin that made Laurie want to drag him behind the beaded curtain into the back storeroom.

Uh oh, she thought, at the same time she casually asked, "Are you visiting for the weekend?"

"Wow, am I that obvious?" Matt shook his head and pushed his hair off his face.

Laurie laughed. "No, it's that you're not tan at all. If you'd been on the beach all summer, you wouldn't have that red burn on your nose."

Matt touched it tenderly. "Yes, it does sting. I was on my way to get some cream to put on it. You wouldn't happen to know where I could find a drugstore around here, do you?"

"You're in luck. Follow me." She led him down to the corner and into Adams Pharmacy.

"I'll wait here." Laurie flipped the postcard rack around and around, picked out a few to send to Nina, Ellen, and Diane, and literally bumped into Matt at the cash register.

"Any chance I can get a tour guide?" he asked. "You seem to know your way around here well."

Laurie laughed again. "Sure!" Then she took the handsome stranger by the hand and out into the bustle of Commercial Street.

Three hours later, after they'd walked all the way down to the Provincetown Inn and out onto the sharp, black rocks of the jetty, heading back only when the tide started to come in, and after they'd exchanged biographical details (Matt, a recent Bowdoin grad, philosophy major, living at home with his parents, probably moving

To Sisterhood!

to Boston in the fall, hoping his graduation money would hold him until he figured out what was next, which, luckily, probably would not involve a tour of duty with Uncle Sam, since his March 18th birthday put him way down in December's first draft lottery; Laurie, psychology major, Radcliffe '72, living in the dorm, no idea of what to do after graduation), and after they'd discovered that they shared tastes in poetry (e.e. cummings, Millay, Browning), and in literature (Laurie was amazed to find that Matt not only had read but had liked *The French Lieutenant's Woman*, a book she couldn't put down when it came out last fall, and that he was the only guy she knew who admitted to having read *Love Story*), and in music (Eric Andersen, Ian and Sylvia, Leonard Cohen), they both realized something important at the same instant: they were *starving*.

"Let me take you to dinner," Matt offered. "It's the least I can do. You've been so kind to show me all the places I never would've found on my own."

"I'm expected home for dinner," Laurie began, but seeing Matt's disappointed look, she changed her mind. "OK, sure, I accept with pleasure. But first let me call them." She walked back into the Inn, first stopping to use the restroom, then calling her mother from the bank of pay phones directly across the hall.

"I've met a new friend," Laurie told Ruth. "And he's taking me out for dinner."

"Oooh, what's he like?"

"Not now," Laurie said, looking over at Matt.

"Go someplace nice," Ruth said. "When do you think you'll be home? Not late, I hope."

"No, not late," Laurie agreed.

"And Laurie?" said her mother. "Be careful."

"Yes, I'm fine," she whispered.

Once Matt was out of earshot, she added, "He's a good guy, totally laid-back. Not at all like the guys I know at school." *They're all so driven, so achievement-oriented*, she thought. *Like her own brothers and her father*. Hanging out with him was relaxing. Except when he looked right into her eyes. That was pretty exciting.

It wasn't even six o'clock, so it was easy to get a table at The Moors. Laurie suggested that they share the two-pound baked stuffed lobster, which she proclaimed "out of this world," and they both started with kale soup, a dish Matt had never even heard of.

"It's a bit spicy," Laurie said. "It has linguica, a Portuguese sausage."

"Do you know absolutely everything about this town?"

"Kind of. I've been coming here summers all my life."

"Yeah, about that," Matt said earnestly, reaching over the soup bowls to take her hand. "What are you doing for the rest of it?"

To Sisterhood!

Laurie blushed. When the singer in the adjacent lounge, a big burly man who looked like a cuddly Teddy bear, began to croon *Close to You*, Matt again looked deep into her eyes.

"This will always be our song," he said.

By the time they'd scraped the last of the bread pudding from the bowl they'd shared, and Matt had paid the bill, and they'd said hello to the live owl who sat perched behind the register looking as if he owned the place, Laurie was pretty sure she'd found her soul mate. But there was only one way to be absolutely certain.

"Let's go see a friend of mine," she said, taking Matt's hand and leading him to a side street in the West End, as the sun was setting. "You'll like her. Her name is Desirée."

✵ Twenty-Five ✵

In the more than two months since the People's Free Health Center story was filed, Nina hadn't seen or even spoken to Dennis. She'd heard he was working in Philadelphia, helping the Party set up some programs there. Nina was annoyed that she felt aimless, waiting for his return. She'd never been this wrapped up in a man, especially one she hadn't known for long.

They'd certainly talked enough when he was in town, and she trusted her instincts about his sincerity and his politics. And as much as she believed in the programs the Black Panther Party was doing for the people, Nina knew that she'd made that gift in large measure to impress him. But she didn't understand the pull he had on her. They hadn't even talked all summer, and she still thought about him all the time.

Get hold of yourself, girl, she told herself one crisp late-September morning. *You did a nice thing for the people in Mission Hill and around the city. Get over him and focus on work. There are more stories out there, and certainly, more men!*

Full of purpose and determination, Nina dressed with extra care, and wearing her new boots, she walked to the *Old Mole* office.

Chaos greeted her. Even though she was early, a noisy staff meeting was already in progress. The gist seemed to be that several of the staff and some folks in the community were unhappy with the direction the paper had been taking. They found it too closed, too elitist, and felt that the staff had no right to speak for all the people. There was talk of the possibility of reorganizing into something more responsive to the various factions of the community, but that wasn't going to happen right

To Sisterhood!

away. After a long discussion, they voted to suspend publication, effective immediately.

"Sorry about this, kid," Perry told Nina. "I don't agree, but the majority of the collective feels this is the way to go. I guess we're both out of a job. And I'm out of a paycheck too."

Stunned, Nina nodded to Perry, not trusting herself to talk. She left and started to walk back home.

What was she going to do for work? It wasn't about money; she'd been an unpaid staffer. And she still had some money left from the trust fund, so paying the rent and buying groceries wasn't an issue for now. But all that unstructured time? Not good for her, not good at all.

She wondered if Laurie was around now that classes had resumed, but lately she seemed to be spending most of her free time with that guy she'd met on the Cape.

Nina wished she'd stayed in closer touch with more of her Dalton or Sarah Lawrence friends. But they were all in the New York area, and Boston was home now.

She missed Ellen and Diane – how happy she was to have made three new friends that first day here – and she and Laurie had kept in touch with them with letters and the occasional phone call.

Should she fly out to San Francisco? She could take a trip up to Napa, do some hiking, maybe… *Oh, no!* she chided herself. Ellen was married now. To Nick. *You sure don't want to mess that up.* Still, Ellen was her friend. Nina still felt kind of guilty that she let Nick get away without teaching him a thing or two about how women's bodies work. She could only hope that Ellen had done a better job. Somehow, she doubted it.

When she got to her apartment, Nina phoned Laurie at the dorm, but she wasn't in. She was probably at Matt's place, or studying at the library. Laurie was taking five courses again, on track to graduate so she could "get out and do something real," as she had put it.

Nina had been doing "real" for a couple of years now, and look how it'd turned out. She wondered if she should finish her degree, but she didn't know what she would study. Suddenly, she was crying. She missed her mother so much. Her mother would have told her what to do.

She didn't have to think about any of this today. She could hang out for a while. Maybe go out later and grab a sandwich.

She put on comfortable clothes, made a big bowl of popcorn, and had settled down to watch whatever old movie was on TV, when she heard a loud knock at the door. She didn't feel like company right now, especially when she was still sniffling. She decided to ignore it. Whoever it was could go away. The knock came again, more forceful this time. *Oh, what now?* she thought. *This day can't get any worse.* Another knock, only this time, it was more of a loud banging.

Just shut up, Nina wanted to scream.

"Nina Rosen?" a loud voice called. "Open up, Nina. It's the police."

Grabbing a handful of tissues to blow her nose, Nina wrapped a blanket around her and peeked through the keyhole. There were two men dressed in police uniforms. A cruiser was parked in front of the house.

To Sisterhood!

But she was careful.

"Identification, please?" When the officer held up the badge, she could see it looked authentic.

She unlocked the door, leaving the chain on.

"Open the door, Nina," the bigger cop said. "We have a warrant for your arrest."

"What!" she screamed, though she took the chain lock off. She wasn't stupid enough to think she could get away, and she certainly didn't want to be charged with resisting.

"Arrest? Are you kidding? What on earth for?"

The policemen barged into the room, knocking the popcorn bowl out of Nina's hands. One pulled out a pair of handcuffs, and before Nina could even blow her nose, he had her hands cuffed behind her back.

"You have the right to remain silent," he began. "Anything you say can and will be used against you in a court of law. You have the right to speak to an attorney. If you cannot afford an attorney…" and the big cop snorted out what Nina guessed was supposed to be a laugh. She wanted to kick him in the balls, but she knew better.

"What are the so-called charges, officer?" She managed to sound calm, even though her nose was running and she couldn't reach up to wipe it.

The one who was reading her Miranda rights kept talking.

They're doing this by the book, she thought.

"Nina Rosen," the bigger cop said. "We have a warrant to arrest you for being an accomplice to murder." And when the other one was finished reading, they led her outside in full view of her landlord and her neighbors, into the waiting squad car.

※ ※ ※ ※

Nina was taken to the main Cambridge Police Station, fingerprinted, and shoved into a holding cell. She hadn't been allowed to make a phone call yet, but she knew her rights. She didn't know what was going on until another guy – she figured by the way he was dressed that he had to be a Fed – unlocked the cell.

"OK, Nina. I'm going to take you to use the phone, and if I were you, I'd call my rich daddy and beg him to come up here from Jew York City and bring the best lawyer money can buy. You're gonna need it, sweetheart."

Nina winced at the slur. She was damned if she was going to let this asshole see she was scared.

"Can you please tell me what this is all about?" she asked with all the dignity she could muster. Her stomach growled loudly.

"Call your daddy," the agent continued. "And tell him you got mixed up with the wrong group of friends. Tell him those Panthers are pinning it all on you."

"WHAT!" The scream came from deep in her gut. She couldn't help herself. This could mean only one thing – that Dennis was in trouble too. Big trouble.

To Sisterhood!

Nina called Perry. Fortunately, he was still at the office sorting out the wreckage. She told him what was happening – at least what she knew – and asked him to get her a Movement lawyer right away. And to please call her father and let him know what had happened. Perry promised to help and reminded her not to say anything at all. She could claim immunity under freedom of the press.

"I don't think that's going to cut it for murder charges," she said sadly. "Just get me someone good and get him here fast, please."

A dour-faced matron brought her a sandwich – peanut butter and grape jelly on stale white bread – and a cup of coffee. It was disgusting, but Nina was so hungry she ate it anyway. Then she was led to the back of the station, to a solitary cell.

The Fed came back. Nina was sure that's who he was, not just a Cambridge detective. She knew that F.B.I. agents were required to tell you the truth if you asked them if they were with the Bureau. He nodded curtly. But she was surprised when he told her he was from the Philadelphia office.

She had a million questions, but she knew enough not to talk. He tried to get her to say something.

"You know, Nina, it will go easier for you if you cooperate with us."

"I want to speak with my attorney." She crossed her arms over her chest, where the agent had been staring. "He should be here soon."

"Suit yourself," the agent said, and walked away.

John Waterstone appeared soon. Nina was glad he was the one Perry had called. Out of Harvard Law for about three years, John was dedicated to the Movement, worked at the People's Law Collective, had successfully defended draft resisters, and was the only lawyer in town who'd been able to get a husband with flying fists put behind bars. *If he can't help me*, Nina thought, *he's smart enough to find someone who can.*

"Hey, Nina." He wore a tan suit jacket over pressed jeans. His long hair curled slightly over the collar of his button-down blue oxford shirt. He smiled kindly and said, "Sit tight and let me find out what's going down."

"I'm not going anywhere. Thanks so much for coming, John."

Less than an hour later, he returned. "They want to take you in and talk to you now. I'm going to tell you all they told me and then once we're in there I don't want you to say anything unless I nod at you like this."

He showed her an almost imperceptible up-and-down movement of his head. "If I don't want you to answer, I'll shake my head a little, okay?"

Nina said she understood.

"It's important that you say as little as possible. Right now, they're fishing for information. They don't know too much."

"I know absolutely nothing, except from that foul-mouthed cop." Nina leaned against the cell bars and lowered her voice. "I figure it has something to do with Dennis Burton. And I haven't even seen him in two months, and we haven't had a real conversation for a long time before that."

To Sisterhood!

John looked at Nina and nodded gravely.

"A bomb went off in the supply closet at the police station in Philly. Not the main one; one of the satellite stations in the Black community. Tragically, the night janitor – a Black man with five kids – was killed. The police are blaming it on the Panthers. They raided the Philadelphia Party headquarters. They claim to have found a huge cache of unregistered weapons in the basement, supplies to make enough bombs to blow up every police station in the city, and more than a kilo of dope and several bags of heroin, ready for street sale."

Nina's eyes widened.

"That's crap. Black Panthers don't do drugs. And they would never be stupid enough to keep illegal stuff like that in the house."

"That's what I think too," John said. "It definitely looks like a setup."

"But how could I possibly be charged? I haven't even been to Philadelphia in years…" her words drifted off, as she began to grasp the terrifying truth.

John shook his head slowly.

"That's right," he said. "They think you paid for the whole thing. You wrote the check to The Black Panther Party – Boston chapter, and that's where the Feds are saying all the contraband was bought. One of the party leaders – a cat named Wayne something – turned state's evidence. I wouldn't be surprised if he were an undercover agent. He's pinning the whole thing on Dennis. Who, he says, did it with your money."

"Oh my God!" Nina began to sweat. "You've got to help me, John! I'm innocent! I gave that money to help buy the van for the health center. And Dennis is innocent too. He wouldn't hurt anyone."

☼ Twenty-Six ☼

By the time the leaves changed color, Laurie had made up her mind. It wasn't so much what Desirée had told her and Matt that fateful August evening – "you two have been together before, and you have a purpose to fulfill together" – but the simple fact that Matt needed her. He still hadn't figured out what he wanted to do for work, or if he should go back to grad school. He'd been keeping busy reading more about the history of revolution and studying the roots of the struggle of the working class. Living on his graduation gift money would hold him for another six months or so. He couldn't take just any shit job, he told Laurie. It had to mean something.

Breathless by the time she'd climbed the stairs to the apartment, she could hear the radio blaring. Edwin Starr was singing, asking what war was good for, and Matt was lying on the perfectly good king-sized mattress they'd found on the street near Tufts. It took up most of the floor space in the room. *The Wretched of the Earth* was upside down on his stomach. He grinned at Laurie as she let herself in with the extra key.

"Hey there, lovely lady," he said.

"Hi yourself." Laurie wiped her sweaty forehead, flopped down on the mattress next to Matt, and gave him a kiss.

"Have you read this yet?" He held up the book.

She shook her head.

"It's by Frantz Fanon. He does a brilliant and scathing attack on colonialism and post-colonial nationalist governments, so we can understand the impact of racism on the emerging African states."

Laurie listened.

Matt sat up, energized by his audience. He clasped the book to his chest.

"We need to learn about the anger of our Black brothers and sisters," he said solemnly. "We can't change our white skin privilege, but we *can* try to understand the history that informs the Black Power movement."

Laurie beamed. She *loved* this man. Matt was so smart and interesting. He could talk about Black Power one minute, and then about meditating to reach Nirvana the next. Laurie was happiest when they were practicing some of the meditation techniques Matt had shown her. They would sit together, quietly, and at these times, she was sure that they were soul mates. She wanted to be with him forever.

"Listen, honey," she said, stroking his hair. "About the money thing? I think I've got an idea."

That evening, Laurie called her parents in Florida to tell them that she'd found "The One." Yes, that fellow she'd met in August in Provincetown. She'd been spending a lot of time with him, no, she wasn't neglecting her studies. But the big news was that she and Matt didn't want to wait. They wanted to get married next summer. Yes, she'd met his parents, and they seemed to like her. No, he wasn't Jewish; his folks were Unitarian. Yes, they lived in a big house in Marblehead, no, not right on the water, but near it. No, they hadn't told them; she wanted to tell her parents first. Yes, she'd write them about the plans as soon as she and Matt had worked them out.

Matt saw the wisdom in her plan. While they didn't need the state to sanction what they felt for each other, they'd get to have a big party, and better yet, get a whole lot of checks and gifts. That should keep them set for a while, at least until Matt figured out what job he could do that wouldn't compromise his value system, or until Laurie graduated and went to work, whichever came first. They stayed up all night talking.

The next day, Laurie wrote to her parents.

"Dear Mom and Papa,

Here are the plans we've been working on for our wedding. Please let us know what you think. Matt's parents are eager to meet you. Would it be all right if they came to Florida for a couple of days while we're down there at Christmas break? Also, please know that the enclosed are only ideas, and all are subject to change. Here goes:

First, the invitations. Matt and I have each made a list of friends and relatives – I'm enclosing mine – you can add or subtract. Matt's parents will go over his. We can order the invitations in March. We'll look at different kinds when we come down in December.

The place we're thinking of for a June wedding is our Wellfleet house, if that's okay. In addition to being near the place we met, we both love it there. It represents serenity (the beach), purity (the light and air), and strength (the ocean). For the convenience of the friends and relatives who work at regular jobs, we're thinking of a Sunday morning. That way, people who want to could drive down on Friday and make a whole weekend out of it. We can serve brunch, buffet style, right out on the lawn, or in the great room if it rains that day.

The ceremony itself is hardest to plan. In addition to our interest in political work and reading, we've been doing a lot of exploration into meditation, and we'd like to try to re-create that calm, peaceful feeling.

We are thinking of seating guests in a multi-layered ring with Matt and me standing in the center, surrounded by our families, who will stand around us in a circle, all holding hands. That way, the vows themselves will be heard only by those dearest to us, while everyone else can be present. We will ask family members and close friends to give a brief presentation, read a poem, or give us a blessing. We will then sign our marriage certificate with our vows written on them beforehand, then pass it around for each guest to sign, then we'll end with music.

As for clothes, we'll both wear white. I will wear a long white gown, sort of quaint, not too fancy, either with Juliet sleeves or sleeveless, perhaps linen. No veil, but a crown or ring of white daisies, with flower-streamers down the back. Matt plans to wear white dress pants and a hip-length white jacket and white shoes. We don't know yet about the others, like maid of honor or best man. We think we'll have everyone wear what they want so it doesn't look plastic. We can shop for my "trousseau" when we come down in December.

About the money thing. I guess you and Matt's parents can talk about that when you meet. Maybe you can split the whole thing down the middle, or maybe you can agree on paying for certain things. I don't know how it works.

OK, let me know what you think. I love you, Laurie."

✳ Twenty-Seven ✳

Nina spent the night in the cell, shivering and hungry. She was wearing her oldest jeans and her red flannel shirt – her "comfy clothes" – that she'd put on yesterday when she was settling down to watch a movie and feel sorry for herself.

She refused to eat any more of the disgusting food. And she certainly didn't expect to be able to sleep, with all the banging around and shouting and police sirens. From what she could tell, she was the only prisoner. But sometime in the middle of the night, she heard them bring in someone else. It sounded to Nina like an older woman, and she'd had way too much to drink. They put her into the next cell, and after a few minutes of mumbling and her asking them to bring her a big steak sandwich, which didn't happen – she got peanut butter too – Nina heard her snoring loudly.

Oh, great, Nina thought, but after a while, she couldn't stay awake any longer and she too dozed off, dreaming of her mother.

Early in the morning, she woke up to hear a noise outside her cell. It was the large police officer.

"Visitors, missy!" he shouted. "Rise and shine!'

Nina stretched and turned around to see her father, disheveled and looking as if he hadn't slept. With him was a tall, distinguished-looking man who Nina vaguely recognized. He was wearing a navy blazer and his hair was cut short.

"Nina, honey!" Herb cried. "Are you alright? Did they hurt you?"

Nina shrugged. "I've been better." She rose from the uncomfortable cot and peered at the other man.

"This is Mr. Friedman, Nina. Arnold Friedman. From Golden, Friedman, and Gaskin. One of the biggest firms in the city. He's the senior partner, criminal law. He's here to help you."

Herb reached through the cell bars and took Nina's hand. "We're gonna get you out of here soon, sweetheart."

"Hello, Nina," said Arnold Friedman. "First I need to talk with you alone. Then I'm going to go before the judge and ask that you be released on bail. It shouldn't take more than a couple of hours, if everything goes smoothly. Do you understand?"

Nina nodded yes, and Mr. Friedman turned to Herb. "Give us a few minutes, would you?"

Herb gave Nina a thumbs-up and tried to smile. He turned to go. "Bernie sends her love, Nina. She says she's getting your room ready for you. Oh, and, um, Muriel sends love too."

I'll bet, Nina thought, and turned toward her lawyer.

"What do I have to do?" she asked.

Mr. Friedman explained the procedure to her, slowly.

"First," he said, "you will appear at an arraignment. It's a formal hearing before a judge, and you will be informed of the exact charges against you. We will enter a plea of 'not guilty' and request that you be released

To Sisterhood!

on your own recognizance. Most likely, though, since this is probably going to be a high-profile case, the judge will set bail, which we will pay so you can walk free.

"I should warn you that, due to the seriousness of the charges, you could be remanded to jail without bail, but I don't think that's likely, because you are being charged as an accessory, you're not a flight risk, and also because you don't have any prior record or other pending charges against you. Plus, your father will be there, and you have a job in the community…"

"*Did* have a job," Nina said glumly. "They closed the newspaper yesterday. And I was only an unpaid staffer."

"I see. Well, you've been productive and volunteering in your community for some time, and there is every expectation that you'll find another volunteer or paid job once this is behind you."

"Not if I'm a convicted criminal." Raw pain swept across her face.

"Now, let's not get ahead of ourselves, Nina," Mr. Friedman murmured gently. "Let me continue." He signaled to the guard, who nodded, then brought him a stool.

As he sat down, he continued. "Probably at the arraignment, the prosecuting attorney and I will discuss your case with the judge. It's likely that I'll find out more about what they think happened and how you are involved. We may discuss a plea bargain, and, if I can convince them that you were, well, let's say it for what it is – framed – we may even be able to get the charges dismissed, or possibly reduced to a misdemeanor. If the Assistant District Attorney makes any kind of an offer, I of course will discuss it with you before I give them an answer."

"Where will I be all this time?" Nina wanted to know.

"Right in the courtroom. You'll be able to see everything that's going on, but not hear the talk with the judge. It's called a 'bench conference,' so you know."

Nina nodded.

"Probably," he continued, "because the charges are serious, they will not be disposed of at the arraignment. The prosecuting attorney may announce that they intend to present your case to a Grand Jury. If that happens, we may give notice that you wish to testify in front of the Grand Jury on your own behalf. But if you do that, you will waive your rights to protection against self-incrimination."

"Will there be any witnesses?" Nina asked. Her mouth was dry. "I can't imagine how there could be, because no one saw me doing anything wrong because I *didn't* do anything wrong!" She got up and began to pace around the cell anxiously.

"Normally, there won't be any witnesses –" he began. Nina cut him off.

"How can these jerks do this to me?" she wailed. "I didn't do anything!"

"Try to stay calm, Nina," Mr. Friedman advised. "I know how dreadful this is for you, and we are going to do everything we can so that you walk free as soon as possible."

To Sisterhood!

Nina glanced up at the ceiling light, and steadied her breathing.

"At the arraignment, a date will be set for the preliminary hearing. This hearing can be really important for us. The state will present evidence to show the Court why you should be brought for trial. I will be able to cross-examine their witnesses. However, it's possible that the prosecution – especially because we have reason to believe that they have a weak case against you – will not want to use their witnesses, and so they may decide to go with the Grand Jury instead. Are you following me so far?"

Nina said yes.

"Now, do you know what a Grand Jury is?"

"I have a general idea, but it would be helpful if you can go over it."

"All right. A Grand Jury in Massachusetts is made up of 23 local citizens. They hear the prosecution's evidence and decide whether that evidence warrants the issuance of an indictment against you.

"I'll go over this again with you later, but know that the Grand Jury kind of works for the prosecutor, because usually, the Grand Jury hears only one side of the case – his side. There is no judge, no one to rule whether the evidence the prosecutor presents is admissible or not. You won't have me or any lawyer to cross-examine the witnesses, and you can't do that yourself. So, the jury won't hear anything at all in your defense. If they find sufficient evidence against you, they will True Bill your case, which means you will be indicted and your case will go to trial.

He paused as she winced, and then went on.

"You have the right to testify in your own defense, but I would have to get permission to present other witnesses, and, as you point out, there are no witnesses to a crime you did not commit. If you decide to do that, I can't be there in the room with you, but I will be right outside in the corridor, and if you need to consult with me, you can ask to step out of the room to do so."

Nina nodded.

"Now, there is a chance that the Grand Jury will not indict you," Mr. Friedman said, "but in this case, I'd say that is not likely. We can expect an indictment and a trial."

"That's all I want to tell you now. It's time for me to go upstairs. Stay strong, Nina. We should have you out of here soon." She smiled bravely, as the guard let him out.

Nina was released on $25,000 bail, which her father paid. She was ordered to surrender her passport and to not leave the Commonwealth. *So much for my warm bed and Bernie's grilled cheese*, Nina thought. Still, she was happy to be out of there.

After the arraignment, Herb said goodbye to his daughter outside the police station.

"I'm sorry, Nina, but I have to get back to the city. I know you're in good hands here. I'll call you tonight." He gave her a kiss and walked quickly toward Central Square, where he hailed a taxi to Logan Airport.

Arnold Friedman held Nina's arm as they walked out into the sunny fall day. "I've got a rental car here. Where can I drop you off?"

To Sisterhood!

"I live up the street." She gestured north. "I think I might like to walk."

"You've had quite a shock, young lady. At least, let me buy you some lunch." Nina smiled gratefully and directed him up Prospect Street to the S & S. Was it only yesterday she'd been planning to walk up there? A lot could change in one day. Now she was charged with being an accomplice to murder. And all she'd been trying to do was help.

Mr. Friedman held the door for her and helped her out of the car, a shiny white El Dorado.

"I know," he said. "It's a bit much, but it's all Hertz had available in the full-sized model." They walked together into the noisy deli.

Nina laughed. Yesterday, when the paper closed and she'd lost her job, she didn't realize how grateful she'd be to be able to walk into a restaurant and order whatever she wanted. She gave a silent *thank you* to whomever might be listening, and studied the enormous menu.

After they ordered, Mr. Friedman looked up.

"Nina, I want you to know something. I was a friend of your mother, may she rest in peace, a very good friend."

"I thought you looked familiar," Nina said. "You've been at our house?"

"Yes, many times. But you were small. I didn't think you'd remember me. Your mother was a good woman, a wonderful friend both to my late wife and to me, and, of course, a valued client of our firm." He smiled at the fond memory. "I want you to know we're going to do everything possible to get these charges dismissed and to clear your name. But it may take some time. We have to go through appropriate channels, play by their rules, and so on.

His expression hardened. "This is no small case, Nina. The FBI is involved. They want to destroy the Black Panther Party. I had my assistant do some research before I flew up here. I was quite shocked by the information he presented to me. They say that the Black Panthers are a threat to America and to the security of our nation. This incident in Philadelphia isn't the first case where it looks like the government may have trumped up the charges. Now, I may be an old fool, but I don't see how feeding hungry children or providing free medical care to the needy is any kind of national security threat."

Nina's shoulders relaxed as she listened. She was afraid that Herb had sent some super-straight establishment type to help her. Of course. Who else worked in one of the largest law firms in New York City? But she was happy to have this kind, competent man on her side. She sensed her mother watching over her, and she smiled again, as she bit into the huge pastrami on rye.

✢ **Twenty-Eight** ✢

As soon as classes ended, Laurie and Matt headed to Florida.

After giving her daughter a great big hug, Ruth welcomed Matt warmly.

"Matt, I'm sorry that Dr. Goodman isn't here to greet you too. He should be right along. He called from the club to say he'd been delayed."

"Club?" Laurie asked.

Ruth laughed. "Would you believe it, honey? Your Papa has taken up golf in his dotage. He's quite good, and it gets him out of the house a few times a week," she added with a wink to Laurie. "You know what they say, 'I married him for better or worse but not for lunch!'"

Ruth smiled affectionately at her daughter. "Look at you!" she exclaimed. "You look so happy! You must be quite a fellow," she said to Matt. "Come, dears, let me show you to your rooms."

Laurie rolled her eyes at Matt behind Ruth's back. She'd already told him to expect the guest room. Not married. House rules.

Matt hefted his suitcase and Laurie's and followed Ruth up the stairs.

"You have a lovely home, Mrs. Goodman."

"Why, thank you dear," she said. "We're still settling in. And please, Matt, call me Ruth. Or Mom, if you like."

Laurie relaxed. This meeting was going even better than she'd expected. She was eager for her Papa to get back.

She didn't have to wait long. As she was unpacking her things in this unfamiliar room, she heard the garage door open and a hearty, "I'm home!" called up the stairs.

Ruth, Laurie, and Matt headed down to the den, where Papa was already looking through the mail. Laurie made the introductions, and Papa reached out to shake the hand of his future son-in-law.

"Welcome to our home," he said stiffly. "I'm pleased to meet you."

Laurie smiled as Matt took his hand firmly.

"I'm pleased to meet you too, Sir," he said. "And I intend to take good care of your little girl." Laurie winced, but Papa seemed to relax. Ruth called out that dinner was almost ready, and Jacob should go up and change his clothes. He came down a few minutes later.

"You children must be starving!" Ruth said. "Why doesn't everyone come in and have some appetizers?" She set out a large platter of deviled eggs, garlicky olives, marinated mushrooms, and pickled beets, along with endive stuffed with mashed anchovies.

The foursome was about to sit down when there was a knock at the front door. Ruth looked puzzled and got up to answer it.

"Oh, my heavens!" the others heard her call from the foyer. "Jacob! Laurie! Look who's here!"

To Sisterhood!

She walked back into the dining room, leading her son Andy, who had his arms full of luggage.

"Look what the cat dragged in!" Andy grinned, dropping all the suitcases and picking up his little sister and twirling her around.

"Ow! Put me down, you big ape!" Laurie squealed.

"And this must be the lucky guy!" Andy said, gently lowering Laurie to the floor, then reaching over to shake Matt's hand.

The door opened again and in came David and Roberta, who'd married last summer after her graduation.

"Surprise!" a beaming David shouted. "Mom, Papa, we're sorry to drop in on you like this but we wanted to meet our new brother-in-law. I hope you don't mind."

"Oh, my!" sighed Ruth. "Sorry? Mind? Not on your life! What a treat!" She grabbed her older son and hugged him tightly, and then did the same to his wife. Jacob got up from the table to shake his sons' hands and give them both a hug. He pecked Roberta on the cheek.

"How did you both get off from work at the same time?" he asked.

"Not easy," said David. "We both traded shifts so we can stay through the weekend, if that's okay. Of course, we're going to have to do double time when we get back, and we're signed up to work Christmas and Christmas Eve, but I figure it's worth it."

He held out a chair for his wife. "Let me hang up your coat, dear. Can I get you some water?"

Roberta shook her head. "I'm fine, David. Don't fuss," she scolded.

"Laurie, how are you? I'm sorry we never got a chance to get that lunch I promised. I've been so busy. But I'll make it up to you soon."

"That's all right," Laurie said. And then, "Can I help you?" to Ruth, who was scrambling to set three more places at the table.

"Yes, if you don't mind, dear, put out more rolls and butter. Fortunately for you hungry travelers, I've made a roast. And it's ready to come out of the oven. And plenty of kugel. Let's eat and you can tell us the news!" Ruth was glowing, now that all her children were here under one roof.

❊ ❊ ❊ ❊

After stuffing themselves with second helpings, Andy and David headed into the den. Roberta and Laurie offered to help Ruth with the dishes, but she shooed them away.

"Go sit and relax," she said. "I've got my system. I'll join you soon and bring some dessert."

"Can I help you, Mrs. Goodman, um, Ruth?" Matt asked politely. He lifted up the large roast platter and carried it into the kitchen.

"Oh, no, that's fine, thanks," she said. "That's all I needed. I'll do the rest. Go sit with the others. Get to know your new brothers."

To Sisterhood!

Jacob came into the den, carrying a basket of kindling. "Who wants to help build a fire?"

Andy said, "I'll do it, Papa," although the Florida night was only a bit chilly. He put kindling over the hardwood logs, then struck the match.

"First try," he boasted. "I'm such a good Boy Scout!"

Laurie laughed.

Roberta turned to her. "So, Laurie, tell us about what you're planning for your wedding. Where? When? And do you want my notebook? I've got the scoop on the best florist, that great photographer, and have you started looking at gowns yet?"

Laurie laughed. "Whoa! Slow down a bit, girl! We weren't going to talk about the plans until Matt's folks arrive the day after tomorrow, but what I know so far is that it's going to be at our Wellfleet house, the third Sunday in June."

"Oh, dear," Roberta said in a quiet voice. "So soon."

Laurie looked puzzled. She gave Matt a questioning glance, *Did I say something wrong?* Matt shrugged and shook his head. *Beats me*, he seemed to say.

David walked over to his wife and put his arm protectively around her shoulder. "You see, Laurie..." he began. "Wait a minute." He got up and went to the doorway.

"Mom!" he called. "Can you come in here a minute? Right now?"

Ruth appeared, wiping her hands on her apron. She went over to stand next to her husband. "What's the matter? Is something wrong? I was still rinsing the –"

"Mom, Papa," David beamed, squeezing Roberta close to him. "We have news. You are going to be grandparents."

"Oh, my!" Ruth shrieked and rushed over to hug her daughter-in-law and to kiss her son.

Jacob walked over too, and they were all surprised to see that their undemonstrative father had tears running down his cheeks. He made no move to wipe them off.

"Such wonderful news!" he cried. "Wonderful!" He reached into his breast pocket and took out an embroidered linen handkerchief, which he used to blow his nose loudly.

"Mazel tov, dear children," he said. "May you be blessed with a multitude." *Those mamzers didn't beat us. Our people will go on, for yet another generation!*

Laurie jumped up to hug her sister-in-law. "I'm gonna be an auntie!" she yelled, at the same time Ruth asked Roberta, "How are you feeling, dear? And when are you due?"

Roberta looked up at David. "That's the thing," he said. "We sure don't want to rain on your parade, Laurie. You too, Matt. But our baby is due on June 23rd. We didn't want to tell anyone until Roberta was past the first trimester. She and the baby are doing well, and we're so excited. But there's no way either of us can travel that week, even to the Cape.

To Sisterhood!

We have to stay in town, to be close to Lying In." David was doing his residency at the famous Boston maternity hospital.

"I'd never hear the end of it if I had to deliver the baby myself on Route 6," he joked. "And you all know how brutal the weekend traffic can be. I'm sorry to spoil things for you. And of course, if she's early –"

Laurie stifled back tears. "I'm so happy for you both!" she said. And looking at Matt, she added, "We'll figure out something else." By the time Matt's parents arrived, it was all arranged.

"Well, at least the most important people will be here," Laurie said bravely. And that Saturday afternoon, shortly after the sun set, Laurie and Matt were married in her parents' living room, by the Reform rabbi from the next town and the local Unitarian minister, who included a reading from Kahlil Gibran. After the rabbi pronounced the seven wedding blessings, Matt stepped on the glass while the proud parents, brothers, and sister-in-law all shouted their congratulations.

※ ※ ※ ※

Laurie and Matt could hardly believe their luck. Though the couple was disappointed that their "dream wedding" wouldn't take place, Ruth promised to hold a big reception in late August in Wellfleet, so all their friends could celebrate their marriage and meet the new baby too. And after they came back to the house from the wedding dinner, "to make up for having to change your plans for your brother," as Ruth put it, Jacob wrote the newlyweds a check that would cover one year's rent.

"And there will be more for you to buy a car," he added. "A good one. Anything except a Volkswagen."

✻ Twenty-Nine ✻

Soon after New Year's Day, Diane bid farewell to Ellen, Nick, and little Sandra, and moved back to Cambridge. Without Theresa or much contact with her parents – after one awkward "welcome back" dinner – Diane was determined to make a fresh start.

It didn't take long to find an apartment and a job, assisting the head cook at a breakfast and lunch restaurant in East Cambridge across from the Courthouse. Cooking, even the simple prep work she'd been assigned, was restful. It had rhythm and certainty. Feeding people pleased her, and she did her best to approach her work as a healing art.

Evenings were still tough for her, and even though her tiny apartment was in a house with others about her age, she was lonely. Without the comfort and solace of alcohol, she had many long nights to think about her daughter and her sister, not to mention the rest of her life.

One of the restaurant's lunch regulars told Diane about his friend who volunteered every Tuesday night at the Arlington Street Church's free dinner program for the homeless and others down on their luck.

"They sure could use more help," he said, "especially folks like you who know how to cook."

That week, Diane joined the team to cook dinner in the church's big kitchen, using food provided by area supermarkets. *This is something Nina might like*, Diane thought, and she decided to give her a call.

Even though some of Nina's political ideas were too radical for Diane, and she was basically a pampered rich kid, Diane liked her. There was

To Sisterhood!

also something sad about Nina. It was as if she were looking for something she'd never find. Or possibly, Diane admitted to herself, she was putting her own feelings onto someone else.

And with the charges against Nina hanging over her head, Diane knew she needed not only a friend, but something meaningful to do.

Nina was indeed interested in the Arlington Street Church's free dinner project and became a regular and eager volunteer each week. Working side-by-side helped to deepen the connection between the two women. They started going to the movies together, and once, on a rare day off for Diane, she and Nina drove down to the Cape to walk on the beach in the freezing cold and to eat warm lobster bisque.

Sometimes, Diane invited Nina for dinner, usually when she was trying out new recipes and needed a taster. She'd been wanting to recreate the delicious chicken dish she'd enjoyed at Ciro and Sal's, back at Nina's 21st birthday. After a couple of tries, she was ready.

While Nina watched from the sofa, Diane cut a whole chicken into quarters and rubbed it with some good olive oil and garlic. Then she sprinkled cayenne pepper and salt over each piece, arranging them in a roasting pan she'd coated with more olive oil. Baking it in a 375° oven for about 45 minutes, she basted the chicken with lemon juice several times while it was cooking.

She blanched six artichoke hearts in boiling water infused with more lemon juice and drained them, heated some butter in a small frying pan. and sauteed a cup of mushrooms until they were barely tender, then added the drained artichoke hearts and some salt and pepper. When the chicken was cooked through, she drained off the fat and set it aside while she heated a sauce she'd made earlier from veal bones with onion, garlic, carrots, celery, herbs, and tomato paste. To the simmering sauce, she added the chicken juices and more salt and cayenne. In a separate pan, she heated three roasted sweet red peppers, cut into chunks. Finally, she arranged the chicken on a bed of rice on a large platter, topped it with the peppers and artichokes, poured the sauce over it all, and served it with a side of crisp, roasted asparagus.

"This is sooo delicious," moaned Nina, after her first bite. "You're an incredible cook, Diane. I loved that pesto spaghetti you made for me last time, but I think I like this spicy stuff the best."

"I always appreciate an appreciative audience." Diane smiled.

Between her work, Tae Kwon Do, and Nina's more frequent company, Diane got through each day, one at a time. Now that she was willing to feel her feelings, the emptiness settled into a sharp ache. And while volunteering at the church one night a week was satisfying, Diane wanted to get involved in something she could put her whole self into. She missed the little bit of community organizing she'd done with Patty. She missed her friend, and wrote to her frequently, making plans to get together as soon as they could.

So when Laurie came stomping into the restaurant at the end of Diane's shift one afternoon, just as Nina showed up for their outing, Diane was both surprised and pleased. Laurie insisted they go someplace warm so they could talk, and when they ended up at a nearby coffee shop, with steaming mugs of cocoa against the February chill, Laurie told them all about the International Women's Day Rally and March, to be held on Boston Common early next month, and invited them to come along. Diane and Nina looked at one another.

To Sisterhood!

"Sounds exciting," Diane said. "Count me in!"

"Agreed," said Nina, "I'll join you. That is, if I'm not in jail."

※ ※ ※ ※

Ellen was out of breath by the time she made it indoors with Sandra, who was squirming to get down. Sandra was crawling everywhere and a few times had even pulled herself up to standing.

"Going to be an early walker," Ellen's grandmother predicted on their regular monthly call, when Ellen told her all that Sandra was doing.

Ellen put Sandra down and shrugged off her own coat, then reached for the baby. When Sandra scooted across the room and yanked on the lamp cord, Ellen scooped her up and gently plopped her into the playpen with her favorite stuffed bear, and took off her jacket.

Sandra seemed content, and Ellen took a few minutes to decorate the front window with the paper Valentines she'd bought on the way home. She was tacking up the last one when the postman appeared.

"Package for you, Missus."

"Thanks," Ellen said, juggling the door with her free hand. She smiled as she saw the Cambridge postmark. She opened it to find a tiny, red cardigan sweater with pink, heart-shaped buttons. Laurie had been sending gifts for Sandra often, and they spoke a couple of times a month, but with school and Matt and her impromptu wedding, she hadn't had time to fly out for a visit.

"When classes end," she'd promised. A note fluttered to the floor.

Hi Ellen, it read. *So glad to hear from you, and happy that all is well with you and Nick and your little cutie. Thanks so much for sending that new picture. She's growing so fast, and she looks like both of you!*

Things here are about the same as when we last talked. We are both okay. Call me Sunday around 4:00 pm my time if you possibly can. I have lots to talk to you about that I don't want to write. Love, Laurie.

Ellen thought about her friend's life. There was always some kind of drama going on with her. But she looked forward to their chats. Right after lunch on Sunday, Nick bundled Sandra into her carrier, kissed Ellen on the cheek, and left to take a walk.

Ellen basked in the rare opportunity to be alone in the house, even for a little while. She brewed a cup of Peets' Major Dickason's®, the one cup per day she allowed herself. Any more than that would keep Sandra awake. Ellen put in a little cream, sat on her rocking chair, read for a while, and then dialed Laurie. She was happy when Laurie picked up the phone and said, "Hey, Ellen!" in that cheerful voice of hers.

"Hey, Laurie," Ellen said, realizing how much she missed her friend.

"Ellen, I'm glad to hear your voice! I told Matt I've got a headache so I wouldn't have to drive up to his parents' house for dinner so I could talk to you. Can I get right to the point? I think I'm going crazy!"

"What's up?"

"It's Matt," Laurie began.

"What's wrong? Is he okay?"

To Sisterhood!

"Worse," Laurie said. "He's boring. I mean he's pretty smart, but all he does is read and listen to music. Except for sometimes when we're trying out new meditation techniques together, he's boring to hang out with. And boring in bed. Boring, boring, boring. Oh, Ellen, I think I totally screwed up by marrying him."

"Oh, dear," said Ellen. "It's only been – not even two months?"

Laurie was on a rant.

"The worst part is making dinner. Listen. This is my life: I get up in the morning and get in the shower. That is, *if* there's enough hot water. I get dressed and when I leave for school, Matt is sitting on the bed listening to the radio and reading. Yeah, we finally got a real bed with some of the wedding money instead of the old ratty mattress he had. When I come home from school, he's *still* sitting on the bed reading and listening to the radio. If I ask him what he did all day, it's, 'Not much. I read some. What's for dinner?'"

"So I make dinner," Laurie continued. "We don't have much money, you know, and Matt got a job right when we got back from Florida because, after all, I'm in school, and my parents are paying our rent, so it's only fair that he contributes *something*. He got this job in the stereo store on Mass. Ave., but then he lost it after two weeks because he got into a big fight with the owner, who Matt said is an asshole. He started getting General Relief not long after he lost his job. And now he isn't even *trying* to find a new one."

"Slow down a minute, honey," Ellen said. "Take a deep breath or something. I'm not exactly following you. What does all this have to do with making dinner?"

"Well, when you get General Relief, they also give you this gross government surplus food. And we have to use it, at least the semi-edible stuff, because with Matt not working, we don't have enough money for food. Most nights for dinner I use up that huge block of yellow processed cheese they give us, throw in canned vegetables, and serve it over government white rice. And most nights after dinner we hang out in the apartment but it's impossible for me to study because he's always playing that damn radio. Even if he uses headphones, I can still hear the music – he puts it on so loud. Then on the weekends, we walk to the big newsstand in Harvard Square so Matt can check out the books and magazines." Laurie paused for a breath.

"Wait a minute," Ellen said. "Didn't your parents get you a car?"

Laurie groaned.

"We can't take the car because then we'd have to pay for gas and the parking meter. Once in a while, he buys us each an ice cream cone, and then we take the bus back. Except for going to dinner at his folks' every Sunday. Thank goodness for their leftovers. And I won't ask my parents for more help. They can't know what a mess I've made."

Laurie started to cry. "I'm not in a good head space now," she said.

"Have you told him how you feel?" Ellen asked gently. "I mean all marriages need some adjustment time. This is all brand new for you both. And it was so fast –"

"Wait, that's not all," Laurie interrupted. "Let me lay this out for you straight. Did you ever – I mean *ever* – hear of a guy who doesn't like oral sex? I don't mean the lazy kind who wants it but doesn't return

To Sisterhood!

the favor. I've known more than one like that who wasn't crazy about performing – though only one who refused outright – but, Ellen, Matt doesn't like it even when I go down on him. I think he thinks it's dirty or something. I can't believe I didn't pay attention to this before!"

"Oh, dear," Ellen said again. This was more than she wanted to hear. Her own sex life wasn't all that exciting, especially since Sandra was still waking up to nurse in the night, and Ellen was exhausted all the time. But then, Ellen didn't have high expectations of Nick, and at least he was gentle and considerate. *Laurie had been so smitten. I wonder what happened,* she thought. "Did you say anything to him?"

"Sort of. But I can't say, 'Oh, darling, by the way, you're the most boring man I've ever met.' And there's more. When we get ice cream, he lets me know that I don't need it. Yeah, I've put on a couple of pounds, but all my jeans still fit. Oh, Ellen, why did I ever marry him? I could be living in the dorm, which is a whole lot more comfortable than this ratty apartment, and going to the dining hall whenever I'm hungry. I've made a big mistake!" Now Laurie was sobbing.

"Well, honey, I guess you were in love."

"Not really. At least, I'm not sure. I think we didn't care about whether or not we made it legal. I think Matt wanted the money he knew we would get for the wedding, even though that was my idea. He's already made me sell one place setting of the silver we got from his family. But I took the rest and gave it to my brother and he put it away for me so Matt can't get his hands on it."

"It's half his," Ellen said reasonably.

"No!" Laurie was vehement. "*I'm* the only one in this family with income. I'm taking five courses. I have to go to the library to study, because I can't concentrate at the apartment because of that stupid radio. Then I write my papers, and I got a job on Saturdays cleaning up mouse crap in the lab at MIT, while Matt sits on his lazy behind and does absolutely nothing!"

Ellen wished she could do something to help. Laurie didn't deserve this. She remembered what Laurie had said – that what had attracted her to Matt in the first place was that he was "so laid back," unlike her own father and brothers and most of the guys she knew at Harvard.

"Are you doing anything at all that's fun for yourself?" Ellen asked.

After a short pause, Laurie said, "I see Nina and Diane once in a while. It seems like they're kind of tight with each other now. Doing some volunteer work at that church in Boston that does all the good stuff, you know, the one across from the Public Garden? And I'm still taking Tae Kwon Do at least one night a week, two if I can squeeze it in."

"That's good," Ellen said encouragingly.

Laurie told her about going to the Somerville Women's Health Center, and how they gave classes in how to use the speculum so women could examine their own cervix.

Ellen thought this sounded kind of disgusting, but she understood the political rationale.

"It sounds like you're meeting some interesting people," she said. "Keep your eyes open, and you'll definitely meet more. Just focus on making your own life as interesting as possible and, of course, on your schoolwork. Give Matt some space to figure out what he wants to do. He can't be happy with the way things are, I guess. Men are so proud, and if he's not able to support you, well, there's that too. I'm sorry you're having such a tough time. I've got to go. Nick's coming back soon and Sandra will need to nurse. Please keep in touch. Let me know how you're doing."

"Oh, Ellen," Laurie wailed, "I didn't even get to ask you how you are!"

"We're all okay. Look, Laurie, I've got to go. I'll write to you soon, I promise. Bye, now."

Laurie hung up, feeling dejected. She'd hoped her friend would have had some advice for her, but no one could help her. Nothing could. She was stuck.

※ ※ ※ ※

In the next couple of weeks, Laurie did meet some interesting people, as Ellen had predicted.

She dragged Matt out at night to whatever lectures or programs she could find. One night they went to a talk by the folks from the new Bridge Over Troubled Waters medical van. Their mission was to bring medical care to the street kids who wouldn't go to a doctor or a hospital on their own. Some of the kids were doing drugs. Some had regular things wrong with them, or cuts and bruises from living on the street.

Laurie's brother Andy was one of the volunteers. Laurie thought he could encourage Matt to help out. But when she asked Matt about it, he said it was cool that med student Andy was volunteering, but Matt wouldn't be of any use to "those doctor folks."

Laurie didn't give up. On her way home from work on Saturday, she stopped in at Free Wheel, which was based in the Ecology Action storefront on Mass. Ave.

The Ecology Action folks had found an old bus and painted it green and yellow. They drove the route of the Harvard/Dudley bus, up and down Mass. Ave. They collected enough donations to cover the day's gas and oil expenses, then stopped collecting for that day. People who wanted to contribute late in the afternoon were told that their money wasn't needed – their ride was free. Laurie wondered what would happen when the bus needed repairs, but no one at Ecology Action seemed concerned about that.

Laurie hopped onto Free Wheel at Harvard Square the next day to get to work. There was definitely a good vibe on the bus. When she got home that night, riding Free Wheel from MIT back to Harvard, she was excited to talk to Matt about it.

"You could drive the bus," she told him. "All you need is your driver's license, and they need more volunteers." She wasn't sure if this was exactly true, but she knew that anything that got Matt out of the house was good. To Laurie's great surprise, Matt agreed to go to Ecology Action with her on Monday.

※ ※ ※ ※

Late in February, Laurie rode with Matt during his shift on Free Wheel. When he parked the bus for the night, they headed over to Boston

University. There was a talk at the Student Union by some folks calling themselves the Red Star Collective.

Laurie liked what she heard. And when the speaker, a pretty, dark-haired woman named Rose, told the crowd that the Collective had recently set up a Boston headquarters and they were looking for a few more people to join, Laurie saw a way to possibly rescue her troubled marriage.

The next day, she told Matt she was going over to Boston to talk with Rose about joining Red Star, and he could come if he wanted. If not, she was going alone. *Anything would be better than living alone with him*, Laurie thought. *Anything to get out of this shitty apartment.* She'd talked with Ellen several more times. She'd called Nina and Diane, too. Laurie was determined to make the best of her own life, no matter how much she'd messed it up so far.

※ ※ ※ ※

On the first of the month, Laurie and Matt moved into the large Red Star Collective house on a sunny, tree-lined street near Porter Square.

On their second day in residence, Laurie, Matt, Rose, Rose's old man Thomas, and the six other housemates gathered in the kitchen for the daily house meeting.

"One of the purposes of this collective," Thomas bellowed, banging his fist on the table for emphasis, "is to smash monogamy!"

Laurie flinched. Thomas was so loud, and wow, what did he mean? She didn't have to wait long to find out.

"Monogamy is one more oppressive institution," he said. "Loving freely helps us overcome our bourgeois sexual hang-ups."

He then went on to outline the house rules for the new residents.

Matt took them all in stride, but Laurie found them strange, even from the perspective of a communard-in-training. You wanted a matching pair of socks? You'd have to get up early in the morning and find two from the communal sock drawer. You wanted to have sex? Then you kept the door open, even an inch, so everything was out in the open and there could be no jealousy. The two resident babies were bottle-fed, not nursed, since you never knew when their moms might get arrested. All the residents took shifts sleeping in the babies' room and caring for them in a twelve-hour rotation.

"That way," Rose explained, "they won't get too attached to just one mother."

Laurie drew the line at shared toothbrushes and public sex, opting for sanitation and celibacy for the two months she and Matt lived there. Since she was still in school, she wasn't required to hold a job as long as she and Matt could cover their share of the rent and groceries. But she still had to do some kind of political organizing work. Laurie was assigned to go to Boston Common on Sundays, to find runaway teenaged girls and bring them to a safe house to crash, so they would be protected from predators.

She liked the work. If the girls were underage and it was safe for them to go back home, Laurie tried to help by calling their parents for them. Most of the time, though, it wasn't safe – there was a nasty stepfather or mother's boyfriend around, so Laurie and the other sisters in the collective helped the girls find a decent place to live and a part-time job, or tried to get them back into school. Matt and some of the brothers did political education on the street, handing out flyers and doing whatever temporary work they could find to earn some money.

Laurie wrote to Ellen:

Political education is the first order of the day. Each morning starts with that six o'clock House Meeting. We're reading The Bust Book (What to Do if You Get Arrested). *And* Seize the Time. *And of course, we all carry a pocket-sized copy of* Quotations from Chairman Mao.

We all went to the rifle range to learn how to shoot. Matt took to it right away, but I hated it. It was so noisy and it scared me. I am still committed to peaceful action. But I understand that it's important to arm ourselves – our Constitution guarantees that's our right – so some of us got gun permits at the police station. I wonder what would happen if the pigs busted in – would we shoot them?

Kisses to that gorgeous girl, and to you and Nick too.
Love, Laurie

Laurie never did get to find out what would have happened in a police raid. After spending evenings reading by candlelight for a month, the Red Star Collective got evicted by the landlord. It seemed that Thomas had neglected to pay both the overdue electric bill and the rent, before he left for covert action training in Vermont.

⁂ Thirty ⁂

On the first Saturday in March, hundreds of women gathered across from the State House on Boston Common to show their solidarity for women's rights.

The last speaker urged the group to walk with her towards Cambridge, and most of the crowd followed. They marched down the street peacefully, except for a few who threw rocks at the Playboy Club in Park Square.

Diane, Nina, and Laurie linked arms as they walked. They joined the other women in singing new lyrics to *Bella Ciao*, which Laurie explained was originally a folk song and then was sung by the anti-fascist resistance movement in Italy.

"We are the women," they all sang, "and we are marching, Bella Ciao, bella ciao, bella ciao, ciao, ciao. We are marching for liberation, We want a revolution now…"

Laurie's hat blew off in the cold March wind, and as Diane stepped out of line to try to retrieve it, she turned to find a woman behind her who had picked it up and was holding it out.

"Thanks," Diane smiled and turned to give the hat back to Laurie.

"Sure thing," the other woman said, staring at Diane for a moment, then looking away quickly.

To Sisterhood!

The group turned onto Mass. Ave. and marched over the Charles River. Soon they were in Central Square, and unexpectedly, the leaders of the march told the group to turn left onto Pearl Street.

When they reached Memorial Drive, the group stopped at a gray stone Harvard building at number 888. One of the organizers, a woman from the Bread and Roses collective, grabbed a bullhorn and explained to the excited crowd that she and some of the others were going to liberate the building, and everyone was encouraged to join in the takeover. The point, she shouted, was to underscore the urgent need for a women's center here in Cambridge, and also to raise awareness of the way Harvard was destroying the Riverside section of Cambridge by tearing down neighborhood housing, against the interests of the community, most of whom were poor and working class.

Like me and my family, Diane thought, the first time she'd thought about herself in the context of her family in quite some time.

"We need affordable housing for the community," the speaker said. "As well as childcare, equal pay for equal work, and basic reproductive rights."

"But you need to know, sisters," the speaker continued, "that what we're doing is an illegal action, at least as far as the Cambridge and Harvard police are concerned, so if you enter the building, you must be prepared for arrest. If you have children at home, or a job you could lose, you don't have to go in – you can support us by bringing us food and other supplies. Again, do not enter the building unless you are prepared to be arrested. Now, who's going to join me?"

Nina, Laurie, and Diane looked at one another in excitement. Nina squeezed their hands, and wished them well.

"I can't go in," she said sadly. "I can't take the risk of getting arrested again. You all go and I'll come by with some supplies and stuff for you later, okay?" She looked wistfully at the building.

As they watched, a few women, who'd gone in ahead of time, opened the windows and unfurled a huge hand-painted banner that read: "Liberated Building," and a smaller one from the upstairs window: "Sisterhood is Powerful."

Diane and Laurie went in, feeling both eagerness and trepidation. It was Saturday, and neither of them had to be anywhere else until Monday morning. As for spending the night, they'd figure that out later. Laurie would have to find a way to call Matt to let him know. They said goodbye to Nina, who again promised to come back later with food, and holding hands, they went inside.

Once inside the building, the women set about making it as comfortable as possible. Harvard University officials soon got word that the building had been occupied, and promptly turned off the electricity and heat. One of the women, an apprentice electrician, turned the electricity back on, so at least the women could see inside the building when night fell. But it was freezing outside, with a stiff wind blowing across the river.

Laurie and Diane recognized a few of the women from the conference at Emmanuel College a couple of years ago, and Molly, the main speaker there, was leading a long discussion about who should be

To Sisterhood!

allowed into the building, the purpose they'd come for, and the politics of who should be in charge.

Most seemed to agree that the building should be a "women only" space, but what about women who brought in children? How old did a boy have to be before he was considered a man, hence, not allowed? After what seemed like hours, during which Laurie was a vigorous participant in the debate, and Diane sat quietly on the sidelines, amazed at it all, she heard a soft voice behind her.

"Can you believe how seriously they're taking all this?"

Guess I'm not the only one who thinks it's all a little strange. Diane turned to see the pretty woman with feathery brown hair and wide brown eyes who'd picked up Laurie's hat on the march.

"Hi," Diane whispered. "With this much talking, you'd think we could've solved world hunger by now."

The woman laughed. "You want to go get a juice or something?" she whispered back. They went over to the makeshift kitchen area, away from the debate.

"Hi, I'm Mona," the woman said, sticking out her hand to shake.

"Diane."

"Are you from Cambridge?" Mona sat at the small table, and motioned for Diane to join her.

Diane said yes, and Mona told her she was originally from Alabama, that her family had moved to Montreal for a while, and she'd been living in the Boston area for some time now.

"Except for spending a few months in Mexico back in the fall of '69. That was a trip."

"I've never been out of the country," Diane said. "Was it beautiful? Did you…"

She stopped when she saw Mona shaking her head.

"I shouldn't even be here at all," Mona said. "Most of my time in Mexico was spent in a hellhole of a prison, first in a little border town, then in Mexico City. It was awful. The charges were finally dismissed but I know the FBI is watching me. I really should be more careful," she added, looking over her shoulder in both directions, pretending to be scared, and laughing again.

What a pretty laugh, Diane thought, *and a nice Southern accent.* "What on earth happened?" Until Nina's arrest, Diane had never met anyone who'd been in jail.

"We got caught in Operation Intercept, but fortunately, after I'd already spent a completely miserable five months in jail, I was released and all the charges were dropped. It was terrible."

"Whoa!" Diane held out her hand like a traffic cop. "You're going much too fast for me. What's Operation Interrupt?"

To Sisterhood!

Mona smiled. "'Inter*cept*.' It was the latest in a long line of Nixon's fuckups. But this time, I got caught in it. What a total bummer!"

Mona explained that the Top Pigs were freaked because their own kids were smoking dope and so, figuring that most of it came from Mexico, they were cracking down on all the drug trafficking.

"Basically," she told Diane, "it was a full-scale effort that had started on September 21st and lasted less than three weeks – that's how screwed up it was – to prevent anyone from bringing dope from Mexico into the U.S. It was timed to coincide with the fall marijuana harvest, because the American supply was short.

"Attorney General John Mitchell and his henchmen had set up blockades at about thirty crossing points along the border. All the U.S.-bound traffic was backed up for miles.

"It was bad," Mona said. "They strip-searched people, looked into babies' diapers, took apart car engines, you name it."

Diane looked stunned. She knew this kind of thing happened in dictatorships, but to Americans?

"But in spite of their brigade of pigs," Mona said, "and royally pissing off all the American tourists, not to mention the small business owners in the border towns, they arrested only thirty-three people the whole time they were pulling this stupid stunt."

Diane leaned closer, as the noise from the main room grew louder.

"Unfortunately, one of them was me. The other was the guy I was traveling with, one of the other Venceremos folks. We'd been in Mexico organizing the travel arrangements to get to Cuba, and we were going across the border to pick up some supplies before heading to Montreal. Unfortunately, he had the money for all the airfares on him. Foolishly, we had two joints, each one in the center of a roll of peppermints. We thought we were so clever."

Mona grimaced. "The Feds saw all the cash, the two joints, and that was enough. My folks sent a good lawyer. I got off. For all I know, he's still in prison. When I left, his parents were down there from Ohio trying to get the American Embassy to help him, but since this was a government bust, I don't think the Embassy was trying too hard."

"OK, I'm kinda lost here," said Diane.

As Mona explained again, Diane listened sympathetically.

"And the damn thing is," Mona concluded, raising her voice. "Now I'll probably never get a chance to go to Cuba."

Just then, the two women were startled by the sound of loud drums. A chant went up from the opposite corner of the large room, and they walked over to join the group: "We are the women, and we are singing…"

"Want to go dance?" Mona asked, and she held out her hand to Diane.

⁜ Thirty-One ⁜

Ellen walked in the door and sighed when she saw the mess. *It was Nick's turn to do the dishes, damn it.* The radio was loud, with Van Morrison singing about rocking someone's gypsy soul. Ellen turned it down. She went into their cozy living room and saw Sandra bouncing happily on Nick's knee. Ellen smiled, and her irritation softened.

Nick got up and gave Ellen a peck on the cheek, handing over the baby, who needed a diaper change. He went into the bedroom, which doubled as his office, so he could grade papers before taking a short nap. It was his turn to fix dinner, but Ellen had a feeling she'd be doing that too.

Ellen diapered Sandra, then fed her some noodles, pureed carrots, and a scrambled egg. When she finished, Ellen tucked her into the new backpack. Soon she'd be ready for her nap. Ellen hoped she could tidy up the apartment before Sandra got too sleepy. Nick had set up a small cot in the front room, and the baby always seemed to be soothed by the sound of the typewriter keys. It was the only way Ellen could get any work done. She didn't have to keep interrupting her train of thought to get up and go to the back of the apartment to check on Sandra.

It had been a rough month, with Sandra cutting a new tooth and choosing the hours from about midnight to 3:00 am to scream about it. Nick had been having a tough time at work, too. His colleagues were giving him grief about not picking up that extra course for freshmen, but with Ellen in school, and his shifts at night with Sandra, he didn't have the energy.

With Sandra happily cooing to herself, Ellen began rinsing the dishes. It was the least she could do. *Nick didn't choose this.* He was good with Sandra, better than she could have hoped. And, she reminded herself, she was eternally grateful that Nick didn't have a clue that the baby girl he adored wasn't his. He would never find out. And neither would Sandra.

Ellen scrubbed at the worst of the mess, and tossed the sponge into the sink. Then she remembered the words of her heroine and role model, Katharine Butler Hathaway: *"I believed passionately that every human being could be happy. I believed that everybody should pursue his own kind of happiness boldly and positively."* Ellen was determined to be a good mother, a good wife, and to make the happiest life for herself, in spite of what she'd lost.

As she headed to the front door to get the mail, she tripped over the coffee table. She righted herself, then checked her foot, which wasn't cut. *Nick's so talented at making things like that*, Ellen thought as she admired the big round telephone wire spool table. She couldn't have lugged it home herself, off the street and up the front steps. She wouldn't have taken the time to sand it again and again so there weren't any splinters, and to apply all those layers of varnish or whatever it was he put on it to make it shiny. The mail had arrived, and Ellen grinned as she picked up the letter decorated with slogans, surrounded by red stars and blue women's symbols:

"Sisterhood is Powerful. Revolution is the Way to Life. Free our Sisters, Free Ourselves."

Laurie. Who else?

Sandra was making little fussing noises. Ellen took her out of the backpack, checked her diaper, which was still dry, and sat in the rocker to nurse her. Sandra ate greedily and fell right to sleep. Ellen gently tucked her into the cot, surrounding her with pillows so she couldn't roll off. She opened the letter.

March 20, 1971

Dear Ellen,

Thanks for your letter telling me about your work, and for the pictures of that adorable little girl!

Ellen, I did what you asked me to do and thought a lot about your choice to do this struggle from inside the system. I mean, I know I'm not one to talk, still being in school and all, but I've made the choice to fight as best as I can. And Ellen, I'm proud of you and amazed that you'll be able to graduate on time, with the baby and the interruptions and all. I'm going to graduate on time too, but I don't have a small person to take care of – just a big one. I understand your choice, though, and in spite of all that went down last year, I still feel that for me, the best place is fighting against the system from the outside.

Nina and I started working with a group called the Mayday Tribe, and Matt is too. He's gotten into political activism in a big way. It's helped me, and us, a lot now that he's doing something meaningful. As you can surmise from the name, the Mayday Tribe is set up to coordinate local people and activities for Mayday. Look, I'll start from the beginning.

"Mayday" is seven days in May – or if you want to be precise – it's part of the "spring offensive": the anti-war actions for the spring. Mayday is based around the People's Peace Treaty, which was written and signed a few months ago by Americans and NLF members (those for the reunification of South and North Vietnam). Its premise is that the people

of America and Vietnam are not at war; the governments are. Hence, "People's Peace Treaty." People all over the U.S. are signing it to show solidarity with our Vietnamese brothers and sisters, and that we're tired of this unjust and unwarranted war. We're tired of the U.S. government making war in the name of the American people, 73% of whom want total withdrawal by the end of the year (per the latest Gallup poll).

In some communities, Vietnam Action committees have started – gathering signatures, holding teach-ins, trying to get the Peace Treaty on the ballot. This is what the liberals, not students and radicals, can do. Lots of older people are involved too.

On April 24th, there'll be a mass mobilization in Washington. The group sponsoring it split politically from our group, so I don't know if we'll be going to that. Here's the rundown on Mayday activities right now:

May 1st: A rock festival on a farm outside Washington.

May 2nd: Mass demonstration to confront the war-makers.

May 3rd-4th: More demonstrations and non-violent civil disobedience to stop the government from functioning. By "non-violent" we mean we won't be trashing, breaking windows, etc., but instead we're going to try to paralyze Washington by blocking bridges and entrances to government buildings by putting tens of thousands of bodies in the way. I am committed to peaceful actions only, though I can't speak for the others. We're expecting at least 500,000 people.

May 5th: A day for mass demonstrations all over the country, a "No-Business-As-Usual" day, and student and labor strikes. People will be lobbying government employees – trying to get them to sign the Peace

Treaty. This is something you definitely can do, even with the baby. Put her in a carrier thingy – there are babies at lots of the peace marches.

Our group is trying to tell Boston people about the planned actions, and trying to arrange transportation and housing. We're leafleting at colleges and high schools and showing films to raise money. Jane Fonda loaned us her own personal copy of They Shoot Horses, Don't They? *We screened it and raised about $2000, which we shared with another anti-war group.*

I'm enclosing some copies of the peace treaty – you can take them to your campus and gather signatures and you can get some friends to do the same. When they're all filled out, send them to the People's Coalition – the address is there – and you can take out ads in your local paper with signers sponsoring them, reprinting the treaty. And then you can try to get it on the ballot for the primaries in San Francisco.

I've also compiled some facts about the war for you (enclosed), so print them up and distribute them on your campus.

Isn't it incredible how Charlie Manson and William Calley are complete opposites, yet they are products of the same insane society?

After Mayday I am definitely going to need a rest, so after the semester ends, Matt and I are planning to take a few weeks for a vacation, travel for a while, or go to Wellfleet. If we go to the Cape, then Nina and maybe Diane can come out for a bit and hang out with us. Nina's having a tough time, and a lot is going to depend, of course, on what happens at her trial, if she's indicted. I hope those Feds go straight to hell!

Any chance you'll be coming back east to visit your parents or anything? I know I promised to come out there, but I'll have to wait and see what happens after Mayday. Think about it, will you? I would love to see you and to meet little Sandra!

Don't let motherhood pull you from the struggle, Ellen – we've come too far and worked too hard for you to give up now. Talk to Nick. Maybe he'll even babysit for a few days so you can come to Washington with us. Wouldn't that be fun?! Love and kisses to the little Williams family.

*Yours always,
Laurie*

Ellen put down the letter. She didn't know whether to laugh or to cry. She looked at Sandra, sound asleep in her cot, and at the mountain of clean laundry waiting to be folded and put away, the dishes and pots waiting to be dried and put on the shelves, and her unfinished paper in the typewriter. Circulate petitions? Put an ad in the local paper? Did Laurie have any idea how much an ad in the *Examiner* would cost? Ask Nick to "babysit?" Take a week off from classes and papers at the end of the term to go to a demonstration? Laurie, Ellen decided, and probably Nina, were totally removed from reality, at least from the reality that was now her life.

As she stood up, another piece of paper fell out of the envelope.

Facts on the War
- An equivalent of the bombs dropped on Hiroshima is dropped on Laos every two days.
- A pregnant Vietnamese woman who drinks a glass of water contaminated by defoliant (virtually the entire Vietnamese water

supply) is more likely to have a deformed child than a woman exposed to the radioactivity at Hiroshima.
- Allied bombing of Cambodia has "generated" more than 1,000,000 refugees (total population – 7,000,000) (*Senate Subcommittee on Refugees* report, 1970).
- Since May, 1964 (two months *before* the Gulf of Tonkin), American B-52s (flown from Thailand) have been bombing Laos.
- Sometime this spring, 17 highly sought-after leases to drill for oil off the Vietnam coast will be awarded by the Thieu-Ky government to international petroleum companies, most of which are American. (*Wall Street Journal*, confirmed in various trade journals.)
- 240,000 refugees have been created from the 3 million Laotians.
- From 1964-1968, air strikes in Laos averaged 60-70,000 yearly. Now, there are 200,000 annually, with a cost of $1.5 billion.
- NVF of Cambodia (Cambodian Liberation Army) has grown from 3,000 before Lon Nol Coup (May, 1970) (CIA-sponsored overthrow of Prince Sihounuk who was leaning to the left) to 115,000 now.
- Desertion rate of ARVN (South Vietnamese Army) is 15% per year.
- In Saigon, it is a capital offense for anyone to publicly advocate peace or neutrality.

Ellen looked at her baby girl stirring in her cot.

"OK," she said softly to herself. "I will do one thing. I will make copies of this sheet and post it around campus." And then she went back to typing her paper.

✵ Thirty-Two ✵

After what seemed like an indeterminable wait, Nina finally got notice that her Grand Jury hearing would be in two weeks. As advised by her attorney, Nina was not planning to testify, and she wouldn't be allowed to be in the courtroom. But she wanted to be as close as she could get. What was going to happen? Would she have to go to trial for a crime she didn't commit? Nina had spent months imagining the worst.

As she walked into the courthouse in Boston in early April, she suddenly remembered the motto of The Dalton School: "Go forth unafraid." She stood straighter, prepared for what the day would bring. She had arrived well before the day's hearings were to begin, so she could take a look at the courtroom in which her fate would be decided.

At the time scheduled for the proceeding, her attorney Mr. Friedman joined her, and together, they sat out in the corridor, waiting.

Nina could only imagine the scene inside. She figured all the jurors would just as soon crucify her as listen to the truth. She guessed that none would be her age. A jury of her peers? Hardly.

Meanwhile, inside the courtroom, the Assistant District Attorney outlined his case against the defendant, Nina Rosen. He presented the facts of the case: that an honest, hard-working father of five children working the night shift as a janitor at a satellite police station in Philadelphia, was killed by a bomb when he opened a rigged supply closet door. The bomb was placed by the Black Panthers. Police commissioner Frank Rizzo called for a second raid in two weeks on the Philadelphia Black Panther Party headquarters, where they allegedly found bombs, bomb-making supplies, and drugs.

To Sisterhood!

The Assistant DA continued his statement, ending with the fact that all the drugs, weapons, and bomb-making supplies were purchased with funds given by the defendant, Miss Nina Rosen, with a check she wrote to the Boston Black Panther Party on May 17th, 1970, in the amount of…" he paused dramatically and turned to the jury for effect. He spoke each word slowly and distinctly, so there was no mistake in what he was about to say. "Five. Thousand. Dollars."

One or two of the jurors gasped. Five thousand dollars was about half the average annual salary of all workers in the United States. Half of what many of these jurors must have earned in a year.

In the hallway, Nina guessed what the Assistant DA must have said. She knew that the jury wasn't going to like the fact that she donated this money to the Black Panthers, no matter how good her motives. These people were not going to be sympathetic to a little nincompoop who gave away her rich mommy's money.

As it turned out, she was wrong. She wouldn't know, until later, when she requested and read the transcript of the proceedings, that the state's only witness, one Wayne Connor, had stated under oath that Nina Rosen had written on the check itself "for the Free Health Center." And then, under further questioning, he had gone on to explain what the Free Health Center was and why the Black community – as well as some white folks who were allies – had supported it. That must have been enough to convince a majority of the jurors that this rich, probably spoiled, twenty-two-year-old from New York was guilty of nothing more than appallingly poor judgement. They found insufficient evidence to bring her to trial. Nina was free – for now.

✳ Thirty-Three ✳

The first thing Sam did when he finally – finally! – was released from jail after nearly eighteen months, was to go home to Ohio, where he slept for three days straight. He'd lost nearly twenty pounds from his already-lanky frame, due both to the case of dysentery he'd had the first week, and from the crappy food they'd fed him.

He just wanted to rest, recuperate, and eat his mother's good home cooking. Any thoughts he'd had about going to Cuba, and helping with the revolution, were gone. He'd spent a lot of time thinking. There wasn't much else to do in jail except watch cockroach volleyball and count the drips of water coming in through the window when it rained.

Still committed to the cause of peace, he'd help out when he could, but never again would he put himself at risk on the front lines. No more peace marches. No more sit-ins. He'd had it. And the supreme irony of this misadventure was now that he'd been in jail, the army didn't want him. He was free to start his life over.

Sam knew how hard his father worked to make a decent life for his mom, his brother, and him, and decided that he wanted, well, he wanted stability. That meant finishing college, either back in Boston or near home while working for his father. It meant that as soon as he was rested and healthy enough to function, he would call Ellen – the girl he wanted to share that life with.

Sam couldn't believe how much he'd missed her, even though he hardly knew her, and how much the thought of her had sustained him through the long days and terrible nights in jail. He'd tried several times to get messages to her via his lawyer, but he never heard back.

To Sisterhood!

He knew there was a damn good chance she'd be supremely pissed off at him. But Sam was confident that once he explained that he never meant to leave her for so long, she'd forgive him. She had to.

He tried calling the last number he had for her – at the apartment where he last saw her – but it was disconnected. He tried Radcliffe, hoping that she'd gotten her wish and been accepted, but they said no one by that name was enrolled. He called Charlie at school and at home in Vermont, finally reaching his mother who told him that Charlie was backpacking across Europe this semester, and if Sam heard from him could he please tell her son to call home?

Ellen had some friends in Boston, but he'd never met them and he didn't remember their names.

Sam went to his mother. "Mom, there's this girl…"

Maisy looked up from her work. She was addressing envelopes for an anti-war candidate running in the local election.

"How can I help?" she asked.

"I'd only just met her before I left for Mexico, and I don't know much about her except that she's from someplace in Vermont. She was living in Cambridge the last time I saw her."

"Do you know anyone who knows her?"

"Only Charlie. They went to the same regional high school and dated a while. But I called his folks and his mom said he's in Europe. There's no way to get in touch with him unless he writes or calls them."

"If Charlie dated her, wouldn't his mom know who her parents are? And where they live?"

Sam smacked his forehead. "You know, I think you've got something." He reached out and gave Maisy a big hug, and got up.

"Where are you going?" she asked. "You haven't even finished —"

"To pack," Sam called, already loping up the stairs two at a time. "I'm going to Vermont!"

Sam borrowed his brother's car and left early the next morning. He had Charlie's home address, which he'd use only if he couldn't find Ellen's in the phone book.

He drove for twelve hours, stopping only for gas, food, and the bathroom. Not finding an address, he pulled up to Charlie's house after dark, exhausted but exhilarated. He was going to find her. He knew it.

He knocked on the door. Charlie's dad opened it and smiled. Though they'd met only once or twice, he recognized the tall, skinny kid who was his son's roommate and friend.

"What can I do for you, son?" *He looked like Charlie's going to look in 25 years*, Sam thought. *Same twinkling eyes, same hair, same build.*

"You see, sir," Sam began, but he was interrupted by Charlie's mother, who chided her husband.

"Alfred," she said, "invite the boy in." She offered Sam a cold drink.

To Sisterhood!

Sam explained his mission. Of course they knew the MacDougall family, Charlie's mother told him, but they lived in King's Lake, about a half-hour drive on back roads, not too easy to find if you didn't know the way. Charlie's mother suggested that he spend the night with them and "tidy up a bit" before he drove over to the MacDougall's. She settled him into Charlie's room, and discreetly left a razor and some scissors in the adjacent bathroom.

Sam set out the next morning with high hopes. But when an older man, who Sam figured must be Ellen's grandfather, answered the door by opening it a crack, he listened to Sam's plea and shook his head. No way was he giving any information about his granddaughter to this tall, bearded hippie. Sam kept pleading, but Mr. MacDougall, or whoever it was, wouldn't say a word.

Sam turned away, distraught. At least he'd had a glimpse of where Ellen had grown up. As the front door slammed and he turned to leave, he heard a "pssst" coming from the bushes.

"I know where she is," a kid of about ten years old said in a whisper. "How much is it worth to you?" After a brief negotiation, the boy ran into the house and came back with a torn envelope.

"Five bucks," he said, and Sam gratefully gave him the money, exchanging it for the envelope.

"Thanks, man," he said.

"It's Ron," said the boy. "I'm Ellen's brother."

Sam was eager to get something to eat before racing over to wherever Ellen was living. As he sat at the local diner, he was not at all prepared for what he saw when he took out the envelope from his pocket. There was no name, only a return address in San Francisco.

Sam was not about to quit now. He drove back to Ohio, rested up for a day, then spent the last of his savings to fly across the country to find the girl he was going to marry. He took a bus from San Francisco Airport into the city, then another bus to a few blocks from the address he'd been keeping safe in his wallet. Then he started walking.

His heart pounding, he smoothed his beard, tucked in his shirt, climbed the front steps, and rang the bell.

The door was answered by a stocky man wearing a flannel shirt and jeans. He was friendly but careful with the stranger at his door.

Sam spoke boldly. "I'm here for Ellen."

The man replied, "Ellen? Why do you want to speak to my wife?"

Sam reeled back as though he'd been hit.

"Your wife? Ellen is your wife?"

The man nodded calmly.

"Guess there's been some mistake here, buddy. I'm sure someone can help you down at the Draft Help office. Why don't you try there?" he said kindly.

To Sisterhood!

Sam quickly turned to leave, so Nick couldn't see him cry as he stumbled down the steps.

When Ellen got home at dinnertime, Nick told her, "You really need to be more careful not to give out our home address, ever. One of those people you counseled at Draft Help showed up today looking for you. Kind of a scruffy looking guy." Sitting down to feed Sandra, Ellen said sure. She'd be more careful.

✷ **Thirty-Four** ✷

On a beautiful late April evening, Sandra was finally asleep, and an exhausted Ellen struggled to finish the paper for her psychology course. There were three weeks left in the term, and if Sandra would nap every afternoon, Ellen thought she'd make it, without having to ask for an extension.

Her professors, at least the two women, had been understanding. With few students juggling motherhood and the pursuit of a degree, they viewed Ellen more as a colleague than as a student.

Ellen was surprised when Nick came up behind her and kissed her hair. She'd made it clear that she was not to be disturbed during her treasured writing time.

"Um, sweetheart?"

Ellen tried hard to hide her annoyance.

"Yes?" she said, still typing.

"Ellen, I need to ask you something," he said, gently touching her shoulder. "I know you're incredibly busy, and that this will make things even harder for you, but, well…" *How could he even ask her?*

"But?" Ellen sighed.

"But, honey, I feel like I need to go to the Mayday demonstrations in Washington. My student teacher can cover for me, and I'd be gone only three days at most. I know how hard it is for you to manage, but

To Sisterhood!

I've been feeling like between school and stuff here, I haven't been pulling my weight and I need to get out there and show Nixon –"

"Fine." Ellen took off her glasses and rubbed the bridge of her nose. "Go. I'll take care of things here." She thought that it might be a whole lot easier to study if it was just her and the baby. After Sandra went down for the night, she could study in bed, and not have to cook meals, and if she needed help, maybe Harriet could come for an extra day.

"Are you sure?" Nick said. "I mean, I'll stay if you want, it's that –"

Finally looking up, Ellen cut him off again. "I said it's fine, Nick."

"I can stay with Patrick, one of my college buddies. He came home from Vietnam pretty messed up. He's in a group called Vietnam Vets Against the War. It won't cost much. Only the airfare, and whatever I need for food."

"If it's that important to you, you should go, Nick. Now please let me finish this paper before Sandra wakes up." Ellen returned to her typing.

The first night Nick was gone, after Sandra had settled down, Ellen got a call from her grandmother. She was surprised because Grandmother rarely called her, though they wrote back and forth regularly.

"Is everything all right?" Ellen asked anxiously. "It's kind of late, your time, isn't it?"

"Everything is fine, dear," said her grandmother. "I wanted to let you know that I've been thinking about you and that sweet little baby girl.

I hope you'll bring her here for another visit before too long. It's hard to believe she's almost a year old already. I so want to hold her again."

Ellen was happy to hear her grandmother's voice. Though her mother had forgiven her somewhat for the disgrace she'd brought to the family, Grandmother had never judged her at all. She'd told her everything: how she'd wanted to go to Radcliffe, and that she'd been accepted for this past year, but couldn't go because of Sandra. Her grandmother had told her that it was often the lot of women to put aside their own dreams for the good of their family.

She herself had dearly wanted to become a teacher, but was needed on the farm, then she got married, then she had Ellen's mother and aunt, and that was that. She encouraged Ellen to continue her education, and to make sure she knew that raising a child properly and with love was the most important thing she could do.

"I know," Ellen said. "I love you, Grandmother." She was surprised to be so emotional. She hadn't realized how much she missed home.

"I love you, too, Ellen Patricia. And I will continue to pray for you and that dear baby."

Ellen hung up, stifling her tears.

With Nick away, Ellen had space to think about her life, what she wanted for herself, and what she wanted her daughter to learn from her. She thought about what it would mean if after graduating next year, she pursued a doctorate. She could teach college. That would allow her to be home in the afternoon once Sandra started school, if she could work out such a schedule.

To Sisterhood!

Ellen felt cheered, even if this plan was a pipe dream for now. She'd start by looking into graduate schools this summer. If she was lucky, she'd get into one of the better schools in the University of California system. She'd been a California resident for a year and a half, so she and Nick could afford the in-state tuition. What a perfect career!

※ ※ ※ ※

At the beginning of May, Nina, Laurie, and Matt took a bus down to Washington. Not having anything else to do this year, or anyone to do it with, Diane figured this might be a good use of her vacation week and decided to go with them. The four formed their own cadre, or "affinity group," since the Mayday Tribe had insisted there was no central leadership for this action. Demonstrators were to work in small groups of four to twelve or so people, who would stick together and look out for one another. At information stations all around the city, volunteers would help demonstrators find places to crash, give written instructions on how to dress and deal with tear gas, and offer tips on where to eat cheaply.

The weekend weather was perfect: partly cloudy with temperatures in the 60s. The group headed over to the Mall, where a rally by Vietnam Vets Against the War was about to start, followed by an action at the Department of Justice.

The first speaker gave an impassioned diatribe against the war. He told the crowd how last week, led by Navy Lieutenant John Kerry, more than 1,000 veterans threw their medals, ribbons, and other honors over a fence at the Capitol building, each one giving their name, rank, hometown, and a brief statement about why they opposed the war.

"A few of us were not able to be here last week," he said, "so we're giving back our medals now." He removed his combat medals from his neck and threw them into a metal trashcan the Vets had set up.

The guy who seemed to be running things said: "And now, I'd like to introduce our next speaker. This is a man who, despite great risk to himself, crawled under fire to save a wounded buddy and brought him back to safety. He returned stateside this month, and although he will be in a wheelchair for the rest of his life, he says it was not in vain, as long as he can continue to protest this illegal war. Here he is: winner of the Purple Heart for being wounded in combat and the Bronze Star for bravery in the line of duty, Private First Class, Tony Giovanni!"

The crowd applauded thunderously.

Diane fainted.

Laurie ran to the first aid station for some water.

"It's not that hot out," Nina said to Matt. "Maybe she forgot to eat?" She was worried about her friend, who'd never been ill like this before.

By the time Diane stirred, Tony had left the stage. She stood shakily, and tried to run to the front.

"I've gotta go get that bastard!" Diane shouted. "Let me at him!"

"Take it easy, honey," Laurie said, putting a hand on Diane's arm.

To Sisterhood!

Diane realized sadly that even if she were able to reach Tony, there was nothing she could say to him. She had to think quickly or risk having to tell the whole story to her friends.

"Guess I got him mixed up with someone I used to know," Diane said, shaking her head and feeling a bit steadier now. "Let's get out of here!"

They skipped the protest at the Department of Justice, going straight over to West Potomac Park. Many of the demonstrators had set up camp – some had been there for more than a week – while others found housing with friends. Matt and Laurie were staying near Dupont Circle with Matt's cousin. His tiny apartment was cramped with his two roommates and the two extra guests, but as Laurie said, "beggars can't be choosers." Unlike most of the protestors, Nina and Diane had checked into a hotel near the Mall.

Diane found this ironic, but Nina insisted, "No tents for me." Diane was only too happy to have a clean bed to herself plus a deep bathtub. She was grateful to have such a generous friend.

"Peace City," as the encampment was dubbed, vibrated with the sounds and sights of an all-night music festival. Large, colorful helium balloons flew overhead to prevent police from buzzing the area with helicopters. The atmosphere felt more like Woodstock than a political action. But folks knew why they were there: "If the government won't stop the war, then we'll stop the government."

Echoing that slogan of the Mayday Tribe, Phil Ochs sang, followed by many other protest singers. Some people were stoned and dancing, and for the most part, everyone was orderly.

So it was a big surprise when early Sunday morning, the U.S. Park Police suddenly revoked the permit to camp. Even before the sun was up, police had surrounded the site.

As dawn broke, they announced that everyone had to clear out – immediately. As fifty thousand protesters, sleepy and groggy, began to leave Peace City, they were doused with a chilly rain. Half of them simply left and went home. Score one for the government. The rest gathered that afternoon at local churches and colleges to continue making plans for the next day.

Monday, May 3rd, dawned cloudy but not raining, with temperatures in the 50s. Laurie and Matt got up at 5:00 am and went to the spot where they'd agreed to meet Diane and Nina. The two women were already there, waiting for them.

They were all dressed similarly: thick sturdy jeans, hard boots, and helmets. Each wore a cotton bandana that could be drenched and used in case of tear gas. Full of energy and excitement despite the early hour, they made their way to Memorial Bridge, the one that led to Arlington. They saw other cadres, plus some cars on the route abandoned by drivers who'd given up even trying to get to work.

Since the Mayday Tribe in Boston had encouraged each cadre to figure out its own method to shut down the government, this wasn't like any demonstration they had participated in before.

"What the heck are we supposed to do?" asked Diane as they watched some protesters tossing trash cans into the road, and others marching and chanting. Unlike the Women's March this winter, there was no clear direction. Matt picked up a trash can from the side of the road,

To Sisterhood!

carried it for a while, and rolled it in front of the traffic. They noticed that others up ahead were sitting down across the road, forming a human blockade.

"We have to prevent workers from getting in to run the government," Nina said. "No Business as Usual!" She pumped the air with her fist.

And then, without warning, the rented trucks came. Dozens of them. And the sliding back doors opened, and out poured what seemed like hundreds of DC's police, swinging away, cracking heads as they stormed through the crowd, lobbing tear gas as they advanced.

Nina and Laurie grabbed hands and started to run. They made their way up 23rd Street toward George Washington University, not turning around to see if Matt and Diane were following. They ran into the first building they saw. The nameplate on the first door read, "Professor Dillon," and listed office hours. The professor did not appear to be in.

A secretary dressed in a mini skirt and pullover sweater came out of her cubicle and yelled at the women, "You can't come in here, this is a private office!"

"The police are gassing us, sister!" Nina yelled back, which was unnecessary because all three of them could smell the gas wafting in from the street.

"Leave. Right now!" the secretary demanded.

Nina shouted, "You've got to be kidding! Go out and get our heads kicked in? I don't think so!"

She yanked Laurie by the hand, pulled her into the bathroom, and locked the door. The secretary, now overcome by the gas, stopped banging on the door and left.

Nina and Laurie, eyes streaming, turned the water on full blast, soaked the bandanas, and used them as wash cloths to try to rinse the gas out of their eyes. Eventually, the noise on the street subsided. The women stayed locked in the bathroom for two more hours, waiting to be sure it was safe to leave.

"I wonder what happened to Matt and Diane," Laurie wailed. She was afraid the police had caught them. "Let's try to find them. I hope they're back at the apartment."

Cautiously, Nina and Laurie turned toward Dupont Circle. They were shocked by the scene in front of them. Protestors had rolled parked cars into the streets to block traffic. Dupont Circle was completely occupied by DC police and the National Guard. Nails thrown on the roads prevented cars from moving.

The women turned in the opposite direction. Unless they could somehow ditch the combat wear, they couldn't move freely around the city without risking arrest. They found an information station, where a brother confirmed what they'd suspected: all of the protesters on Memorial Bridge had been arrested.

Once again, Nina took Laurie's hand and led her into a coffee shop, where they ditched their helmets, bandanas, and boots in the bathroom. They tucked in their shirts, washed their faces, and ran Nina's comb through their hair. Walking outside in their socks, they went next door to a variety store which, luckily for them, sold thongs. They took off their socks, slipped on the rubber sandals, and sauntered as casually as they could back to Nina's hotel, looking like tourists out for a stroll.

They were astounded as they watched the news that night. Of the 25,000 people who'd been out on the streets, some 7,000 were arrested, in what the commentator said was likely the "largest mass arrest in U.S. history." More than 10,000 troops were under direct orders from the Attorney General to arrest every demonstrator on sight. According to the report, protesters not only had blocked the bridges leading in and out of the city, they'd built barricades, thrown large rocks and glass bottles onto the roads, and let air out of the tires of stalled cars, in an effort to stop traffic.

President Nixon had refused to give Federal workers the day off, and the government continued to run as usual, the newscaster concluded solemnly.

After Nina had called for room service, and both women had taken showers and changed into Nina's spare clothes, Laurie decided to go back to the apartment to wait for Matt. With fresh clothes and her hair braided, she could pass for any student. She figured it would be safe to walk back, but Nina came downstairs with her and put her into a taxi. Nina wondered if Diane had gotten arrested, or if she'd found another place to stay, but there was no way to contact her. Nina would have to wait until she showed up at the hotel.

After a restless sleep, and still no sign of Diane, Nina woke at 6:00 am. She noted the date with some irony: May 4th, exactly one year after the Kent State killings, and two years since she'd first met Ellen, Diane, and Laurie at the Female Liberation Conference. She wished she could call Ellen, but it was only 3:00 am in California. She hadn't spoken to Ellen lately, and she thought she should try to stay better connected.

After ordering breakfast, she called a friend from the Mayday Tribe.

"There will be more cops out there today than us," he told her. "It's gonna be a trip!" He explained that the protests would be focused on four places: Dupont Circle, Scott Circle, Mount Vernon Square, and Thomas Circle.

Nina dressed carefully in her extra pair of heavy jeans, but since she'd ditched her boots yesterday, she had to wear loafers. She walked to Dupont Circle and found it cordoned off by a ring of hundreds of Marines. She assumed there were Marines, or some kind of troops, at the other sites. She definitely didn't want to be out there alone, but she didn't want to give up either. She couldn't risk getting arrested again. She was still figuring out what she should do when she saw a man, also alone, walking toward her.

"Nina?" he said. "Nina Rosen?" Nina stopped, astonished. It was Nick. Ellen's Nick.

"Nick, is that you?" Nina laughed. "I guess we're among the few left standing." She reached out and gave him a hug.

"What the heck are you doing here? Is Ellen with you?"

"No," Nick said. "She's home with the baby."

Nina smiled. "Did the other people in your group get arrested yesterday too?"

To Sisterhood!

"I guess so. I kind of lost them somewhere around Scott Circle. Just missed getting my head cracked open there too."

"Well, there doesn't seem to be much the two of us can do here, unless we're feeling suicidal. Let's go get a cup of coffee." Nina took his hand and led him toward her hotel. *I can finally do Ellen a favor*, she thought. *I think I know how I can help her.*

※ ※ ※ ※

Nick flew home early Thursday, completely exhausted. He played with Sandra for a little while, then crashed, and didn't wake up until almost dinner time. He hardly said a word while he ate, and didn't say much before he left for work in the morning.

Nick couldn't put it off any longer. He waited until Friday night, after he'd read *Goodnight Moon* to Sandra. He was sitting in the kitchen, his head down on the table, when Ellen came in.

"Are you okay?" she asked, touching his back. "You've been awfully quiet since you got home. I'd like to hear all about the action –"

Nick sat up, interrupting her. "Look, Ellen, there's something I have to tell you."

Nick's forehead was wet. Ellen wondered why he was sweating.

He continued: "In Washington…after it was over on Monday night and the people I'd been with got arrested, I guess, because they never made it back to the apartment, and then Tuesday morning I got up and I was all by myself, but the Marines were everywhere, and I didn't know where to go, and then I ran into someone."

Ellen was still.

"Someone you know. Well, I used to know her too. Your friend, Nina Rosen."

"Nina!" Ellen exclaimed. "You saw Nina! I'm surprised she'd be at the demonstration, since she finished that mess with the Grand Jury not that long ago. I'd have thought she'd want a break from all this. How is she? I haven't had a good talk with her since the night after they let her go."

Ellen recalled that conversation. Relief that Nina was okay and out of trouble, and then what was next for each of them. Finally, Nina had asked Ellen how she and Nick were doing, and what having Sandra had done to their love life. And Ellen had told her the truth.

"Ellen, wait," Nick said. "Nina and I – well, neither of us got arrested, but so many other people did. Then on Tuesday, like I said, there was hardly anyone left on the street, and I literally ran into her. I mean, it wasn't planned or anything."

"No, of course not. You didn't know she was going to be there. You didn't even know that you were going until last week. And you haven't seen her in what – a few years?"

Nick twisted his hands, looking more and more uncomfortable. But he couldn't stop now.

"Right, well, we went back to her hotel room and then...we hung out, catching up, and later we shared a joint, and a whole bottle of Chianti. And then she, well, she...well...I guess there's no easy way to say this.

To Sisterhood!

We went to bed together. Ellen, I'm so sorry." He was crying now. "It didn't mean anything. I don't want to hurt you."

Nina, how could you! Ellen thought. *I told you our sex life wasn't that great lately, practically nonexistent, but that doesn't give you the right...*Nick wiped away his tears as he waited for her to speak.

"Ellen, say something." He was sobbing now, mucus from his nose running down his chambray shirt. *He's not that cute anymore.*

Ellen stared at him. Him, she could understand. He was a guy. But Nina was her friend. Why would she do this? *Nina, what were you thinking?* She took a breath. *Eddy, help me out here!*

"Ellen, please," Nick cried. "Oh, honey, I'm so, so sorry."

Okay, Nick, she thought. *Now we're even. Well, clearly not all squared away, but I can't come down hard on you. So, okay.*

She folded her arms across her chest as if to protect herself. "And...?"

"And it will never, ever happen again," he said. "I swear it. I love you. I love Sandra. I love our life. It was a mistake. A big drunken mistake. Will you – can you please, please forgive me?"

Ellen said softly, "I guess I haven't been a good wife to you lately."

Nick's shoulders relaxed a little.

"I know this sounds stupid, but you've been busy with the baby and your schoolwork and all. I think I *have* been a little bit jealous..."

"Yes," said Ellen, "and I probably haven't been as attentive to you as I should have."

She reached out and touched Nick gently.

"Just this once," she said softly. "But don't do it again. Ever. I mean it, Nick."

He nodded, and took his wife into his arms. "Ellen," he repeated. "I'm so sorry…"

Mostly, Ellen was tired. And she couldn't understand what sisterhood meant, if it included sleeping with your friend's husband. She was going to have a serious talk with Nina soon.

⌘ Thirty-Five ⌘

Diane returned to the restaurant after her so-called vacation. She didn't mention her arrest to anyone at work. Not one person on the staff seemed to have heard of the demonstrations, let alone connect the Diane they knew with those "no-good Commie bums."

Although it would be some time before the ACLU succeeded in getting all the detainees' charges dropped – there'd even been some talk of the protesters getting monetary compensation – Diane keenly felt the stigma of her arrest. Having lost track of Matt when the arrests began, she was penned into an outdoor arena with thousands of her fellow protesters, without police following usual booking procedures. Sleeping on the ground, with only the most basic of provisions, killed any desire she had to continue in the anti-war movement, at least in public. And seeing that bastard Tony being honored as a war hero, that was more than she could handle. She would stick to her cooking, and vowed to keep things simple in her life. She was determined to lay low and not get into any more trouble.

She tried to enjoy her work, even if it was frying burgers and making sandwiches for her regular customers, most of whom were construction workers and courthouse clerks. At the end of May, she earned a small raise. That gave her the confidence to approach her boss about adding a couple of new items to the menu – some of the lighter fare that she'd so enjoyed in California.

"No one here wants to eat rabbit food, Diane," her boss laughed. "But go ahead, if you want to add something like that, give me a cost breakdown and what you think we could charge. I'm willing to try it."

Diane was excited to do some research on plant-based cooking, and one night after work, she called Nina and they headed over to the library. While Nina browsed in the new fiction section, the helpful librarian directed Diane to the Seventh-Day Adventist vegetarian cookbook, *Ten Talents*. She took it home, eagerly testing one recipe after another, until she came up with her own version of a cashew burger she thought her customers might enjoy.

She brought a sample from home for her boss to try. "Not too bad," he said grudgingly. "What do you need me to buy?"

Diane gave him a short list of ingredients, and soon, "The Nutty Burger" appeared on the menu.

A few brave customers tried it, and gave it good reviews, but it didn't go over as well as Diane had hoped, so when the supplies ran out, she went back to frying beef burgers with onions.

Diane continued studying and teaching Tae Kwon Do a few nights each week, where she sometimes saw Laurie. On other nights, she spent time with some folks she'd met working at the Arlington Street Church free dinner program.

Mona had been at Arlington Street a few times, helping in the kitchen. After they'd cleaned up together one Tuesday, Diane asked her if she'd like to hang out some time, or catch a flick at the Orson Welles.

"Sure," said Mona. "I'd like that. Where do you live?"

Diane told her she had a small apartment in a house on Kinnaird Street, and Mona answered with delight, "Hey, we're neighbors! I live on

To Sisterhood!

Putnam, right near the furniture store. It's a great night. You feel like walking home?"

"Sure," Diane said, "and yes, you're almost right around the corner. Do you have roommates?"

"Two," said Mona. "A straight couple, Julie and Jay. And their two adorable cats."

Diane laughed. "I never had a cat but I always wanted one. My mother claims she was allergic. I don't think my landlord allows pets though."

"You can come visit ours anytime. Porgy and Bess, they call them."

Diane laughed again. "Gershwin fans, I take it?"

"You wouldn't believe it!" Mona said. "I go to bed listening to *Summertime* and wake up to *I Got Plenty of Nothing*."

"Actually," said Diane, whose grandfather had loved Gershwin too. "I think it's '*Nuttin'*.'"

"You know that!" Mona linked her arm through Diane's. "Louis," she said, out of the corner of her mouth, "I think this is the beginning of a beautiful friendship."

Diane looked amazed. "My number one, all-time favorite movie."

"Mine too," said Mona. "Isn't Ingrid Bergman the most gorgeous girl you've ever seen?"

"Hmm, she's pretty, I guess," said Diane. "My favorite is Sam. Dooley Wilson. You know, the Brattle is going to show the film next month. We should go."

"Absolutely," Mona said.

They spent the next hour walking home, up Beacon and over the bridge, laughing and swapping more favorite movies, and music, and TV shows. Then the conversation turned more serious, to Cambridge politics and what Harvard was doing to the neighborhood.

"Did you hear," said Mona, "last Monday the Cambridge City Council voted down the resolution by the people from the Riverside community to deny Harvard a demolition and building permit for the Treeland site?"

"That stinks," said Diane. "I've been kind of out of touch lately."

"I was there," said Mona. "It was pretty intense. "Saundra Graham – you know, she's the head of the Riverside Planning team? – said, 'Harvard, you're *not* going to run us out of our city. We have no place to go, and we're not going to run.'"

"Catch me up," said Diane. "I know that Harvard wants to build apartments at Treeland and that the neighbors want low-cost housing. Do you know what Harvard's planning for the site?"

Mona snorted.

To Sisterhood!

"Get this," she said. "Twin luxury towers with 278 units starting at $300 a month! Harvard also retains the option to turn these apartments into dorms after, I think, 20 years."

"And they don't pay anything at all to the city?" Diane asked.

"Well, they do pay about a 2% fee in lieu of a tax to the city even though they don't have to. But that's much, much less than they would have paid if they weren't a so-called nonprofit."

"I probably should get involved again," said Diane. "When's the next meeting?"

"I'll find out and let you know," Mona said. "Hey look, we're almost home! Are you still hungry? It's not that late. We could go up to Inman Square to that cool vegetarian restaurant, Corners of the Mouth. It's run by a collective. Good food, not expensive."

Diane shrugged. "I'm beat. But I'd like to try it another time. I've got to get up at 6:00 am for work. Where do you work?"

"At the Goodwill store up at the corner," she said. "But I don't have to be in until 10:00 am. I can wake up at quarter of, throw on my jeans, run a comb through my hair, grab a cup of coffee, and be on time. No one cares much what I look like."

"Do you get first crack at the good stuff people bring in?" Diane asked.

"Sometimes. I got these boots," she said, showing off her Tony Lamas. "Aren't they cool?"

When Diane nodded appreciatively, Mona continued, "They're the El Rey model. The same ones Sandi Prati wore."

"Who?" said Diane.

"Sandi Prati, Miss Rodeo America, 1964," Mona said. "I thought she was wicked hot when I was thirteen. There weren't that many women role models for us."

"Hmm," Diane said. "My sister and I liked Penny on *Sky King*."

"Oh, you have a sister?" Mona said. "Me, I'm an only. I think my parents thought one curtain-climber was enough. I guess I was kind of a wild child."

Mona looked at Diane, whose whole posture had shifted. She sagged against the telephone pole.

"Diane, did I say something?"

Diane shook her head. "No, it's fine. I'm just wiped. I've gotta go to bed."

"Sure," Mona said, looking puzzled. "Why don't you come into the store sometime? I work until 6:00 pm every day except Tuesday."

"OK, thanks, I will." Diane turned quickly in the direction of her apartment. "It's been fun, Mona. I'll catch you soon!"

"Bye," Mona said softly to Diane's back, wondering what had just happened.

To Sisterhood!

❋ ❋ ❋ ❋

June 22, 1971

Dear Ellen,

So much has happened! I'm enclosing Issue #3 of the Cambridge Street Sheet *— a weekly paper Matt and I have been helping with. I helped Nina write the Grand Jury article on page 3, but a couple of paragraphs got lopped off the end.*

Other than that, I've been pretty busy. I'm taking Tae Kwon Do on Sundays and Thursdays. I'm helping with the women's dinners on Tuesdays. The Women's Center is opening next week, and I'm on the crash pad committee. Did Diane and Nina ever tell you the whole story about how the Women's Center got started last March? A large group of women, organized by the group Bread and Roses, took over an unused Harvard building that was scheduled for demolition so Harvard could build some more plastic sky-rise apartments for their students while the poor people in the neighborhood would be forced out. The women supported the community's demands for more low-income housing, and we wanted to show the need for a women's center. We occupied the building for a week and a half.

Anyway, it came to a showdown between us and the Cambridge police, so we left, but not until our needs had been publicized and made widely known and an anonymous donor — who we think might've been one of the Radcliffe deans — donated $5,000 for a permanent center. Others gave $1,000 or $100 or whatever they could afford, so now we own a big house in Cambridge. It's on Pleasant Street in Central Square. It's got 12 rooms — a living-room/lounge with a women's library; an office with an information switchboard; a women's law commune so we *don't need piggy lawyers; a clinic, so we don't need piggy doctors, especially gynecologists; a crash pad for runaways and girls who come from other cities to stay for a few days, so they don't have to sleep with some guy they meet on Boston Common just to get a bed. Then there's a large meeting room/karate room/dance room, a gay women's center, and on and on. We've needed this for such a long time! Any of your women friends or classmates are welcome for a couple days if they visit Boston. You and Nick, of course, can stay with Matt and me. Anyway, we'd love to see you.*

We missed you at Mayday. Nina says to give Nick a special "hi."

Love,
Laurie
Free Our Sisters! Free Ourselves!

"'A special hi', my backside," Ellen muttered. She waited a few days before she wrote back to Laurie. As for Nina, well, she'd get around to calling her sometime, but for now, there were dishes and laundry to do, and all that babyproofing to figure out, now that Sandra was walking.

✺ **Thirty-Six** ✺

After all the excitement of preparing for Mayday and then going to Washington, the prospect of living alone with Matt again was stultifying for Laurie. Since returning north, they'd been staying at a large house with the rest of the Boston Mayday Tribe, but the lease was up and they all had to move by August 1st. Laurie and Matt would have to find a place in Cambridge soon, before her classes began.

She'd convinced her disappointed mother not to throw them a big wedding reception, saying it was too late after the wedding, and that it felt more like a grab for gifts than a celebration.

This would be a good time to visit Ellen and finally meet little Sandra. Matt had no interest in going. One of his buddies had recently opened a pizza shop and needed temporary help.

"Do it," Laurie said. "It's only for a little while, then we can look for a new apartment."

Matt agreed, and Laurie was glad she could get away. She couldn't wait to finish school, and then – who knew? She wanted to travel. She wanted to see everything there was to see. The trouble was, she didn't want to see it all with Matt.

✺ ✺ ✺ ✺

When she arrived in San Francisco, Nick was at the gate.

"Ellen was going to come get you," he said, taking her bags and hugging her awkwardly with one arm. "But as she was leaving, Sandra started fussing and since she's cutting a tooth, Ellen put her down for an early nap and sent me instead."

"Thanks so much, Nick. Wow! I'm finally here!"

Nick steered her toward the exit and the car. He switched on the radio, and they drove north on the 101, listening to *Riders on the Storm*.

"It's hard to believe he's gone," Laurie said. She'd been upset to hear of Jim Morrison's unexpected death early in July. "And this seems to be the last song he recorded."

"I know," Nick added, shaking his head. "And how weird is it that he died exactly two years to the day after Brian Jones?"

In half an hour, Nick pulled up in front of the house. He got the suitcases out of the trunk while Laurie bounded up the stairs.

Ellen stood in the doorway, holding a smiling baby. "Welcome, Laurie," she said. "I'd like you to meet our Sandra."

"Oh, what a cutie pie!" Laurie said, hugging them enthusiastically. "She looks like you, Ellen!"

"Hi, Sandra," Laurie reached out to touch the baby softly on her cheek, which made her giggle.

Ellen had prepared a special dinner for their guest, and Sandra was on her best behavior, her antics making Laurie laugh several times.

To Sisterhood!

"Ever think about it?" Nick asked, followed swiftly by "Ow!" as Ellen kicked him under the table.

"What was that for?" The women shook their heads at his bluntness.

Wiping strained beets off Sandra's face, Ellen said, "Let the girl graduate first. I mean, we're living proof of how tough it is."

"Gotta get this little one tucked in." Nick took Sandra from Ellen and started upstairs. "I'll leave you two lovely ladies to catch up."

"So…" Ellen began, as Laurie said, "Tell me everything…"

And they talked until long after Nick had fallen asleep, about motherhood and marriage and the reality of their new lives, which had changed dramatically since they'd last been together.

※ ※ ※ ※

Laurie woke at dawn. She lingered in bed, listening to the sound of the birds, and then to Sandra's cheerful babbling.

Over pancakes, Ellen asked Laurie what she'd like to see first.

"Everything!" Laurie exclaimed. When Ellen laughed, she added, "I'm the tourist. You decide."

After breakfast, they drove to the Japanese Tea Garden and wandered the grounds, pushing Sandra in her stroller until Ellen announced, "This little one is kind of stinky."

As Ellen went to the ladies' room to change Sandra's diaper, Laurie sat on a bench in the Zen garden and tried to calm her breath, using some of the meditation techniques she and Matt had been exploring. Before long, Ellen came up next to her.

"What is that you're doing?"

Laurie explained that she and Matt had been doing some research into ancient meditation practices, but there were so many, it was difficult to know which would work best.

"What are you hoping to get from a practice?" Ellen sat next to her on the bench, jiggling the stroller as they talked.

"That's a great question," Laurie said. "I guess I'd like to be calmer and get clear about what my next steps will be after graduation. I'm still not sure what I want to do."

"You can do anything you want," said Ellen. "I know you said you'd like to travel, and that you want to do healing work. What about joining the Peace Corps?"

"You know, I've been thinking about that!" Laurie's enthusiasm made Ellen smile. "I'd get to do two of my dreams at the same time. The only thing is, I haven't discussed it yet with Matt. I'm not sure he'd want to serve. And while I think I'd go without him, I don't know if the rules allow that if you're married."

"You won't know unless you ask him." Ellen tucked a light blanket around Sandra, who was sucking her thumb and looking drowsy.

To Sisterhood!

"You're right, but who knows what he'd say? These days, all he seems to want to do is read. Though now he's helping his buddy at his new pizza shop." Laurie shrugged. "Probably that's all a philosophy degree will get you these days, unless you're going to grad school. Now that he got a high lottery number, he's not motivated to do much. You know, I was first drawn to him precisely because he's laid back. Well, I guess there's laid back and then there's supine."

Ellen laughed. "But it seems like the two of you have done some exploring into alternative paths – meditation and such. That's fascinating. All Nick and I talk about is whose turn it is to do the dishes and keep the laundry moving. God, this little girl sure makes a lot of laundry!" Ellen looked down fondly at her sleeping baby.

"You know," said Laurie. "I envy you. You have a purpose, a reason to get up in the morning. I'm not sad; I feel like I'm kind of drifting."

"And I envy you your freedom," said Ellen. "Not that I'd trade her for the world, but you still have all your options open."

"What are you going to do next?" Laurie leaned forward, elbows on her thighs and hands cupping her chin.

"It's amazing, but with Nick's help," Ellen said as she smiled down at her baby girl, "I'm going to manage to graduate on time, next May. And I'm strongly considering going on to grad school. I want to make a difference, teaching other women – and men too, of course – some of the ideas and principles you and Nina and Diane and I first learned about at the women's conference."

"Speaking of Nina," Laurie said. "Have you heard from her lately?"

When Ellen shook her head, Laurie went on. "Diane mentioned that something went down between the two of you, but she's so loyal, she wouldn't say what it was."

"You're very perceptive, Laurie. But it's better that I talk with Nina first. And I've been so busy…"

She was interrupted by a cry from Sandra. "Mama!" the baby held up her arms.

"To be continued," Ellen said as Laurie laughed. They headed back to the car, and as Ellen tucked her daughter into her car seat, Laurie looked at mother and child.

Yes, she thought. *That's for me. But not yet. And maybe not with Matt.*

The two women spent the next several days visiting major tourist sites – Fisherman's Wharf, Ghiradelli Square, a trip over the bridge to Sausalito, and a longer excursion up to Sonoma to visit a couple of wineries; then relaxing at home in the evenings.

When it was time for Laurie to return east, Ellen took her aside. Removing her glasses, she put her face close to Laurie's.

"Look at me, Laurie. I want you to think about applying to the Peace Corps. I called them yesterday and found that the application is due in September for next summer. Just fill it out and you have all year to make a final decision. With your psychology degree and your desire to see the world and to heal, you'd be a natural."

To Sisterhood!

Laurie's eyes filled with tears. "You're a dear friend, Ellen. Thanks for looking out for me. I'll definitely give it some serious thought." She wiped the tears with her sleeve and laughed.

"What a couple of saps," she said as Ellen teared up. "You'd think we're never going to see each other again." Neither of them could have known that it would indeed be a long time before they were reunited.

On her way to board the homebound flight, Laurie was jostled by a bearded, long-haired guy wearing a three-piece suit with flared trousers and well-shined shoes.

What a strange-looking dude, she thought.

"Do you know where you're going?" he asked.

"I beg your pardon?"

"Hello, sister," he smiled. "I asked if you knew where you were going."

"Well, Boston," Laurie said, indicating the overhead flight schedule board. "What about you?"

She had time to learn what he meant, as Jaipal was seated next to her.

By the time the flight landed at Logan, he'd told her all about Transcendental Meditation®, and convinced her to sign up for instruction at the Student's International Meditation Society, near Radcliffe. One week later, after paying a fee and bringing fruit and flowers, Laurie was initiated and received her secret mantra.

After her first visit, she insisted that Matt come with her and, to Laurie's surprise, he too was an eager student. Unlike Laurie, who'd jumped right in, Matt took time to research some of the health and other benefits that Transcendental Meditation® offered. They both started a daily morning practice, and Laurie felt hopeful for them as a couple for the first time in a while. For one thing, Matt was getting out of bed in the morning, and he'd found a part-time job at a used bookstore in Harvard Square.

Once she and Matt had settled into their new apartment, Laurie started classes, continued working at the MIT lab, and spent all her spare time at the Society. She barely had time to sleep or eat. She did, however, do as she'd promised Ellen, and sent in her Peace Corps application. Two of her professors and her supervisor at MIT agreed to provide references, and all were encouraging and supportive. Matt said he would complete an application too, but Laurie never asked him about it and didn't know if he'd followed through.

She didn't see her friends again until late September, when she called Diane and Nina and asked them to meet her at the new restaurant in Harvard Square.

When Diane and Nina arrived at Grendel's Den, they were startled by Laurie's appearance. She'd lost a lot of weight. She wore frayed bell bottom pants with a white-on-white embroidered shirt, with pearl buttons down the front. She had on two strings of love beads – the kind Diane had last seen in high school – and what looked like an expensive pair of handmade sandals. A rainbow-colored scarf twisted through her hair, which hung down to her collar in a fat braid. Frizzy strands stuck out, which, to Nina, made Laurie look like a crazed toddler.

To Sisterhood!

They ordered from the eclectic menu, and Laurie waited until they'd all taken a few bites of salad, before she spoke.

"You've both been such good friends to me and supportive of all the political work we've done. And now I need to walk a different path."

Neither Diane nor Nina said anything. They waited for her to go on.

"I've been hanging out with some folks this summer," Laurie continued. "At the Student's International Meditation Society."

"You mean the group run by the guru the Beatles follow?" Nina asked.

"Maharishi Mahesh Yogi," Laurie said and smiled. "He can show you the way to peace and harmony and love." She twisted the strands of love beads around her forefinger.

Nina said, "Tell me more." Diane glanced at Nina, who looked like she was itching to take out her reporter's notebook but didn't.

Laurie explained that how, with only two twenty-minute periods of meditation a day, she already felt lighter and calmer and could handle difficult situations better.

"But how will meditating stop the pigs from busting people and how will it stop the war?" Nina wanted to know.

"Maharishi says that meditation is the only way to peace."

"Laurie, what a cop-out!" Nina blurted. "You mean to tell me that after all we've been through, all we've done together on the streets, you're gonna give it all up to sit on your behind and chant 'Om' all day?"

Laurie spoke calmly. "Nina, Diane, why don't you come with me and Matt to an introductory program? I think you both can use a little more peace in your life."

Nina shook her head. "I thought you wanted to travel and 'see everything there is to see.'"

"I'm learning that there's so much to see by turning inward, not outward," Laurie said, raising her hands together in a gesture of prayer.

Diane looked at her friend. She sounded serious. She shrugged, squeezed Laurie's hand, and said she had to run. But before she left, she looked around the cool new restaurant. *I wonder if they're hiring.*

"Gotta go too, Laurie," Nina said. "Good luck on your different path thing. It's sad to think that the Movement's losing you to some old, fat Indian guru who probably just wants your money. It's hard for me to understand all this."

"Please keep in touch, Nina."

"Sure." Nina walked away, again shaking her head. She figured it might be some time, if ever, until she saw or heard from Laurie again.

※ ※ ※ ※

"Could you believe that?" Nina said later to Diane on the phone. "It sounded like she forgot to come down off a bad acid trip."

To Sisterhood!

Diane wasn't amused. "It's too bad, really, to lose her to a bunch of weirdos. But maybe it's just another one of her exploration things. I mean, she didn't drop out of school. She's still enrolled. She never actually put herself on the line."

"That's not true," Nina said. "She was at Mayday, and at the takeover of 888."

"Yes," Diane said. "But she didn't sleep in the building. I know you couldn't risk it, but I was there, and each night, she said she was going out 'for supplies.'"

"Well, you told me she did bring in supplies…" Nina said.

"Yeah, from her rich daddy's allowance!" Diane wasn't even sure why she felt disappointed. She too had decided to step down from activism. Maybe because Laurie had every advantage that Diane did not.

Changing the subject, Diane asked, "Have you spoken to Ellen recently?" Diane wanted to hear Nina's version of her story about Nick, without letting her know that she already knew what had happened from Ellen's point of view.

"Um, no, not since Mayday." Nina was vague.

"Maybe you should give her a call," Diane said, wondering if she'd ever understand anyone, or what they did, or why they did it.

⁂ Thirty-Seven ⁂

Despite a stern warning from her lawyer, Nina felt compelled to go to Dennis's trial in Philadelphia. It was early October, and she still hadn't found a full-time job, though she'd had a few freelance gigs for the local paper, and even one assignment doing background research on Cuba for a small literary magazine. On the train, she reflected on the relationship that never had a chance. She didn't know Dennis all that well. She just knew that she trusted him.

Before she entered the Courthouse, she paused on the steps, considering what it would mean for Dennis if he were sentenced to more time in jail.

She slipped into the back row. He looked thinner, but somehow harder, as if he'd spent all these months getting tough. He didn't see Nina. That was how she wanted it.

While Nina watched the preliminaries before the opening statements, she caught the attractive, young assistant defense attorney looking at her questioningly. She nodded slightly, and he returned hers with a small shake of his head: "You shouldn't be here."

After Nina had pleaded with her father to help her friend Dennis, saying she'd use whatever was left of her trust fund to pay for his lawyer, he'd reluctantly asked his attorney for a referral. Arnold Friedman made a couple of phone calls and found that Dennis already had representation, someone he knew well and respected, an older Movement lawyer named Leo Markowitz, and that Dennis's parents had paid the retainer, with many friends and church members offering help. His attorney had been frank with them: it was going to be a tough battle, and the most they could expect was that the murder charges would be reduced to manslaughter, which at least carried the chance of parole.

Markowitz had been on the defense team for the Portland folks accused of pouring blood on draft files. His young associate, Neil Tierney, "a real sharp go-getter," Mr. Friedman explained, had been with the firm for a year, having started his career as a public defender.

"Leo's the best there is," Friedman said, "but since the government is pressing charges, I've got to tell you, there's not too much of a chance of Dennis being found innocent." He strongly cautioned Nina to stay away from the Philadelphia courtroom. But she couldn't help it. She had to know that it wasn't Dennis who'd set her up. Dennis had never trusted Wayne. He had to be an infiltrator, he had to be.

The prosecutor, Edward Cranston, was about to start his opening statement. He stood, straightening his Brooks Brothers tie. He began by telling the Court that sometime during the night in question, Dennis Burton and Mitchell McGee went into the Philadelphia police station, asked to use the men's room, and left a bomb on a timer, which then exploded in the middle of the night, killing Mr. Harlan Q. Thorton, a 45-year-old janitor with five children. Mr. Thorton, the prosecutor said, was a hard-working Black man.

"We intend to prove, Your Honor," he said, "that the Black Panther Party intended to kill one or more police officers but ended up killing one of their own people. And that they did this with malice aforethought, and had planned not only this bombing but several others."

Apparently, explained Cranston, as soon as the officers on duty heard the bomb go off in their own building, they immediately knew it had to be the work of the Black Panther Party.

"Objection," said Leo Markowitz, pulling himself up to his full height. "Your Honor, that is speculation on the part of the prosecutor." He ran a hand through his gray hair.

"Counselor?" asked the judge. "How would the police know that it was the work of the Black Panther Party?"

"Thank you, Your Honor," Cranston said. "It was the way the bomb was constructed. It was similar to bombs left in other cities. It had all the hallmarks of an unsophisticated explosive."

Markowitz again said, "Objection!"

"Yes, Mr. Markowitz."

"How could they know how the bomb was constructed merely by hearing it?"

"Thank you, Counselor," the judge said. "Help me to understand this, Mr. Cranston."

Cranston explained that recently, a series of unexploded bombs had been recovered by the FBI, so this event, while tragic, did not come as a surprise. And when the officer on duty saw the two defendants enter the building "to use the rest room," he was already suspicious.

Markowitz objected. He told the judge he would show that the two men were nowhere near the police station at the time and this story was a complete fabrication.

"You will be given that chance. For now, I'm going to allow Mr. Cranston to continue," said the judge.

"So, understanding that this bomb may have been only one of more planned attacks, the Philadelphia unit of the F.B.I. obtained a warrant to search the premises of the Philadelphia chapter of the Black Panther Party. They attempted to enter the house peacefully by identifying themselves as police officers in possession of a search warrant. Instead, they were immediately fired upon. Fortunately, all the shots fired missed the officers." Cranston paused dramatically and looked around the courtroom. "Then Officers Grabowski and Mellon used force to open the door, and told the shooters to drop their weapons. They did so without resisting, and the officers apprehended three suspects."

"Are those suspects in the Courtroom today?" asked the judge.

"They are, Your Honor."

"Can a witness please identify them for the record," said the judge.

Edward Cranston pointed to the three men at the defense table, and named them, one by one. "Mitchell McGee, Dennis Burton, and Wayne Connor."

"Thank you, Counselor," said the judge. "You may continue."

"The officers handcuffed the suspects and had them lie face down on the floor so they would not continue to be a threat. Officers Horton and Marsh were called in as backup. They proceeded to search the house in compliance with the warrant. No one else was in the building at the time, and nothing remarkable was found until the officers reached the basement. There the officers found several unregistered weapons, including three semi-automatic Colt 1911 .45 ACPs, and six .357 Magnum revolvers. They found more supplies to make bombs of the same type that were detonated in the Philadelphia police station. And they found a large cache of drugs, prepared for street sale."

Cranston paused to take a handkerchief out of his breast pocket and used it to dab his brow.

He looked meaningfully at the jury.

"These weapons and bomb-making supplies were designed to be used against the same officers who are paid to protect and defend you."

Markowitz was on his feet.

"Objection, Your Honor. There is no way the officers could have known what these items were intended for. Unless in fact, they were planted there to frame the defendants –"

"Sit down, Counselor!" The judge banged the gavel hard. "Your objection is sustained, but I must caution you to refrain from speculation of your own. You will have your chance shortly to present your case."

To Sisterhood!

"Sorry, Your Honor," said Markowitz, trying to look contrite. "And thank you."

The judge nodded to Markowitz.

"Go on, Counselor," he said to Cranston.

Nina watched in horror as the prosecution presented its main case and their witnesses, who turned out to be – no surprise – members of Commissioner Frank Rizzo's police force.

On the afternoon of the third day, the defense presented its case.

"The defense calls Dennis Burton to the stand."

"Do you swear to tell the truth, the whole truth, and nothing but the truth?" Dennis was asked.

"I do." Dennis sat up straight in the witness chair and looked directly at his attorney.

"Good morning, Mr. Burton," said Markowitz. Dennis nodded hello.

"Can you please tell the Court where you were on the evening in question?"

"Yes, Sir." Dennis sounded calm and confident. "I was at the Fuller Street Baptist Church, doing preparations for the next morning's Free Breakfast Program for Children."

"Can you tell us your duties there?"

"Yes. I set the table, put out the glasses for juice, and help get all the supplies ready for the morning shift cooks, who come in at 6:00 am to prepare the food."

"I see," Markowitz said. "And how long had you been doing this job before you were arrested?"

"About two weeks."

"And what did you do before that?"

"I served as Acting Minister of Information of the Boston chapter of the Black Panther Party."

"Can you tell us what you were doing here in Philadelphia?"

"Yes. Two of the Boston chapter members, myself and Wayne Connor, were sent here to help the Philadelphia chapter organize a free medical program like the one we started in Boston."

"I see. So why were you working at the Breakfast Program?"

"We all help out where it is needed, and there was no more work to be done that day on organizing the medical program."

"I see, said Markowitz, changing tactics. "Can you please tell the Court what you received on Sunday, May 17th?"

"You mean the check?"

Markowitz said yes.

To Sisterhood!

"I received a check from Nina Rosen in the amount of $5,000," Dennis said.

"Did Miss Rosen say anything at all to you when she handed you the check?"

"She did. She said she wanted to contribute to the Free Health Center – that's the one in Boston, where we both live."

"Did she say anything at all about how the money should be used for guns, or bomb making supplies, or drugs, or even if it was a general contribution with no strings attached?"

"No, Sir," said Dennis.

"And what was her reaction when she saw you open the envelope and look at the amount?"

"She didn't see me open it. I didn't open it until I got back to Headquarters. She had wrapped the check in a plain piece of paper and she specifically told me to open it later."

"So she didn't see you open it?"

"That is correct, Sir."

"Did anyone else see you open the check?"

"Yes."

"Who is that?"

"Wayne Connor."

"Is Mr. Connor in this Courtroom today?"

"Yes."

"Can you point him out for the jury?" Dennis pointed to Wayne.

"Mr. Burton, at what point did you first suspect that Mr. Connor was an informant for the Federal Bureau of Investiga –"

"Objection, Your Honor!" shouted Cranston, jumping to his feet.

"Sustained. The defense attorney's last question will be stricken from the record," the judge instructed the Court reporter. "And Counselor, I caution you to refrain from these tactics."

"So only Mr. Connor and you knew about the donation to the Free Health Center?"

"On the evening it was received, yes."

"And after that evening?"

"Pretty much everyone in the Boston chapter knew of the gift, and that it was to be used to help purchase the van for the health center."

"And was it indeed used toward the purchase of the van?"

"Yes, it was."

To Sisterhood!

"Do you recall the purchase price of the van?"

"Not exactly, but it was close to $48,000, fully equipped."

"When you say 'fully equipped,' you mean…"

"That it came loaded with shelves, and a refrigerator to keep the perishable medicines, and cubicles for exams, curtains, furniture, and the like."

"Where did the rest of the funds come from to purchase and equip the van?"

"Many community groups and individuals in the neighborhood made contributions, and that money was also used."

"Can you tell the Court the amount of those other donations?"

"Approximately $43,000."

"Leaving how much to buy guns, bombs, and drugs?"

"Objection," said the prosecutor.

"Sustained," said the judge. "Mr. Markowitz, can you please refrain from leading the witness?"

"Sorry, Your Honor," said Markowitz. "I am trying to establish that there is no possible way that either Miss Rosen's gift – nor any of the other funds collected from the community – were used for anything other than that for which they were intended – to help those in the

Black community in need of medical care and assistance." His voice rose as he concluded, "and that the Party did not have the means – nor the inclination – to purchase guns, bomb-making supplies, or street drugs at all."

"Kindly proceed," said the judge.

"No further questions, Your Honor."

"Mr. Burton, thank you. You may step down." Dennis stood up, looked directly at Nina, and gave her a shy smile.

At exactly that moment, Nina felt certain: Dennis was going to be found guilty.

Nina had seen enough. She slipped out of the building, walked for a while to clear her head, then found her way to the train station. She didn't return the next day to hear the travesty that went down during cross-examination.

She found out later that Dennis was charged with being an accessory to murder, only because he could prove he was not in the police station when the bomb was planted. He was sentenced to 10-15 years in prison in Philadelphia, and would not be eligible for parole for at least five years.

His attorney, citing family ties, educational background, and employment record, asked that instead, Dennis be incarcerated at Walpole near his home in Massachusetts. The judge denied the request.

✳ Thirty-Eight ✳

For the fall 1971 term, Ellen scheduled her classes in the late afternoon and evening, so either she or Nick could be home with Sandra. Sometimes they traded off childcare with another student couple, Maggie and Scott, who lived across the Bay in Berkeley. Their Moira was three, a pretty, dark-haired, child who adored Sandra. The two couples became close, sharing potluck dinners and sometimes going to concerts together, when they chipped in for a sitter for both girls.

With Nick teaching and Ellen in school, they adapted easily to academic family life and gradually let go of their political friends who didn't have kids. And now that they had an active toddler, their time for anti-war work was limited.

Ellen applied to local graduate programs and went to a couple of interviews. She found them unfriendly to women, because, as one admissions officer told her, every woman who got accepted was taking the place of a man, who presumably needed the degree to support his family. As their daughters napped, she talked this over with Maggie, who invited her to join several graduate students, faculty wives, and their friends, who were forming a consciousness-raising group.

"Explain, please." Ellen was intrigued.

"Well," Maggie said, tucking her legs under her on the sofa, "a CR group is composed of women – usually, but not always, from the same social circle, or they could be neighbors or colleagues – who are likely to share your concerns about being a woman. If you're colleagues, you might focus on issues at work. If you're neighbors, you might talk about children, or marriage."

She paused. "Wait, was that Sandra?" Ellen got up and peeked into the bedroom. "Nope, both sound asleep. Tell me more."

"From what I've read," Maggie continued, "it's a chance to examine our lives to better understand the nature of women's oppression and sexism, and get a woman-centered perspective on ourselves, how society views women, and what we can do about it. It sounds like an opportunity to have people listen – really listen – to your ambitions and concerns. It creates a feeling that you're not in this alone, and gives women the opportunity to replenish our energy and our strength."

"Do you have to tell your secrets?" Ellen did need to know.

"No one has to say anything they don't want to." Maggie said calmly. "Look, it's just forming, so I guess we all get to make up the rules together."

"Sounds interesting," Ellen said. "Now, should we close our eyes for a few minutes too before the girls wake up?" She stretched out on the thick rug on the floor and put a soft throw pillow under her head, gesturing for Maggie to stay on the sofa.

※ ※ ※ ※

On a mild November evening, Ellen and Maggie walked up to a large Victorian house in Maggie's neighborhood. A woman with frizzy red hair and a big grin opened the door, saying, "Welcome! I'm Anna."

Maggie introduced herself and Ellen, who offered their hostess a plate of freshly baked brownies.

"Yum! Thank you," Anna said and gave a big hug to a startled Ellen.

To Sisterhood!

Seven other women were already there, sitting on overstuffed sofas and pillows on the floor, chatting comfortably while sipping wine and munching on snacks.

Maggie and Ellen were surprised to see that most of the women were much older than they. Maggie shrugged and said, "I didn't know what to expect," and Ellen whispered back, "It's okay."

A couple more women arrived, and once they were all settled, Anna clapped her hands and said, "Let's get started. I have absolutely no idea how to do this."

A tall brunette, who looked familiar to Ellen, introduced herself as Beth, and said she was on the faculty at State College. Ellen remembered her now; she taught somewhere in the Science Building.

"Why don't we take turns each week acting as facilitator?" she suggested. "I'm happy to lead off."

The other women nodded their assent, and Beth continued, "maybe we should go around the circle and introduce ourselves, and say what brought us here tonight? Then we can write down a list of possible topics to discuss, and go from there. Does that work for everyone?"

"Before we begin," Beth said, "let's set a few ground rules, so we all feel safe. Confidentiality, of course. What we share stays in this room."

"No judgments," added a slim woman of about thirty-five, who introduced herself as Andrea.

"And no interrupting!" shouted an older woman, who didn't give her name.

After much laughter, the women began to brainstorm topics they wanted to discuss. Beth took out a pad and wrote down the suggestions: the division of labor in a marriage, childcare, finding a job when one is older, health issues that doctors don't address well, and a lot more. She then asked for a vote on which topic they should start with.

"How about we all go around and introduce ourselves and say a few words about what our lives were like as young women?" Maggie said.

The women agreed, but the short answers Maggie was expecting turned into pieces of each woman's life story.

"My mother was a heroin addict," Andrea began. "When she got out of the mental hospital, she took me to San Jose, where she would shoot up and nod out in front of me. I liked to go to my friend Sally's house. She had a normal family. I mean, like, they had meals at regular times." She shook her head ruefully and continued.

"I was fourteen when I picked up drugs. When I started my period, my mother gave me a Seconal and a tampon and said 'just relax.' Drugs made me feel better. They took the place of nurturing. Made me feel good inside. Dropped out of school, and flew to Nevada. I found my father living on a commune. He was the father of 28 children."

A couple of the older women gasped and one laughed. Andrea smiled, and continued.

To Sisterhood!

"I lived by myself in a teepee. They used different drugs: mushrooms, LSD. I felt smug. I used better drugs, like crystal meth. I was hip.

"There were a lot of Chicanos in town, tough guys who wore black leather. I was enthralled. I was hungry. I met a guy from the motorcycle gang. We were both nineteen. I wanted a baby. I wanted to belong to someone. My biological clock started ticking at age fifteen. If I had a child, I would have someone who was always with me. When I was pregnant, I didn't need drugs because that empty hole was filled up. Everything was fine between us. After my daughter was born, her father and I didn't stay together. I drifted." Andrea looked up at the ceiling, as if remembering, and sighed.

"Heroin. I'd wanted to try it for so long. I wanted to know what my mother felt. Mother's little helper. It made me feel fulfilled. My needs were met. I could be less frustrated and take better care of my kid."

She gave a self-deprecating laugh. "That's what I thought. Then things got pretty bad pretty quickly. I did eventually get clean and sober. I'm gonna spare you the gory details." She laughed again.

"I married again, then left that alcoholic marriage. I got my GED at night school when I had a teenager and a two-year-old. Then I started losing control. I never wanted to be that way with my kids. I was on welfare, alone with two kids, in nursing school, and one morning I was in a hurry to get to an exam. On the way out the door, the little one dawdled."

Andrea put her face into her hands for a minute, then looked up again. She took a breath, then continued bravely.

"I threw her across the room. I had so much rage. I was still learning to tolerate my own feelings without chemicals. I called the school health plan. They had parent classes at a time I never could've gone at a cost I'd never be able to afford." Andrea paused, and glanced at Beth.

"Then I met Beth here – well, she's my biology professor. She told me about this group of parents on campus who are struggling with anger and exhaustion and stuff, and we meet twice a week, and we can bring our little kids. It's been a blessing. I haven't laid a finger on either of my kids – though my fifteen-year-old really can get on my nerves – and I'm taking it one day at a time. Truthfully, sometimes just one hour at a time."

She fidgeted, and looked at Beth for approval, who gave her a small nod.

"Wow," Maggie said. "Um, I mean, thanks, Andrea, for sharing your story. I mean, I thought I have it hard when my husband leaves his smelly gym clothes on the floor. I'm just blown away."

Beth said gently, "Yes, Andrea, you're an incredibly strong woman, and Maggie, this isn't a contest. We all start out with what we're dealt, I guess, and we go from there. Who wants to speak next?"

An older woman of about sixty, with stylishly cut silver hair, raised her hand shyly.

"Hi everyone, I'm Esther, and I live next door to Anna, and she invited me. I guess I'm the oldest woman here, so it could be I have some wisdom to share? Anyway, here's my story.

I grew up in a religious family. I remember the synagogue of my childhood. I was restless in the hard wooden pews, and bored with a

To Sisterhood!

language I couldn't quite get, even though I went to Hebrew School twice a week."

Esther laughed. "It's no wonder I haven't been inside a synagogue since my cousin Izzy's Bar Mitzvah." She stood up to stretch, and continued standing as she spoke.

"And when I fell in love and got married to a gentile, a lovely man I met at school, my family sat shiva for me. They cut me off, just like that. I lost my way. I began seeking other forms of spiritual enlightenment. Then after ten years of marriage and two sons, my husband got bored with my search, and he left me too. My family refused to take me back."

Ellen observed that as Esther told her story, she seemed to grow taller and more confident.

"I got a job at the branch library," Esther continued, "and moved into an apartment with the boys, who, thankfully, turned out mostly okay. They are both good to me, and so are my daughters-in-law. I'm very lucky. And now I have a darling baby grandson, so I'd have to say, life is good – much better than when I was young. That's all. Thank you." Esther took a little bow and sat down, as the others murmured thanks.

A small woman with curly blonde-white hair, who had been squished down in a beanbag chair, raised her hand and then sat up straight so she could be seen.

"Well, Esther," she began. "I think I have you beat on the old lady thing by a few years." Everyone laughed.

"My name is Lucinda. When I was twenty-one, I was married to a promising young doctor nearly ten years my senior, in a big society wedding. I was just out of college and eventually we had three children. When he turned forty-five, he sold his practice to a younger colleague, and began to hire out to do consulting in his specialty, cardiology. He was invited to give lectures at medical meetings, public health conferences, everything. He travelled all over the world, and much of the time, I travelled with him. We sent the kids to a good boarding school and brought them with us during their summer and school vacations." She gave a small smile and continued.

"We went skiing in the Alps, and scuba diving in the Bahamas, and had tea at the Ritz in London, and even met the Queen on one trip! It was an exciting life, and I was a good wife, in the old-fashioned sense of being loyal and supportive."

Some of the other older women nodded knowingly. Ellen took off her glasses and wiped them clean, listening intently.

"He was tender to me, he treated me well, and I always knew he loved me. The children and I never lacked for anything. He was quite successful in his job and made what you would call a comfortable income. But he had a very big ego, an ego that needed stroking all the time. I shouldn't have been surprised – but I was – when I found out about the first extra-marital affair. He confessed when I found the ticket stubs to a play I hadn't attended on a trip I didn't go on. At least he had the decency not to lie to me about it! He cried and said he was sorry, blah, blah, blah. And then it happened again. And again."

Lucinda hugged herself as she went on.

"And, although I was very hurt, I saw that he had needs that I could not fill. It wasn't sexual – that part of our marriage always worked. It's that I couldn't be there twenty-four hours a day telling him how wonderful he was. He needed younger, more beautiful women to do that. For years, I turned a blind eye. He was very discreet; he never did anything that would bring shame to me or to the children. Well, besides the basic fact that he was a philanderer!"

The woman sitting next to Lucinda reached over to pat her shoulder, and Lucinda smiled.

"On my 50th birthday, he had to be out of town. I was supposed to go with him, but I had a meeting – by then I was a trustee at our public library, and it was the annual meeting. He sent me a lovely diamond necklace, and a note that read: 'To Lucinda, the lovely mother of my children. My best girl.' And I thought: 'Wait a minute. I signed up for *only* girl. Not *best* girl.' I didn't want to be in a competition anymore.

"When he came home from the trip, I told him I was through. I wanted a divorce. He was so sad. He told me he'd often thought I 'would do this to him' one day – he didn't seem all that surprised. But on top of all the sadness and hurt, I was in for the shock of my life." She paused to take a deep breath, as if trying to keep back the tears and pain.

"For when we got down to the nitty-gritty of the divorce, it seems that he had been hiding assets for years. My lawyers found that he owned oil wells, had invested in pork belly futures, precious metals, everything. And it was all in his name. My lawyers tried hard, but I ended up getting only the house – which had a mortgage I couldn't afford – and spousal support until my Social Security kicked in. The amount he gave me was just enough to rent a small apartment, not even big enough for all the kids to come home at the same time. It seemed as though 'the mother of my children – best girl' thing was good only as long as I was willing to be the little woman, support his huge ego, cook for him, raise his kids, and shut up about all his mistresses.

"Well, I got angry. You know what I did? I sold that necklace and put a down payment on a little house out in the country, near where I'd grown up. And, last year, at age sixty-five, when the support checks ran out, and the meager Social Security checks began, I had to go to work – for the first time. I found a job as the secretary to the minister of our local church, and it's good to be useful. You know, I'm not unhappy – but this is not the life I signed up for. Not at all."

She fished in her pocket for a hanky and blew her nose, then turned to the woman on her right.

"OK, your turn," she said, no longer wanting to be the center of attention.

"Thank you, Lucinda," Beth and Maggie said at the same time.

A soft-spoken, heavyset woman of about forty-five was next. "Hi, everyone, I'm Martine." The others called out their hellos.

"My husband is a judge. Yes, my husband. We are still married, because he refuses to give me the divorce I desperately want. He keeps dragging out the legal process, because he doesn't want to have to pay support. He has a temper. I knew that when we got married. But I didn't know how bad it was." She shook her head.

"He pushed me down the stairs. I went to the emergency room with a broken arm and bruises on my face. He was all solicitous-like, and told them that I fell. On the way there, he threatened to kill me if I said anything else. He said I was confused and that I had been drinking – I *never* touch a drop of alcohol! – and that who would believe a stupid cunt like me? Yes, those were his words. Of course, the ER doctors believed him – who would doubt the word of Judge Alvin Peterson?"

Martine paused as she looked around the room, When she saw the care and concern on the faces of the others, she was able to continue.

"When it happened the next time, I left, literally with the clothes on my back, and went to stay with my second cousin, someone Alvin didn't know at all. He couldn't find me. My cousin and her husband were kind to me, but I couldn't stay there forever. I bought an old VW bus, and I've been living in the bus for the past six months, working at temporary jobs when I can. I got a membership to the YWCA, where I could shower every day. Somebody needs to bring that man down!"

One of the other women got up and crossed the room to give Martine a hug. She spoke to her for a few moments and Martine started to cry.

Beth said, "Maybe we should all take a break for ten minutes or so? Get some snacks, use the bathroom, stretch our legs?"

When the group reconvened, Martine was smiling broadly and sitting next to a pretty middle-aged woman with dark skin, who was wearing a long colorful skirt and dangly earrings.

Martine raised her hand, and Beth called on her.

"I know I already had my turn, and I don't want to hog the floor, but Susan here" – and she had to stop to wipe the tears that started again, freely running down her cheeks – "Susan is a widow with a great big empty house, and she's just offered to let me move in with her until I can get back on my feet."

Everyone smiled and a few women clapped. One woman who hadn't yet spoken offered to help Martine find a job when she was ready, and Martine gratefully accepted.

Another woman, whose name Ellen didn't catch, told of being fired for refusing to take her boss's advice to "wear shorter skirts" to the office "so we can all enjoy your pretty legs." Other women told their stories: new love after loss, challenges with teenagers, partners who were supportive and those who were not, medical problems, aging parents who needed care, demanding bosses – tales of struggles and joys, heartbreak and happiness – in short, the stuff of women's lives.

When it was finally Ellen's turn to speak, she talked about her longtime desire to go to Radcliffe, and a little about how she ended up in the Bay Area instead.

She told the group about her involvement in the women's movement beginning in the spring of 1969, and how difficult it was to keep doing political work with a toddler to raise, and a household to run, in addition to going to school.

"Still," she said, "I feel pretty sure that academia is the right place for me, and I'm becoming more interested in studying – and eventually teaching about – women's issues. I've heard about the groundbreaking program down at San Diego State – they have a brand-new

To Sisterhood!

department of women's studies. And I've begun putting in some applications for doctoral programs, and had a few interviews. But it feels like I'm getting a lot of pushback, just because I'm a woman."

A few of the others nodded. "Have you tried talking to Sonya Miller here at U.C. Berkeley?" asked Tula, who'd told of being passed over for an academic promotion. "She's the only tenured professor in the sociology department. Sounds like that could be the right place for you."

Beth chimed in. "I've heard that at Berkeley, there's a group of women who organized a course in Women's Literature. Right now, it's being taught by grad students, and it sounds fascinating. Some of them are beginning to do advocacy work to hire and promote more women faculty."

Ellen was interested. "Well, it sounds like I have a lot to learn. Thanks so much for the tip. I'll definitely get in touch with Professor Miller."

As Ellen and Maggie brought empty cups and plates to the kitchen and gathered their jackets and bags, the other women continued to chat.

"Wow!" Maggie breathed as she walked Ellen to her car. "I honestly don't know whether to cry or scream."

"That was intense," Ellen said, wiping away a tear. "I mean, I thought…" she was unable to continue, so just gave Maggie a brief hug and said goodbye. *None of that is ever going to happen to me*, she thought as she headed toward home.

✲ Thirty-Nine ✲

Wearing her new negative heel shoes, which the other cooks swore by but took some getting used to, Diane stood in the kitchen of Grendel's Den, where she'd been working for six months. It was an ordinary late March day in Cambridge, with clear skies and temperatures expected to rise to 50° by early afternoon. She'd been for a walk earlier and spotted a single purple crocus blooming in the square outside the restaurant. Everything was humming along smoothly in the kitchen. Diane had no idea that her life was just about to change significantly, this time for the better.

The radio newscaster announced that the proposed Equal Rights Amendment, having passed the House last October, was approved yesterday by the U.S. Senate in a vote of 84-8. Now three-fourths of the states had to ratify it, and it would become law.

It's about damn time, Diane thought, as she drew her knife slowly across the stone, tilting it slightly on the diagonal to get it really sharp. She looked at the Japanese lettering on the box lid.

"I wonder what that says," she mused aloud, catching the attention of Shane, the head chef. "It could be 'Best Knife Sharpener Ever' or 'Cooking is Groovy.'"

Shane laughed. "Just cut the onions, and don't worry about it, Diane," he said. "We're running out of spinach pie again; let's get going."

As she reached for the bag of onions, Diane thought it might be helpful to learn another language. Two years of high school French made it possible to ask what day it was – and boy, if you were in Paris and

To Sisterhood!

didn't even know what day it was, you'd be in trouble. She knew how to count to twenty, the days of the week, the months, and how to find the bathroom. She'd tried to practice her French with Mona, but Diane felt it was hopeless. Mona had encouraged her, but the accent and pronunciation of the Québécois French Mona spoke wasn't the same as what Diane had learned in school, so she'd given up.

She rinsed the knife, wiped it on the kitchen towel, and cut the top and bottom off the sweet onion. First, she made vertical slices, then swiftly rotated it a quarter turn and sliced again, and it was now a small mince. Scraping it into the glass bowl, Diane quickly reached for a second onion. After she finished, she went to the cooler to grab another bag of spinach to rinse, when Katy, a waitress who also sometimes assisted with the cooking, poked her head into the kitchen.

"Someone's here to see you, Diane. Shane said it was okay to let her back. And before you ask, yes, I prepped the romaine and bell peppers for the Greek salad."

"Thanks, Katy."

A petite, blonde woman walked into the kitchen.

"Diane Romano?" she asked.

"Yup, that's me." Diane set down the knife and wiped her hands on her apron.

"I'm Naomi Cooper, and I'd love to be able to chat with you about cooking when you're not on duty. Can I leave you my phone number?" She took out a business card and handed it to Diane.

"Sure thing," Diane said politely. "May I give you a call tomorrow afternoon after my shift? Is that good for you?"

"Anytime. If I don't pick up, just give your number to my answering service so I can find you." Naomi walked out, leaving Diane puzzled as to who this woman was and what she might want.

She didn't have to wait long to find out. Shane came bouncing into the room. "Naomi Cooper was just here asking for you!" he exclaimed. "What did she want with you? Did you talk to her?"

"Whoa, slow down," Diane said. "Yes, that's who she said she was. But who is she and how do you know her?"

"You're kidding, right?" Shane looked stunned. "Do you mean to tell me you never heard of Naomi Cooper? *The* Naomi Cooper? The youngest and hottest chef on the east coast? The one who wowed New York a couple of years ago? Her restaurant, JoJo's? Where you can't get a reservation for weeks, months sometimes? I'd heard she was planning to open a second location in Massachusetts. I thought here in the city or possibly on the Cape."

I wonder what she wants with me? Diane thought again. *Guess I'll find out tomorrow.*

As it turned out, what Naomi wanted was Diane. Over coffee at an out-of-the-way place near Kendall Square where she wouldn't be recognized, Naomi explained that she hoped to bring Diane in as sous chef at Naomi's new restaurant in the Boston area. The concept was based on using fresh, locally grown ingredients, farmed in and near

Massachusetts. Diane asked if she'd been inspired by the local food movement in San Francisco.

"Yes, exactly," Naomi said. "We all have a lot to be grateful to Alice Waters for," mentioning the dazzling young chef who'd opened Chez Panisse in Berkeley last August.

The two women talked for more than an hour, about Naomi's hopes and plans for her new location, and about Diane's background, experience, and career goals.

Naomi put down her coffee mug.

"This has been delightful," she said, shaking Diane's hand. She smiled broadly as she offered Diane the position. Working under Naomi, Diane would have a hand in creating the menu and input into hiring the staff. When Naomi named a starting salary, Diane almost gasped.

"Yes, it all sounds wonderful," Diane said. "But I have to ask – why me? I'm not even in charge here at Grendel's and I don't know much about managing a restaurant or how to control costs or –"

Naomi interrupted her. "Because I heard that you're a wonderful cook, creative and daring, and you're organized and a hard worker," she said. "And you don't have a lot of bad habits to unlearn. I want someone I can train as we work together, and then, when I'm comfortable, I would leave the kitchen and management of the restaurant entirely to you – in a few years or so. We'd have to see how it all goes."

"How do you know so much about me?" Diane sipped the last of her coffee, which was now cold. This was a lot to handle all at once. "And why would you be willing to take a chance when you've never even tasted my food?"

"It seems that your friend Nina thinks very, very highly of you, and of your cooking."

"How do you know Nina?"

Naomi explained that she'd been a friend of Nina's at Sarah Lawrence, where they'd met on the debate team when Nina was a freshman and Naomi a senior, and they'd kept in touch. While Nina dropped out after her first year, Naomi graduated and went on to train at one of the most famous culinary schools in the world, opening her own restaurant at the age of twenty-five.

Naomi paused in her story, and again asked Diane if she would be willing to consider her offer.

"It's definitely a terrific opportunity," said Diane, "but I'm curious to know, so I'll ask you again – there are a lot of other people you could have asked, most with more experience. Why me?"

Naomi took a breath and let it out, looking directly at Diane.

"Nina told me that you'd been through a pretty rough patch, and that this job could make a difference for you. And, Lord knows, an excellent chef with a strong work ethic could really make a difference to me. So, what do you say, Diane? Shall we give it a try and see how things go?" She smiled brightly.

"I say 'yes'," Diane grinned as she reached out to shake Naomi's hand. "And thank you, Naomi. Thank you so much!"

※ ※ ※ ※

On June 1st, 1972, San Francisco State College officially became "California State University, San Francisco." After President Hayakawa spoke, Ellen stood to receive her degree. Nick and Harriet watched proudly, Nick holding a squirming Sandra on his lap.

Thanks in part to the connection she'd made with Professor Sonya Miller in the Sociology Department at U.C. Berkeley, Ellen had been accepted into its doctoral program for the fall. She and Nick had decided to move close to the Berkeley campus this summer. Nick would commute to San Francisco for the coming year, then start looking for another job closer to their new home.

Ellen was comfortable with their decision. While she hadn't realized her dream of graduating from Radcliffe, at least she'd been accepted into a prestigious grad school. And her new dream was to teach at the college level, and earning her doctorate at Berkeley would be a significant step toward that goal.

Taking Sandra from Nick, Ellen looked at her beautiful daughter and wondered how differently her life might have turned out had she stayed in Cambridge. She thought, briefly, of Sam, and where he might be, and why he'd never gotten back in touch with her. And she knew that, as promising as her future looked, she would never again be totally at peace. She would carry a profound secret that she could not tell without destroying lives around her – for the rest of her life. She said a short prayer for Sam's well-being and offered a silent *thank you* for the precious gift he'd given her.

※ ※ ※ ※

Two weeks later, on June 15th, Laurie was awarded her bachelor's degree, with her whole family in attendance. Laurie – and Matt – were on their way to the Peace Corps. Meditating together for the past ten months had brought them to a better place in their marriage. Matt realized how much his lethargy had been affecting Laurie and he'd promised to do better. After lengthy discussions, they decided that serving together in the Peace Corps for two years would give them a new direction and purpose.

They hadn't yet received their assignment, and were due to report for training in July. They'd be staying with a host family, at least for the first few months, and then find housing in their new community. At the suggestion of the coordinator, they'd spent time meeting with returned volunteers and learned about their experiences. Laurie had asked them to describe things she and Matt wouldn't think to ask. She realized she'd miss two years of her baby niece's life, and that she and Matt would likely find themselves way beyond their comfort zone.

Still, Laurie was excited to be heading off to a new country, a new adventure, and a way to realize, at least for now, both of her goals – to see the world and to help heal it.

※ ※ ※ ※

Ellen, Nina, Laurie, and Diane all would be eligible to vote for president for the first time in November. With the recent passage of the 26th Amendment, the voting age had been lowered to eighteen, and both parties expected a huge youth turnout.

By June, Nina had undergone a major change of heart. After seeing Dennis get royally screwed by the Feds last fall, and after Mayday failed to stop the war, she'd become disillusioned. Not as much as Laurie, of course – Nina wouldn't drop out of political activism completely. But she was twenty-four now, old enough to realize that it might be more effective to work within the system. She decided to volunteer for George McGovern's campaign. While she liked the People's Party candidate, Dr. Benjamin Spock, Nina felt McGovern had a much better chance of winning. He was one of the Senate opposition leaders against the Vietnam War and was in favor of civil rights, as well as a number of other liberal causes.

Nina reported to headquarters, down by the Berklee College of Music. The paid staffers, all men and recent Ivy grads, wore jackets and ties, at least at the beginning of the day, and all of them smoked, which Nina found disgusting. They reminded her of Rod – smug, arrogant, but devoted to the cause. Nina knew she could handle it, especially since she'd be out in the field, not in the office, much of the time.

She and the other volunteers were trained in talking points about the candidate and the things he stood for, and were sent out in pairs – usually a man and a woman – to ring doorbells in blue collar neighborhoods in Somerville, East Cambridge, and Cambridgeport. They were given handouts to leave. Nina quickly learned not to talk about the war at all, but to focus on McGovern's domestic policies, as many folks had sons, brothers, or husbands in the service.

She appealed to their sense of goodness: "Have *you* ever been hungry? Do you think it's fair for little children to be hungry?" Nina described the candidate's efforts to expand the food stamp program. While she knew she was good with people, this was a different kind of getting-to-know-people skill than she used as a reporter, and she learned something new with each visit.

She wished she could go to the Democratic National Convention in Miami Beach next month, but she had no standing as a delegate. She did, however, put up posters wherever there was an appropriate space: "**McGovern**ment for the People."

While she'd have been happy to continue to volunteer on the campaign full time, Nina had to figure out what she wanted to do next for gainful employment. She'd been contributing articles for the alternative paper, the *Cambridge Phoenix*, but didn't feel like she fit in. She was self-aware enough to appreciate the irony of writing for an underground weekly while working for a straight, albeit anti-war, candidate. But she wanted to make a difference however she could, and she wasn't going to risk going back out on the streets.

There was a lot of discontent at the newspaper's office. And when the editor was fired in a dispute with the owner, the staff decided to strike in solidarity.

By the second week, the strike was resolved but the editor was not reinstated. That Friday, the entire staff was informed that their services were no longer required, and that their paper had been purchased by the owner of the rival paper. The *Phoenix* staff decided to continue to publish anyway and created a new entity called *The Real Paper*. Nina was thrilled to be included in this new venture.

She called Diane to take her out to dinner to celebrate. Diane said she'd been planning to try a complex recipe from a new cookbook, *The Vegetarian Epicure*, and said she'd come over to Nina's with the ingredients and cook there.

To Sisterhood!

Diane was busily chopping walnuts into a fine dice while Nina was telling her all about the new newspaper, when the phone rang.

"Excuse me a minute, will you?" she said to Diane, who turned her attention back to stirring the bechamel sauce she was going to use on the walnut-cheddar balls.

"Hello," Nina said.

"I'm looking for Nina Rosen," said the caller.

"This is she."

"Nina, this is Neil Tierney. You may not remember me. I was the assistant defense attorney on the Dennis Burton case. We met briefly in Philadelphia back in October – well, we didn't really meet, but we saw one another in the courtroom."

Nina pulled the phone cord into her bedroom for more privacy.

News of Dennis! Was he okay? Would he be getting out of jail early?

"Yes, Mr. Tierney, how can I help you?"

"Neil," he said. "Please call me Neil. And I know you're probably hoping to hear word of Dennis, and I'm sorry to say there's no change – that is, no update on early probation."

Nina let out the breath she didn't realize she'd been holding.

"Ohhh…" was all she could manage.

"And unfortunately, there probably won't be any, at least not until McGovern is elected and Nixon is out of office."

"We can hope," Nina said. "I've been working on his campaign –"

"Nina," Neil interjected. "I'd like to hear about that, and all you're doing, and that's the reason for my call. I hope you don't mind that I asked Leo to ask Arnold Friedman for your number."

Again, Nina asked, "Okay, how can I help you?"

"Well," he said, and Nina heard something other than the sharp, confident attorney she'd seen in action at the courthouse. "I was calling to see if you'd like to go out to dinner with me on Saturday night. I'll be in Boston, and I thought…" again, he paused, sounding more like a nervous high school student than an accomplished adult.

"Oh!" Nina said, not sure what to think. "Yes, we can have dinner."

"How about Anthony's Pier 4? I know it's a big tourist place, but then, I'm kind of a tourist and I've heard about their famous popovers…"

"You know, Neil, I've never been there either. I'd like that."

The two chatted for a few minutes more, and Neil told Nina he would come for her in his rental car, before he said, "Nina? One more thing?"

"Yes?"

"Well, this might not matter to you, but Leo said to be sure to tell you that "Tierney" is my grandfather's name on my father's side. My

To Sisterhood!

father's mother was Epstein – and so my father, and of course, my mother, Rebecca Levin, are Jewish. Leo thought you'd want to know."

Nina laughed. "I don't do too much in the way of religious observance. But, yes, I do appreciate you telling me. I know Malka and Ben – they're my Bubbe and Zadie – they would be smiling."

Now that's a curious development, she thought, grinning as she put down the phone.

"You're not gonna believe this," she said to Diane, who was straining onions from the sauce. "I just got asked out on a date."

She told Diane about Neil Tierney and how he'd let her know he'd tracked her down through their mutual acquaintance.

"Sounds like the guy's interested," Diane said, as she chopped parsley.

"Could be," Nina said, trying to recall what he looked like. "It's been a long time since I've been with anyone."

"Yeah. About that. Maybe you ought to call Ellen and share your good news about the paper with her. Maybe about this guy, too." Diane knew Ellen still hadn't completely forgiven Nina.

"I don't think she wants to talk to me," Nina said.

"Why don't you write to her instead? Then she can take the time she needs to listen to what you have to say, and to respond if she wants."

So the next morning, Nina took a sheet of new letterhead and wrote:

Gail R. Shapiro

August 10, 1972

Dear Ellen,

We haven't been in touch for a while, and I'm hoping you'll read this in the spirit of friendship and apology. The news here is that the Phoenix, *the alternative paper I've been writing for, is defunct. The owner refused to negotiate with the Employees' Union and he sold out to the competition for $600,000. No former* Phoenix *staff members were offered jobs and so theoretically we're all out of work. However, we got together some money and found some advertisers, and we're putting out a new publication,* The Real Paper, *as competition. No one's getting paid here yet, but several offers have been made to buy it, so we should be salaried again in a few weeks. I'm totally psyched!!*

I trust that you and Nick and little Sandra all are doing well, and again, Ellen, I'm sorrier than I can say for how I hurt you last year. And congratulations again on your graduation! I'm proud of you, and happy that you're off to grad school to make your dream come true, even if it is on the other coast.

So here I am working on this new paper – my dream may be coming true too. Diane said she called you about her incredible new job, feeding one hungry soul at a time. And I hear Laurie's got her assignment and she's off to the Peace Corps to help save the world. Ellen, we are all on our way!

Yours in sisterhood and solidarity, Nina

⁂ **Acknowledgements** ⁂

Enormous gratitude to all who helped me create this book:

Those who read early drafts and offered encouragement and support, including: Kathy Berlin, Susan Fahlund, Nancy Haverstock, Sandi Peskin, Susan Reich, Becky Sarah, Arline Shapiro (z"l), Dan Shapiro, Harold Shapiro (z"l), Rita Shapiro, Steven Shapiro, and Gil Wolin (z"l).

Sarah Hutcheon, Reference Librarian, Schlesinger Library, Radcliffe Institute for Advanced Study, for steering me in the right direction.

Michael Brian Murphy, for reading and correcting many drafts, and for being by my side every step of the way.

Lynn Klamkin, for more than fifty-five years of friendship, and astute writing guidance.

Margo Melnicove, for a sharp eye and an even sharper red pencil.

Joanne Wilkinson, M.D., Robert Wolin, J.D., and Melvin Norris, J.D., for reviewing medical and legal details. (Any errors are mine.)

NaNoWriMo, for the jumpstart, and the team at BookLocker, for bringing the story to life.

And to my sisters, especially those who organized the May 4th, 1969 conference, and the takeover at 888 Memorial Drive, who are still out there fighting for justice and our rights.

⌗ Questions for Discussion ⌗

1. Ellen, Laurie, Diane, and Nina come from very different backgrounds, and view the world in very different ways. Can you identify with any of them? If so, whose world view is the most like your own?

2. *To Sisterhood!* takes place at a time when the nation was as sharply divided as it is today, perhaps even more so. Are there lessons you can learn from this period, 1969-1972, that apply today?

3. Each of the women struggles with the government's involvement in what she believes is an unjust war. At one point, the narrative reads, "[…] Laurie realized there were two ways to heal the world. You could work *against* the bad, or you could work *for* the good." Do you agree? Which path feels right for you?

4. How do you respond now when your government passes laws or commits acts with which you strongly disagree?

5. Each of the four women faces several choice points throughout the novel. Consider Diane, Ellen, Nina, and Laurie. Did each make the right decision each time, in your view? What other options did each have?

6. How do you think each woman's relationship with her mother informed her life choices?

7. What has been an important choice point in your own life? What factors did you consider as you made your own decision? Looking

back, would you make the same decision now, or would you do things differently?

8. *To Sisterhood!* describes several significant historical events in this three-year period. Were there any with which you were not familiar? Did any surprise you?

9. If you're not old enough to remember this era, can you talk with your grandmother, mother, aunt, or older friend and ask her to share her perspectives and experiences with you? If you were, can you share your experiences with the younger women in your life?

10. What do you think the future will hold for each of the four women?